RIVERS

THE CROW BROTHERS

S.L. SCOTT

Design: RBA Designs

Photographer: Nikita TV

Editing:

Jenny Sims, Editing4Indies

Marion Archer, Making Manuscripts

Marla Esposito, Proofing Style

Kristen Johnson, Proofreader

*Dedicated to those who **Dream Big** and **Love** with their whole heart.*

PROLOGUE

Rivers

THE RAIN DOESN'T bother me.

Gray clouds and dark skies fit my mood better than sunny days have in years.

I'm better off without her.

The lies come easier these days. I used to mentally stammer over the words even if I wasn't voicing them out loud. I thought it would become second nature to tell myself she was wrong for me. *That I was wrong for her.* When we were together, she was a girl becoming a woman and a beautiful fucking mess of emotions. When we were together, I was a boy becoming a man, a fuckup compared to who I wanted to be.

But I loved her. Loved us. I loved every fucking emotion and remember them like it was yesterday.

Only it wasn't. It was five fucking years ago.

"I'm better off without her." I repeat the lie, still not believing a damn word. The words are bitter on my tongue, such a contradiction to how sweet the memories taste.

She was my everything.

Until she wasn't.

My fingers tighten around the steering wheel, and I exhale a slow breath. The raindrops become sprinkles and then stop altogether. As if the universe is clearing the path for me to follow my heart, I get out of my 4Runner and lean against it, facing the school.

Five years have dragged since I walked away, leaving my heart broken at her feet. I can't go another day pretending she wasn't my every-fucking-thing. That's why I'm back. For her—Stella Lilith Fellowes.

Star of the night.

Star of my life.

I miss her so fucking much, but I begin to debate if I have a right to be here at all.

What am I doing?

She hates me. This is such a bad idea. It's after five, so she might not even be here. I open the door but still when I hear, "Rivers?"

Closing my eyes, I take a deep breath and am slow to exhale. It starts drizzling again. Is this a sign? Will we always be trapped under a dark cloud, or can we find blue skies again?

When I turn around, my breath stops hard in my chest.

She's absolutely stunning.

I've rummaged through a box of photos a million times. I've watched video upon video on the loneliest of nights. I've had dreams that feel so real that I wake up expecting her to be next to me.

But my memories don't do her justice.

I only remember the girl.

Before me now stands a woman. The woman she's become without me. Her brown hair is pulled up, but some strands have escaped, the misty air making them stick to her skin. I can't stop from smiling.

She's better than any dream could ever be.

The white shirt she's wearing reveals lace under the wet fabric. Too much of her legs are covered by a skirt, but I still remember the great shape of her calves. Her glasses slip down, but she pushes the middle back up the bridge of her nose. She never wore glasses when we were together, so it serves as another reminder of what I've missed.

"God, you're beautiful." I don't mean to say it, but I don't regret it either.

She gifts me with the smile I've missed every minute of every year we were apart, but it fades away too fast. "What are you doing here?"

What am I doing here?

There are so many possible answers, and while all of them are true, none of them are right.

I miss her. I love her. I'm so fucking sorry for ruining everything.

My first album set the charts on fire, and all I wanted to do was come home and find her because celebrating this achievement or any without her was never in the plans. Shutting the car door, I shove my hands in the back pockets of my jeans and shift. "I needed to see you."

She moves her bag to her chest and wraps her arms around it. "Needed?"

"Wanted?"

The rain still touches her, but she makes no move to leave, willing to brave the elements just like me. "Are you asking me, Rivers?"

"I wanted to see you." Shaking my head, I know I'm fucking this up. "I wanted to come because I needed to see you."

"Why?" She looks around as if to make sure there are no witnesses before she comes closer, keeping some distance between us.

I take a few steps but don't invade her space like I want to. "When did you start wearing glasses?"

"Did you come here to ask about my glasses?"

The answer to that question isn't what she really wants to know, but maybe she's stalling like I am. It feels good to be this close to her, to be talking to her again. I smile, and this time, it tempts one from her. But she's stronger than I am. She held out longer, didn't take my calls, didn't return my texts, never contacted me.

We stand face-to-face with a thousand unspoken questions jostling between us. I could take another step, two maybe, and breathe in the faint smell of oranges. I could extend an arm and touch her. But I don't. She's not mine anymore, and as natural as it would feel to do either of those things, I know there's an ocean between who we are and who we used to be.

Glancing at one of the few cars that remain in the parking lot, she says, "I should go."

As I try to come up with something to say, I start memorizing everything about her in case I'm not given another opportunity.

She doesn't wear a ring on her left hand.

I used to kiss the soft skin behind the earrings that dot her earlobes.

A simple thin gold necklace highlights the delicate curve of her neck.

Even though raindrops coat her lenses, her green eyes still shine behind them.

When my gaze dips to the lace that clings to the skin I used to kiss, I search for the one thing that will always bind us together. She turns to leave, so I say the first thing I can think of to keep her here. "Your earrings. I remember buying them at a stand in South Padre during spring break."

Two fingers touch her right earring and spin the little turquoise teardrops. When she looks back at me, she replies, "You did. I remember."

Relief washes across her face, and she finally smiles as if we've come to an understanding. The smile is smaller than I want, but more than I deserve. "It was good seeing you again."

My heart lurches in my throat, desperate to keep talking to her, even if only for a minute. But I can't find the words when I need them most. "Stella—"

"Goodbye." She turns on her heel and heads across the parking lot. Water splashes under her feet as she moves quicker than necessary.

With each step she takes farther from me, my mind races faster. And by the time she's backing her beige sedan from the parking spot, I'm next to her window. She takes a deep breath and exhales before rolling it down. "It's good to see you," I choke out.

Her glasses are on the seat next to her, and she tugs at the seat belt across her body. Although she peeks up at me, she's quick to look away again. With her head down, she says, "It's hard seeing you on TV and hearing your songs on the radio . . ." When her eyes find mine again, her shoulders drop as if she's given up. "But hearing your voice, and you standing so close that I can touch you but . . . but can't. It . . . Why are you here, Rivers? Tell me, because I was doing just fine, and now . . ."

The rain isn't to blame for the water in her eyes.

I am.

Pressing my hands against the car, I lean over, looking

into her eyes while ignoring the lump burning in my throat. "Because I've spent five years regretting every day that didn't have you in it. Can I see you again? Can I come over and talk—"

She shakes her head, and then says, "It's too late for us, Rivers."

"But I just want to—"

"I'm taken."

Of all the things I expected to hear, that wasn't one of them. My hands fall off the car as I take a step back. "Stella?"

"No, Rivers. Just . . . no."

She pulls away, and I realize I wasn't prepared for that. I wasn't prepared for goodbye. I look at the sky, broken open and raining, and that familiar feeling returns. What I've felt for so long.

Empty.

1

Rivers

I was a disaster years in the making.

Haunted by my mother's death, I tried to drown myself in booze and drugs to cover the pain. But when I eventually lost Stella, I lost myself for good. Traveling through the past five years like a ghost, I don't even recognize this life as my own.

As soon as the cab dropped me off from the airport, I threw my stuff in the back seat and took off to see her before I changed my mind. Two hours later, I shift my SUV into park, sitting in the driveway of my brother's house knowing I'm going in there alone. I didn't think showing up at her work unannounced would have her dropping her life to breathe life back into mine, but it didn't exactly go as planned either.

Sometimes, I get caught up in the image I portray in my day to day. To the outside world, I'm the bass guitarist for a world-famous band. My face is on the cover of magazines, and I have the world at my fingertips. But they don't see the dark I carry inside, the grieving I never do because the devastation overwhelms me. I've become a master of disguise, hiding who I am on the inside.

Smile for the camera.

Play for the fans.

Do the paparazzi dance, pretending nothing's fucking wrong.

A week ago, I was at a party in New York City celebrating my band's success. Surrounded by my brothers and bandmates, our producer, mentor, and idol—Johnny Outlaw—his wife who helped us launch a line of apparel, Holli Hughes, and our manager, Tommy. I dragged my hand along the glass edge that separated me from the street fifty-five stories below. *The world at my fingertips. The toast of the town. All the money in the world.*

Something inside me is unsettled. *We're* unsettled because we never closed that chapter of our lives. We ended too fast, drastically, and without parting words to satisfy a broken heart to carry on and find someone new to love, but my heart is incapable of loving anyone but her.

Fame can't heal a broken heart.

Money won't fill a body missing its soul.

Only a soul mate can reconcile the two. And Stella is mine.

Six days, five interviews, four performances, and three cities later, I set my suitcase down in the living room and toss my backpack on a chair. Letting my jacket slide down my arms, I throw that and my hat on the chair. I look around the old house, not knowing what to do with myself.

I had gotten a text before leaving Vancouver this morning that my sister-in-law, Hannah, had the fridge stocked for me. Jet, my oldest brother, Hannah, and my nephew Alfie moved out of this house a few months ago when they made Los Angeles their new home. Since they had my niece a few months ago, the house here in Austin hasn't been a priority. I'm taking advantage of the vacancy before it goes on the market. It will be a nice crash pad for the next ten days.

Dead tired, I drag my ass to the fridge and pull out a beer while taking a quick tally of the food inside. I'm pretty set while I'm here. I hold my beer up in silent praise for Hannah.

My stomach growls, so I take a pizza from the freezer and heat the oven.

It's weird to be back in Austin, a place where Stella exists not but a few miles away. I was drawn to her the moment I heard her say my name again. That connection we had before was still there. I wanted to touch her, kiss her, and hold her again. It was painful to keep that distance between us, going against every fiber of my being.

She looked so beautiful, my pretty little mess, except she's not mine. Her words come back like a vengeance and gut me once again. *"I'm taken."*

Taken. Such a strange way to say she's dating someone. *Taken?* Not *I'm in a committed relationship.* Not *I'm seeing someone.* Not *I'm in love with someone else.* But taken. *Taken?* She's taken with some guy? She's not available?

I shove the pizza pan in the oven and lean against the counter. Drinking my beer, I stare at the oven between gulps. I finish a can before the oven timer goes off and grab another. After seeing her, drunk is not a bad state for me to be in.

Eating.

Drinking.

Passing out.

I pound down the Totino's pizza and five beers before I'm lying on the couch staring at a TV I've not turned on.

The blank screen allows my thoughts to flow back to Stella five years ago.

My clothes are on the lawn, my textbooks flying through the air and landing at my feet when I show up outside our apartment. Stella's yelling so loud that I make the mistake to try to quiet her before the cops are called. "Shhhh. Calm down, Stella."

"How dare you tell me what to do! Screw you!" She flings a book in my direction, but it falls short from hitting me. "Where's your new girlfriend, Rivers?" She disappears inside again, but I can hear her loud and clear, along with the whole apartment complex. "Or did you have sex with Naomi and actually think you could come back to me?"

When she steps out on the balcony, yelling for me to confess, I can only repeat the truth, "I didn't cheat on you, Stella."

"Really? What happened then?"

Her eyes are crazed, her mouth pressed so tight her lips pale. Her hands are bound in fists from her fury as she stares down from the second floor. My mind spins as I stumble between what I can tell her and what I can't. I stupidly gave my word to Naomi to keep her secret until she's settled. "Stella, I can't tell you."

"Why not?"

"Because she asked me not to tell anyone."

"Why would she ask my *boyfriend to do something that he can't talk about? You understand the problem with that, right?"*

"I do, but I also need you to trust me when I say—"

"I can't believe you did this to us. I can't believe you would hurt me like this." As tears run down her cheeks, she screams, "I hate you, Rivers."

. . . Stuffed and almost drunk, I let my eyes dip closed, hoping I wake up with less pain than I feel in my chest. Just for a second . . .

A knock on the door startles me awake. I rub my brow

and open my eyes. My wits are a little hazy as I try to manage the jet lag from flying half the day.

Another rap on the door rattles my head, and I stand. "Okay, I'm fucking coming." I glance at the time before I swing the door open. "It's eleven fucking fifteen, what the fu—"

"I'm sorry. I know it's late." *Oh fuck. My pretty little mess . . . I'm wide-awake now.*

She's breathtaking. Stella's hair is long, longer than she used to wear it. It flows over her shoulder with a slight wave that reminds me of when we used to sit on the banks of the Pedernales River watching the water flow over the rock bed.

Her face is clean of makeup like she used to be when she came to bed. Downplaying her great body, she's hiding it beneath a pair of skintight fitness pants and baggy old white Hanes T-shirt that hits her mid-thigh. She always looked amazing in everything she wore, but when she wore my T-shirts was my favorite.

I used to read her so well, but now, I'm not sure what she's thinking. I must stare too long because she asks, "Why are you back?"

"I live here."

A car drives by, drawing her attention to the street behind her until it passes. She crosses her arms and keeps her eyes to the side. "I don't understand."

"You haven't in a long time."

When she looks back up at me, she licks her lips before tugging the bottom one under her teeth. "What does that mean?"

My heart beats hard in my chest, and I start to wonder if she can hear it. "Why are *you* here?"

"To know why you are."

"Can't I come home?"

"Yes, of course you can. As far as I know, you do regularly. But why did you come to see me?" She shifts and sighs, her arms falling back to her sides. When she pinches the bridge of her nose, she squeezes her eyes closed. The green pastures of her eyes find mine again. "You were in Vancouver this morning." She was never afraid to broach a subject head-on.

"It was time I came back." I could tell her I needed a break from being hounded by the paparazzi. These days, the band, my two brothers and our other guitarist, are generally stalked everywhere we go. With a successful album still hanging around the charts after a year, we became an overnight success story. Only took us eight years, but it's a catchier headline to pretend our rise to fame was instant. "I wanted to see you again."

"No." Her tone is steady, her reply curt. "You don't get to decide that on a whim when I'm still trying to recover from the last time I saw you. You screwed up, Rivers. Not me."

I shouldn't love hearing her say my name when it's at the end of an accusation, but it sounds so good rolling off her tongue. I remember the way she used to say it as if I was her everything. *When I* was *her everything.*

I lost my anger over losing her without getting a fair shot to fix things a long time ago. Maybe it was selfish to come back without warning. But if I had, she wouldn't be here now. So I get why she's angry, but it doesn't change the fact that I can't live without giving us one last shot at redemption. "Is that why you came by? You had to get that off your chest?"

"There used to be so much I needed to get off my chest when it came to you," she says, narrowing her eyes. "But that was all lost when I moved on. The real question is, why are you doing this to me now?"

"I'm not trying to do anything *to* you. I wanted to see you. It's that simple."

"Nothing's simple when it comes to us."

"You're right, but I still wanted to check in on you and Meadow."

Her head jolts back. "Don't you dare pretend you care about me or my sister. And if that's the only reason you came by, then let me put your concerns to bed. Meadow and I are doing just fine."

I run my hand over my forehead and into my hair in frustration, not sure how to break through her barrier of anger. Her pretty eyes follow the motion of my hand, and the tension in her tight expression seems to falter. "Look, Rivers. You showing up at my workplace out of the blue was about you. Did you think about what I might want? Or how I would feel? If you showing up would be good for me?"

She makes a good argument, and as much as I want to blame the beers or the jet lag, I can only blame myself. A feeling of desperation, of losing her again, of her slipping away fills my gut and moves higher to my heart. "You're all I think about." I went about this all wrong, blowing this chance the minute I showed up not thinking this through and not putting her first. "I'm sorry, Stella. I knew you wouldn't take a call from me."

"You're right." When she backs away, I reach for her before I can stop the automatic reaction. When her eyes catch me, she stills. I slowly drop my hand to my side again. I fucking hate doing it, but I do anyway. Her voice is quiet, the fight weighing her down by the way her shoulders lower, and then she says, "You made your choice a long time ago—"

"You made it for us," I reply, matter-of-factly, keeping my

tone as neutral as I can, hoping she'll stay. "I would have made a different decision."

"No," she says, raising her voice. "I may have thrown you out, but you left. I wasn't worth fighting for then, so I'm not going to make amends now. Don't waste your life waiting on something that will *never* happen."

"You can't walk away—"

"Watch me." She challenges me with a tight-lipped smirk.

As much as she wants to be the one in charge of this fight . . . err, *discussion*, her body language—the way she peeks back at me, the look of curiosity in her eyes, and her hesitation to actually leave—tells me otherwise. I'm grappling, taking a risk by pushing a button, but she's leaving me no other choice. "You sure you want to do that?"

She stops and turns back around. She doesn't realize I think she's stronger because she stays.

"You know me, Stella. Want to know how I know? Because I'm in your blood, baby. There is no you without me, and there's no me without you."

Her gaze stays locked on the chipped paint of the porch when she braces her hand against the column. I wish I could take away the pain she carries inside, and the uncertainty that should never cloud this beautiful woman's mind. Her eyes flash to mine, grounding me to the spot, but then the fire inside dims. "Please don't show up . . . again."

She gets her message across with less edge this time, but it makes me curious what dulled her spirit. It would be quicker to read *War and Peace* than trying to read the myriad of emotions flickering through her eyes as she says one thing but still looks at me as if it was a question. I answer her the only way I know how—being upfront and direct. "You came over to tell me you didn't want to see me again?"

She pauses on the steps and then without responding walks down the path toward her car.

Good or bad, if I didn't cause some old feelings to rise inside her, she wouldn't have bothered to stop by. "Hey, Stella?" With the car door open in her hands, she stops with one foot in already and looks back. "It's damn good to see you again."

Shaking her head and rolling her eyes, she gets inside the beige sedan that is just so wrong for her and slams the door closed.

The gears grind as she takes the corner down the street, causing me to chuckle. I wait out on that front porch until I can't see her anymore and then head inside. The lock clicks, and I head to the bedroom not only feeling like a stranger in this house but also in this city that's my own hometown. Is this a home if she's not in it?

The bedroom is full of hand-me-downs and thrift store finds in need of a bonfire that somehow survived my older brother's bachelor days. Jet and Hannah took what they wanted when they moved to LA over the summer and bought new stuff for a house in the Hollywood Hills.

Still wound up from the late night visit, I need to vent. I'd call and bug Tulsa, my youngest brother and the band's drummer, but I'm pretty sure he meant what he said when we parted ways in at the airport. *"Don't call me. I'm going to be indisposed for the next three days."* He clicks his tongue. *"Buried deep inside—"*

"Got it," I said, cutting him off.

He's still a newlywed, though it's been a few months since he got hitched. He and Nikki, his wife, go at it like fucking rabbits. That reminds me, I need to text our band manager, Tommy, and tell him to stop booking me in hotel rooms next to theirs.

Although I flew home with a bandmate, Ridge Carson, I decide not to bug others with my fucking issues. He came back to Austin to have a break, not listen to me complain.

While mentally taking a count of the days until I have to be back in LA, I walk into the bathroom.

One month until the band has to be back in the studio.

Ten days before I head back to California.

Nine days to figure out the next chapter in my personal life. I start the shower. When steam starts filling the small bathroom, I undress with a grin lingering on my lips from my late-night visitor.

With my career on the rise, and my family settled in LA, it makes sense to relocate permanently. But I'm here to either say goodbye forever or be hers forever. And I won't know the answer until I've given it my best shot.

Stepping into the shower, I wash my body—over the three crow tattoos that represent my brothers and me, then clean the skin where the star that is there for my once true north marks my skin.

My smile fades when I think of her earlier parting words.

Taken. I really fucking hate that word.

2

Rivers

THE SUN SHINES through the window blinding me too early in the morning, reminding me of how I used to spend early mornings in my mom's arms when I was little.

My mom loved the mornings, especially around sunrise before everyone woke up. With my arm draped over my eyes, a distant memory comes back, one I hadn't thought of in years.

I can't sleep, too excited to see what presents I'm getting for my birthday. I climb out from the bottom bunk and tiptoe out of the bedroom, making sure to not wake my little brother on the top bed. As soon as I enter the living room, I see the presents, and my eyes go wide as I count seven—one for each year. My mom's tradition. I can't wait until I'm twenty. Twenty whole presents.

Sneaking a closer peek, I'm about to ease the tape off a big box when I see a figure on the front porch. My mom. I thought I'd be up before anyone. Dang. I set the present down and walk to the door that's cracked open. When I try to spy on her, she says, "Is that my birthday boy?"

Does she have eyes on the side of her head? Nothing escapes her.

I open the door and go out. The sun makes her brown hair golden in the early hours, and her brown eyes shine when she looks at me with her arms wide. I move into her warm embrace and lean my head on her shoulder. While rubbing my back, she says, "Happy birthday, Rivers."

"Am I bigger like Jet now?"

We maneuver until I'm seated on her lap. She chuckles. "You're getting there. You'll be grown before you know it and too soon for me."

"You don't want me to get big?"

"I want you healthy and happy." Tapping my nose, she says, "Boop. To grow old, and yes, big and strong."

. . . I don't remember much else from that day. I don't know what presents I got or what kind of cake I had. I remember her, though. I remember her holding me while we watched the sunrise together, feeling safe in her arms, feeling loved.

Walking to the window, I lean my hands on the sill and bend down to catch the sunrise, wishing I could watch it with her again.

Kids don't understand the concept of time, life, or death. They shouldn't have to. Fuck, I still don't get why she had to die. Seventeen years will never be enough.

I open the window, allowing the slight chill in the air to invade the room. It feels good after sweating out my nightmares.

The sun rises above the trees, and my gaze lifts to the golden-pink skies. The beauty of the heavens makes me wonder if my mom can see the mess I've made of my life. I may have all the material things a person could desire, but I don't have that happiness she wished for me.

I hate that I've disappointed the two women I've loved more than life.

All the money in the world doesn't matter when you fail your family, fail yourself, and fail the one person you thought you couldn't fail. Bestselling albums, sold-out tours, and more money than the devil can sin with are all empty accomplishments when you have no one to share it with. When there's no one to be proud of you.

No blame falls on Stella for my fuckups. She tried her best to save me. When my mom died on my seventeenth birthday, the pain tormented me. By eighteen, I was trying to drown myself in whiskey. When that wasn't working, I was looking for any way to take my mind higher than in the depths of hell it normally resided.

Moving back to the bed, I lie down, wanting this constant regret to stop taunting me.

When it came to fights, disagreements, or hurt feelings, my mom used to tell me that hope wasn't dead until the person we hope *in* closes the door. Last night, Stella tried to close that door, but my gut tells me she left it cracked open. Her visit gave me a kernel of hope. She's not the only one who's riding the line between conflict of the heart and mind. This middle ground I've been dwelling in for years is slowly killing me.

My head swims with memories of how Stella and I used to be.

Stella Fellowes, the prettiest girl in school, sits under the big oak tree at lunch, like most days. While I stand at a distance, I wonder if she's ever noticed me?

I live in Jet's shadow, and Tulsa snags all the attention when he's around. As a middle kid, I've learned to let them own the spotlight while I tend to disappear in the background. I never really minded until now.

But Stella's not just a pretty face. She's smart and talks to anyone, unlike the other popular girls. Jet told me he thinks she's cute but called her a kid like me and told me to make a move before someone else did.

I take a deep breath, then blow it out, gathering any stupid courage I can muster, and head for the tree because today is the day I find out if she even knows me. Her head is down, her full attention on the book in her lap.

At first, she doesn't see me standing there beside her. I'm about to go back to the cafeteria, thinking I might have made a big mistake coming over, but before I have a chance to leave, she looks up. "Hi."

"Hi," *I reply. Not very smooth. Say something. Say something. Say anything. God, I need to fill this deadening silence.* "I play guitar." *What the heck? I'm screwing this up so badly.*

I turn to leave, knowing I just blew any cool I might have faked. But then she says, "I heard you in the music room the other day. You're very good. My dad told me there are different types of guitar. Which one do you play?"

"Bass. It's the unsung hero in a band. There's no glory in it. That usually goes to a lead electric guitar, but the music's better because of the bass." *What the hell? I sound so dumb.*

She smiles, putting me at ease. "Do you want to eat lunch with me, Rivers?"

She knows my name? She knows my name! Holy, what universe is this? "Yeah." *I sit down before she has a chance to change her mind, and ask,* "What are you reading?"

"Pride and Prejudice." *She flips the cover over to show me. It's been read a few times by appearances.* "I've read it before. Sometimes I just like to revisit characters."

"Like they're real," *I say, chuckling.*

"They are to me." *She closes the book without worry of losing her place in the story.* "Tell me about your music. Do you play in *the school band or take lessons? Have you played long? Who taught you?"*

It's still hot out, though it's mid-October, but fall is coming. A breeze blows her shiny hair into the air like a little hurricane of brown strands. Trying to tame them, she pats it down and then tucks it behind both ears. She's one of the few girls who doesn't cake on the makeup. She wears just enough to highlight what I already find so pretty instead of taking away from her beauty.

Sea green eyes stare into my boring browns, and her curiosity, her genuine interest shines. I reply, "My mom taught me some basics on her acoustic guitar when I was younger, but my brother Jet mostly taught me." My heart pounds in my chest as I get caught up in her eyes. "What else did you ask?"

She reaches into her brown lunch bag and pulls out a sandwich. "Did you bring lunch today?"

If I told her the truth—I left it on the kitchen table because I was so nervous about seeing her today—she'd laugh at me. "No."

"You can have half of mine."

"It's okay. I can grab a soda from the cafeteria."

"You need food, Rivers." I love the way she says my name like it matters.

Stella hands me half the sandwich, which was cut diagonally. She says, "It's bologna, but it's what was on sale this week. My mom only buys the weekly special."

"Yeah, my mom too. My dad's not around, and there are three boys, so I'm used to bologna. I actually like it, though. Thanks." I take a bite.

When we finish the sandwich, we talk about her favorite books and my music while eating the chips and sharing an orange.

She didn't just share her lunch with me. I knew right then that she was sharing her heart. That was the day I fell in love under the oak tree. I've only ever loved her since.

3

Rivers

UNTIL MY PHONE starts buzzing across the nightstand, I didn't remember I'd made plans for today. "Fuck." Grabbing the phone, I answer it. "I'll be there in ten minutes." I hang up on Ridge before he has a chance to speak.

I lie there a few extra seconds and scrub my hands over my face. My body feels heavy as though it's part of the mattress, but I push up just as my phone buzzes again. *Fuck me.* This time I answer and put it on speaker. "It's lunch, not a fucking emergency. What the fuck, man? I said I'll be there."

"Rivers?"

My eyes dart to the screen when I hear her soft voice come through, filling my heart with hope. "Stella?" I'm greeted by silence but still hold it to my ear. "Stella?" Then the line goes dead. I try to call her back, but she doesn't answer.

I'm wide-awake now but have no clue why she called, so I immediately text her: *Call me back.*

I watch dots creep across the screen, and then stop. "*Fuck.* Come on, Stella." I wait a minute and then send another text: *Please.*

What feels like an hour passes. Of course, it's only about thirty seconds, but then she calls. *Thank God!* I almost drop the phone trying to answer it. "Stella?"

"Rivers—"

My stomach drops. "Hey, how are you?" She's texting and willing to call me. My mind spins to worst-case scenarios. "Is something wrong? Are you okay?"

"I'm . . . I don't know how I am." She releases a breath into the phone as if she's given up. "I didn't know if I should contact you again, but I had to."

"You can call anytime." *I just need to hear your voice, baby. I've missed you so much.*

She laughs nervously. "I came over last night to tell you not to contact me again, but now I'm the one instigating something I shouldn't."

She knows her limits, and I've become a hard one for her. *I hate it.*

Or maybe she's dating an overprotective asshole who wants to control her every move.

I used to be an overprotective asshole when it came to her, but I never wanted to control or change her. I just wanted to protect her from the other assholes out there. Now here she is, and she's dating one of them. My head hangs forward, my own guilt for this mess eating at me. "Is this about you seeing someone else?"

"I shouldn't have come over last night either," she says as if the visit is a sin she needs to confess to. "I shouldn't be calling you now. What message am I sending? I'm hot. I'm cold. I'm on. I'm off. You know what I am?" She rushes the words when she says, "I'm weak. You make me feel weak,

Rivers. So I can't do this because just your presence messes with my head. If I open the door to you even a little, you'll work your way back into my life as if you never left." She chokes up. "Please don't do this to me."

Another crack in my heart deepens, and I close my eyes. "What do you want me to do, Stella? Forget you exist? It's been five fucking years, and I haven't managed to do that yet." I hate the plea in my tone. I hate how desperate I sound, how weak she makes me. I'm at the mercy of this woman, and she wants nothing to do with me. But for her, I'll plead. "Please, baby."

The sound of her tears echoes through the silence between us. "I can't. You've already reopened the wounds I thought were healing."

She's so careful when she speaks of our breakup, not wanting to tread on the grave of our relationship or disturb it. I'll fucking tread on it. I'll disturb it if it gets us talking. "I don't want to do this over the phone, but I deserve a chance to tell you what happened."

"You had a chance and didn't take it. I've had to live with that." She starts to speak, "I can't do this . . ." and then goes quiet. A pause turns into silence.

"Stella? I'm begging for your time. Ten minutes. Half an hour. Anything. Please."

"If I give you ten minutes, it won't change anything. The damage is done." I hear how she struggles to say what she thinks needs to be said. I hear her heart breaking through the line. "*We* aren't the same people, and *our* situations aren't the same."

She's taken. *What the fuck am I doing?* Am I willing to destroy the happiness she's found for my own selfish reasons?

True love isn't burdening her with my personal ambitions. True love is letting her be happy whether it's with me or someone else.

I can't do it. I don't want to. I can't give her up. She's my everything.

I have to, though. I have to walk away, though the pain is already rivaling the day I walked away the first time. I begin to speak, but my voice cracks, revealing the fractures in my heart, so I stop and start again. "I'm sorry I hurt you. I'm sorry I couldn't tell you the truth back then. I'm sorry . . . I'm just sorry about everything."

Her sobs are heard even though I can tell she's attempting to stifle them. "Stella?"

"Yeah?"

"Do you really want me to let you go?"

She sniffles again. "I need you to let me go."

"Then I'll let you go, but I will always love you."

The pain overwhelms me, and my mind goes fuzzy. I don't think goodbyes are exchanged. There's nothing good about saying bye to her. *Forever.* But when I look at my phone, the call has ended.

I slam it on the bed behind me, wanting to smash it, wanting to destroy the conversation that will remain our last. "Fuck!" I shout, my hands trembling and my muscles tightening in rage. I can't eat with all this anger coursing through me. Getting up, I take my phone and text Ridge: *I can't make it.*

Ridge: *Lazy ass fucker.*

Ridge: *Beers later?*

Me: *Yeah. Gallons.*

Ridge: *That bad?*

Me: *Worse.*

Ridge: *Sorry, man.*

Digging a pair of shorts out of my suitcase, I pull them

on. Everything's dirty from traveling, but that won't matter ten minutes from now when I'm pounding out my anger on the concrete.

I pull my sneakers and a pair of socks out, slipping them on after snapping on my wristwatch. I'm pushing myself today, and I want to know how many damn steps I cover.

Ridge: *Maybe not gallons. We have an album to record, and your bros will kill me if I let you drink yourself to death. But doubles are on tap tonight.*

I don't know why that makes me laugh, but it does. I didn't know him two years ago, but after traveling with Ridge on tour, he fits in like we've known him our whole lives.

Me: *Doubles then.*

Opening the fridge, I pull out an energy drink and down it. Not a good meal, but it will give me the hit I need to cover some miles. I head out the back door and around to the street.

It's not a straight shot to the trail that wraps Lady Bird Lake, but it's under two miles, so I head that way, wanting to see some water. I need the peace it brings.

Another reminder plays back with every step I run.

I'm taken.

You make me weak.

Like you always do.

Like you always have.

Please don't do this to me.

My feet come to an abrupt stop near the lookout point. I anchor my hands above my knees, bending over and gasping for air. I thought running would clear my head and heal some of my heart, but the more air I take in, the more I realize that nothing's going to heal me. *Except her.* It's been years of fucking torture, and it's not getting better.

I'm not getting better.

I'm getting bitter.

Please don't do this to me.

Her words haunt me. All this time I thought it was her doing this to me.

The misunderstanding in the favor I did for a friend grows into a tornado, gathering strength as it travels the distance from then to the here and now. We're victims in this tornado of emotion's path, our love destroyed like our innocence.

There's nothing left of me worth salvaging in the aftermath. When I think of her, see her beauty on the inside fighting to shine through again, I wonder if she's the same as she was before we were leveled to nothing. Is there anything left of the girl I once knew?

Or has everyone taken what was good, so pure, and twisted her into what she has to be to fit in? Does the man lucky enough to call her *his* know the value of her worth? Does he treat her the way I should have, the way I once did? Is *he* worthy of *her* love? *Am I?*

No.

I press my hands against the rough bricks, letting the jagged cement dig into the palms of my hands. These are the same hands that play a bass guitar like I used to touch her, hitting her high and low notes with ease and finding the sweet spot by memory. Every time I hold the guitar she gave me, it's almost like I'm touching her again—the strong strings, the bass beats, tightening and loosening to adjust to her needs, her desires, craving that sound she makes when our melody comes together.

We shouldn't see each other.

My head falls forward, my breath still hard to catch, but I don't think it's from the running. When I open my eyes, I see the blood staining the mortar, and I pull back, not feeling the pain but knowing my hands have given me the only salvation I've found. *Music.* Without the band, I wouldn't be here, but without her, do I want to be?

Instead of damaging my hands, I should be living the high life—fucking a different groupie every night, blowing cash like cocaine, being fucked-up enough not to notice the difference when I'm down.

But I've been there. Not so much the groupies but everything else. Knew changes had to be made.

Giving up drugs wasn't hard.

Losing her was. Facing a reality of never having her again the hardest of all.

The pain of that day is fresher than the blood that slides to the tip of my finger and falls to the ground when I start jogging, my mind still caught in the vortex of my remorse.

A favor for a friend destroyed us. But . . . *will the truth make a difference?*

Or do I walk away and live with this regret for the remainder of my days? Do I leave her be, so she can find her happily ever after without me?

Just like when my mom died, maybe I've never had a choice. Maybe I was meant to lose her too.

.

4

Stella Fellowes

WHEN IT COMES TO MUSICIANS, they're passionate about more than just the music. They're passionate about everything from the people who surround them, to love, to breathing, living life to the fullest, snorting, creating, demolishing. Nothing was done with less than his full effort, including our demise.

Sitting in the driveway, I put the car in park and cut the headlights. It's been a long day at work, so talking with him this morning feels like it was a long time ago. I leave the car on, letting the song play out. I shouldn't even be listening to The Crow Brothers, but their music was always so damn good. I know all the old songs by heart. *Still.*

It's as if their music is ingrained in my heart just like Rivers East Crow is. I wish I were strong enough to turn off the car and end the songs before the album finishes, but like all those years ago, I'm still weak to it . . . defenseless against him.

Seeing him standing in the rain waiting for me brought back all the feelings I worked so hard to bury. I wanted to run to him, jump into his arms, and forgive him. But I lost him and my best friend all in one swoop. *How do I move past that?*

Rivers and I were inseparable from the moment we met. We changed a lot in those years—together and separately, but I always thought we were soul mates, each other's one and only, soldiers for true love.

At seventeen, his mother's death shook our once solid foundation. While he fell apart, I tried to hold us together. I chose to love him through his pain, love him so hard in hopes of healing him again because it didn't matter how far he fell, I knew where his love lay. *With me.* But somewhere along the way, I lost myself. Young love does that, over-shadows all else. He was my world, and I refused to lose him to partying, drinking, drugs, and the fame he was gaining around Austin.

But I trusted too much, loved too hard, and held too tightly to the memories of what we used to be.

Now he's back, looking more handsome than ever. I missed the slight wave to his hair from wearing ball caps. I missed the way I could see his emotions in the deep seas of his eyes, the rolling tides, and everything he tried to hide from the world. He could never hide from me. Those arms used to embrace me, protect me, but now, his hands were in his pockets as if he didn't know how to act around me. I miss the rough touch of his calloused hands.

But why is he back?

A knock on my window startles me, and I scream, holding my hand to my chest. Brian. *Shoot.*

My other complication.

The downside of having a friend and coworker as your landlord? Some days, I don't want to chitchat, but it feels like I have to because of who he is.

I turn off the car, and the music ends before I pop the door open. "Hey," I say, getting out but not making eye contact, praying he doesn't ask me what I was doing.

"Hey. What were you doing? You've been out here for a while."

The door closes behind me, and I set the alarm while hurrying to the front door of the guesthouse. "Yeah, I thought I left something at school."

His voice is right behind me as he matches my steps. "Did you?"

"No," I say, keeping my eyes on the tile floors when I walk through the door. I hang the keys on the hook and maneuver farther inside. I stop to block the entrance, but he's already standing in the doorway.

Concern weaves its way through the creases in his forehead, and worry is seen in his eyes. "Are you all right?"

"Fine."

My answer is greeted with a hard look before his expression softens. "I worry about you. You're working a lot later these past few months."

"I've been updating the class syllabus. We got a little off track during the benchmark testing." I give a fake smile that hopefully passes his scrutiny. "We still have to cover everything."

"Very true. The curriculum is set." Brian's hair is swept neatly to the side, his part perfectly in place like it was when he left for school this morning. His yellow button-down is wrinkle free and reeks of his job as a principal, successfully hiding any work he did today.

Looking at this man, a man who has been a good friend, I can't help but compare him to another. His eyes are a pallid shade of Rivers's soulful brown ones. I shake the comparison away.

This man who was once my school's principal has become a friend, and he was there four months ago with a helping hand. *"I have a guesthouse . . . until you get back on your feet again . . . reduced rent. It's no trouble . . . it will be good to have some company . . ."*

Wordlessly, he takes a step onto the welcome mat. "If you're up for hanging out, I'm home tonight." I've tried to keep my distance, careful not to lead him on. We're coworkers—not roommates, not lovers, and not dating. Despite the clarity I've always tried to provide, he still looks at me with lingering hope.

"Thanks," I say, pulling the door until it's almost closed. "I'm going to take a long bath and get to bed early."

"Sure. Sounds like a plan." He starts back to his house. "Have a good night, Stella."

"Have a good night." I close the door and lock it before leaning against it and releasing a breath that seemed to be lodged in my throat all day.

Since school started, I've struggled to find my old routine. I don't know what's wrong with me. Besides the issues with my family, my mind has been elsewhere, my thoughts touring with The Crow Brothers. It's impossible to avoid them at this point. *Would I be with them now had we stayed together?*

No. Don't go down that road. Too much water under that bridge. But I've missed them.

I never could have afforded to go to Jet's wedding in California, but I couldn't bring myself to reply to his wedding invitation either. No seemed so final and yes just wasn't possible. After missing Jet's wedding, I would see one gossip piece and lose hours in regret, brokenhearted all over again.

I came so close to texting Tulsa when I heard about him getting married. I miss my honorary little brother. But I couldn't bear to be told about Rivers and couldn't bring myself to smile on the outside even though I was happy for him. I don't like to think of that time. It may have been the best time of his life, but it was my worst, just a month after being viol—

I wasn't in a good place.

I'm still not.

It's a period of my life that's a black hole of nightmares I don't want to get sucked back into.

I should be happy. My finances are finally getting back on track. I have a good job that I used to love and a nice place to live.

It starts to rain outside, and I move the curtain to the side to look out the window that faces Brian's house. He's looking out his kitchen window and waves. I send him a little wave, wishing I had the capacity to appreciate him. *But I can't.* Not how he wants.

I had begun to believe that I had lost the ability to feel much more than dissatisfied and anxious. Those seem to have been the dominant emotions since . . . my throat squeezes, and my fingers tighten around the curtain. I force myself to remember that night months ago in hopes of eventually ridding the memories forever.

But when I saw Rivers, a rush of different emotions washed through me. I don't know how I held myself together in front of him. Maybe I didn't, but in a lot of ways, if for no other reason, I'm grateful for his return. It's intoxicating to feel every nerve in my body again.

He's not my salvation like he once was.

Rivers has moved on and succeeded.

Living life in the limelight.

Watching from afar, his new life suits him.

I let the curtain fall and lean against the wall. Sinking to the floor, I close my eyes and drop my head to my knees, withering while he thrives.

5

Stella

I DO a double take when I see Brian on the other side of the slim glass window carved into the classroom door. The knock causes the students to stir as they look up from their test. Hurrying to answer it, I crack it open, and ask, "What are you doing here?"

Whispering, he asks, "May I see you in the hall?"

I look back at the class before I step out. "What is it?"

"I need two favors."

"My kids are taking a test. I should be in there. Can this wait?"

"I was planning on asking you last night, but I decided against it since you weren't yourself."

That was the real me, whether he chooses to acknowledge it or not, but I'm not going to fight to prove otherwise. "What do you need?"

"I need you to take the lead for the Halloween dance."

"You're asking me now? This couldn't have waited?"

"Mrs. Warner needs you to take the lead since she got as she says, 'shafted with homecoming' this year."

"Look, I can't add another thing to my plate, Brian." I check on my class again. "I told her I would help her, but to take over? That's too much right now."

"It's the only other major dance besides homecoming and prom. The kids love it, and if you can't do it, it's getting dropped this year." *Talk about being pressured.*

I sigh and lean on the wall, feeling cornered. I really don't want the added stress, but he's right. "The kids love it. Fine. I'll do it."

He pats my shoulder. "I knew we could count on you. You're always dependable."

Dependable?

Ugh. Who knew at twenty-five that the only compliment I'd be receiving these days would feel more like an insult. The sound of the soft soles of his dress shoes against the floors as he walks away draws my attention.

Looking down at my own soft-soled shoes, I tap my foot several times trying to make them clack, to echo down the hall, but I'm punished with the sound of sensible, responsible, and comfortable instead. *Ugh.*

I go back inside the classroom and quietly shut the door so I don't disturb the students' concentration. Sliding back into my chair and tucking my legs under the desk, I scan the room of high school students again before I open my laptop to look up Halloween themed dances. Music disrupts the quiet, and I scramble to turn it off. All the students look up and some start giggling while I fumble through my thirty open programs to find my music player. I hit mute instead.

Sasha, a student who sits in the front row, laughs behind her hand, and says, "Good taste in music, Ms. Fellowes."

Josh, one of the star football players and Mr. Popular,

sitting in the back, says, "I saw The Crow Brothers over the summer. Kick-ass concert."

It's been three days since I talked to him on the phone, and sticking to my request, he hasn't contacted me since. But my heart still clenches from the mention of their name. I try to steady myself and get control back. "Language, Mr. Baird."

Just when I return my attention to the laptop, he adds, "Sorry, Stella."

My gaze shoots up, directed on him. "It's Ms. Fellowes."

"My apologies, *Miss* Fellowes." With his hand over his heart, he smiles, but I know that kind of smile. It's a smirk that used to work on me when I was younger and much dumber.

I don't need smirks or handsome faces, great abs, or hands that . . . *shit*. Coming to my rightful senses, I say, "Everyone back to work, or you're not going to finish before the bell."

When the class settles back into their test, I find the music player and hit stop but not before glancing at the band name and song title—The Crow Brothers, "Daydreams."

My mind reaches into my memories and pulls the night Rivers wrote that song to the forefront.

Wrapped in the new sheets we recently treated ourselves to, I relish the softness of them against my bare skin. Keeping my eyes closed, I snuggle into Rivers's side despite the sunshine sneaking in under the shade.

When he starts to move as if he's climbing out of bed, I throw my arm over his leg and hold on. "No, stay with me. All day."

I feel the heat of a large hand cover my back, and I smile against his hip. He says, "Let me get my guitar. I'll be right back. Promise."

His voice is so sexy, deep, and full of dirty promises. I release my arm and watch as he stands—his body would make the cast of Magic Mike *envious. Olive skin over carved muscle. Two lower back divots lead my gaze lower to the smooth indentations on the sides of his ass. The muscles in his back flex as he bends down to pick up his acoustic guitar.*

He turns around, and there's just enough hair on his chest to dust the tips of my fingers across when he sits down. Rivers has changed over the years we've been together. I watched him become a man. He used to be a few inches taller than me at fifteen, but then nature made a masterpiece, stealing the peaks of physical perfection and creating the man he became. At six foot two, he stands almost a full foot taller than I do. His body eclipses mine, but I feel safe, protected, his love felt in his shadow. I willingly move into the darkness and find his welcome embrace on the hardest of days.

"A melody came to me while watching you sleep." Settling back on the bed, he kisses my forehead while strumming. *"It starts off soft like this."*

He plays a few chords and then tightens a string to tune the guitar, strums again, and closes his eyes. His fingers play the melody in his mind.

I say, "It's pretty."

"Like you, my love."

Rolling onto my side, I close my eyes while he creates a song, and I memorize the purity of this moment. There's been a shift in his life, and I've been trying to keep up. He's partying harder and drowning himself in the after-parties. Sometimes, I drink and sometimes I don't. I always observe.

I used to be right there at his side, but he seems not to notice a difference lately. So moments like these when we lie in the place where we're building a home and life together, it's easy to forget our late-night struggles. I drift off into the peaceful illusion.

. . . I look up just as the bell finishes ringing. Popping up from my chair, I call out over the noise of talking, chairs skidding against the linoleum, and bags being packed. "Your test should be on my desk before you leave the room, or you'll get a zero. Thank you and have a great weekend."

"Ms. Fellowes?"

"Yes, Sasha?"

"Mrs. Warner said you were taking over the planning of the Halloween dance."

"I just agreed during class," I start, realizing I was set up. They already planned for me to take it on whether I wanted to or not. I really need to get a life, so I can learn to say no. "Yes, I will be."

"Great," she replies with a wide smile. "I'm on the student decorating committee."

"Oh, good. If you have any ideas, let me know. I'm drawing a blank on a theme right now."

She nods excitedly. "I have a whole folder of ideas. I started planning during the summer."

"Wow. All righty then. We can organize an after-school meeting with the committee next week."

"I'll email the team."

"Thank you." When the class clears out, Josh leisurely struts his way to the front and sets his test down in front of me. I hate his arrogance. Everybody at this school bows to him because they want another division championship, but his athletic career isn't my priority. His education is. I say, "You should get going or you'll be late for your next class."

As if I didn't say anything at all, he asks, "I was wondering what a teacher does on a Friday night. Do you go out or like to stay in?"

"That's none of your business, Mr. Baird. Have a good weekend."

His eyes stay on mine a beat too long, making me uncomfortable. I stand my ground, keeping my body stiff so there's no room for interpretation. He swings his backpack over his shoulder and laughs while walking to the door. "If you ever want a break from that rut you're stuck in, come by the lookout off the 360 bridge." I watch until he leaves. He's such a cocky little shit.

I came into this field starry-eyed, wanting to make a difference in education and help shape young minds. Everyone warned me about teaching high school. They told me to work in an elementary, but I was drawn to the subjects. I realize now they were right.

It took me a few years to adapt and make enough changes to start garnering respect. It's ridiculous that a pair of glasses with non-prescription lenses, wearing my hair in a low bun, and loose-fitting clothes can throw off hormonal teenagers. Even though the changes were necessary, I miss being me.

I had also hoped to find not just peers once I settled into my first job, but also new friends. It didn't work out that way. I'm too broken to make real friendships. Nobody knows what I've endured. I've become a master of protecting my secrets. Meadow doesn't know, and no one else ever will. I lost so much of myself in the past few years that I have nothing left to give.

It's funny, though, because Rivers looked at me like he was seeing the old me. If I wouldn't have been in so much shock, I could have appreciated that more. In the quietest of moments when my mind is open, I will savor that look on Rivers's face since I may never see it again.

Sadly, Josh's words ring true. *"Rut you're stuck in."* I am in a rut. I used to go out all the time, at least three nights a week. Grabbing my phone, I call my sister, Meadow.

Only two years younger than me, most mistake us for twins. She hates that, and I love it. She's a gorgeous girl with a strong sense of herself. With a few short-term relationships behind her, she's currently single and has been begging me to go out for weeks. "Hey, what's up?" she answers.

My heart races from the adrenaline, and my words rush out, "Want to go out tonight?"

"Now that's the sister I know. Yes, I want to go out. Where and what time?"

Standing, I start packing up my stuff, excited to break out of this rut. "La Condesa at seven?"

"Perfect. I'm getting off work now. Are you driving or calling a car?"

"I'll drive. I can pick you up."

"Come get dressed at mine. This has been a long time coming. Let's make the most of it."

She always makes me smile. "I'll see you soon."

"With wine."

"Yes," I reply, "with wine." Tonight feels like a good start to some much needed trouble. I need to find myself again. And if anyone knows how to find that, it's my sister. But only the best kind of trouble, the fun girls out for a good time kind.

I head home to pack and then back out to Meadow's. When she opens the door, I hold the wine and my bag up. Laughing, she grabs the wine, making me whine. "Hey, thanks for the welcome and the help."

"Get your ass in here, sis. Let's get to drinkin' and lookin' our best. We have a date with destiny. Are you ready?"

"More than ever."

6

Rivers

Ridge empties the contents of the Taco Bell bag on the coffee table just as I sit on the couch and set down two beers. Shuffling through the options, I ask, "Where's my double stuffed?"

"Weren't you ever taught that you get what you fucking get and you don't throw a fucking fit?"

Chuckling, I toss a beef Meximelt at him. "It went a little differently back then."

"Too many fucks?"

"Yeah. Pretty much. My kindergarten teacher didn't say that version." Spying my two requests, I reach over and grab the double stuffed tacos and kiss my delicious pretties. "Come to me."

After shoving half a Meximelt into his mouth, he pops open the beer can and washes it down. "Wanna head downtown later? The Dahlgreens are playing Mohawk tonight."

"Man, I haven't seen those guys in a few years. They're back from New York?"

"Moved back over the summer. I told Sheckler I'd stop by."

"Yeah, it'll be good to get out."

It's weird how much things change when you're away. We didn't know the doorman at Mohawk even though he knew us and let us skip ahead of the line. We missed the first two bands but arrive while The Dahlgreens are still setting up.

Grabbing beers from the bar, we head over to the side of the stage. Sheckler, their lead singer, nods when we approach, a large smile spreading. He stands to greet us. "Crow. Carson. Good to see ya. What brings you to town?"

I hand him a beer, and then we shake hands. "Trying to take care of some unfinished business before heading back to LA."

He and Ridge fist bump as he says, "Cool. You staying for the show?"

"That's why we came out. Don't let us down," I joke.

"Yeah, I'll try not to." He turns over his shoulder, and to his bandmates, he says, "We've got celebrities in the house. Don't fuck it up."

The guys laugh. I used to party on the regular with them in my bad days and created some of my worst memories with them. They've cleaned up, as I have, for the most part.

Ridge is a lot like me and doesn't need the spotlight. With a few people now staring at us, he asks under his breath, "Think it's safe to stay?"

Looking around, I nod. "It's cool here."

Sheckler tightens the mic, and asks, "So how's the big time? As great as we all dream?"

Ridge replies, "Better."

Knocking Ridge on the arm, he adds, "The pussy or the profits?"

"Both," Ridge says, laughing.

Sheckler also chuckles. "It's good to have The Crow Brothers gone. We're getting more of your old gigs and maybe even some of the ladies you guys left behind broken-hearted." Coming to the side of the stage, he adds, "Not that you're interested or anything, but I saw Meadow Fellowes and your ex in here earlier."

I lower the beer and lock eyes on his. "I'm listening," I say, giving him my complete attention.

"Still don't know how you left that pretty all alone. Was Naomi worth it?"

I tug at my collar, hating that gossip persists in spite of how hard I tried to tell the truth. "Nasty rumors, man. We never hooked up. The whole situation is jacked up. I was only helping her out; a favor that ended up fucking me over with Stella."

He looks over his shoulder when his name is called, giving the drummer a nod. When Sheckler turns back, he says, "That sucks, Crow. Maybe you should go talk to her. I've not heard any updates on her." He signals to the front corner of the bar. "I stopped by to say hi but had to get back to set up." He makes sure my eyes are on him before he says, "She's looking good. And her little sister—*damnnn*. If I didn't have a girlfriend, I wouldn't be here talking to you fuckers."

Jealousy rises like bile in my throat, and my grip on the beer bottle tightens. He's a fucker for even thinking about them that way.

I turn around and scan the crowd, but it doesn't take me long to find her. *Fuck.* My chest constricts, and I hit my fist against it twice, hoping to loosen the sudden ache. *Why does she have to be so goddamn gorgeous?*

It's only been a few days since I've seen her, but every time feels like the first time again when it comes to her. Just enough light filters over the bar where it reaches her and her sister for me to see her smile and laughing, engaged in a conversation with Meadow.

Meadow was like the little sister I never had. She could be as annoying as Tulsa sometimes, but other times, she was a good girl, sweet as my mom's apple pie. I used to greet her dates after working out. My muscles were taut, my shirt covered in sweat. I let them know from the get-go not to fuck with my family.

Her parents never gave a shit if she was out late or dating some loser, but Stella and I did. The day of the breakup, Meadow delivered my guitars to me after Stella locked me out of the apartment. I begged her to help me, to get Stella to talk to me. Making a call, she did her best.

Hugging her goodbye wasn't easy. She wiped her tears on my shirt and told me to keep trying. I did, but anger came after the grief, and I stopped trying.

Standing in my brother's apartment, I realized we might be over. The shock settled in, the pain engulfing me. I didn't cry when my mother died. No. I was too busy trying to pretend it wasn't happening to give her death an ounce of honesty.

I cried for Stella.

I let my fucking emotions pour out of me and dropped to my knees. Her words troubling me now just as they did then. *"You promised me you would never hurt me, but you did. You betrayed me, Rivers. You destroyed me."*

That's when I knew I had fucked-up beyond repair.

I look back, and Ridge asks, "That's her?"

"That's her."

My shoulder is clapped. "Seems time hasn't healed old wounds, my friend."

I put my back to her, not knowing what I should do, but hoping she doesn't see me. "I must seem so fucking weak to you."

"We're friends, Rivers. You can talk to me. I've been there. The difference is my ex cheated on me, so it was a lot easier to walk away. The night we ended was beyond fucked-up."

Running my hand through my hair, I glance back once more before saying, "I'm the one who fucked-up. I made a bad decision."

"Thought you said you didn't cheat?"

"I didn't, but she thinks I did."

"Tell her then. Maybe she'll forgive you."

I'm already scoffing before I can think otherwise, because part of me is angry that she didn't believe me. Didn't trust me. It took time to see how bad things had looked to her. Understandable why she reacts to me the way she does now.

Please don't do this to me.

"I'm thinking she's not quite ready." The band starts warming up, the sound blaring through the speaker next to us. We work our way back to the bar for another round. I lower the beanie over my brow, hoping to remain unseen by any fans. It would be good to hear the full set from The Dahlgreens, if possible.

I lean my hands against the cement bar top and look down the length to the far end, stealing glances around other patrons. Stella and Meadow are looking around, so I rest my elbows and lower my head, glancing toward the stage. The band starts jamming, and the audience turns to watch. I realize Stella is going to have to look past me to watch the band. *Shit.* I catch the bartender's eyes, and she heads over. She asks, "What can I get you?"

There's no fucking way I'm letting this opportunity pass me by. Looking out of the corners of my eyes, I know exactly what I have to do. "Three bottles of Dos Equis and three shots of Jack Daniels."

She reaches into the cooler and sets the bottles in front of me, then slides a bottle opener to me. While I pop the tops, she pours the three shots. "On me, good lookin'."

She's cute, but she's no Stella. Reaching into my wallet, I pull out a fifty and hand it to her. "Thanks."

Impressed, she says, "Thank you."

I nudge Ridge. "A beer and shot for you." Grabbing the two shots and bottles from in front of me, I turn to duck out. "Be right back."

"You sure you want to do that?"

I shrug. "I don't have a choice." There's no way I can't talk to her one last time.

Walking toward the door, I veer when the bar ends and make my way through a few groups packed in for the show. I stop and stand near but will have to push through some guys to get closer. Watching her and Meadow, she leans in to talk, her hair falling to the side, blocking the side of her face from me. It hits halfway down her back, and the soft wave is enticing to hold like I used to when we would venture to wilder times in bed.

I don't know why I'm still here when I could be there, and why is my heart beating against my rib cage? I know the answer—this is it. My last shot. She already ended us, so what's the worst that can happen?

When I step up to stand next them, Meadow casually looks back and then up at me before gasping. "Rivers!"

Stella's head whips to the side, and her mouth falls open

before she catches herself, and asks, "What are you doing here?"

Her defenses are up. I get it. My walls feel high as the night sky right now, but I push past them. "Hi."

She stands as if she doesn't know what to do with herself. Her fingers fidget with her jeans, and then she runs her hands along her backside. Maybe she's nervous too.

Not able to stop myself, I admire how good those jeans look on her. Her eyebrow rises as she shifts under my gaze. She says, "I thought . . . we weren't supposed to see each . . ." I'm not sure if I like how flustered she appears to be. This could go south fast.

I stand my own ground, though, and hold up the peace offering. "I saw you and Meadow sitting here and thought you might like some drinks."

Meadow takes a shot glass and a bottle. "Thank you," she says with a smile that puts me at ease.

"You weren't even old enough to drink when we last had a drink together."

She laughs. "Neither were you."

"This is true."

Okay, this is good. Meadow's good with me being here. Then I look at Stella whose shoulders are practically at her ears. She crosses her arms over his chest. "I don't need you buying us drinks, Rivers. We can afford them."

"Um," I start, not sure why she's so offended. "I didn't buy them because I thought you couldn't. I bought them . . ." *Shit. Why did I buy them?* To get into her good graces or to give me a reason to talk to her? Either way doesn't change the fact that she told me to stay away from her.

I'm just about to rethink this really terrible plan until I come up with a better one when she takes the shot glass and downs the whiskey. After scrunching her nose, she takes the beer and chases the hard liquor down.

Unexpectedly, she pokes me in the chest and looks up at me. God, I miss her looking at me like I hung the stars. That's not the look I get this time, but it makes me want to try my damnedest to put those stars back in her eyes. "Thank you for the drinks, but you, sir, are not welcome to stay here staring down at me like that."

"Like what?"

There was a slight smile before, but it fades and her eyes dip to the floor between us. "Like you care about me."

"I do care about you."

"Don't throw bullshit lines at me. You don't know me anymore. You can't possibly care about me when I'm basically a stranger."

"Stella, come on. I'm just—"

"Leaving. Please, Rivers . . . I can't do this." Moving around me, she works her way through the crowd toward the restrooms.

I'm not sure if I should—Meadow pushes my arm, stopping me from second-guessing myself, and says, "Don't just stand there. Go after her, silly."

I don't have to be told twice.

7

Rivers

CUTTING THROUGH THE CROWD, I see her get in line up ahead, but by the time I make my way over, she slips inside the bathroom.

Side-eyed by the other girls waiting in line, one snaps her fingers and points at me. "Hey, you're Rivers Crow."

The small hall is full of chatter until that moment. Another girl gasps and her eyes go wide. "Oh. My. God."

Phones are pulled from purses, and I'm touched on my arm, my ass, my back, everywhere all at once. *Shit*. This is a really bad idea. The bathroom door swings open and my star, my beauty, grabs my wrist. "Hands off, ladies." Then I'm pulled toward her, loving every second of her touching me again. "Come on, Riv."

One long stride and I'm in the women's restroom. Alone with her. A smirk pops out without my permission. The door is closed and locked to the sounds of squeals and my name on the other side. "What are you doing?"

"Saving your ass." The right side of her delectable mouth rides up. "Thanks would be nice."

"Thanks, but quick question. Now that you have me in here, what do you plan to do with me?"

Her body is relaxed, her shoulders not stiff and at her ears like they were earlier. She taps her fingers on her hip that's kicked out and accentuates the curve of her waist. I receive an epic eye-roll before she turns and says, "Window."

Looking over her, because I can, I see the window cracked open above the sink. "You want me to climb out?"

Jiggling the doorknob, she shrugs. "I can feed you to the groupies out there instead if you prefer."

And right there, right now, I see the girl I used to love so much when I was younger. She was lighthearted and quick-witted, and this girl in front of me is my Stella. I can't ignore the light in her eyes, the sense of adventure she sees this situation to be. She's laughing at me, and I fucking love it.

Right now, though, I need out of here. Even though I know what I should do, I drag it out as if I'm actually debating. I like sharing this private space with her . . . even if it is a bathroom.

Someone banging on the other side of the door startles her, and the magic is lost. "You should go." Moving around me, she cranks the old window open all the way.

"Only if you're coming with me."

"And leave Meadow?"

"Text her when we're outside. I'll text Ridge."

"Who's Ridge? A long-lost Crow brother?" She snorts with laughter, covering her nose with her hand. "Ridge. Rivers. Jet. Tulsa. Get it?"

"I get it." I just don't laugh at the joke, but she still has me grinning. Looking at her more closely, I ask, "Are you drunk?"

"Nope," she replies, emphasizing the *p* and shaking her head. She runs her hand over my chest and up. "I might be tipsy, though."

If memory serves me, and it does on a regular basis when I'm in the shower thinking about her, she gets so turned on when she's been drinking. I take hold of her hand because her touch feels so good. The knocking gets more insistent, and the sound of my name being called from the hall seems to bring her back to the sadder version of our reality, the reality where she's not mine. She backs away, so I ask, "Are you coming, or are we staying?"

Stella Lilith used to have an adventurous side, but I think it's been a while since she broke a few rules. "Will you climb out first?"

There's my girl. "Yep." I press down on the sink, hoping it doesn't fall off the wall. It looks old, so I'm not sure it can hold my weight. But it's getting louder in the hall, so I climb up, grabbing an exposed pipe above the window, and maneuver my legs through the opening. Good thing we're on the ground level. Pushing off, I land on my feet in the alley and turn around. "Stella?"

She peeks out and by the way her lips are twisted and her eyes are looking at the cement, she's nervous. "I don't want to fall."

"I'd never let you. Not to the ground anyhow."

For a second, she looks confused, but her brow relaxes and a small smile appears. "You'll catch me?"

"Every time."

She disappears, and I can hear her climbing onto the sink. Her legs slide out the window until her ass rests on the metal sill. "Ready for me, Rivers?"

"All my life."

"For real," she says, her nerves causing a slight shake to her tone. "You're going to catch me, right?"

"Always." I take her by the ass, and say, "Put your legs over my shoulders."

"What? No."

"Yes. I've got you. Then all I have to do is back up as you slip out."

"I'm not as light as I used to be. Are you sure you can handle me?"

I work my way under her so her legs are over my shoulders. "Don't worry about me, baby. I can handle you all right."

Her thighs squeeze my neck. I like to think it was the name I slipped in there, but it's probably because she's anxious to do this. She slips out a little more, and our eyes meet. "You're sure you're ready?"

"All you have to do is let go. I have you."

Releasing the pipe, she ducks her head to the side while I support her back with my hands, holding her until she clears the glass. Helping her upright, my face is against the jeans that cover her vagina and she's squeezing my head with her legs so tight I don't know if I'm going to live. *What a sweet fucking way to die.*

I back away from the window, and her legs loosen just enough from me to get a breath. I ask, "You okay up there?"

She's holding my head. "Don't drop me."

"Never." I start laughing, but she wobbles and leans forward. "I can't see. Loosen your grip. I've got you."

"Put me down."

"What's the magic word?"

"Now!"

"Tell me you're more fun than this these days."

"I'm not. I lead an incredibly boring life. That should send you running."

I lean back and am met with those green eyes I've dreamed about for years. "Nothing could send me running anymore."

Her hands rest on my shoulders, and she cocks an eyebrow. The smile on her face reaches her eyes where I see a flicker of the stars I adore inside. "Are you going to put me down?"

"Do I have a choice?"

That elicits the sweetest of laughs. "You're ridiculous."

"Am I?" I lift her so she can move her legs beneath her. She holds me as she begins to slide down the front of my body, but as soon as she's eye level, I tighten my arms around her again. "How taken are you?"

The light reflecting in her eyes dims, and she presses her palms against me. I set her down on her feet and start a silent prayer that she won't walk away.

Stumbling, she looks up when I catch hold of her waist, and says, "I can't forget what happened. I've tried, and I couldn't then and that wasn't even with you standing in front of me."

"I get it. But, Stella, it wasn't what you thought it was."

"How do I know what anything was?" She looks at me with narrowed eyes. "I wasn't even worth telling."

"That's not true."

"No, that is true." She gulps in a breath. "You put another woman before me—

"I gave her my word."

"You gave me a lot more than your word, and you chose her over me. I'll let you decide how bad that might hurt. Spoiler alert," she says abruptly. "It didn't just break my heart. It crushed my soul."

Crushed. Broken. I did this by not fighting through my own hurt feelings. "I'm sorry. I know it doesn't matter that I say it, and it fixes nothing, but I am sorry."

"You're right. It fixes nothing." She looks down at her shoes and sighs in disappointment. "I've spent years trying to figure out why I wasn't enough for you to choose me that night."

"It wasn't like that." *Christ, I feel like we're talking in riddles.* But outside a bar isn't the place to talk. Not now. I need time with her. I need to go back to that night and explain it from the top. Not just a quick-fix apology that says little.

"Then what was it like? Or can you not tell me that either?" She laughs humorlessly. She starts to walk away.

"Stella, I didn't cheat on you, but I understand why you think I did. We need to be somewhere quiet—"

She stops as if I have the answers to the universe. "A part of me thinks it's dumb I still care about that night, but you broke more than my heart. You broke us." Dropping my chin, I dare to look up at her just as she huffs. "But to answer your question as to us—I'm taken, Rivers. *Very* taken."

8

Rivers

STANDING at the entrance of the alley, she texts Meadow, and I text Ridge. I want to keep talking to her, to get this anger out until we don't have anything but our hearts bare before each other. But when I look at her, she refuses to make eye contact with me.

Meadow's the first one to see us, and she rushes to her sister. "Where did you guys go?"

Relief washes over her face, and Stella releases a long breath. Grabbing her sister's arm, she pulls her a few feet away just out of earshot . . . or so she thinks, and eyes me suspiciously. "Out the window," Stella replies like it's perfectly normal to climb out a window when you want to leave a bar.

Meadow scrunches her nose. "What? Why?"

"Groupies, but that doesn't matter." Stella and Meadow glance back at me, but I turn toward the opening of the alley and watch the partiers walking by. I hear her whisper, "I need your help."

"What's going on?" Meadow whispers back.

"I've been drinking—"

"I know. I've been drinking with you."

Stella waves her arms in annoyance and rolls her eyes. Sooo Stella. She turns her back to me when she catches me watching her and lowers her voice, but an alley carries sound. "Have you seen him?"

Meadow glances my way and smiles at me, then waves. "Yup. He's right there."

I chuckle and pretend to not listen because this game is too fun not to play. While they whisper, I check my phone and then text Ridge again: *Where the fuck are you?*

My ears perk up when I hear Stella say, "I told him I was taken."

"Taken? Like dating someone? Why would you do that?"

I hear a tiny whimper, and even though I can't see her, I feel the weight of the pause. I take a step toward her, wanting to dry her eyes but am given a death glare. She tugs Meadow around and leans toward her ear. "I'm taken *with him* again. And I can't be. This is terrible, Mead. Help me."

"Aww, sis. Come here." I glance back and catch Meadow's eyes on me while she hugs Stella. "That's not terrible."

Ridge finally shows the fuck up with his arms out, getting all the attention. "I'm here. What's up?"

Stella pops straight up, swiping under one of her eyes. When we look at her, she says, "Nothing to see here, people."

I'm about to finally go to her, tempted to bring her in for a good hug—for her and me—but Ridge spies the ladies, smiles, and asks, "Why are we in an alley?"

Pointing my finger at him, I say, "Good point. How about we get out of here?"

Is he fucking strutting? His swagger needs work. Making a beeline to Meadow, he sidles right up to her. "I'm Ridge. What's your name?"

"Meadow," she replies leaning a little closer to him.

Stella snaps her fingers between them. "Hey."

Ridge turns to her. "You must be—"

Meadow says, "This is my sister, Stella."

"Ah," he says as if a light bulb went off. I don't say her name much, but in a drunken moment in Dallas, I did, and then I couldn't stop as if I had to get it out of my system. I blamed being back in Texas, so close in proximity but still a world away from her. He glances between Stella and me, and then to Meadow. "Are we hanging out in an alley for a reason, or should we go somewhere to get more drinks?"

She raises her hand. "I vote more drinks."

I watch Stella carefully. She said she was tipsy, but I still don't think she wants to spend time with me. Meadow asks, "What do you think, Stel?"

I don't speak *sister-to-sister*ese, but I think Meadow might be on my side. Clueless, I let them figure out what they want to do and hope their decision swings in my favor.

Stella looks at me and then at her sister. "I'm out for the first time in forever, and I'm kind of having fun." I note the "kind of" part of that sentence. She asks, "How do we avoid what happened back there because that was not fun?"

"You didn't like having your legs wrapped around my neck again?"

She blushes as her lips part, then she laughs and back-hands my chest. "I meant the groupies."

"How about Ego's?" Ridge offers, a smirk settling across his face as he eyes Meadow. "Dim lighting. Private . . . mostly."

"Can't get much darker than Ego's," Meadow adds. "Love it." She heads down the alley. "Come on, kids."

Stella glances to me, standing in place. I can feel her hesitation from here, but then she follows her sister, and I follow her.

Stella stands on that stage, captivating every member of the audience. The spotlight shines on her, and I've never seen her so much herself, singing Lana Del Ray's "White Mustang" as if it's just the two of us. If her eyes aren't on me, they're closed. The way she holds the microphone to her mouth makes me envious of the proximity of those full lips I remember leaving kisses on my body, the heat of her breath against my skin reminding me how cold my life has been without her.

Although she always had a great voice, she had no interest in singing for a living. But for me, she would. I'd play guitar, and she'd sing, or I'd sing to her, or we'd just listen to the melody. Simpler days. Perfect times.

Meadow's elbow slips my way, bumping into mine. When I turn, she says, "You took my sister with you when you left."

"What do you mean?" I glance up at the beauty with the sultry voice and then back at my partner in crime who's helping me see things in a new light.

"She's hasn't been herself since you guys split, Rivers. But tonight, I'm seeing glimpses of that light in her eyes. I've missed it." Stella's karaoke song ends, and she steps down from the stage. Meadow leans in, rushing her words. "If I could change anything in the past, it wouldn't be something for me. It would be for her."

"What would you change for her?"

Meadow's gaze looks just past me and mine follows. Our conversation ends abruptly as Stella steps closer. I stand ready to get another round when Stella eyes me. "Another round?" I ask Ridge and Meadow who say yes. Turning to Stella, I ask, "Another—whoa!" Tripping into my arms, I catch her before she falls too far.

She gasps; her mouth wide open, matching her eyes. "Oh my God, Rivers." Her grip is tight on my biceps, so I flex.

"Are you all right?" I ask, holding her beneath me. I set her back on her feet, but she still holds me.

"Good. *So good.*" A little squeeze of my arms, and the left side of her mouth rides up.

Just when the rest of the bar fades away, and I finally get to look into those pretty eyes, over the walls the beers have lowered, Ridge says, "Are you going to get it on?"

My head whips to the side to face him. "What?"

He says, "Are you going to get the drinks?"

"Drinks?"

He holds an invisible glass and acts like he's gulping. "B. E. E. R. What did you think I said?"

Stella steps away, releasing me as I shake my head. "Forget it. Be right back."

"Are you getting the beer or what, man?"

Annoyed, I snap, "I'm getting the fucking beer." I glance once more at Stella before I leave.

When I reach the bar, she comes up right beside me. "Hey."

Pleasantly surprised, I tap my hand against hers. "Hey."

While we wait for the bartender to come over, I say, "You're still a great singer."

"I'm one hell of a good shower serenade and car singer."

She taps my chin. "You, sir, are still a charmer, but your charms won't work on me."

"Oh yeah?"

"I've spent years building a tolerance, making myself immune to you."

Without touching her, I lean in, inhaling her sweet scent, and whisper in her ear, "Immune, huh? Guess we'll find out."

When she doesn't reply right away, I tilt my head back to see her eyes, those gorgeous eyes. Her lips are parted, and she takes another deep breath before whispering, "Totally immune. See?"

I smile. "Clear as day." *Fine, I smirk.*

Lifting on her toes, she presses her lips to the shell of my ear, and says, "Another round?"

"Beer or us?"

She lowers before me, and I already miss the feel of her breath against my skin. "We need something stronger. Shots?"

"Shot to the heart." Whipping my beanie off, I rub my hand over my head just as the bartender presses his palms to the bar, and asks, "What can I get ya?"

"Four Jack Daniels shots." I'm tempted to buy the bottle. If I can't get the girl, I'm damn well getting drunk.

Some guy is singing a song about a ring of gold when I close the tab and take the glasses back to the table. As soon as I sit down, Stella taps her shot glass against mine, and says, "Bottoms up, big boy."

We shoot the shots, and while she recovers from the whiskey, I ask, "Where's your boyfriend tonight?"

Her expression sours and not from the alcohol. While Ridge and Meadow talk about the tour we just wrapped, Stella is staring at me. "You don't have a girlfriend?"

"Nice deflect. But okay, fine. We can go around in this circle, but we'll always end up back where we started. No. I don't have a girlfriend."

"Have you since...?"

"Since us? No."

Resting her chin in the palm of her hand, she asks, "Why not?"

Eyeing her, I find she's still cute when she does things like that which remind me of her when we were younger. Feeling bold, I ask, "Have you thought about me over the years?"

"Yes," she answers so easily.

"I never stopped thinking about you."

She sits up but lowers her gaze to my hand as I turn the empty shot glass around. "We shouldn't go there, Rivers."

"Why?"

"Because I can't think clearly when I'm around you. Add in shots of whiskey and my mind is muddled with too many emotions."

I keep pressing forward. "I almost contacted you so many times."

"But you chose not to."

"I did call you. You didn't answer."

Her hands go to her chest in mock offense. "Oh, I'm sorry. You tried for two weeks," she scoffs. "I'm glad I was worth two weeks of attempts."

I rough my hand over my head, trying to figure out what to say to keep her talking versus setting her off again. "I got mad, I guess. I was on the verge of doing a lot of things I shouldn't like barge into our apartment. Coax Meadow into getting you to meet me. I sat outside your school like a fucking creeper trying to get the nerve to talk to you. But I was so angry that you gave me no option to tell you my side."

"So what? You left me to save yourself?"

"You forced me, Stella."

"No one forces you to do anything," she says. "I know you. Don't try to bullshit me, Rivers."

"I'm not . . ." Someone bumps into me when they pass by, drawing my eyes away from her. "Let's go outside."

She walks past me without argument. We weave through the tables together and out the door until we're standing alone inside the parking garage where the bar's located.

The thick air lingering from the hot day seems to revive her, giving her strength. She walks out of my reach, and I let her, keeping the distance she appears to need. Her back is to me, her head down. "Stella?"

This time, she doesn't run or leave. She turns around and lets me see the pain as it pours from her eyes streaking her cheeks. "What do you see when you look at me, Rivers?"

"I see an amazing woman before me. You're beautiful. Successful."

She smiles sadly. "You see the girl I used to be, and I haven't been her in a long time."

"What happened?"

"You took most of me with you when you left." Scuffing the sole of her shoe on the cement, she lifts her eyes to me. "So much has changed. I've changed."

Meadow's words come back to me on the tail of Stella's declaration, matching the sentiment.

"Who are you now?"

"Oh no. I don't have to define who I am just because you're back. It's not going to be that easy."

"Easy? Do you think this has been easy for me?"

"You left pretty damn easily."

"I left because you told me to."

Rushing me, she shoves me in the chest, and yells, "You can't blame me. I didn't cheat on you. I didn't leave you." Her words echo through the garage. "You did this. You, Rivers!"

I grab her wrists and hold her steady. "I'm sorry. I fucked-up by leaving with her, but I've told you, I did not fucking cheat on you."

Surprise colors her fine features. "So you didn't cheat on me physically, but you did cheat on me emotionally. But what's worse is you left me here to face those men—" She suddenly turns her back to me, covering her face.

"What men?"

Turning around, she gulps back her tears. "I hate you. I hate you for ruining what was good. I hate you for coming back. I just . . . hate you so much."

Each of her words stabs me in the heart until my love for her bleeds from me. "I would never hurt you on purpose. I swear to you."

"But you did."

Fucking tears—hers become mine, but I refuse to let them fall. Seeing hers hurts enough. "What can I do? I'll do anything."

Her tears stop falling as she looks into my eyes. Taking a deep breath, she closes her eyes and then exhales. When they reopen, she says, "Please just leave me alone, Rivers. I loved you with everything that I am, and it hurts too much just to see you. That's the *anything* I need you to do. I need you to let go of what we used to be. Don't stay in Austin for me."

The door opens, and Meadow walks toward her sister, shaking her head. I want to tell her that I tried, but her harsh glare keeps me silent. With her arm around Stella, they walk toward to street. Seeing her pain and feeling it through her words cut deep. I did that to her, and it might be too late to fix it.

Ridge stands next to me, and says, "Didn't go so well, huh?"

"You could say that."

"I just did." He adds, "Meadow's hot."

"Not now, Dave." Yeah, it's a punk-ass move to call him by his real name, but what-the fuck-ever. I'm in a mood. I head toward the street, following the ladies, but give him a friendly salute with my middle finger.

They've made it to the corner, and Stella's arm is in the air to hail a cab. Running off instinct, panic makes me pick up my pace and start running. Just when Stella sees me, I take hold of her, the two of us swirling until I slow the momentum from running to capturing her in my arms. Then I kiss her like I've wanted to for so long.

Holding her to me, her feet are off the ground. Her arms wrap around my neck, and she kisses me right back. My lips are greedy, hers soft and sensual. When I begin to pull back, she becomes possessive.

My girl.

My woman.

Star of the night.

Star of my life.

Our lips slow, and we begin to part. Her eyes remain closed until I set her back on her feet.

Exhaling, she leans her forehead against my chest. I wrap my arms around her and hold her at the corner of South Congress and Riverside as if it's only the two of us in the world. Ignoring the traffic and the honking cars, the cheers and the shouting telling us to get a room, I kiss her again because damn, I'm kissing Stella. "*My Stella.*" Again.

When she looks into my eyes, the streetlights reflect off

the glassy surface. A slow clap draws our attention to Meadow and Ridge, who are both laughing. Meadow says, "About time."

There's enough light to see a pink deepen Stella's cheeks. That's when I know for sure. She's not seeing anyone else. "Hi." I can't ignore how good it feels to hold her in my arms again.

But I don't want to do anything tonight that she'll regret tomorrow. She was pretty damn firm when she said she doesn't want me in her life. I want her back forever, so putting the brakes on now is probably the wisest move I can make.

Standing next Meadow, Ridge asks, "What are we doing?"

Stella turns to me. "What are we doing?"

"I want to keep kissing you, Stella. But we've been drinking and you're—"

She nods like it's coming back to her. *Fuck, I hate being the good guy.* "You're right. I should go." She takes a step back, and I already hate the distance. "Right ..."

I touch her cheek because she's just so damn beautiful I can't resist. "This is not goodbye. I promise you if you let me, I'll build us back from the ground up. But tonight, you need rest."

"Yes, you're right. You know me when I've been drinking."

"I do know you." I've given control back to her, so she thinks this is her idea. It's the only way to remain unscathed in the sobering morning hours. "More than anyone, Stella."

She takes my hand and holds it between us. "Okay. So, I'll ..."

"Yes, I'll see you soon." I close the distance once again and kiss her on the forehead. This is the right thing to do because this is focusing more on her than me. I can only hope she'll see that this time we'll be different, that I've changed, that I've grown up.

All it takes is for me to come clean, and then there's no stopping us.

9

Stella

THE CAR PULLS into Meadow's apartment complex and stops. We hop out and trek past one building to hers in the back. Once we're inside, my shoes come off first, and then I pop the top button of my jeans. "God, I can finally breathe."

My sister tosses her keys on the coffee table and slips off her heels. "I was prepared to come home alone."

"For about five minutes there, I was prepared for you to come home alone too."

"So what happened?" She pulls off her shirt as she walks into her room.

I kneel over my bag but realize I forgot to grab a tee to sleep in because I usually come over more casually dressed. *Shoot.* I can't wear this top. It will mess it up. Pulling my jeans off, I grab my toothbrush and head to bathroom. "I need to borrow a shirt to sleep in."

"No prob."

While she goes to her dresser to get one, I load up my toothbrush and hers. "I put it on the couch for you."

Brushing my teeth, I lean against the counter and try to focus on the act instead of what happened tonight. But I can't. I stop brushing and look at my lips in the mirror. They tingle from his kiss, from the kiss I gave him back. I touch my bottom lip, liking the deeper shade of pink and how it's fuller, a little swollen.

When my lips were pressed to his, I forgot about him leaving and about Naomi. I forgot the pain of our time apart and how I was forced to pay a debt.

It felt good. He felt so good I was tempted to take it further. But I didn't need to. For that moment, I felt happy and free to be me again. "I think when he pulled back, he healed a little piece of me."

Meadow pulls her brush from her mouth. Her face scrunches, and she asks, "By not kissing you again?"

"I liked kissing him, but when he put the brakes on, I realized he listened to me. He heard my needs. That he'll wait . . . I don't know. I just find that so incredibly sweet."

She spits in the sink, points the brush at me, and rolls her eyes. "Good grief, Stel. I've had too much to drink to overthink this with you. We need sleep and clear heads. None of this is making any sense right now, and the alcohol makes everything worse. I would have jumped him, but that's me." After rinsing her mouth, she says, "And you need to really think about why you told him you're dating someone because you'll only be able to move on if you're honest with him."

"The Crow Brothers are on top of the charts. He's got more than he ever dreamed, Mead. *So why now?*"

"You." Before I can protest, she eyes me in the mirror while tapping her brush against the edge of the sink. "Just hold on to how you felt at the end of the night. You were happy. Now the alcohol is sloshing your brain. I'm going to bed. Stop thinking and try to sleep."

After spitting and rinsing, I reply, "You're right on one thing. My mind is ruining a perfectly good night." Grabbing a washcloth, I clean my face free of makeup. Walking out, I cut through the bedroom and into the living room. "This is why I never go out. I overthink everything and then regret sets in and ugh. Do you think it was chance or destiny that we ran into them?"

"You're doing it again. Stop overthinking this. Sleep."

"Why can't I just enjoy the night for whatever it was?"

"Because you care," she calls from the bedroom.

I snort. "Pfft. I think that's a little heavy-handed—" Picking up the shirt, I hold it in front of me with both hands. "Really, Meadow? Not funny."

"I think it's quite funny." She comes into the living room but detours into the kitchen. "Anyway, it's just for sleeping."

I'm about to toss it at her, but my grip tightens instead of loosens, and I hold it to my chest. It's not like anyone will really know. I'll be sleeping in The Crow Brothers shirt, not staring at it all night. I put on a good show of irritation for her sake, though. "I'm too tired to argue." I swap tops and grab the pillow and blanket from the closet to set them up like I did for months before I rented the guesthouse. The routine almost feels ingrained in me as a phantom ache returns to my back, pulsing from where it used to hurt every morning. I lie down and punch the pillow under my head a few times. "I think my overactive brain is dooming me to a life of singledom."

"Here's a reality check for you." While she fills two glasses with water, she says, "You won't be single because you're cautious after getting burned. You'll be single because you're still hung up on Rivers."

"I—"

"Eh! Nope. I'm not going to listen to it. You two either need to deal with your issues, or you move on once and for all. But when I say deal, I don't mean kiss or have sex to cover up the past. The past will always come back to haunt you. I mean *talk* to him, really talk to him about everything. Sober. Get it all out there so there's nothing that can hurt you again moving forward."

"I wasn't going to sleep with him."

"You were tongue fucking him. When you stopped, I saw that look in your eyes. And if *I* saw it, *he* saw it."

"He kissed me first."

She mimics my higher pitched defensive tone, "You kissed him back. Nana nana boo boo." After bonking her head with her hand, she adds, "My point is you guys were a bunch of jumbled hormones of I-want-to-but-I-shouldn't-but-I-really-want-to. Just deal with your issues already so we can all get to the happily ever after part."

My mouth is hanging open. "Just deal with it?" I'm lost for other words. She knows what I went through after the breakup. She knows how much he hurt me. Her speech might be full of truths, but she needs to work on her bedside manner.

I'm too offended to remain lying down, so I stand and start pacing. She sets a glass down on the coffee table and points at it. "You should finish that before bed."

"Why are you doing this to me, Meadow?"

Standing in her pajamas, she crosses her arms over her chest. "As your sister, I'm obligated by blood to tell you the truth. As your best friend, I'm trying to break it to you as gently as possible. I saw how he looked at you. I saw how he hung on every word you spoke. But you know what else I saw?" This is clearly a rhetorical trick question, so I cross my arms over my chest in some sort of weird protest and refuse to answer. "I saw how you looked at him and how you hung on his every word. It's not over for you two. And if I was a wagering woman . . . okay, fine, I'll bet you five dollars that this is just the beginning."

"Hope you've saved your lunch money, sister, because I ain't buyin' it." I sit down, not even sure if I'm making sense. She's right on one thing—my head is fuzzy. I slip my legs under the blanket. "You know what I am buying? Sleep. Good night." I drop my head back on the pillow dramatically and close my eyes. "Hit the lights on your way out."

"You're being stubborn, and you know where that will leave you? Alone in singledom." She hits the lights, but before she shuts her bedroom door, she adds, "Destiny."

"What?"

"That's what brought you two together tonight. Give into your fate, sister. Good night."

I'm left with my mouth hanging open. I open my eyes and lift on my elbow to look over the arm of the couch. As soon as the light from under her door goes out, I sit up.

"Destiny," I grumble. She might be right, though. All the hate I've held on to over the years disappeared as soon as hope in the form of soulful eyes that have never looked at me as less than perfect showed up with whiskey shots, beer, and a smile I couldn't deny. Rivers Crow owned my heart for what feels like most of my life, and tonight it's clear—he still does.

I wrap my arms around my middle, hugging the shirt to me in an attempt to hold myself together, but I can't. All I thought he healed tonight shatters all over because if tonight is all we'll ever have again, it's not enough to mend this broken heart. I break down in the quiet of the night where no one has to see my nightly routine. I touch my lips;

they're still raw from the scruff that looks so sexy on him. It felt even sexier as it scraped across me, marking me as his, even if just for the night.

I wanted him. I wanted him touching me in all the ways I remember, the ways I dream about, the ways I crave. No man has ever made me feel like he does, which is why the pain of that day still bears down on me with the weight of the universe.

He broke me. I can't forget that, but I don't hate him. I want to so much, but my heart can't seem to rage the way my head wants to. The fact of the matter is this. Losing Rivers wasn't the only thing that has hurt me. I've been down and have had to pick myself up many times over. *And I always get up and fight for another day.*

I was the one who had to face my mother when my father couldn't. I was the one who had to give her an ultimatum as she rolled her suitcase down to the end of the driveway where her new boyfriend waited to take her away from us forever.

I was the one who was strong enough to go back inside that house and face my sister one week before her senior prom and tell her I would be there when her mother chose not to be.

It was *me* who faced the criminals extorting my dad during the lowest point in his life. It was me who begged for more time to pay back the debt. It was me who ...

My tears fall, exposing my quiet sobs.

When I had nothing left to sell, I sold myself.

The bedroom door opens, and Meadow comes out, silently sitting next to me on the couch. She puts her arm around me and pulls me to her shoulder. She thinks I'm crying over Rivers, so I let her. I can't taint her with my sins. "You've closed your heart off for so long, Stel." With her arms around me, she says, "But you deserve happiness." I lean back and look at her. Her smile is kind, and I remember how much she's been there for me over the years. She doesn't know everything I've been through and never will, if I have my way, but she knows how much I loved Rivers. "Do you know why Rivers is back?"

Shrugging, I shake my head.

She says, "For you. I know it. I saw it tonight. He feels just as awful as you do. What I don't understand is why you won't talk to him."

"What if I talk to him and nothing comes of it but more pain?"

Taking my hand, she gives it a little squeeze. "That's exactly why you need to talk to him. *Sober.* Heaven knows I was ready to hump Ridge right there in the middle of Ego's for all to see. Would I do that sober?" She shrugs and then laughs. "Yeah, I would, but that's me."

I laugh because she always manages to lighten my mood.

She continues, "But you, dear sister, have always been more guarded since . . . *since him.*" She hugs me, wrapping her arms around me. "So it's okay to take things slow. Just don't go so slow that the door closes on this second chance."

When she stands up, I lie back down, and say, "Don't get ahead of yourself with this second chance business. There are more than a few conversations that need to be had that probably won't end well."

"Do what it takes, but don't waste a day. Ridge told me they're only in Austin for a short time, and then they're going back to LA again."

"Yeah, no pressure there. Anyway, that's the exact reason I should forget this whole thing." I wipe the hem of the shirt over my cheeks. Looking behind me, I shake my head.

"That's just it. If he's just going to take off, where does that leave me, but alone again?"

"You're going to have to dig deep on this one. I'm not saying you should date him again if you guys can't get there, but isn't it worth a conversation?" She taps the wall. "Get some sleep. Also, drink your water or you're going to feel like shit in the morning. Good night for real this time."

"Good night." *God, I'm thankful for my sister.*

I sit up enough to drink half the water before I set it down again and let my mind swim in a replay of tonight.

Spinning in his arms with his lips pressed to mine, I'm lost to the stars and the light, the weight of him against me, and the soaring of my heart.

I gasp when I sit up, my heart racing as my eyes dart around to land on something familiar, something that will clue me in to where I am. The curtains. The sunny yellow and white fabric never did block the morning sunshine. *Meadow's apartment.*

Looking around, it must be early. There's still a golden hue to the light that wants to break in. The bedroom door is still closed and the tiny apartment quiet. I exhale the initial emotion that startled me awake and then touch my feet to the floor.

My heart continues to race as I stand and then immediately regret it. Holding my hand to my head, I make my way to the coffeepot and turn it on. Dashing quickly into the side door to the bathroom, I splash water on my face, but I wish I could take a shower. I'll do it later. I don't want to wake Meadow this early on a Saturday.

Back in the kitchen, I stick the mug under and let the machine work its magic. Filling it with a lot of creamer, I stir and head for the shared patio area for this block of apartments in the front.

It's not private up here since it overlooks the parking lot, but this is the side where the sun rises. I sit in one of her two plastic chairs and sip my coffee. Most residents of the complex are still asleep since it's the weekend. There are a few people starting to jog or getting an early start, but I'm alone for the most part.

"Good morning."

I freeze with the mug to my lips. Surely, that's a figment of my imagination. There's no way Rivers can be here. I don't know the time, but I know it can't be later than six thirty. Leaning forward, I peek through the railings and look down.

I might swoony-sigh a little. *Okay, I do.* Out loud. I almost hate myself for finding him so attractive. The eyes don't lie.

Standing up, I lean against the rail. He's just one floor down, so fortunately we don't have to yell to be heard or the neighbors might skewer us. I ask, "What are you doing here? How did you find me?"

"Meadow told Ridge you were staying over last night."

That little traitor. "How do you know where she lives?"

"She's listed online. She should really fix those privacy settings. By the way, I like that shirt on you."

"What?" Looking down, I realize I'm wearing his band's shirt. *Shoot.* This doesn't make me look hung up on him . . . nope, not at all.

Totally does.

"Nice panties too." *Oh God.* I jump in surprise and spill a little of my coffee. *Ugh.* I forgot I wasn't wearing pants. I turn to go back inside, but hear, "Wow. There's that great ass."

He's utterly incorrigible. I roll my eyes because he's got some nerve commenting on my ass as though it's here for his enjoyment. But I like the compliment . . . ugh. I hide my smile, not wanting to feed his ego. "Go home, Rivers. I'm not coming down, and I haven't even had a sip of my coffee yet, so it's way too early to do this dance with you."

"No worries. I'll come up cuz if there was one thing we were always good at, it was dancing together, even if just verbally."

I open the front door to hurry inside, but I realize if I shut the door, he'll knock and wake up Meadow. I huff my annoyance and leave the door open while I slip my jeans back on.

His tall frame fills the doorway, drinking me in like a man who needs water. Then that smile that won me over years ago—boyish charm mixed with bad boy sexiness—appears, and I'm weak to him once again. With his hands resting on either side of the opening, he leans in without breaching it. "About last night . . ."

10

Stella

ALTHOUGH RIVERS HAS SEEN me naked more times than I can count, I still rush to zip my jeans. He hasn't seen me in years after all. My body's changed, just as his has. Lord have mercy has his body changed. I bite my lower lip just thinking about his broad shoulders and what I can tell must be amazing abs based on those magnificent biceps I tried and failed to squeeze last night. I release my lip and mentally berate myself for even thinking about this infuriating man.

With his eyes on me, though, naturally, I struggle. Damn. It's like the world is conspiring against me wearing clothes with him around. Feeling the weight of his stare on me, I peek up.

"Need help?" he asks.

"Nope. I sure don't. I have it all under control."

He saunters in anyway, owning the room, his body, and judging by how the lower half of my body clenches, he owns mine too. *Still.*

Damn him.

One finger lifts my chin until our eyes meet. "Let me try." Kneeling in front of me, his face is level with the front of my jeans . . . and what's under that denim.

I suck in a breath, and my words fly out on the exhale, "You really don't have to—"

"I know. But I like the view. And I'm pretty good at working a pair of jeans." He looks up at me with a smug grin on his face and winks.

My gaze goes to the door in annoyance because I see his ego is as big as it ever was. He really shouldn't affect me like he does. I zoom between hot and cold with him, not able to settle in the middle. He's screwed my emotions all up between the past and the present. "I just bet you do."

The zipper slides down, and then he slides it with ease all the way back up. "There you go. You just needed me to work you over."

"Or a pair of pliers." Not wanting to give him too much credit. His ego might explode. "I thought it was broken."

Standing in front of me, he says, "You'd be surprised what you can fix with the right touch."

"You do that a lot."

"What?" His deep voice carries. So I grab him and drag him back to the porch and prop the door open with my shoe.

"The way you talk to me in double meaning. Everything seems to have two purposes—one that serves the situation and one that serves you. Do you really think I'm that naïve not to notice?"

"I don't think you're naïve. Quite the opposite. I think you're very aware of what's going on here." *Annnnd* he smirks.

"Instead of leaving me in suspense, just tell me." I wave my hand between us. "What's going on here?"

"We're getting to know each other."

"Oh, no, no. I'm not looking to travel down memory road with you, so you're wasting your time if you think showing up here unannounced looking all handsome will make me just forgive and forget, you can move along to someone who appreciates a smooth talker because that's not me anymore."

"You think I'm handsome?"

Scoffing, I say, "Figures that's your takeaway."

"It was a joke, albeit a bad one." He sighs. "Look, Stella, last night was not as awful as you want it to be."

"Why would I want that?"

"Because then you could close this door and feel justified doing it. Right now, you're struggling to find your footing because you don't hate me as much as you once did. This is a good thing. This is a starting point."

My patience wears as he gets closer to the rawer parts of my heart. "Just say it, Rivers. What do you want?"

"You got your say. I want mine." His expression is missing the arrogance I expected to see. Instead, it's just him with a crease between his eyebrows, worry in his eyes, and a frown. He shouldn't have to beg.

I just dumped my thoughts on him without asking, but he's taking my residual animosity and greeting it with reasoning. "Okay. That's fair."

"Generally speaking, I'm not a liar." His jaw tightens. He closes his eyes and seems to struggle with what he should say. "But I lied to you. I'm sorry. You were my life, and you ended us without so much as a discussion." I grip the door-knob tighter, my heart beating for the man in front of me as all the memories—good and bad—rush back, making my heart hurt.

Coming closer, he lowers his voice as if his own pain is coursing through him. "I'm only in Austin for a short time, but I'm only back because of you. I want a chance to explain everything when we're not rushed to get out the words and we have time to hear them. Then if you decide we're over, we're over. I'll leave you in peace. It won't be easy, but I'll accept whatever you decide."

I find myself leaning in, wanting to touch him, to ease the lines in his forehead and give him what he wants because he's not demanding it, he's asking with his heart on his sleeve. And maybe I'll get what I need to put this, *us*, to bed for good. "You're not going to change my mind, but I'll give you a chance because I think it would be good for both of us to have closure."

"Closure?" The word wounds him as pain flickers across his face. "That's not what this is about."

The last thing I want to do is inject promises into his pain when I'm still cautious and not quite sure what he wants from me. "What is it about then? We'll never be able to pick up where we left off like nothing happened."

"I agree. I'm not looking for that. I also don't want to rush this conversation."

"What do you want then?"

"A new beginning." He centers himself, staring directly into my eyes, refusing to be deterred from his goal. "Name the time and place and I'll be there." His determination gains steam, and a small smile appears.

"I'll figure it out today and text you. Will that work?"

His grin grows. "That will work." Leaning down, he kisses my temple, and then whispers, "Thank you."

Tilting my head, I brush my cheek against the roughness of his jaw, but I stay right there until both of our breaths come out a little harder. I close my eyes and swallow the emotions building in my chest before I turn and take a step back. "I'll text you."

"I'll wait for you."

I'd point out that he did it again, waiting for me instead of waiting to hear from me, but I know what he's doing, and I can admit I like it. Since this, whatever this is between us, feels so good, I decide to tease him. "I'm going in now, so I can finally drink my coffee, you stalker."

He chuckles. "I only pull out my best stalker moves for you."

"I'm flattered. Now go. It's not even seven in the morning."

With his hands up, he says, "Going. Going. But don't forget about me."

"I've tried but never could."

"Good." I'm sent a wink before he heads down the steps.

Leaning over the rail to get one more good look at this man, I say, "For whom?" when he appears from the stairwell.

"Guess that remains to be seen, but I'm feeling pretty damn good right now." He opens the door of his SUV, and asks, "How about you?"

I wave my hand. "I can't tell you all my secrets, or what will be left?"

"The whole world and when we burn through that, the universe."

My knees weaken. He was always a poet with dreams bigger than the lives we were born into. His success comes as no surprise. I just wish I could have been there to watch his star shoot across the sky. "Save your lines for your lyrics, pretty boy."

That makes him laugh again. He starts the engine and

rolls down the window. Resting his arm out, he looks back once more at me and gives me a little wave.

I stand there for a few seconds before I go back inside, not ready to see him leave. When his car pulls out of the parking lot, I actually mourn the loss. He was once my life. We're not kids now, so we need to talk as adults and then move . . . and then . . . *and then what?* I think that's the crux of the problem. A few days ago, Rivers Crow was but a painful memory. But now, he's in my present.

Beginnings. That's what he wants. Logic tells me I'd be stupid to even consider it. *"You've closed your heart off for so long, Stel. But you deserve happiness."* I hear what Meadow is saying, but will letting him into my heart equal happiness?

We need to talk, but I wonder if we'll discover there's too much water under this bridge to go back to what we once were.

"Morning."

I jump, covering my heart with my hand. "Good lord. What the hell, Meadow?"

She laughs. "Jumpy much?"

"Yes, when people sneak up on you and catch you off guard, especially before seven a.m."

"So what was going on outside?"

"Nothing."

"Really?" She puts the K-Cup in the coffee machine and presses the flashing button. "Nothing?"

"Nope." She doesn't need to know that I just made a date —*Ugh.* Not a date. An appointment . . . with Rivers. Yes, that's what it is. That's *all* it is.

"I heard voices."

"That was just me. Umm . . . talking to myself."

She turns around and studies me. "You sure? It sounded like Rivers."

I drag out my sip of cold coffee and shrug. When that doesn't satisfy her, she stares at me just as the coffee machine gurgles. She turns her attention to the coffee thank God. When she finishes adding creamer and takes a sip, she heads for the bedroom. She's already out of sight when she says, "I have a date with my bed and bad TV movies today. I'm glad you have a date with Rivers."

"It's not a date," I call, loud and clear.

"Sure."

I get up in a huff, tilting my head. "It's not a date, Meadow."

Her eyes are glued to the TV as she sips her coffee while snuggled in bed. "Okay. Whatever. Have fun."

"It's not about having fun. It's about finalizing—"

Shifting her gaze to me, she asks, "Finalizing what? The breakup? Who are we kidding? That was finalized years ago."

I lean back on the arm of the couch and fall back, leaving my legs dangling over the side. "You're exasperating."

"Actually, you and Rivers are exasperating. Hence, why I'm happy you're finally going on this date."

"It's not a date." I drape my arm over my eyes.

"Whatever you say. Where you going on this date anyway?"

"Oh my God, I can't with you." I swing my legs off the couch and go to my bag. Realizing I didn't pack clothes for today in my rush to get over here, I look down at the shirt that covers me. My cheeks feel hot to the touch just thinking about that smile on his face when he caught me in this shirt, braless.

After pulling out my flip-flops and packing my heels

from last night, I zip my bag closed. "You enjoy your movies. I'm going home."

"It's not your home. Also, we need to start looking for a place since the two bedroom in the next building we were supposed to get renewed their lease."

"Between our measly salaries, it's not going to be good. Prices have skyrocketed in the past few years, but I'll start looking again."

"Me too. Also, keep me posted on your date," she says, laughing.

I'm not going to bother going back in there to give her my resting bitch face, but I will correct her. "It's not a date."

"I let you live in your fantasies, so let me live in mine."

"You fantasize about me and Rivers going on a date?"

"Yes. Now leave me to it. Later, gator." The volume on the movie she's watching is jacked up just as the scary music starts playing.

That's my cue to leave.

On the drive to the guesthouse, I think of Brian and how I need to tell him as soon as I secure a new place. He's been more than generous by opening his home to me when I was evicted. I often think about what my father has told me. "Be with someone reliable, someone who won't abandon you out of nowhere." *Oh, the irony, Dad. Reliable.*

Reliable is like a rash Rivers got rid of a long time ago. That and my heart. But then he shows up being kind and begging for time, and I can't say no.

I pull into the driveway and park in front of the converted garage. Brian's dressed for exercise and stretching on the patio. I open the door and ask, "Going jogging?"

"Before it gets too hot. Need help with your bag?"

"No, I've got it. Thanks."

Reaching into the back seat, I grab the bag and lock the

car. While I walk to my front door, he says, "Nice shirt. Good band. Saw them a few times in college."

My body tenses as I stand frozen on the porch behind him. Looking down, I catch a glimpse of the crow design feeling equally protective and exposed.

Protective of Rivers and the band to any potential scrutiny, I fold my arms over my chest, feeling as if he can tell I kissed Rivers Crow last night.

He says, "When I get back, I'll shower, and we can go to breakfast if you're hungry?" *Crisis averted.*

His even-tempered nature makes him a great principal. He doesn't blow up or overreact. He likes to get the facts, to have a plan, and to follow protocol, but he's stepping out of his usual boundaries by wanting to go out. I momentarily pause, thinking it over. I owe him so much that this will be a good opportunity to thank him for the hospitality he's shown me. "Okay. Yes. I'll be ready."

Beyond the teachers who talk about him in the teacher's lounge, I overhear the girls in my classes comparing him to a cross between Bradley Cooper and Matt Damon. I don't see it, but apparently, he's "like a hot dad." The phrase itself bothers me, but it does make me wonder how I overlooked something everyone else so obviously sees.

He's been a good friend, but that's all he'll ever be to me. Is Meadow right? Am I still so hung up on Rivers that I can't appreciate a handsome and kind man? *Is that why I need to talk to Rivers? To be free of that connection? That bias? And if I do talk to him, will it actually free me or hook me again?*

"Great. I'm off."

"Have a good run," I reply.

Life is strange and unpredictable, and I have no idea what the next few days will bring. *"I'll wait for you."* I guess that's where I start.

11

Stella

ONE MIMOSA in and I'm ready for another. So is Brian. "They're light pourers with the champagne," he says, looking for the waitress. He's nervous, which is unsettling. *Why is he so nervous?* "Would you like another?"

I'd like ten because he's right. There's barely any champagne in these drinks, and I need the hair of the dog. Is it inappropriate to order a beer at this hour? Probably. "Yes please." Our drink order is placed when our breakfast plates are set down.

He asks, "Would you like a bite of my Eggs Benedict?"

"No, I'd feel like a traitor to my pancakes." I snort laugh. It's a terrible joke, but I'm hungover, and after waiting almost an hour to get in here, my brain is too tired to be clever. "You know, like Benedict Arnold. The traitor from the Revolutionary War. Get it?"

"Ohhh. I get it now." He still doesn't laugh, though.

"Goofy teacher's joke, I guess." I'm too hungry to care. "These blueberry pancakes smell like heaven. Want a bite?"

"They look too good to pass up."

I wait for him to cut off a portion, but he seems to be waiting on me. "Take what you want."

"I was hoping you could maybe feed me a bite."

"Why?"

Oh. Does he think this is more than friends grabbing a meal together? The last time I fed a male food was Rivers when . . . *Oh, no.* "Um, Brian, I'm sorry."

"For?"

"For giving you the wrong impression. I just thought this was something casual, two friends eating out."

I see the disappointment trickle into his eyes. "It is." He fixates on his napkin on the table. "Just friends." When he looks back up, he asks, "But would a date with me be so awful?"

He could provide the security my mom always told me to want.

The predictability my father insisted was a good trait.

My heart beats in protest.

"No. No. Not at all. I've just always considered you a colleague and friend. In our positions, we shouldn't tangle in new territory."

"There's nothing in the policy that would stop us."

There's also nothing that has drawn me to him. I feel terrible as he stares at me waiting for an answer to a question I haven't asked. "I'm not in any position to date someone. There have been so many changes in the past few years, emotional things that I'm dealing with. I think it's just safer right now, better for me, if I focus on fixing me." Reaching across the table, I cover his hand with mine. It's not warm like Rivers's was, and there's no electricity between us. We're more physics than chemistry. "I'm sorry, but please know I value our friendship."

His hand is pulled back as he leans back in the booth. "Yeah. Okay. Friendship. Value. Got it."

Clearly, he's upset. Now I feel even worse. "I'm sorry."

"Don't worry about it. I was just seeing if there was something more between us, but there doesn't seem to be."

Not the best for my self-esteem, but I'll take the lumps now while his pride is injured. We'll be fine, but if we're not, I guess I'll deal with that when it comes. "Right. Nothing. Okay then. If you'll excuse me, I'll be right back." I slip out of the booth and go to the bathroom.

I should have never come out this morning. He's been supportive, but I'm not dumb or blind. What I hoped—us being friends—doesn't seem to be possible. This was a bad idea. I won't make the mistake again. I won't lead him on or cause him more hurt feelings by staying in the guesthouse longer than I need to either. I've tried to be a good tenant and not invade his space when it seems more obvious than ever that invading his space is what he's wanted all along.

Finding a new place to live was already a priority, but now it's been put on a rush.

I move in front of the sink and wash my hands. Wetting a paper towel, I press it against my face. I've made such a mess of things. Looking in the mirror, I stare into my eyes, searching for the life that once lived there but can't find it.

Is this how I want to spend the rest of my life? Stuck in some . . . *rut*? I'm not interested in Brian, and I don't think it has to completely do with things not being resolved with Rivers. In this case, we just seem so different. I don't want to live in this mire of *singledom*. I wonder if it's possible that the dark clouds of my past are clearing? I didn't lie to Brian. I am dealing with very emotional and difficult issues at the moment, yet my heart—okay, and body— wanted to cling to Rivers last night *and* this morning.

Somehow, I think being that honest with Brian would be more hurtful than not, and that's not something he deserves.

───────────

My ex is a member of one of the biggest bands in music. It's a lot to process and something I never really have. The band of three brothers became four when Ridge joined them. The Crow Brothers were signed by Outlaw Records. The label was started by Johnny Outlaw, the lead singer of one of the biggest bands in the world, The Resistance. After their first full album was released, it shot to the top, like they did.

The fame.

The money.

The records.

None of that mattered when it came to Rivers. I just loved a boy who once loved a girl.

Life has stolen our innocence away.

Their music video comes on my laptop, and I close my eyes, thinking about what Rivers said this morning. He's making an effort and in charming ways. I didn't ask him how long he'd been out there waiting on me, but for that alone, I owe him a chance to speak his piece. We may have ended horribly, but I can see how agonized he is. And despite how much pain I endured, I still hate the idea of him being hurt. Maybe talking to each other can heal some of the wounds.

I pick up my phone ready to text him, simply because I want to see him again when a soft rap on the door causes me to set it down.

Brian.

"Coming."

Swinging my robe around me, I tie the belt as I unlock the door and then open it. "Hi."

"Hi. I wanted to check on you and to clear any bad air. I feel bad about this morning."

"There's no bad air."

He shifts and glances over his shoulder. When his eyes return to mine, he says, "I still owe you an apology. I'm sorry for making you uncomfortable."

"You don't have to apologize, but I'm glad we talked. I consider you a friend, and I'd hate to lose you."

"You won't," he replies, a smile appearing. "I value our friendship as well. It's been nice to have someone renting this place who I know." Looking me over, he asks, "Are you not feeling well?"

I laugh. "No, not really. I drank too much last night. Today is payback."

"What did you end up doing?"

Tightening the belt and looping it around my hand, I keep the details vague. "I went out with Meadow."

"Did you go to dinner?"

"We grabbed tacos and then went to see a band play downtown, ran into some old friends, and . . ." I pause because I almost said I had fun. A sudden need to protect my time with Rivers washes through me. We all laughed a lot, and hell, I even climbed out a window with a rock star while we escaped a mob of groupies. That was unexpected fun. "It was a good night."

"Good. So are you attending the fall banquet? The PTA will be honoring me."

"Yes, I'll be there and congratulations."

"Thank you. Maybe we can ride together if you'd like?"

I consider my answer carefully. I don't want to lead him on in any way, and I'm learning that I must keep my boundaries. When I see him patiently waiting, I'm blindsided by an irrational thought.

No. It's too crazy. I can't. I shouldn't. It would be ridiculous. Fun . . . maybe. It would be a great way to get Brian to look elsewhere for his companionship. Rivers always did look good in a suit. Maybe I should. Hmmm . . . No. Rivers and I are nothing more than passing ships. He'll be gone so soon, I'm not even sure if I'll get a goodbye. It was ridiculous for me to even think he's an option.

"I have a lot going on this week. Probably best if we take our own cars."

"Yep. Sure. Will do." Turning to go back to his gardening, he picks up the weed whacker and glances back at me. "Sorry for the noise."

"No problem." As soon as I close the door, I lock it and lean against it. Have I lost my damn mind? What was I thinking? Rivers asked me for more time, but this may completely blow up in my face.

Rivers Crow is hard to miss and looking better than he should. I spot him the second I walked through the doors of Highball. I immediately start second-guessing myself, my feet becoming heavy with every step I take toward him.

I'm so conflicted when it comes to what he wants and what I need. Are they one and the same? I can't help but hope he's changed—*for the better*. I know I have—*for the worse*. Is it time to forgive even if I can't forget? Why does just the sight of him make my heart still hurt so much?

Rivers stands from the red vinyl booth to greet me. He's nervous, dragging his palms down the front of his jeans. "Hi. I'm glad you texted."

"Me too." I don't mention how hard it was to make the move, but the ball was in my court. He gave me that courtesy, so I'm giving him the same.

He greets me with a kiss on the cheek. "Thank you for coming."

My eyes dip closed as I take in the scent my body knows by heart. "Tell me what I'm supposed to feel because my thoughts are muddy."

With his head against mine, he whispers, "Just go with what comes naturally. If it's anger, tell me. If it's something else, tell me that too."

My forehead touches his shoulder, and I'm tempted to wrap my arms around him, but I don't. "Thank you."

When our bodies part, the intimacy still lingers. He asks, "Would you like to sit?"

I push myself into the half-moon booth and dump my small clutch on the table. "I felt like we needed to talk in person."

The bartender comes over. "Our waitress hasn't shown up yet. What can I get you?"

"Water for me," I say.

"Iced tea please." When the bartender leaves, Rivers says, "I like talking to you in person. How are you feeling from last night? I think you drank more than you copped to."

Laughing lightly, I say, "I did. I feel better after eating and getting some sleep today."

"No hair of the dog to help with that hangover?"

"I had mimosas for breakfast."

He smiles. "Nice. I remember when we had mimosas on Easter once. Your mom got so mad since we weren't twenty-one. Mimosas in bed sound better. You get vitamin D and the cure while hanging out at home."

"I wasn't at home. I was at Kerbey Lane for breakfast."

Chuckling, he says, "I thought Meadow would have been sleeping all day. She told Ridge that she has a pretty rigorous school and work schedule, but today was her day off."

Our drinks are set down along with a menu. "Happy hour starts soon," the bartender says while he walks away.

"Look, I want to talk to you about something that I need to clear up."

He takes things with ease, not seeming to stress over the potential confession. "All right."

"Since you returned, my feelings have been based on our past. It's not fair to judge your past actions or to hold the past against you, but I'm clearly still hurt. The reality is that I don't know you anymore to judge you by any other means."

"Fair enough. Could I ask you to try to stop judging and start feeling? Do you feel the same connection I feel?" Leaning forward, his eyes are set, his words firm, but his expression softens when looking at me.

I feel so much I can't be a good judge of what's right or wrong when everything with him always felt right.

That fire in his eyes I remember so well is still seen. "You know me, Stella. I'm the same guy you once loved. The same one I hope you can love again."

"Why? Why do you want me to love you?" It's exasperating trying to weed my way through his confessions. I can't seem to reason why I'm the one he wants when he can have anyone, including the supermodel from the tabloids. I must seem so small town in comparison. "You have the world at your feet. You have women clamoring to touch you as evidenced by the groupies last night. You can have anyone in the world, women much more sophisticated than I am."

"You underestimate yourself."

"Maybe it's that you don't know *me* anymore. I'm not the same little girl you left."

"I don't want a girl. I like the woman you are."

I swipe at the strands of hair that have wriggled free from my ponytail and then tuck my hands under my legs. "I wish I could live up to whatever image you have of me, but my road has been a lot different from yours."

"I want to hear everything I missed."

Resting my chin in my hand, I reply, "It's not glamorous. It's not even pretty. If I tell you all the crap that's happened . . ." I stop, not sure how much to give him. I like that he still sees me as beautiful. My voice lowers, and I'm tentative to speak. "You won't see me the same."

"Try me."

"Okay." I take a deep breath and let it all out in a hurry to get it off my chest. "I'm twenty-five with a job I thought I'd love, but I don't. My mom ran off with a medical sales manager, leaving my dad after twenty-one years of marriage. You know what he did after that?"

Rivers stares at me, but I can't read his thoughts. He knew my parents. They were always on shaky ground. He doesn't seem surprised by the news, but he holds nothing but compassion and interest in his eyes. I say, "He drank and gambled his way into so much debt that my sister and I dropped out of school for a year to work full time so he didn't lose everything." I sigh, the visuals, even with time and space from what had to be done, flash through my mind. "Trust me, Rivers, you don't want me anymore. Some things will never wash off, and I have scars that are never going to heal."

"I'm sorry," he says, angling toward me as if he has no control of the pull between us. I understand the feeling. It's why I showed up today. "I'm so sorry you went through that. I never wanted to leave you—"

"But you did. And when the horrific happened, I blamed you too. Which I now know wasn't right. It wasn't your fault. It was my father's. It was those disgusting men. But I felt so . . . abandoned. You, Jet, Tulsa, and then my mom, my dad. It was hard. And . . . well, now it's just Meadow and me."

"Shit, Stella." His hand flies to my hand on instinct, but he seems to stop himself. Resting his head against the tips of his fingers, he asks, "Do you need financial help now? I can help you—"

"No." I'm not sure if I should be flattered or insulted. Everything I did to pay that debt eats at my soul, sending me to hell with the imagery. But hearing him offering to be here for me now soothes some of the loneliness I've felt for so long. If he knew how much I struggled . . . he would hate it. "No. I don't want your help." I handled it on my own. "I didn't tell you to beg for a handout."

"That's not what I meant. If I can help you, I will. Any way you want." *If only it was that simple. If only his presence now could solve my problems.*

"It's just too late. I'm catching up, making it work. Slowly, but it's happening. It's irrational to blame you, but that's part of my anger. I think I wanted . . . I needed you to help me emotionally. I lost you, and then I lost my mother, our home, our cars were sold or repossessed. *I* was sol—" I come so close to crying but don't, holding the hurricane of emotions inside. "I've learned that what's done is done. There's no changing the past."

Reaching over, he wraps his hands around mine that are clenched together on the table between us. "I hate what you've gone through because of your parents. I hate what you've gone through because of me. If I could turn back time . . . If I could change the past, I would have been there for you and Meadow."

"But you can't." I hate that I cry when I'm upset. "Can I ask you something?"

"Anything."

"Earlier today, I was wondering why now, and if you're here because your brothers are both married?" Surely, that's not the reason to bring him back to town in hopes of patching things up with me.

"You could say that. But not for the reasons you probably think. I've missed you being in my life, Stella. I haven't felt right for a long time now, and watching my brothers find their other halves made me finally admit that I still love you." He looks down as if the confession steals his strength, as if he's a weaker man for admitting the truth.

Tension forms a line between his brows, and when he looks back up, the molten chocolate of his eyes silently pleads with me. A calm washes over him, easing the angst trapped in his expression, and then he says, "I love you. I never stopped. I want you back. I want to be yours again, and I want you to be mine." The words are heavy like the deep breath he takes. "And I know that may not happen. But I can't go through life not having tried with everything I have. Not anymore."

12

Stella

THE WAY the light from the far windows flows in causes the gold flecks in his deep molten chocolate eyes to shine brightest. I always appreciated how handsome he is. Me, and thousands of other women . . . maybe it's millions of women now that he's world famous.

The University of Texas ball cap he wears makes him look like a college kid again. Also, it helps him blend in, which is what he's probably trying to do. He didn't blend in back when we were together, and he doesn't blend in now. He's just lucky it's a weird time of day—past lunch but too early for dinner.

"You love me, so you came to Austin and want me to take you back?"

"That's the dream, but I know it's not that easy. For one, you have a boyfriend."

A boyfriend . . . I almost forgot the defense mechanism I put in place to protect me. I take a sip of water and lean back, sliding my hands out from under his and knowing it's time for me to confess. I won't hide in the shadows of my lies even if they're only little white lies. Shame fills me. "I lied to you. I believe my intentions were of a different nature, but it was still a lie."

The right corner of his mouth tilts up ever so slightly when he asks, "What did you lie about?" And maybe I'm looking to justify what I've done, but his eyes are bright with delight.

Embarrassment heats my chest, and my heart pounds. "I thought telling you I was seeing someone else would send you away."

That clears away any joy he was finding in the situation. "Do you still want me to go away?"

"No. But I don't trust my heart around you."

Resting his elbows on the table, he dips his head down. He lifts his cap off with one hand and slides his other through his hair. I catch a slight shake of his head too. I know I've disappointed him, maybe even hurt him, though I didn't mean to. I'm quick to add, "I'm sorry. You came back out of the blue and surprised me at work. I don't know what you expected. I just know that I couldn't even think straight. I wanted to leave as fast as I could, not realizing the true purpose of why you were there."

"What are you saying, Stella?"

"I'm not dating anyone."

He sits back, his body slumping against the vinyl while keeping his eyes on me. A small smile finds its way onto his lips, and then he licks them, sustaining my rapt attention to the small detail. "I understand your hesitation. I even understand your anger. We were left in an ugly place." Sitting forward again, a renewal of excitement flickers in his eyes like it used to years ago when he'd concoct the craziest of plans. "Let me show you how beautiful we can be again."

"We have so many demons, Rivers." I push down how natural it feels to be around him again, how comfortable it is to be open and honest without worrying about repercussions. "In a way, you chose Naomi over me, and then you left. Now you're back but only for a few days. I'm not sure what to think or do."

"You're here. You took the first step, and that's all I could ask for before. But now, I want to ask for more." Reaching over, he slides his hand under mine—palm to palm, the tips of his calloused fingers tap along my wrist, igniting goose bumps up my arm. "You said I don't know you anymore. Give me the chance to meet who you are now, and I'll show you who I am."

There's such a sweetness to his tone and genuine kindness in his eyes. That's the Rivers I always knew until we started barreling toward our end. But seeing him like this and hearing him ask for that chance makes me want to give it to him. "I can't let go of the past until we address it. So if I give whatever this is—this friendship—a chance, and we get to know the people we are today, I'll still need to talk about what happened and how I was hurt. That's never gone away, but maybe talking through it with you can help heal us. That's a starting point. So if you think that would work for you as well, I'm open to this idea."

His smile grows. "I leave later this week."

My smile matches his. "Then we shouldn't waste any time."

Am I breathing too heavy?
   Can Rivers hear me?
   Can others?

My heart is beating too loud?

Does he think I'm just some small town girl compared to the women he meets in LA and New York?

Wonder how many women he's been with since he was with me?

Ugh. Not the mental picture I wanted.

Watch the movie.

Watch the movie, Stella.

Watch the movie.

He's so good looking. Wonder if he knows my heart is racing for him?

Don't look at him again. He'll think you're weird or clingy or—"Hi," he says when I try to sneak a peek at him.

I smile because he is. "Hi," I whisper, matching his tone in the dark theater connected to Highball. But then I giggle because I'm sitting next to Rivers Crow again and other than the giddiness blooming inside, this feels more right than wrong, and I love it. I slip my hand into his on the shared armrest, and our fingers weave together.

We kissed last night, and I can't seem to stop thinking about it and how I want to kiss him again. Attempting to seem cooler than I am, I force myself to watch the new superhero movie, though I'm only interested in watching him. Leaning over, he asks, "I thought you wanted to see this movie."

"No. I just wanted to spend time with you."

He bites his lower lip as he looks at me and then touches my cheek. "I'm glad. I like spending time with you."

He's shushed by a woman a few aisles in front of us in the nearly empty theater but chuckles. His hand touches the side of my neck and slides his fingers into my hair.

I suck in a breath when I realize he's going to kiss me. My favorite part of last night was when this man was kissing me. I close my eyes, wanting to feel instead of think. Our lips touch, and the pressure gently increases until our mouths are locked in a sweet embrace.

When I part my lips, our tongues touch, and the kiss deepens. Taking it slow, we angle toward each other, not caring one bit if anyone looks at us not hiding at all in the back row. Music blares as a scene changes in the movie, and we open our eyes, sitting back in our respective seats with huge smiles on our faces.

Giggling behind my hand, I glance over at him as I lick my lips. "This getting to know each other again might be more fun than I first thought."

"I promise more fun where that came from." He gives my hand a little squeeze and smirks as he turns back to the screen. We don't make it two minutes before the armrest is lifted and he's in my space, my head against the back wall as he kisses me like I'm the star of the movie. He's always been a star to me. "Hey, want to get out of here?"

"Please do," the lady says over her shoulder.

"Yes," I whisper and then say loudly, "I do."

"I love hearing that every time you say it."

As we walk down the steps in the dark hand in hand, I realize what he means and stop. He looks back, and since he's a step down, we're a little closer to eye level than usual, though he's still a good five inches taller. "I do?"

"I do too."

The woman says, "Bravo. Now take it outside before I report you to the manager."

Nodding toward the exit, Rivers says, "C'mon."

We hurry out of the theater and into the sunshine, stopping on the edge of the parking lot. I ask, "What now? We're in two cars."

"Want to go back to the beginning?"

Learning to trust someone who broke it is not easy. But everything about him right now reminds me so much of how we were together when things were good. "Yes." *Trust.*

I'm learning to trust the journey I'm on. Though my mind spins in ways that tell me to protect my heart, we have this one chance to start slow and build back what we once lost. I have so many thoughts on what happened, and one day, we're going to have to deal with that, but today's been nice. Last night was good. He said he didn't cheat. He said he's sorry. I can't sit on the fence when it comes to him. I'm either all the way in or all the way out. Maybe I need to not just trust in him, but also myself and stop second-guessing everything. It feels good to be with him, but I can't just let everything go without discussing it first. "It's beating a dead horse, but I'm choosing to believe you. I don't need the dirty details, but I do need the basics." He crosses his arms and stares at me, searching my eyes for some sense of my thoughts on the matter. I don't want any further misunderstandings. "You said you didn't cheat."

"I didn't."

I slow things down and search his eyes right back. I always did love the way his warm browns always comforted me. "I want answers, but I also don't want to cry, and I don't want to be upset right now."

He reaches for my hand and holds it again. "I get it."

"You didn't cheat. That's the important part. The rest—"

"The rest I'll tell you before I leave Austin. I promise."

"You promise, but you need to talk to her first?"

He nods. "I gave my word."

"I'm frustrated, Rivers, and I'm going to hold you to that promise."

"I won't let you down. Not this time."

"Thank you."

Kissing my knuckles, he lowers my hand to his side. "Thank you for giving me your trust again." He asks, "We can go in your car if you'd be more comfortable?"

Double meaning.

It's not just about a working air conditioner or having a newer model car. He's giving me the right to leave. He's giving me an out. Most of all, he's willing to take this slow. It may not go anywhere if I can't get over the past. But he's trying, so I will too. "Mine, it is. Where to?"

"It's a surprise." We start walking to my car when he asks, "How much time do you have?"

"I'm all yours all night."

"Music to my ears."

When I look at him, he's smiling, which suits him. I realize I've caught quite of few of his smiles in the past twenty-four hours. I pull my keys from my pocket and dangle them in the air. "Want to drive?"

"Absolutely." He unlocks the door with a push of the button and walks me to the passenger's side. Our hands are still joined when I lean against the door and pull him close. "I liked kissing you."

Moving against me, he traps me between his arms. He kisses me and then says, "I really like kissing you, Stella Lilith."

The effects of his dulcet tones affect me down to my knees, and I take him by the shirt and pull him even closer. We kiss again just because it feels so good.

When we separate, he moves around and opens the door for me. "I need to run to the store before we hit our destination."

Once we get to the nearest grocer, I wait in the car because he's still insisting on keeping it all a surprise. Time in the car isn't wasted. I text Meadow: *I've spent the past few hours with Rivers.*

Then I go about checking my emails but get a text back in record time seconds. *O.M.G!!!! Tell me everything!!!*

My phone rings, and I laugh when I see her name on the screen. "Oh my God. Tell me everything, Stella. Do not leave out a single minute."

Whispering as if someone will overhear me talking in my own car, I reply, "Actually, I'm still with him. He's in the store right now. He's taking me someplace, but it's a surprise."

She squeals. "Where?"

"I don't know. I just said it's a surprise."

"Sorry. I'm too excited. How did this happen?"

"I listened to my heart and followed it. I also texted him about—"

"This is it! This is your date?"

"It's not a—wait, yes, it is. It's a date. I'm on a date with him."

She squeals again. "I'm literally so excited that you would think it was me on a date with a rock star."

"Rivers."

"Yes, Rivers, but he's a rock star now."

Rock star doesn't fit the image of who I know him to be. Sure, he was famous around Austin, and I always knew he and his brothers would make it big, but they were still Jet, Tulsa, and Rivers to me.

When I see him coming out of the store, his head is down. A guy and a girl are following close behind him with their phones aimed at him, watching his every move. He gives them a little wave and then lowers his gaze to the ground again. "I need to go, Meadow. He's coming back."

"Have the best time."

"Thanks," I reply, still watching him. I don't know why I suddenly feel sad, but I do.

He opens the back door and sets the bag on the floor-board. When he opens the driver's door, his smile is still genuine, but it's lost some of its luster from before. I ask, "Is everything all right?"

The car is started, he adjusts his hat before he backs out, and we leave. "It's fine."

"Want to talk about it?"

His gaze finds mine briefly and he asks, "How do you always know when something's bothering me?"

"I guess in some ways I still know how to read you."

I thought he would jump at that, that maybe I do still know him better than I'm admitting to, but he lets it go and turns on the radio instead. We listen to music until we pull into a parking lot and he shifts the car into park.

Taking in the scenery, I smile. It's been a long time since I've been here, but I remember being here with him. "What are we doing here?"

"Going back to the start."

13

Rivers

"WHAT ARE YOU UP TO?" Stella asks.

Pretending to zip my lips, I pick up the grocery bag in one hand and hold her hand in the other because if she's letting me hold her hand, then I'm going to damn well hold it.

We walk across the high school lawn to the old oak tree. What a pair we make. Both of us are smiling like fools who got caught making out in the janitor's closet during school hours. We would know. I set the bag down and then point. "You were sitting right about here."

"Do you want me to sit?"

"Yep." I nod and give her a wink.

She sits down and leans against the tree. Stretching her legs out, her cutoffs ride high on her toned legs. She's a major distraction, but I pull my gaze away so I can begin the romancing. Going back to my bag of supplies, I reach in and pull out the book I found in the back seat of her car. I also pull out the brown paper lunch sack.

When she sees the items, her mouth falls open, and her hands cover her chest. "This is why you went to the store? Rivers," she says, sounding more emotional over the gesture than I expected. "This is the sweetest thing that anyone's ever done for me. And you used to do some pretty darn sweet things."

"I'm glad you like it."

I sit down so I'm facing her, our legs stretched out and parallel. I gently knock her hip with my foot. "What are you reading?"

She turns the book over in her hand and shows me the cover. "*Until I Met You.*"

"What's it about?"

A grin graces her lips. She's onto me, but she loves it. "Well," she says, pausing to think. The smile returns, and she leans forward, her enthusiasm too big to keep her contained to one spot. "It's about a couple who decide to determine their own destiny and fight for their love."

Resting back on my elbows, I say, "Sounds like another couple I know."

"Really?" She quirks an eyebrow. "Who?"

I know she's teasing, but damn if she isn't the cutest doing it. I can play along. "I'm looking at the better half."

She leans back on the tree, settling in. "Are we fighting for our love, Rivers?"

Staring right into her eyes, I say, "I sure hope so."

"You're quite the romantic these days."

"I always was when it came to you."

I hope she remembers me that way. If not, I definitely have more work cut out for me than I thought. Even when she looks down, I can still see the smile that reaches her eyes. Under dark lashes that flutter when her gaze meets mine again, she says, "I won't deny we had something very special."

I rub my hand over the top of her bare leg. "I like those shorts on you."

"They're just old cutoffs."

"They look good on you."

"Thanks." She hates being the focus like that, but she is so fucking gorgeous, and I want to shower her in attention. Grabbing the bag, she asks, "Did you bring lunch today?"

Hearing her repeat the same thing she said to me ten years ago takes me back as if it were yesterday. I'm just as unsure now of where this will go as I was then. "No, not today."

"That's awful. I bet you're hungry."

"Starving."

"You can have half of mine."

"I shouldn't take your lunch."

"You need food, Rivers." The words tumble out as if she had them memorized. She digs the sandwich out and starts laughing. "It's a bologna sandwich. I don't think I've eaten this since I moved out of the house." She pulls out a half cut on the diagonal and hands it to me. "Why didn't you have lunch that day?"

"I did. I just forgot it at home. I had planned to talk to you that day. My lunch slipped my mind until I was standing near you and realized I had left it on the table." I eat half of my half sandwich in one bite.

"Ah. My mom bought bologna in bulk and froze it. Freezing it made it rubbery. I once swore I would only buy freshly cut deli meat when I grew up." She laughs to herself as if the memory isn't as funny as it once was.

When her smile turns into a frown, I ask, "Are you okay?"

"I don't understand my mom. It's like once we became teenagers, she dusted her hands and was done being our mom."

"Do you still talk to her?"

"Not often. She was vacationing in Mexico on my birthday, so I didn't hear from her. And then at Christmas, she said she would be back to spend it with Meadow and me, but we sat in Meadow's apartment until five waiting. She never showed, so we took the dinner we made over to my dad, wished him a good holiday, and went to get In-N-Out Burger."

"Why didn't she show? Did you find out?"

"The guy she's dating has grown kids, and he talked her into spending it with his family instead." Her eyes flash to mine, and she sits up, her hand resting on my leg. "Oh Rivers. I'm so sorry. Here I am whining about not seeing my mom when—"

Sitting up, I say, "It's okay. It doesn't get easier not being able to see my mom or hear her voice, but it is what it is." I slide my fingertips under hers and add, "She loved you like her own."

"I think I loved her more than my own. I feel like a horrible person for saying that, but your mom was . . ." A wistful smile on her face causes me to smile too. "She was amazing. Did you know she gave me one of her dresses from high school to wear to homecoming?"

"I didn't know that." There's an ache that never seems to subside from the death of my mom. It flares anytime she's mentioned, like now. I rub the spot on my chest. "But it doesn't surprise me."

It's dark, but I can still see Stella so clearly from the lights shining near the path. She says, "When we got nominated for homecoming court, she was so happy for us. I remember her pulling me into her room and offering me one of her old dresses. She said we could have it altered, or I could change it however I wanted." Stella pauses as she looks at the brown bag in her lap, seeming to lose her appetite.

"Hey," I say. When she looks up, I move a little closer. "What's wrong?"

Reaching over, she takes my hand in hers. "My mom ripped the dress I picked out. I apologized through tears to your mom, and you know what she did?"

"What?"

"She hand sewed the tear and blamed the fabric for not being high quality. She knew it was my mother, but she never said a negative thing about her."

"I never heard her say a bad thing about my father either, and that asshole left her with three little boys to raise on her own."

"You're so much like her in your temperament and care of people. I mean," she says, smiling and peeking up under those long lashes. "What happened with us aside, you've always been the one there for everyone, including your brothers."

"Do you mind if I ask what happened to the dress?"

"Louisa knew I couldn't afford much . . . or anything really. So she gave me free range of her three dresses."

"I remember that dress on you. I didn't realize it was my mom's."

"We kept it our secret. I never felt more beautiful than when you looked at me that day."

"The dress. It was blue."

"Your favorite color."

"Your eyes are my favorite color, but blue after that."

Stella tilts her head to the side, showing me those beautiful green eyes. "Your mom altered the dress herself and then took me shopping for shoes."

"I thought you bought the dress, and she was just tailoring it to you. As soon as dinner was done, she would go to her bedroom and work on it. You would have thought it was a wedding dress by how she treated it and wouldn't let me see. She told me I should see it on you the first time."

Although I know Stella's happy right now, tears fill her eyes anyway. "The dance was three days before . . ."

I nod and take a deep breath. The call replaying in my head. *"There's been an accident . . . Louisa Crow . . . Come now . . ."*

"I miss her every day," I say.

"I do too."

"You looked incredible in that dress."

"You looked pretty incredible in that suit, your highness."

"I only won because I was escorting the queen."

She sighs. "It's funny how being crowned homecoming prince and princess of the junior court meant so much to me back then. I felt like that meant we would always be together."

"We get to determine our own destiny."

Holding up the book again, she says, "Like Hazel and Jude."

Reaching forward, I press my hand flat against hers in the air between us. "Like Stella and Rivers."

"Just like them." She takes a bite of the bologna sandwich, and while she chews, she digs an orange out of the bag. "You thought of everything."

"I thought of you. You always smelled like oranges."

"They're my favorite."

"I used to be your favorite."

"Maybe you will be again."

A flashlight hits our eyes, temporarily blinding us. "You can't be on school property after hours."

Squinting, I hold my hand up to block the light so I can see. A cop stands there, lowering his light the ground beside us. "Sorry, Officer. We were reliving our first date."

"I'm sure that will earn you some bonus points, but you need to pack it up and move off the property."

Stella says, "Yes, sir. We will."

I had just enough time to shove the small sandwich in my mouth and get up before he was rushing us toward the car.

We're laughing as we load into the car and pull out of the parking lot. But what I love most is the way she casually rests her hand on my leg like she used to. It's as if there's been no time away from each other. "Where to next, Romeo?"

"I'm fucking starving. That little sandwich wasn't enough to tide me over."

With a laugh, she looks me over. I work out for many reasons, one of which is because touring is hard, and if I'm not in shape, I wouldn't be able to play at the level I do. But I like the way she lets herself linger on different parts of my body, appreciating it in ways that make me want to flex and tighten for her. She says, "Well, you're much bigger now. How about we grab something, and I don't know, do something adventurous?"

"Adventurous, huh?"

"I have an idea, but first, burger or tacos?"

"Burger."

The remains of our fast food dinner are abandoned on a table right next to our clothes. "The first time we ate lunch under that oak tree, you asked me what type of guitar I played."

"Yeah." She smiles as if she's busted. "I heard you in the music room and asked my dad about them. He dabbled but never committed to the instrument."

"You asked him about guitars because of me?"

"I had these thoughts, little daydreams, about us being alone one day, and it would give me something to talk to you about so you hopefully didn't look at me like I was an idiot."

Wearing a deep pink bra and bright yellow thong, I take in that incredible body of hers as she swims away from me, across the pool, and rests her arms on the side. She drags her hand over her wet hair, and says, "I had the worst crush on you. Every girl in school was in love with one of the Crow brothers. You were mine."

"Your love?" I wink.

"More than."

Swimming toward her, I keep my head above water, and say, "I still am."

That pink bottom lip is tugged under her teeth, and a sly smirk takes claim of the other side of her mouth.

"You're still mine?"

"Wholeheartedly," I say, "It took me a year to build up enough courage to talk to you that day. It would have saved me a lot of trouble had I known you liked me. My friends were laughing from the corner of the building where they were spying on us. Jet had the same lunch period and told me he'd kick my ass if I continued to drag this out. He was tired of hearing about my 'pining' as he called it."

Kicking her feet in the water in front of her, splashing

me, she says, "I like the idea of you pining over me. Did you make Jet proud?"

"Yeah. He patted my back and then put me in a headlock of pride after school." I chuckle from the memory. My brothers were always my best friends. My mom used to say the three of us had to stick together no matter what. That long after she was gone, we'd have each other. *Thank fuck we did. Life would be nothing without them too . . .*

Her legs lower, allowing me to get closer. I swoop in against her and plant my feet on the bottom of the pool. Only the stars and moon above, and lights on the sides of the pool shine, but her eyes look at me like I can do no wrong. "Do you know how incredibly sexy you are?"

"Not anymore."

"That's a damn shame. I plan on reminding you. No games. No beating around the bush. Just truth in action."

"Are you going to keep talking about action or make a move, Rivers?"

I take her face gently in my hands, and whisper, "Make a move." Tilting my head, I bend my knees, and press my lips to hers. Soft and supple, welcoming with that hint of possession that gets me hard. Her legs come around my waist and her arms around my neck as I slide my arms around her back, so her back isn't scratched by the rough edge of the pool. As our kisses deepen, my body presses to hers, steadying us in the water.

"Rivers," she moans in my ear when our lips part, clinging to me as water laps around us. "What are we doing?"

Although I know she means more than this moment, I keep her in the present. "What do you want to be doing?"

"Kissing you."

"Then I'll kiss you till the sun rises."

The giggle that escapes tickles my ear. Her happiness makes me feel invincible. I made her laugh. I made her moan. I made her—"Rivers?"

I spin us in the water so I'm against the side instead, not wanting her to get a scratch on her body. "What?"

"Where are we anyway?"

"Right here together. Just you and me and a whole night ahead of us."

She smiles and runs her hands over my shoulder and up my neck. When her hand reaches my jaw, she replaces it with her lips and kisses me all the way to my ear. "No," she whispers. "Who do you know who lives in these apartments?"

"No one. Just wanted to get you naked as soon as I could."

She flails and sinks under when she pushes off. When she pops back up, she starts swimming back to the other side but stops to look back. "You're absolutely crazy. You know that?"

Crazy about you. "You wanted adventure." I swim after her and catch her just past the middle of the pool.

"Adventure. Not to get arrested for trespassing." But I see the twinkle in her eyes. I see how much she loves this even if she won't admit it.

Our feet don't touch, so I grab her waist and lift her until her legs are around me again. With her hair slicked back and all of her wet wrapped around mine, she's a siren who speaks to my basic instincts. *She always did.*

I could try to hide my physical reaction, but I don't. Instead, I move my hands lower and hold her ass harder so she feels every last inch of how she affects me. Her breathing matches mine, but watching her chest rise and fall so heavily before me makes me want to slip inside her like I used to.

She kisses me again before she says, "We should go before the cops are called."

"I can handle them, but if you're worried, we'll leave." I carry her to the edge and set her on the side. I hop out right after but notice how she walks without hiding her body from me. That yellow thong isn't hiding anything and when she turns back to me, I see my tattoo peeking out from under the lace of her pink bra. "What are you doing?"

"Admiring you." No need to lie. "Your body is just . . . you're really fucking sexy."

Tossing my shirt at me, she says, "So are you. Get dressed. You're making it hard to keep my hands off you."

"If that's the case," I reply, standing up and taking my boxer briefs down. They're soaked and I have no problem going commando in my jeans. "I just might stay naked all night."

She gasps when she sees me and quickly turns her back to me. What can I say? I'm hard for the woman.

"Rivers," she admonishes.

I come up behind her and wrap myself around her. "What is it, baby? Did you forget what I look like? How about what I *feel* like?"

"Jeez," she says, "I must have." She's squirming, and I'm not sure if she's trying to wriggle free or get a better feel of the situation.

Holding her hands to her cheeks, I see how she's forgotten what it's like to be around someone she can be free with, someone she can be herself with. So, I run my hands down her body—the sides, her hips, and slowly bring them up to her waist. "Maybe you need to do some exploring of your own, Stella."

I'm given a playful jab with her elbow into my ribs. "Good grief, you're ridiculous." When I set her free, she turns around to face me and slips on her shirt that clings to her wet skin. "You've fed me, and you've wooed me. What's your next move, Romeo?"

"Romeo, huh? What would Romeo do with you?"

Sidling back up to me, she wraps her arms around my middle and tugs my ass toward her. "Kiss me again?"

Is it stealing if she wants me to kiss her? I add a little body grind when I finish kissing those sweet lips. "We're wet, Rivers." *Damnnnnn.* She knows how to tease a man. "Should we go home?"

Fuck. I was hoping to spend more time with her. "I can take you home." I start to pull back to get dressed.

She moves back against me and winks. "I meant your place."

Oh.

Fuck. Yes. I want to take her back to my place.

14

Rivers

I'M NOT NERVOUS.

I'm not even worried about what will or won't happen tonight. Being with her again confirms I made the right decision to come back here. Things are happening naturally with just a little help, but they are going in the right direction.

And although I'm not sure her being "taken" would have stopped me from going after her, I'm so fucking glad she's single.

I pull off my shirt and slip on gym shorts while she's in the shower. She was cold on the way back to Jet's house since her clothes are wet. I tossed them into the dryer while she showered to warm up.

The shower turns off, and shortly after, she comes into the living room wrapped in a towel. But when I automatically drag my sweaty palms down the front of my shorts like a fifteen-year-old standing in front of her again, I realize maybe I am a little nervous. I like what's happening between us too much for it to end so soon.

Standing across the room, I take her in. Hair messed from towel drying, face clear of makeup—she's breathtaking. She rolls her eyes while laughing . . . probably at me, but I can handle it. "Stop staring. You're making me self-conscious."

"I'll never stop staring at you. You're fucking beautiful."

"You keep saying that." She moves into my arms and leans her head against my chest over the tattoo that's solely hers. "You can have anyone."

"I don't want anyone." I kiss her head. When she closes her eyes and her arms tighten, I realize she is opening herself up to me. She's beginning to put her trust in me. I can't . . . I won't screw this up again.

She asks, "Do you have a shirt I can borrow and a spare pair of boxer shorts while my clothes dry?"

"I got ya covered." I want to cover her with my body, but I'll get the next best thing.

I go into the bedroom and scrounge around in my suitcase. With her standing behind me, she asks, "Guess you really aren't staying long. You haven't even unpacked."

The teasing fun is gone from her voice, which causes me to look back. With the shirt in hand, I stand, giving the clothes to her. I rub her bare shoulders, selfishly because I want to touch her soft skin, and because I want to make her feel good, comfort that change in her tone, and make her happy again. "Just because I'm leaving doesn't mean I'll be gone forever."

"What are your plans?" The sincerity shines in her eyes but is disturbed with the worry I hear in her voice.

"We have practice for a few weeks to nail the new songs

before we head back into the studio to record our next album."

"So you'll be gone for a while?"

"A few weeks, a little longer." I hate to think about leaving, but the reality is, when I signed on the dotted line for these record deals, I also signed away some of my free time. "I have to be where the job requires me to be."

"And that's LA?"

"That's LA."

"Job," she repeats as she turns and goes into the bathroom. She shuts the door just enough for me not to see her changing, but leaves it open enough for us to hear each other. "What happened to playing because it was your passion?"

"I still do. I can't imagine doing anything else. What would I do with my business degree anyway? All I know is music. All I feel is the beat. I won't ever be someone who finds a nine-to-five or wears a suit every day. And now I won't ever have to."

"Would you leave if you could stay?"

A lot has happened over the time I've been back, but she still doesn't know where things will go between us. Neither do I. I just know I like being with her and that I still love her. "I'm living my dream, Stella. But there are times I have to do what's needed to continue. It's no different than when I was here except I'm paid more."

"We haven't really talked about your life and how it's change—Oh my God! You're kidding me with this, Riv. I swear you and Meadow are plotting together." She comes out with the shirt outstretched in front of her. "Really? This is all you have?"

"I quite like seeing you in my clothes again. And if I

recall correctly, you used to steal my band shirts to wear. What has Meadow been up to?"

"The shirt you saw me in this morning was her doing."

"I always did like your sister."

My pretty little mess stands there with wet, messy hair and her hands on her hips. I lean down and kiss her as her hands run over my ribs. When I return to my full height, I say, "I should shower."

She doesn't release me, though. Instead she moves against me and rests her cheek on my chest. "How bad is it that I like smelling you again?"

"The chlorinated version?"

Laughing, she replies, "Yes, even the chlorinated version of you."

Wrapping my arms around her, I give her whatever access she wants. "We used to have the best sex after a gig. I was so fucking sweaty, and you were so turned on. You turned on turned me on."

"Your shows were aphrodisiacs."

"Well then, smell away."

She giggles but pushes off and climbs onto the middle of the bed, resting back on her elbows. "My favorite was when I could smell your scent on me."

Taking her in from her toes up to the top of her head, I rub my thumb over my bottom lip, visually enjoying every inch of this woman. "So what you're saying is you don't want me to shower?"

Her finger summons me to come hither, and she replies, "That's exactly what I'm saying."

I get my ass there and climb right over her. Settling between her legs, I hold my chest above hers. "You're a dirty girl, you know that."

"I'm hoping to get a lot dirtier." Fingers weave into my hair above my ears, and she nods.

"I don't even have to play a show?"

"Nope. Though I want to hear you play again, you only had to feed me a bologna sandwich this time."

Chuckling, I lower a little more of my weight. My dick is hard and getting harder being with her like this. "Tell me what you want, Stella."

"I'm sorry I lied about dating someone else."

"Want to know the truth?" Her eyes widen, and I say, "I knew you were single."

"You did?" Her mouth drops open.

"I overheard you talking to Meadow in the alley."

Her hands press to my chest, maintaining the distance. "And you let me carry on like that?"

"I could have called you out on it, but I was still trying to figure why you were lying. Though the reason makes me feel shitty, I understand why you did it."

"I'm sorry. Really, it wasn't even about you. It was about me and my issues."

"We both have our issues. Let's not talk about them tonight. I lost myself years ago, and this is the first time I feel myself again. I want to bathe in the hours I get with you." Lowering down, I kiss her cheek, then whisper, "Do you know how many times I thought of you and making love to you again?"

She says, "Don't tell me. Show me." I lift enough to see her eyes—the desire and want, the need and . . . love. "We haven't had a sip of alcohol tonight, but I feel tipsy around you."

"You just forgot how intoxicating I am." God, I want to touch her under that shirt, kiss her neck, and lick that Crow tattoo like I used to. When she smiles, I kiss her until those lips embrace mine. I kiss her until her hands slide under my shirt, and I kiss her until her body begs mine for more.

"Do you have protection, Rivers?"

I've never had unprotected sex except with her, but life sure has a way of fucking things up. It's sad that we fell apart enough to need a barrier between us now. "Let me get a condom."

I hope me leaving her alone with her thoughts doesn't change the heat building between us. I dig through my suitcase, promising God I'll be a better man if he will grant me this one favor. Please let me find just one condom in this messy suitcase. I've fucked around on tour but don't keep a replenished stock. I would just hit up Ridge or my brothers when I was in need and had run out.

The familiar sound of a wrapper has me scrounging through dirty clothes and smelly sneakers only to discover it's a coffee receipt. *Fuck.*

"It's okay if you don't," she says.

My head whips around to see her propped up and watching me. "I don't think—"

"I mean, it's okay if you don't have a condom and we don't have sex. We can do other stuff." She's sitting there looking perfect while waiting for me, and all I see are a million thoughts flashing through those beautiful greens.

I get up and lie down on the bed next to her. Pulling her close, she rests her head on my chest and drapes a leg over mine. "It's not what you think, Stella."

"What do I think?" The tips of her fingers drag the front of my shirt up and she traces the curves of the muscles in my stomach.

"You're thinking I've been fucking my way through three tours now and not thinking about you."

"I hope you weren't thinking about me when you were

with other women. Some might find it flattering, but I think it would be disrespectful to them." She pushes up and looks me in the eyes. "I wouldn't want you thinking about someone else when you're with me."

When, not *if*.

"I guess we need to talk about it. The reason there are no condoms in my bag is because I haven't wanted to be with anyone in a long time. But—"

"I know you've had sex with other women, Rivers. I'm not dumb, and I've seen the articles out there. I even know about the Victoria's Secret model you dated for a while last year."

I'm already shaking my head. "It's not true. She was a friend. She came to an event with me, and I escorted her to one of her events. That's all."

"The Victoria's Secret Fashion show airs on TV. The cameras flashed to you when she blew you a kiss with those huge angel wings on her back. I mean, does she eat? How did she hold those things up?" Anger slips into her tone.

"She does eat, and believe it or not, she's nice." Taking her chin between my fingers, I angle her so her eyes meet mine again. "But we never dated. We went to those events as friends. She could have gone home with anyone she wanted."

"But she went home with you, right?"

Man, I don't want to answer that, but I have to. Full disclosure. Honesty. "Yes. But we only slept together two times because we really were good friends. It was . . . fun, not a relationship."

"I remember our fun being more than a little."

"I've never had what I had with you with anyone else. God's honest truth."

A quick peck is placed on my chest. "She's gorgeous, and

her body is perfect. I can never compete with that. My body has changed."

Pulling her on top of me. I kiss her forehead and then her mouth before I say, "Don't you see, Stella Lilith? You never had to compete. You had me all along." I kiss her again. "I could never date anyone seriously else because they weren't you."

"It's okay that you slept with others. I don't love it, but you were free to do so. I also hate thinking about it, but I won't hold it against you."

I stroke her hair and push for what I want to know. "You dated others. You had a boyfriend, if not many." I don't ask a question because, like her, I hate the thought of her with anyone else. I feel rage inside just thinking about some asshole touching my girl.

"I . . ." She stops and I hear a hard swallow. "I did a few years ago, but—" She stops abruptly.

"Stella?"

Exhaling a shaky breath, she whispers, "I was never good for anyone else. My heart was never in it."

"Where was your heart?"

This time, she smiles before replying. "Touring with a sexy bassist for The Crow Brothers."

I grin, and it's goddamn smug as fuck. "For the record, I didn't have sex with as many women as you think I did. I left that for Tulsa." I kiss the top of her head.

"Oh Tulsa," she says. I'm sure she's rolling her eyes.

"I'm not innocent, but most nights, I just wanted to be alone."

"I understand that too well." She lifts her head, and says, "We really are a sad pair."

"I can't say I'm sad right now."

That brings a smile back to her face. "I can't either."

My guilt gets the best of me, so I lay my sins at her feet and let her be my judge and jury. "I only had sex after we broke up to try to satisfy a physical need. Emotionally, I was never satisfied. Fuck, the sex wasn't even good."

Her hand caresses my cheek as if my sentence has been stayed for the time being. She kisses my chest. "I believe you." Kissing my chin and then my jaw, her breath waves across my skin. "I believe you." She tugs my earlobe gently between her teeth and then whispers again, "You know why?"

"Why?"

"Because I'm in your blood, and you're in my blood. There's no escaping what we had."

"Have," I say, my eyes closing as I breathe her and her words deep inside so they reach the deep recesses of my being.

Her lips press to mine, but she doesn't kiss them. There are so many thoughts buzzing around my head, but the main one is, *Shit. Too fast.* Because in my head, there is no escaping what we had, and what I believe we still have. She's here. With me. Allowing me to kiss her.

And then she says one simple word, and my heart soars. "Have."

15

Stella

I CAN'T BREATHE.

I'm going to die.

I'm going to explode into a million little pieces.

Rivers looks up, and asks, "Are you okay?"

"No."

Sitting up in alarm, he eyes me. "No?"

"This feels too good."

Then that gorgeous smile of his shines, and he chuckles. "Is too good a thing? Kissing you, touching you, making out with you is incredible and feels good, but I don't want to stop. I mean, too good means too much, right?"

"No." *Please don't stop.*

"No?"

We've been making out for at least an hour like teenagers, taking things slow. He rounds each base with deliberate care. More like deliberate torture for me, but it feels too good to rush this.

I'm about to lose my mind, but I pull him to me again

anyway, ready to lose my mind to the ecstasy. "Not too much. Perfect. Keep going."

He chuckles against my neck and starts kissing me again. A hand is up my shirt just below my bra, tentative, careful, taking things so slow that I'm going to burst. My eyes close, my head falls back against the wall, and I moan in delight. "God, yes. This so much. More of this."

If him kissing my neck feels this good, I might legit die under his magic mouth if he goes any lower. My memory still serves me well when it comes to that act. He says, "This shirt is big on you," and then tugs the collar to the side exposing my shoulder and quickly staking claim to the bare skin with his mouth. "Do you know how good you taste?"

"No," I repeat the word, mindless of anything else to say because I'm feeling too much, the universe in every one of his delectable kisses.

"Then you're missing out." He licks his lips and waggles his eyebrows before tracing my collarbone with the flat of his tongue and moaning as if I'm his favorite dessert.

With his other hand, he finally attempts to go further, the tips of his fingers just under the wire of my bra. "Am I going too fast?" he asks. "Tell me if you want to slow down."

"Slow down? No way. I want to speed up."

"I'm starting to think you're sex starved."

"Famished." I wiggle until my back is against the wall and he's no longer over my chest. I touch the top of his head, driving my fingers into the thickness of his dark hair. Pushing enough to get him where I want him—his face to my vagina, I ask, "Ready for the second course?"

"Famished." He leans in, kisses me between the legs, then tugs the material back between his teeth. "Ready to take these off?"

Oh yes. Yes. Yes. Yes. Yes. "So ready."

He pops the elastic waistband of the boxers he loaned me and chuckles lightly, then starts to slowly pull them down as if he's savoring every new exposed inch of my skin. The shirt still hides my torso, but when the boxers go flying over his shoulder, he eyes me in a way that makes me want all my clothes off—deep umber-colored hungry eyes. His tongue drags over the fullness of his bottom lip, and then he says, "I want to see my tattoo."

His tattoo.

Not mine. *His.*

Just like me.

With him still positioned between my legs, I take the hem of the shirt in hand. Why is my heart beating so fast? "Don't look, okay?"

"We don't have to do anything."

"I want to. I do. It's just . . ." I look away from him. "I feel like I'll disappoint you."

"Never. You could never, Stella. You're better than any memory I had. You. Here now. You're . . . I don't feel deserving to be here."

Sitting forward, I run my nails through his hair to the back of his neck and pull just enough for him to know I want him to come to me. Moving against my body with ease, the muscles in his shoulders flex as he kisses me. He leans back enough for me to hold him lightly under the jaw. How can he still love me so much? After all this time, after all the hurt and pain? *I lost myself years ago, and this is the first time I feel myself again. I want to bathe in the hours I get with you.* God, I want that too. "How does someone who has the world at his feet miss someone who only held him back from his greatness?"

He was always mine. He was my reward at the end of all my long days in student teaching and hard work at school.

Though his muscles were firm and strong, his soul was my soul's soft place to land.

After The Crow Brothers' second nomination and first win— big win—for Band of the Year at the Austin Music Scene Awards, my man has never been sexier owning that stage. I used to think his beats matched my heartbeats, but I was wrong. My heart beats to his—musically, physically, emotionally, I'm in sync with this man.

Jet accepts the award with Tulsa piping in his ecstatic two cents. Rivers doesn't need the glory. He's won for doing what he loves to do, for doing something that pays the bills for us to have a better life one day. While his brothers thank the fans, Rivers stands in the back with his eyes on me, thanking me.

When his brothers head for the side stage with the award in hand, Rivers hops off the front. Coming up the aisle, he starts into a jog.

I know what he's doing. I would do the same—our breath, our beats in sync.

The auditorium isn't that big, but guests aren't allowed where the nominees are seated. The bands themselves take up too many seats. That doesn't bother me. He deserves all the glory.

He's been my rock, my partner, my lover, my whole heart since the day we first spoke. Even though I don't need any recognition for loving him, he needs me.

God, do I love how much he needs me. He's not alone in his needs because they're rivaled by my own. We've been inseparable for years and taken this journey together.

Although I'm trapped in the middle of the aisle, I stand so he can find me in the crowd. Other musicians and fans here to celebrate the best Austin bands watch one of the best there is run toward me. He stops at the end of the aisle and huffs his disapproval. Not deterred, he steps up on the armrest. The fans lift their arms, letting him walk right over them until he drops back down in front of me amongst cheers and hollers. Taking my face between his hands, he says, "None of this would be possible without you, without your support. My win is your win, baby. I wouldn't be here without you. I love you."

He kisses me with no hesitation, my lips meeting his in a kiss that speaks to my heart and my head. The clapping starts slow and builds fast to a loud roar as we get lost in each other like we do every other time. Though, it's usually without an audience. Our lips part but hearts are hooked together. "I love you," I whisper, opening my eyes slowly.

. . . He didn't return to his seat up front after that kiss or the next four. He chose me instead. That night, we celebrated by making out until my lips were swollen and his beard had scrapped along my chin so much that my skin was pink.

Consumed was a word others always used to describe us.

Rivers and I preferred *in love.*

This is the Rivers that has come back for me. The way he kisses my neck, the movement of his hard body against mine as we lie on this bed feels so much like my cherry on top for the hell I've been through.

"How can you look at me the same when so much has changed?"

A hand slinks under the side of my shirt and rests on my bare hip. Leaning down, he kisses my chest over the fabric still covering me. "Loving you is my greatest honor and hurting you my biggest regret. No matter where I was in the world, my heart stayed here with you. You were more than my girlfriend. You were my sanctuary, my haven."

"What am I now?"

"My home." *And somehow, I think he's my home too. Again.*

16

Rivers

DESPITE THE RUMORS AND REPUTATION, I never claimed to be smooth. But looking at Stella's face, I see what I thought was only possible in my dreams, the flicker of hope that I prayed for shines in her eyes. Maybe I am the Romeo she likes to teasingly call me.

My mind is not racing, not searching, or lost. My soul is at peace and my heart calm. We were so close to exposing more than our regrets and feelings. We were so close to sharing our bodies. But holding her in my arms, in this bed, in the quiet of the night again feels like the home I've been missing.

She feels like home.

"Rivers?" she whispers.

"Yes?"

"Is it bad to want to move forward physically when there's not a perfect bow on the resolutions to our past yet?"

"I don't know. Most important to me is your happiness.

So do we pull the Band-Aid off? Maybe. I'll follow your lead. I want us to date again. I want us to be . . . *us* again."

Lifting her head, she looks up at me with a sweet smile before scooting higher and leaning back next to me. "What about the others we've been with?"

"I can't say anything about you being with others while we were apart."

Her shoulders rise and fall quickly. "What if I want you to know?"

Her confession causes me to tense. "You only have to tell me what you want me to know." For her, I'll go where I don't want to. For her, I'll go where she needs to be.

Since the conversation is steered into choppy waters, she shifts, adjusting to the tide as it turns. Sitting up, she eyes me. "I've been with two other men."

The topic is unsettling and angering. My jealousy spikes through my veins as I silently repeat to myself that I don't have a say in what happened after we broke up.

She adds, "I needed you to know that."

"What do you want me to say, Stella?"

"I don't need to hear words. I need to feel this love you say you still have for me because there was no love with either of them."

"We can make love. We can fuck. We can do whatever you want, but it's not just being here that will bring us together again."

"I don't understand what you mean, Rivers."

"We had a show last summer and a rare day off to ourselves in Denver. Tulsa was off fucking around doing who knows what, probably chasing Nikki around. Jet went back to his room to call his wife, and I went to my room to do nothing. I didn't have anyone to call or spend time with. I didn't have anyone who made me want to chase them. So I sat there in the room staring out the window for an hour before I walked out of the hotel and just kept walking. I ended up a few miles away standing in front of a building that had graffiti on the side brick wall." Raising my arms, I can visualize it so clearly. "Painted in familiar green was the phrase: the truth will set you free."

"That's from the bible."

"You know I've never been a religious man. My father left years prior, before my mother was taken too soon. I had a lot of fucking blame to dole out, and I took some of that out on you."

"You took it out on yourself—your body, your mind, your heart. You chose to slowly kill yourself for something you aren't responsible for."

Reaching between us, she takes my hand and folds her fingers with mine. "Why did that quote speak to you?"

"We were destroyed by lies. I need you to know the truth. All of it." Looking into her eyes, I say, "But it wasn't just the quote that spoke to me."

"Familiar green. What does that mean?"

"You have unique green eyes. They're the ones that I see when I pray to be set free from the lies."

Her lips part just enough for me to see the center of that upper lip that I want to kiss and nip. Her hand holds mine tighter. "Let me be the one to set you free."

My mouth pours the truth at her feet, hoping she can survive the flood. "I did not have sex with Naomi."

She leans forward, dropping her head into her hands. "Rivers," she says my name as if her patience has worn thin. "People saw you with her."

"Fucking John Cables, her ex, saw me at her house."

Her ponytail whips around when she turns to face me. "I don't understand."

"I know you don't, Stella. I swear to the God I know and pray to on the daily that I never wanted to hurt you."

"I don't know what to think." Slipping out of bed, she walks to the window and looks back. The room is lit by the moonlight, but it's enough to see the fire raging in her eyes. "*The truth will set you free.* Can you tell me more? Because just thinking about that night is ripping me apart again. Please set me free from this torture where you left me."

"I didn't do it. I didn't touch her, Stella. And I wasn't there for any other purpose than to help her." I climb out of bed, slowly, careful not to send her running. Walking to her, I take her hands in mine, which is a good sign that she'll let me, and bring them to my chest. I close my eyes as her palms warm my skin.

My eyes open again when she says, "Look me in the eyes, in these familiar green eyes that you see when you pray for peace, and tell me the truth." Tears form and fall as she pleads, "Please stop my heart from hurting."

I look directly into her eyes, sharing the truth the best I can. "I wouldn't do anything differently, and you wouldn't want me to. I helped a friend in need. You weren't supposed to be hurt because I didn't think you'd think the worst of me. But I can't break a promise—"

"That's it? That's all you're going to tell me?"

The moonlight reflects in her eyes as she stares into mine. "I told you I didn't have sex with her, and I helped her because she needed help. I should have gone about things differently, but as for where my love laid, I never stopped loving you."

"We didn't have secrets until then."

"You're right. We didn't have secrets, which was why I thought you'd trust me regardless of what you heard. But you chose to believe the lies. I hate that trying to do the right thing ruined what was already so right. Please believe me, Stella. If I had cheated, there is no way I would have come back for you, because there was no way I could have forgiven myself. I'm not that person, and I never was."

Her shoulders relax, and the emerald rage I saw earlier in her eyes calms into a soft sage I love. I need her to believe in what we were; otherwise, we can't move forward. "Maybe because there's been time and distance, and I've grown up, but I believe you, Rivers. I believe that you couldn't sit here now looking me in the eyes and lie if you had cheated. I believe you're too good of a man to do that." She touches the collar of my shirt, gently stroking like she used to do when she was deep in thought. "I'm sorry. We can't take it all back though, can we?"

"No, baby. But I'm here, and if you want me, I want us to move forward. Together." *Desperately. With all my heart.* I watch her take a few deep breaths as a war rages within her. *Please choose us, Stella.*

Her gaze dips to my shirt, and her hand slips under, navigating my chest and tracing the star by heart.

"Take this off. I want to see it."

She always found comfort in seeing the permanency of her effect on me. I'm willing to do whatever she wants me to do. When I lift my shirt, she lifts hers and removes her bra, baring her body as I bare mine. Her fingertips bypass my three crows to trace the star that's inked on my chest, over my heart, for the star of my life.

I mimic her light touch and outline the crow she wears permanently on her skin for me. There's something heavy in the moment, in the light touch that I feel beneath the skin. She whispers, "I remember when we got these."

"I do too."

I can't call it a smile, but it's not a frown I see on her lips. "My dad was furious."

"Your mom told me that my brothers and I were a bad influence."

"She called me a whore."

I remember that too well, and it pisses me off to this day. It also makes me feel sad for her. "You were a good daughter. She was a terrible mother."

"Yeah. I didn't regret getting the tattoo, though."

"Did you after we broke up?"

"Every day until—" She stops and takes a deep breath, then exhaling slowly.

My gaze slides up from her fidgeting hands to her eyes again. "Until?"

"Until I had more important things to regret than a tattoo I got out of pure love."

Taking her hand, I press mine against it, holding them between us. "Pure love. How did two innocent kids handle a love that was too big for the two of them?"

Now I see the smile I adore. "Our love was never too big for us. The world just couldn't handle something so good."

"You make references to regrets beyond your family. The world's treated you badly?"

"Standing in front of you makes me believe it can be good again."

I run my hand down the curve of her waist as she runs hers over my stomach muscles that lead her lower. "You don't even understand how much your body affects me."

She giggles softly. "I have a pretty good idea."

Her hot hand takes hold of my erection, drawing every ounce of blood to the spot, and I find myself holding my breath and releasing harshly. "Fuck, that feels so fucking good." Detouring, my hand slides between her legs. I move into the heat of her hand, her stance loosening before me, her body welcoming me by parting for me. Her exhale comes with a small whimper that I remember like the melody of my favorite song. Dipping my head down to her shoulder, I say, "Let me make you feel good. Let me remind you that the world doesn't have to be so bad."

When I reach the valley between her leg and promise land, I pause and meet her eyes. Her breathing has picked up, each breath verging on the next in rapid succession. This is new; my memories of her were much more comfortable when we were together. "You doing okay?"

"It's been a while."

"For me too."

Surprise colors her expression. "Really?"

But she stops stroking me and I just need her to start doing it again. "Please."

She grins, and her hand begins moving again with the right amount of pressure to her grip. "Sorry." While I stroke the soft skin of her bare pussy, she squeezes her eyes closed, struggling to reopen them again. "That feels so good." Her focus is divided though when she asks, "How is it that it's been a while for you?"

"How?"

"Why?"

"Just don't stop, okay?"

"Okay, but why?"

Fuck this and the twenty questions. I slide my middle finger between her lips and when her eyes close and her mouth opens, I kiss her—deep and long, like I want to be with her in other ways. Finding the secret entrance, I dip my finger in and pull back to her dismay. "Don't stop."

I'm going to make her forget her name by the time I'm done with her. I drag my finger along her slick center and up, bringing it to my mouth. "Do you taste the same, baby?"

The guard she was building in angry protest to the vacancy I've left lowers again. "You tell me."

I suck my middle finger in knuckle deep and pull it out slowly, sucking all of her off me. "Better."

She lifts up on her toes and presses her lips to mine but doesn't kiss me. Instead, she drags the tip of her tongue across the middle of my lips and says, "I cannot wait to taste you again."

Fuck me. I bend down and lift her naked body up so her legs wrap around my middle. It would be so easy to push against the wall and fuck her hard and fast, to come inside her while she comes around me.

But that's not what this is. Tonight is about beginnings not endings. There's still no way I'm missing the opportunity to lick that sweet pussy until an orgasm coats my mouth. We kiss as I carry her to the bed and set her down.

Climbing to the middle, she lies back, her body ready for me with pert nipples and spread legs. I kneel beside the bed between her legs and start kissing a trail up the inside of her thigh. She shivers, and says, "I've missed your mouth on me."

I'm not beneath a challenge, not only to make her mine but to also make her forget the time we spent apart. I owe her no less. "I missed my mouth on you too." I never mind giving her what she deserves. I've come from her coming. I can't wait to feel her legs stiffen around me, to know that I've caused her body to give to me her sweetest pleasure. Me. I do that to her. Fuck. I'm turned on. I'm fucking licking her skin, my girl, my woman, my soul's body is mine right now for the taking as she gives me all access to possess her like I used to.

"Move higher on the bed," I direct. She's quick to obey and gives my body the room I need to dig my hips into the mattress, knowing the pressure against my cock can get me off before she has a chance to. *Do I want that?* Fuck, yeah. I'll take coming against the mattress in exchange for her coming any day all day long. I want her to come, to take what I can give and give me the symphony of her ecstasy.

I don't know why that little space at the apex of her legs, the valley of her leg gets me harder, but I have always love that part of her body so fucking much. I flatten my tongue, teasing her.

A groan causes me to look up. With her forearm over her eyes, she almost appears to be in pain, so I stop. "Stella?" When her head pops up, I ask, "Everything okay?"

The line of her brows softens, and she nods. "I want you . . . I want this. It's just been a long time, and I'm caught up in my head."

I move up higher because her comfort in what we're doing wins out over anything I need or want. Lying next to her, I kiss her before I stroke her hair back. "What's going on in your head?"

She caresses my cheek. "Being with you like this makes me feel like a teenager again."

"Me too. It feels good to be with you again." I slide my hand down her stomach and lower between her legs, this time going straight between those pretty little pussy lips and deeper inside her. "I like touching you. Do you like that?"

"Oh God, I love it." Her eyes practically roll to the back of her head, and she drops down on the mattress. I kiss her forehead and then nose, cheek, and chin, and her neck, lower to her chest, and then to the tattoo that will always mark her as mine.

One of her hands tugs at the hair at the back of my head,

and this time, she moans in a weighted sigh with a slight smile on her face. "That's it, baby. Just feel." I start a slow fuck with my finger before I add another. Her body moves, reacting every time I push in or pull out. I rub my thumb over her clit, and her back arches, her legs tightening around my hand.

I keep going, fighting through the tension of her thighs around my hand. While I kiss her nipple and gently take it between my teeth, my cock presses against her hip, and I thrust to ease the ache, falling into rhythm with my hand and the ways her body takes me in.

My hair is tugged as her fingers fist. "Rivers. Rivers."

"My Stella Lilith. My star of night."

"I'm close. Faster. Faster. Please."

I go deeper and fulfill her request by moving faster. She's already so wet for me, and when she cries out, "Oh," I watch her come, the visual better than I remember.

Full, pink lips parted. Eyes squeezed closed and tits exposed. Her breath is caught in her chest, and I slow my hand as she comes back down, bucking from the sensitivity. I stay put until she comes down from the high she's riding. When her body relaxes onto the mattress and her eyes open, I kiss her chest and then pull slowly out of her. She stops my hand and says, "I liked you in me." Kissing my lips, she takes hold of my dick that's about to explode. "I can't wait to have more of you inside me again."

But she doesn't release me. She grips and slides her hand down to the base of my cock and back up. Then again. I wrap my hand overs hers and tighten her hold around me. "Keep going. So close." Trapping our hands between us, I can't stop my body from gyrating against hers chasing my release. "Feels so good, baby."

Keeping my eyes open, I watch her tits as they bounce

for me. I stare at the tattoo on her chest and listen to the music our bodies make when coming together. "Oh fuck, Stella." I drop my head to the pillow above her head. "Fuck," comes out in a string of slurs as my body pumps in her hand.

Still holding my hand over hers, I release when I come. My eyes squeeze closed, and flashes of heaven pepper the inside of my lids. I lie back and spread my arms out. One slips under her and I pull her close. The other goes wide as I try to recover my breath.

She doodles over my chest as her leg drapes over mine. Doesn't matter that we've made a mess all over us. She wraps around me anyway. Resting her chin on my chest, she smiles, and says, "If this is just the beginning, I like it."

"God, I've missed you, Stella. You're just too beautiful and too fucking amazing. I want to win your heart back so bad."

She kisses me on the chest, and I sigh with her touch. So gentle, yet almost possessive. It's been so long since I've felt like this. "If it matters, you're already way ahead of where I thought you'd be when it comes to making *us* a *we*. And I'm really starting to like *us*." *Thank God.*

"I love us."

17

Stella

IT'S A SATURDAY NIGHT. I'm glad I can sleep all day if I want tomorrow because I can't sleep at all. I also can't stop staring at Rivers while he slumbers or wipe the smile from my face. I can't believe I'm lying naked in bed with him and we did what we did.

Whether I should be or not, I'm giddy. Ridiculously so.

Not one regret has slipped into the little world of this bedroom. Not one doubt. Trying not to burst at the seams from excitement, I realize that I feel the best I've felt in years ... maybe even since we were together years ago.

His body is sexy, his face handsome. He's physical perfection—strong with broad shoulders, lean and tall. That's just superficial stuff, but it's a darn good package.

What that package holds inside is more precious than my own heart. An aura that can lighten up a room or bring it to its knees in his darkness. A soul that feels so full of hope when he looks at me that it's tangible. I can touch it, hold it, and reattach his soul to mine.

I want to bury myself in his arms to recapture the protection of his love. He makes that feel possible. Rivers makes everything feel possible again.

His heart beats in sync with his every emotion in the clear depths of his soulful eyes. There are no games with him. When he wants something, he's all in. He makes me believe in us again.

One eye opens and then his other. Reaching down, he takes my hand and brings it to his mouth to kiss not once, but three times. "What are you doing?" he asks. His voice is rocky like the cliffs of a rough morning, laced in seduction that speaks to my heart in rhythm and tone.

"Staring at you."

His chuckle is deep, a reverb heard in his chest. Seriously, can he be any sexier? I'm thinking no.

But then he is. Grabbing me quickly, he flips me onto my back under him. His breath tickles my neck before he kisses a little too roughly. That's going to leave a mark. *At least I hope it does.*

His hardness pushes between my legs, and I have my first regret of the night—putting the boxer shorts I had discarded earlier back on and him putting his on. I have no idea how I look but how he looks at me makes me feel beautiful. Lifting up, I kiss him, then whisper, "We can do more .. . if you want."

"No protection," he says on the cusp of his regret by the discontent on his face.

"I don't care," I say, getting caught up in the heat of the moment. "We never did before."

"I haven't earned your trust so don't give it away so easily." His hips push into mine. "Even if this does feel fan-fucking-amazing."

"But I said I believed you."

"I know. It means a lot to hear you say it, but I want you to feel it, and I don't know if you do yet."

"So if I feel your truth," I say, slinking my hand between us. "I get this? Because if you ask me, I'm feeling a lot of your truth right now."

He chuckles, his mouth falling open and his eyes dipping closed before he takes a deep breath and exhales. "You play dirty."

"No, you're playing too clean."

"Too. You love that word. Too good. Too much. Too clean."

"Too turned on. I want you. If that's wrong, then I don't want to be right." I shrug and then move my hips to meet his while wrapping my arms around his neck. "Doesn't that feel good?"

"Too good," he replies with a smirk. "Especially too good considering we don't have a fucking condom."

I should care, but ever since I started letting our past go and feeling instead of thinking last night, I want to rub against him. So I do, and he lets me, kissing my shoulder, collarbone, the other shoulder, neck, under my jaw, and landing on my lips. Our tongues swirl together as our bodies grind against each other's.

Like we used to do as teenagers, our make-out sessions got heavier until there was no reason to wait to have sex. We were in lust, but more importantly, we were in love. When I open my eyes, it's so easy for me to see why, and it has nothing to do with his looks. His love pours from him, his need for me almost dark around the bright center. We're not just a one-time love affair or a relationship gone bad. We're more than that. We're eternal.

I kiss him again and again, missing the sensation of losing myself in him. Despite the thin layer of fabric between us, we move together and I'm feeling as one with him. I suck in a harsh breath and dig the back of my head into the pillow as my muscles tense and my mind goes black. "Yes. God." Pushing. Pushing. I reach the peak as energy surges through me.

Rivers's breathing is erratic in my ear and a moan follows as the length of him feels like steel against my soft center. He grounds a grunt with my name, hot breath hitting my ear before the weight of him sinks me deeper into my pleasure.

I tighten my arms around him, willing to drown in this bliss even deeper. My heartbeat starts to calm just as he rolls off me. His eyes remain closed, and his voice is deep, relaxed when he says, "What are you doing to me, woman?"

"Killing you by way of ecstasy."

"Best way to die."

When he looks at me, I ask, "What does this mean?"

His hand finds mine, though, his eyes never leave me. "What I want is you to want to explore the idea of us again."

I snuggle against him. "I like exploring with you."

He laughs lightly, but when his arm comes around me, I can tell by his hold he's afraid of what's to come. "In the morning, let's not make this awkward. Let's not be who we were last week. Let's be the us we are right now, the us when our guards are down and we're free from the outside world to just be still in each other's arms. Can we do that?"

He's right. The sun seems to shed light on unwanted emotions in the brightness of a new day. Is the world capable of ruining what's so good between us right now? I hope not. "Morning won't change what we are tonight."

The top of my head is kissed, but no words follow. I eventually slip out of bed to clean up and then he takes my place right after. We silently climb back into bed and resume our position in each other's arms. My eyes are heavy from the long day, but my heart feels light from the man I spent it with. I kiss his bare chest right in the middle of the star tattooed over his heart and let my mind drift away with the hours.

We've moved around this morning in relative silence, the wanderlust of last night evaporating in the sunlight. Although he dried my clothes, I choose to keep his Crow Brothers shirt to add to my growing collection. He doesn't say a word, though I've caught a smug smile or two when his eyes glance between the shirt and my eyes.

He puts my car in park but leaves the engine running. With his hands firmly at ten and two on the steering wheel, he says, "When can I see you again?"

"Yesterday was fun."

His smile brightens. "It was."

The banquet comes to mind. Do I take the risk and ask him? It's not his world and asking him would mean bringing him into mine. I'm not sure what he'll say, but I ask anyway, "There's this thing."

His interest is piqued as an eyebrow rises. "Yeah, a thing?"

"A work thing. A banquet thrown to honor the staff and administration at the private school where I teach." I start fidgeting with the loose strings of my cut-off shorts. "You can come. I mean, I'm sure that sounds so uninteresting compared to the stuff you do in your life, but it—"

"I'll be there."

"You will?"

"Yes. If you're going, I'll go to support you."

"But you don't even know when it is."

"Doesn't matter. I'll make sure I'm there. You can text me the details and what to wear."

I rest my hand on his leg. "Just like that? No details needed?"

"If I'm in Austin, I'll be wherever you want me to be. Just like that." He leans over, and we kiss. When our lips part and our eyes open again, I say, "Tuesday."

"Tuesday," he repeats with a smile. "When can I see you before Tuesday?"

"What are you doing today?"

"If you're free, let me take you to dinner."

"What about the hours between now and then?"

Leaning back against the headrest, he says, "I'm supposed to meet with Ridge to fuck around on some tunes we're writing."

"I might be speaking out of turn, but I'd love to hear you play again. Maybe you can fuck around with me. Meadow and I could come over and bring food to cook out. Beer as a bribe to let us hang around you rock stars."

"You don't have to bribe me to spend time with you. It's all I've wanted for years, so I'm definitely up for it. I'll get a hold of Ridge. You get a hold of Meadow and let me know."

"Sounds like a plan."

He pops the driver's door open and says, "I guess I should go."

When he gets out, he comes around and opens my door before offering me a hand out. I remember his mom always telling me that she would make sure her boys always treated women with respect and kindness. She raised them on manners and with good hearts, filled their bellies with food, and their hearts with boundless love. She was a good mother. The best actually.

I'm not released the moment I'm on my feet. Quite the opposite. I'm pulled into his warm embrace, making my heart race as we avoid an inevitable goodbye. I've always been sensitive, a little shy, a little wild, and bewildered by the breadth of our love. Today I'm reminded why. Because I could be me when I had him. With Rivers, I was the Stella he saw in me.

His Juliet to my Romeo.

Are we fated to end so tragically?

That seems impossible with the feelings that flow so freely. "I don't want to let you go," he whispers.

"You're not. You'll be with me all day until I see you again later. Everything we said, everything we did will replay because the memories allow me to relive each amazing moment we just shared."

"You're quite the romantic for someone who said we were too much, or did it feel too good?"

"Both, but I can still get used to all the *toos* you want to throw my way." We hold hands while walking around the back of my car. I slip into the driver's seat, and with one hand on the roof of the car and the other checking my seat belt, he leans in, and says, "Kiss me goodbye."

I kiss him, but there's no way it's a goodbye. It's a promise to see him later. The door closes, and I put the car in reverse. I don't look back at him because I'll be tempted to stay. But when I begin to drive away, I do it anyway, catching a glimpse of him in my rearview mirror. He's standing where I left him, and with one hand slightly raised, he waves.

Pumping the brakes, the car comes to a stop, and I push the gearshift into park. Opening the door, my seat belt comes off, and I fly through the parking lot of the theater and bar where we left his car yesterday.

The grin on his face was worth the effort, but when I fly

into his arms and kiss him, I realize *he* is worth the effort. Angling my head to face his, he asks, "What are you doing, crazy girl?"

"When we kiss, I don't want it to be a goodbye."

"What do you want it to be?"

"A hello."

He kisses me again. When I flatten back down on my heels, the wind whips around us, and the hot sun bears down in the middle of this parking lot, and he says, "Hello."

"Hello."

18

Stella

WITH ONLY MY shirt from yesterday and my purse in hand, I lock my car and walk to my door. The key is in the lock of my front door, but before I have a chance to turn it, I hear, "Good afternoon."

Looking over my shoulder, I see Brian sitting on his back porch. I just want to get in and clean up. My hackles go up, bothered that I have to play nice, which is really unfair to him. Keeping my voice light, I joke, "Good afternoon? I thought it was still morning." I turn the key.

"Must have been a good night to lose track of time."

I open the door, but stop and look back, not liking his tone, which seems to be more accusatory than friendly. "Yeah . . ." I let the word fade off, hitting the door with my shoulder. "Have a good—"

"Another Crow Brothers shirt in the span of twenty-four hours. New obsession?"

Stopping, I turn back, thinking I'm reading too much

into it. He's just being social. "Former obsession that's come back." That fits Rivers as much as the band, if not more. I step inside but stay visible. "How are you today?"

"Good."

I hang the purse on the hook and toss my shirt to the couch. Going back outside, I stop at the edge of the porch and lean against a column. "The yard looks great. All the hard work has paid off."

"I winterized the yard early this morning." He points at the far-right corner. "I'm thinking about a garden over there next spring. Maybe a hot tub near the house over here. What do you think?"

I think you're very lonely. Sitting down in a patio chair, I look at where he's referring. "It would be great." Turning back to him, I look at him, really look at him while he watches over his yard. "Can I ask you something?"

"Sure."

"Why don't you date? You're attractive, fit, own your home, and have a good job."

"Nobody wants to date a principal, even one for a private school."

"You're more than your job. That's something I'm slowly being reminded of. I sort of lost who I was."

"You've changed since we first met. You seem happier." If only he knew the truth. *No. Wait.* I don't want anyone to know what's happened to me.

"I hate to admit, but we met when I was at my lowest. I needed a job and tried to hold it together long enough for you to want to hire me, but I was a mess inside."

"You were the most qualified, and even though you say you were a mess, you nailed the interview. Mrs. Warner and myself both agreed you were a good fit for Rostinal Private."

"Can I be super honest with you and it stay between us?"

"Of course."

"I think Mrs. Warner wanted someone to dump all her crap on. A lackey."

"Is this about the Halloween dance?"

"No, it's about the dance team before we found someone who actually knew what they were doing to take over. It was a judge last spring for the annual art exhibit. It was science fair, and now it's about the dance."

"You can say no," he says, with a slight smile.

"Can I?"

"Private schools run differently that public schools, Stella. With a smaller staff, we're asked to cover several areas all at once. I worked the library for two months last year during Renee's maternity leave. I just did what had to be done."

"We should have a better budget. The families of our kids are millionaires. There are Porsches and Mercedes littering the parking lot."

"It's frustrating. But our budget will grow next year. I have a proposal I'm working on that will give us some breathing room. In the meantime, this banquet matters. I need to be in top form to schmooze these parents into large donations. Anything you can do Monday night will help the school."

"I get it. I'll do my best." I'm tempted to tell him about Rivers, or maybe a warning is more applicable, a little heads-up about the celebrity who will be attending. Just in case things fall through, though, I think it's best if I wait and see. Not that I'm having doubts of him keeping his promise to me, but more that I don't know if he's in control of the life he leads anymore. That's something I want to ask him about later. How much freedom does he have? How free is he to say yes or no?

Let's face it. I have a billion questions for him, including if he gets the wish he says he wants—me—how do I fit into his new life?

I guess it remains to be seen. We have three days together before he leaves. I don't want to waste any time overthinking this, or us.

―――――――――――

"Steaks?" Meadow points at the butcher counter. "Guys love steaks."

"I do too, but we can't afford the good cuts. How about burgers and hot dogs?"

Excitement strikes. "Burgers and jalapeno poppers. I'll make the poppers. We need to get the Deep Eddy Vodka and mixers too."

"Grapefruit vodka is on the list." We wrap up our grocery shopping. Right before we reach the car, I say, "Oops. Forgot the Blue Bell. You go to the car and I'll run back in."

"'Kay."

I didn't forget the ice cream, though I did use it as my excuse. I rush through the store grabbing what I need and a half-gallon of vanilla ice cream and head for the checkout. Outside, she's waiting in her car for me in the front. We're quicker at the liquor store, and then we're on the way over to the house.

I'm trying to keep it casual with my sister. She is easily excitable when it comes to Rivers and me, and I not only don't want to set her up for disappointment if nothing comes of us, but I also don't want the pressure or innuendoes tonight. I just want to have a fun and relaxing time.

As for her and Ridge, hell yeah, I'm going to tease. "You said Ridge texted you?"

"We texted back and forth yesterday," she replies with a shrug. "I guess when you asked me about today, Rivers had asked him. Ridge texted to ask if I was coming over."

"And?"

"And what?" She glances over at me. "I'm coming over. Oh and he said he'd bring the beer."

"Nothing else? What did you text about yesterday?"

"You really need to get out more if living vicariously through me is your idea of excitement these days."

Opportunity falls right in my lap, and I smile. I could tell her about my time with Rivers, but it might be more fun to keep the secret a little longer. She parks out front, and Rivers comes out before I have a chance to get out of the car. "Hey Meadow," he says, taking her by the shoulders and kissing her cheek. "How's my little sis doing?"

"So Hollywood of you, Crow," she teases but also blushes.

He replies. "Too much?" He winks at me. I think it's the too much bit, but I'll happily take that wink and send him a wry grin in return.

"I'm going to start kissing everyone on the cheek. I'll start with Ridge." Meadow laughs and pops the trunk. "All good here. And you?"

"Go on in. I'll grab the bags. Ridge is out back."

I shut my door while he comes around. Looking back at the house, he seems satisfied and says, "I have something special for you."

"Oh yeah? What is it?"

Cupping my face, he says, "Hello," then kisses me the way I used to long to be kissed.

Although I'm weak in the knees, I manage not to melt into a puddle of goo at his feet. "Hello."

"How are you, Stella Lilith?" he asks with such genuine kindness that he elicits my smile.

"I always loved when you called me that."

"I always loved calling you that." We move around to the trunk, and he starts pulling the grocery bags out of the car. "Glad you came over."

"Me too. Meadow and I thought we'd get the food together, and you and Ridge could grill."

"Sounds like a plan."

We walk inside, and I spy Meadow hanging out in the backyard with Ridge. Now's the time. Reaching into the bag, I hide the box behind my back. "I have something special for you too."

"Oh yeah?"

Revealing my surprise, I hold it between us, and whisper, "I bought condoms." He laughs so heartily that I check that Meadow and Ridge aren't coming inside. "Shhh. They'll hear us."

Looking over my shoulder and out the window, he says, "They're too caught up in each other to care what we're doing in here." Taking the box from me, he smiles to himself. "Come here."

I follow him into the bedroom but wait just inside the room. He opens the nightstand drawer and pulls out a matching box. "Great minds think alike." I laugh this time, so loud that I cover my mouth. We walk back into the kitchen, and as he digs into a grocery bag, he adds, "I like this side of you."

"The horny side?"

Tapping my nose, he says, "Definitely that side, but the carefree side. It's only been a few days, but you've really opened yourself up for me. This is the real you, the you I knew. It's great to see you comfortable in your own skin."

My defenses would usually fly up, but I know what he means, and I agree. "I feel relaxed with you."

Taking me by the hips, he wiggles me back and forth. He peeks out the window and then pulls me to him. With my middle pressed to his, he says, "Since I'm making confessions, I've slapped jack a few times to the naughty teacher image in my head."

I laugh. "I'm not sure if I should be offended because I'm not. I like that you've done dirty things while thinking about me."

"It's not the first time." He smirks. "It definitely won't be the last." Taking a step back from me, he pulls out the burger buns and says, "Medium well from what I remember," just as the back door opens, and Meadow and Ridge come inside.

I pull back, leaning against the counter. "Ready for a cocktail?"

Meadow holds up her can of Honey Pils. "Did you know Robert Earl Keen makes beer?"

"The musician?" I ask.

"Yep. It's so good."

Meadow's not much of a beer girl, but since Ridge offered, she's drinking. Turning to Rivers, I ask, "Mind if I make a drink?"

"Make yourself at home."

It's funny because when I think about the time we've spent together since he's been back, I *have* felt at home. I've found myself thinking about him while at school and alone in my car while driving. I get a little fluttering of butterflies when I know I'm going to see him and find it hard to resist that charming smile. Meadow was right. I was holding on to the past to protect me from getting hurt again. But with Rivers, I feel more myself again. So even though I'm at Jet's house, I do feel at home because it has nothing to do with where I'm located but *everything* to do with him.

19

Stella

WATCHING Rivers and Ridge play is incredible. Sitting under the stars and listening to the songs they've written, the tunes they created, that they now play their guitars to in a private backyard concert has me remembering how much I always loved watching him perform.

His eyes find mine between the verses and mixed in the melody. I love the way the veins in his arms match the music in their rhythm. His fingers manipulate the instrument he was born to play. Between the notes that beat like my heart, striking chords deep inside, I realize that he wouldn't be where he is without sacrificing who we were.

Cause and effect.

Destiny.

Fate.

Sacrifices have to be made. They're a side effect of the dues that have to be paid on the road to fame. He's doing what he was meant to do. It's hard to stay angry when I recognize the role I played in making the journey to his dreams coming true.

The charcoal has burned out, and we've eaten plenty. I finished my third drink long enough for the ice that was left behind to melt in the unseasonably warm night. Meadow gets up to go inside but asks if anyone needs anything. Ridge sets his guitar down and stands, "I'll go with you."

Rivers's hand flattens against the strings, the music ended. He leans forward, and whispers, "Can you stay the night?"

"What will I tell Meadow?"

"The truth?"

I laugh. "That would be wise, but are we ready to let others in on this little secret?"

"Doesn't feel little to me. You're all I think about, Stella."

"Rivers . . ." I don't know what I want to say other than his words warm me on the inside and heat my skin even more than I already am.

"Don't do that. Don't close yourself off to the possibility."

"I'm not so carefree if I start caring about tomorrow."

He sets his guitar down in a lawn chair next to him and gets up. Standing in front of me, he holds out his hand in offering. I take it and stand, stepping into his space. While our feet straddle each other's, he raises one hand into the air as his other settles on my hip. I rest my free hand on his shoulder and clasp his other and we begin to sway to the sound of nature that surrounds us.

"How can I keep your mind off tomorrow until after tonight?"

I reply, "This is a good start."

"Tell Meadow and stay with me, Stella."

"It could get complicated if others know."

"I'll tell the world if you let me." We twirl under the star-filled sky.

"What happens when you leave, Rivers?"

"You come see me."

"I have a job. I can't just leave when I want."

"Ah. The key is that you *want,* though. Am I reading too much into this?"

I move against him, resting my cheek on his chest. "You're reading me as well as you always did, but I don't know what to make of you."

We move apart, and his arms go out. "I'm exactly what you see, Stella."

The back door squeaks when it opens. Ridge steps out and then Meadow, but they stop on the patio. He says, "So we're going to take off."

Shifting, I say, "Oh. Okay, um . . ."

Meadow says, "We're taking off. Rivers, will you make sure my sister gets home safely?"

"Wait, what?"

Rivers replies, "Thanks for coming over and bringing the food."

She eyes me, and then him. "I'll pick up my car in the morning. Thank you for having us. Call me after work tomorrow. Okay, sis?"

"I will. Be safe."

Rivers adds, "Treat her well, or I'll kick your ass, Ridge."

"I have every intention—" The death glare from Rivers stops him, and he changes course. "With complete respect."

They hurry off again, the door slamming closed after they go inside. I look at Rivers and say, "Guess I don't have to say anything about us at all. Tell me he's a good guy because we have a love match on our hands."

"He's just like me," he replies, chuckling.

"That bad, huh?" I poke him in the stomach, forgetting how hard his abs are until my finger jams against his hard muscle.

Taking my finger, he kisses the tip, and then asks, "You're stuck with me now, pretty girl."

"There are worse places to be stuck." I head for the porch. "C'mon. Stop wasting time. I have to get up early in the morning. That means I need to hit the hay now."

He follows behind with his guitar in hand. "Is this just a ploy to get me in bed to use up all those condoms you brought over?"

"Absolutely. All three of mine and then we'll use your pack. So get your ass in gear and let's go to bed."

"So demanding. I like it."

Inside, I see Meadow's car keys on the counter with a note that she'll pick up her car in the morning. Rivers says, "It's weird thinking of her all grown up."

"She's not. She's twenty-one."

Sitting on a barstool, he twists the caps of two bottles of water and hands one to me. "She's older than you were when we were together."

"Barely. I just don't want her to pay later for mistakes she makes now. If she can avoid some of the pitfalls I fell into, then I feel like I've done something right."

"Were we a pitfall?"

"We were a volcano waiting to erupt." I grab the tortilla chips and park on the stool next to him. "I've thought a lot about what really went wrong with us. Although I felt blindsided by the Naomi situation, I should have been seeing the signs of our downfall before then."

He eats a chip and chases it with water. "The drugs."

"The drugs. The change in the crowd you were hanging

out with. They never really accepted me. I was a nagging girlfriend keeping them from clinging to you too much."

"Too much," he repeats, echoing the phrase that's becoming a running theme. "I once defended you to this weed dealer working a party."

"What did you say?"

"I told him not to talk shit about you. You weren't going to call the cops or cause trouble."

"You shouldn't have had to defend or vouch for me. You never did before then."

He angles toward me to stare into my eyes. "I was a motherless bass player who'd lost my rhythm. I also lost focus on what was clearly in front of me."

"Which was?"

"*You*, my north star." Embarrassment seems to filter through his features, and he gives himself a small reprieve by sipping his water. When he sets the bottle down, he turns back to me. "You still looked at me like I made magic every time I was on stage, as though I could do no wrong, but I did you wrong while I spiraled downward. I'm sorry I dragged you to rock bottom with me. I thought I lost everything when I lost my mother. I didn't. I lost everything worth living for when I lost you."

Covering his hand, I try to comfort him from the weight of his words that seem to burden him even when he's sitting next to me again. "If I tell you something, will you please not hold it against me?"

"I'm not looking for an enemy when it comes to us. I'm looking for an ally." He turns his hand over, so he's holding mine. "You can tell me anything and trust me to protect that information."

And I know in my heart of hearts that it's true. How can I look at him now and justify why I didn't trust him years ago?

Actually, the answer is pretty clear. He *was* lost. The years took their toll on him, on his heart and his compass when it came to us. He was struggling.

The man in front of me isn't that boy who couldn't see beyond the next day. This is a man who has lost and grieved and somehow made something amazing of himself. *And that man,* that's the man I never gave up on, the same man who came back for me.

So he needs to hear this. He needs to hear that he wasn't really ever alone, not in my heart. "My heart never let you go." And there it is, clear as the sky outside. My love served up on a platter for him. *Even in my darkest moments, I never let him go.* But right now? He deserves to know what I did, because for him to have my heart, I need to give him the truth. *My* truth. My *soul-destroying* truth.

Standing, I walk to the opening to the hall. He follows and takes hold of me, kissing my neck. I say, "I want you, Rivers. I want you to make me forget the past."

He stills, lifting his head from where he was kissing me and looks me in the eyes. "I wish I could take away the bad and leave you with only the good memories. I can't bury what we were, but I'll do everything to change what we are."

"What we are?"

"A second chance."

A second chance. I'm being given a second chance with this man I've loved since I was fifteen, a man I never stopped loving. This is it. He means what he says, and his words fill me with the hope he's held in his eyes since he showed back up. We'll bathe our souls in each other's love, but only if I cleanse mine first. "I want that, but I can't—"

"Can't?" Panic rises in his irises like a time-lapsed moon racing the dark.

Staring at the design of his T-shirt, I swallow my pride

like I did once before, and share the only secret I've never told anyone. "I need to talk to you about what I've done."

Holding my chin between his fingers, he raises it until I'm looking into his eyes. I can't hold eye contact. Not with him. Not while I share the most shameful and painful part of my life.

Will he still want me?

Will he still feel the same?

Will he want that second chance he's convinced himself he needs?

If he walks away this time, this time forever, what will become of me?

I place my trust in his hands. If we're to be a better version of our tainted ending, I have to lay down my weapons and show him the scars I bear inside and let him decide if he still wants me.

We walk down the hall and into the bedroom. Once inside, I slip out from his shadow and walk into the moonlight of the window to shine light on my dirty deeds. I keep my back to him and cross my arms over my stomach, the memory as horrid today as it was then. "I had sex for money."

20

———

Rivers

STARING at the back of Stella's head, the words brush by me incomprehensible. She doesn't move, standing statue still after she tells me she had sex for money.

I'm not horrified.

I'm not mad.

I'm not anything.

Numb.

Yes, I'm numb.

"What?" I ask, needing her to repeat what she said because I must have heard wrong.

Disgusted. Not by her, but her father.

She turns back and looks at me as I remain in the darker side of the room. "I was paid money for sex."

Why does my chest hurt? Why is my heart racing? Why the fuck would she sell her body for money? "Why?"

"For the money," she replies as if the reason is more than obvious.

"I don't understand."

"I've barely come to grips with it. I thought . . . well, before we go any further, you should know. You might not want to sleep with me."

"How much money?"

"Ten thousand dollars was the original loan. The interest brought it to fifty thousand."

"What the fuck?" My fingers slide into my hair as I try to wrap my brain around this information. "Fifty thousand dollars?"

"Yes."

"I didn't mean how much were you paid. I meant how much money did you need?"

Her back is to me again, and she opens the window before sitting on the sill. "I didn't need the money. My father did. I paid a debt to free him from it."

"What do you mean? What are you saying, Stella?" I can't keep the edge out of my tone as anger flames in my veins.

She says, "We sold the house, our cars, all of our belongings to pay off his gambling debt, but it wasn't enough to cover what he owed. We still owed the fifty thousand dollars."

"Not you, *him*." My tone causes her to jump and she turns to face me. "*He* owed fifty thousand dollars, so why were you paying off his debt?"

"It's all I had left to sell."

"Yourself?"

"Yes."

Fucking Christ. I sit back, trying to not let my anger get the best of me. If it does, I'll say something to upset her, and that's the last thing I want to do. As painful as this should be for her, she appears numb. Speaking in facts as if there are no consequences to the act, as if emotions weren't drowned in the reality of what happened that day. "Your dad let you sell yourself to pay off his debt? Jesus, Stella. He's supposed to fucking protect you from evil, not sell you into it. I should have protected you."

"*You?* Rivers, you weren't even here. You weren't here because of my stubborn hurt feelings. If I would have slowed down and listened." She closes her eyes again, but then opens them, and says, "As for my father, he didn't know. He still doesn't."

I stand, my hands fisted at my sides. "You were violated. You were raped. You wer—"

"That's where you're wrong, Rivers. I was violated in ways that . . ." She releases a shaky breath. "I was given a choice. I, alone, made the decision."

I stare at her until my vision blurs. My heart stopped beating long before I noticed. I take a breath, trying to sound as neutral as she does, though the information is new to me. "What was the choice?"

This time, she gets up before she speaks, coming to me.

My heart.

My soul.

Star of my life.

Star of my night.

My pretty little mess with the sadness in her eyes puts her hands on my chest before landing the last blow. "Me or Meadow."

"What do you mean, Stella?" I can't remain calm or neutral any longer. "What does that mean?"

"They said—"

I take her by the elbows, tempted to hold her in my

arms, but I need to see her face. I need to get answers. "Who said?"

"The loan sharks. When my dad hit his lowest point, he put it all in, everything we owned on a loan as collateral and then borrowed more money on top of that. He lost it all hours later in the basement of a strip joint in two hands of poker."

"Who are the loan sharks?"

I find life in her eyes again as she seems to awaken from a nightmare. "I can't tell you."

"We need to report them to the police, Stella. Just give me a name and I'll do it."

"No, I don't know."

"You don't know the name?"

"No, they used code names. There were three men. Two called each other colors—brown and yellow, like in *Reservoir Dogs*. The third was called Boss."

"What did you mean about you and Meadow?" I'm still holding her, wanting to hold on to her forever. "What did they make you decide?"

Her gaze shoots away from mine. "Rivers, you don't want to know the details. It won't change anything anyway."

"I need to know. When was this?"

She looks back at me. "Do you really want to know all this? How will it help?"

"I want to know. I want to know how I can help you."

"You can't help me."

"I need to however I can. Please tell me how."

She says, "It was six months ago, but how are you going to change the fact that I was taken in a car and parked outside the restaurant where Meadow works and asked point blank if it will be me who works off my father's debt or my little sister? That's the choice I had to make. So as much as I would have never chosen to sleep with their boss, I wasn't raped. I'm responsible for the decision I made. I was picked up at the times and dates *I* chose."

I feel sick for her. "Could you have paid the fifty K?"

"No. I didn't have five dollars to my name at that point."

"It was only fifty. You should have called me. I could've helped. I would have helped you."

"Only? Jesus. Our lives can't be more different than they are now."

Fuck. "I didn't mean that it's a drop in the bucket, Stella. I didn't have much until last year, and then I got more with the tour and the album. But you have to understand I would have given my last dollar if you asked. I would have then too."

"I couldn't have called you. It would have been humiliating. But I prayed at one point to have the option. I had no options, though. There was only one question asked of me —my sister or me—so there was never a choice. I had to protect my sister. I chose for her not to be tarnished. I chose for her never to have to endure what I did. By choosing myself to go, I chose to keep my sister safe."

Feeling violent toward these fucking scumbags, I say, "Because you saved your sister from being raped doesn't mean you weren't. This was an attack." She sits on the bed, her shoulders weighed down.

Her strength is a source of inspiration, but her experience a reckoning of our past devastation. She gave herself, something that is precious to her and to me, for the sake of her father's losses. Fuck him.

I'd understand if she didn't want to do more. I'd understand and I'd wait while holding on to how her body came alive for me last night, remembering the look of lust mingled with something more when she stared into my eyes.

Kneeling in front of her, I rest my hands on her legs. "They made you decide who was going to be violated. Because you chose to sacrifice yourself doesn't take the blame off them. You were forced to do something you would have never done. I'm so sorry you had to go through that. There's nothing I can say to take your pain away. Please know that I will do anything in my power to help you. Anything."

Resting her hands on my shoulders, she says, "I don't want you involved. I want to forget it ever happened. The only reason I told you is because I thought you had the right to know that I've made decisions that change this, dirties it. Dirties you by association with me. You bought condoms before you knew the situation. Now that you do know, I won't hold it against you if you decide you don't want this to happen with me."

"Because you made a decision in a no-win choice doesn't mean you wanted it. You had to do what you had to do. I won't hold it against you for protecting your father and your sister. I will hold it against your dad and the fuckers who did this to you, though."

Releasing some of her tension, she says, "It was the last time I . . . it was the last time my body was with someone else."

"I should have never left. It was a domino effect that I started. I want you to know that I meant what I said before. Before we're together, I want you to trust me. One hundred percent. To find comfort and pleasure when we're together. If you're not ready, I'm okay waiting as long as you need."

"I don't want to wait." Inhaling, she closes her eyes as if

she needs the moment to recover. When her eyes settle back on mine, she says, "I've waited years for this."

When I rub her leg, my smile brings one to her lips. She adds, "I want to be with you again, but it's not for selfless reasons."

That makes me chuckle. It's funny how attraction works. She's always drawn me in. When I was fifteen, it was a crush. I didn't know her. I saw how she was with others, but for the most part, it was physical attraction.

Now I'm looking at the most stunning woman in the world who feels sullied and not good enough for the man who sees her inner beauty. "You could have had sex with a hundred guys. Though I'm glad you didn't because my ego is pretty fragile these days, but you had the right. An act that didn't involve your heart, or the soul you hold inside, doesn't change what I feel for you. It doesn't matter because I fell in love with you long before now and money paid can never amount to what we have. What we have is real. It's right now. It's organic and evolving. Fuck them. They can't change us."

I take her and kiss her because when she said she wanted to forget the past, I realize it's not only *our* past she's trying to forget. Her arms come around me, and she kisses me with everything I know she has to give.

Her need is felt in the way she tugs at my shirt and then opens the front of my jeans. Her desire has her kissing me with intensity as if I'll pull away and leave her if she doesn't. "Stella," I say against her head when she looks down to undress me.

"Rivers." Her hands still, and she looks up at me. "Don't treat me any different. Please. I need your rough hands on me. I need you to show me how much you want me. I'm not breakable. If I were, I wouldn't be here now. So make love to me, but don't be too gentle."

Too gentle. Too rough. I'll find what feels good to her and be whatever she needs. I'll take those fucking images that live in her head, troubling her, and erase them by loving her so much that they'll be distant memories.

Taking the hem of her shirt, I lift it up over her arms and head and set it aside before removing mine. My jeans are popped open, so I take them off along with my boxers. I'll be vulnerable for her so she won't ever feel alone.

She takes off her bra and then the rest of her clothes. Standing there, she says, "Your tattoos look so incredibly sexy the way they cover your muscles. Three crows and a star for the superstar you are now."

Taking her hand, I hold her palm over the star that will only ever have one meaning. "This star is yours. Always was and always will be. It's only for you."

Smiling, she says, "You're lucky my name isn't Portia or that star would be a pig."

"Is that what Portia means?"

"Unfortunately, yes. Guess we can't name our daughter that."

I pause my hand and look up from admiring the way her stomach has a gentle slope. I realize what she said was off the cuff and doesn't mean anything, but I can't help from pressing a little firmer on her belly and wondering what it would be like if there was a baby inside her. *My baby.*

Realization fills her eyes, and they widen. "I didn't mean . . . um, I'm not rushing anything. It was—"

"I know. A comment. Nothing more." Slipping my other hand around to her backside, I hold her there and she lets me, well aware of what I'm doing. "But what if it wasn't."

This time, she slips out of my hold and backs toward the

bed. "I don't want to talk about that now or tomorrow or nine months from now." Moving onto the bed, she pats the mattress beside her, and says, "Stay with me here in the present."

I can do that. She's incredibly distracting, her legs parted with a slight bend at the knees. This is the here and now. All I've wanted for five years is this, is her. Moving onto the bed, I reach for the box of condoms and pull one out.

She watches with rapt fascination as I cover myself. Bending down, I'm not gentle like she requested, taking what I want, when I want. I spread her legs to fit my shoulders and return my hand to her stomach, letting it span the width and adding pressure as I kiss that sweet, pink pussy of hers. When her back tries to arch, I hold her in place and slide my tongue through the softness of her lips.

A moan is followed by my name that's spoken from deep inside her belly. I don't stop. I take just like she wants me to.

Selfless.

The word destructs on the tip of my tongue as I taste her sweet nectar. Making room, I lean back enough to replace my mouth with my hand and slip a finger inside her warmth. I'm a skilled guitarist. I know how to make her come using all I've learned and playing her like an instrument.

I'm just not sure if I'm ready to let her have a release. I'm thinking of keeping her on the brink so we can come together. Stella grinds against my hand, seeking relief. I pull out and replace my finger with my cock one big inch at a time.

A gasp and then a harsh intake of air draws my attention to her pretty face. "How do I feel, baby?"

"So good. So much." Her eyes open lazily as she takes a slow deep breath and looks into my eyes as I hover over her.

Her hands drift from my shoulders to my jaw. "I want all of you, Rivers. Your body, your love, this look in your eyes forever. Kiss me." *Fuck. Yes. Forever.*

I push in a little more, causing her eyes to close with the motion. My lips touch hers, and she whispers, "I was always here waiting for you. I was always yours . . ." I push in farther, her words driving me to take more. "To love." Further, the feel of her engulfing me begins to cloud my thoughts. "To fuck."

Fuck. I thrust all the way, as deep as I can go. Her head goes back, her words cries of desire. I kiss the underside of her chin and fuck.

Fuck.

Love.

Fuck.

Not gentle.

Driving home everything I've wanted to tell her since the day we broke up. "I love you." I fuck her selfishly. I fuck her to satisfy my own needs. I fuck her into an apology. "I'm sorry if I hurt you."

"Don't say sorry," she manages between panting breaths. "You feel so good."

I rest on my forearms and take her wrists in hand before pulling them above her head. Our palms press together. Our fingers entwine. Her body is stretched beneath me when I kiss her lips, showing her how much I care about her. "I meant I'm sorry for what I'm about to do to you."

Just as her mouth opens to take in more air, I fill it with my tongue and start chasing the high only she could ever give me, wanting to hear her as I fuck her hard and fast.

Her moans aren't filled with pain, but encourage me to keep going, to keep taking, to keep erasing every bad thing of our past. With her legs around me, she says, "Harder. Yes.

So good, baby." I want her to feel how good our future can be, to beg for more. "I'm close, Rivers. Faster. So close."

When her body tenses, her nails digging into the top of my hands, a jolt of electricity strikes like lightning inside me and I thrust until I let go, my body floating with hers into heaven.

My north star guiding me home.

21

_____

Rivers

"RIVERS?"

I open my eyes. My head is on the pillow next to hers, my mouth at her ear. My body is heavy, the weight of my release zapping my strength. Did I black out? Can someone black out from feeling so much all at once, even if it's all good?

Her hands push against my shoulders, and she turns to face me. Our noses touch. "I can't breathe."

"Sorry." I roll to my back and lie beside her.

A smile rolls across her face. "I liked it. I like you on top of me relaxed."

I chuckle. "Until the running out of air part."

"Yeah." The top of her head leans against my shoulder, her hand between us moves to rest on me. "You weren't gentle."

Shit. "Did I hurt you?"

"Yes, but in ways I wanted." She shakes her head. "I make no sense." She turns onto her side to face me and runs her hand over my chest, stopping over my pounding heart. "Sometimes pain is pleasure. Like when you used to . . ." Pausing, she licks her lips and looks down. "I used to love when you'd be behind me and pull my hair or squeeze my breasts. It was a turn-on. An ounce of pain to produce so much pleasure." Her breathing had regulated, but it picks up and deepens as she slides her hand between her great tits and lower . . . lower . . . lower. Two fingers slip into the slickness of her pussy, and she starts to circle her swollen clit.

Although her eyes struggle to stay open, she does for me. Watching her touch herself is better than porn. My breathing deepens to match hers, my cock getting hard again. I yank the condom off and drop it beside the bed. "Can you come twice?"

"I can come multiple times."

Holy fuck. This is the most delectably sinful sight I've ever seen. "You've learned some tricks."

"No tricks. Just treats and a lot of alone time over the years." Tilting her chin toward me, she says, "Kiss me."

I don't want to miss the show, but I'll do what she wants. I kiss her, and as our tongues tangle, she takes my hand and lowers it to her other until I replace hers. I rub around and down, circling, teasing until she's writhing and gripping my wrist.

There are no breaks or ease in the way our mouths make love and my hand makes her come. I slide through her slick center until she grabs my hand and humps. My knuckles hit the sides of her thighs, my hand bigger than the space she's left for me. "God," she says, "I love how rough your hands are. How strong you are—*Oh God.* Yes. Yes." She bites her bottom lip and squeezes her eyes closed as her body tenses and then she's slick against my hand.

There's a sense of pride that fills my chest from making her come again. "How'd you do that?" I ask, fascinated by the woman she's become.

She laughs, though she looks exhausted. "I didn't. You did."

Holding the back of her head, I pull her close until her mouth is pressed to mine. I kiss this goddess. I kiss her again just because I missed her so much. I missed kissing her like this. "God, I love hearing you say that, but I fucking love watching you go after what you want. You ready for another?"

Still grinning, her eyes are closed. "I'm good, but if I can help you out, let me know." Sleep hits her hard, and soon, I run my hand over her hair and kiss her forehead.

"Sweet dreams, baby."

"Sweet dreams," she whispers on the cusp of sleep.

"I love you, Stella Lilith. Always have. Always will."

"Rivers!"

I bolt upright and accidentally hit myself in the face with my hand. Fuck. "What?"

Stella's running around the room pulling her clothes on. "I need to go. I'm going to be late for work."

"What?"

"School." My hands are tugged from where I was rubbing my eyes. She's wide-awake and looking so goddamn beautiful I automatically start pulling her toward me.

"C'mere, baby. Let me make love to you. I'll make you feel so good again."

"No. No. No. I'm late."

"Like your period?"

She huffs and pulls back until she's standing beside the bed. Rolling her eyes, she says, "No. For work. Wake up. I need you to drive me home."

"What day is it?"

Her perfect tits are hidden behind her T-shirt when it comes over her head. "Must be nice not to worry about what day of the week it is." I'm popped with a pillow. "For real. Get up. I need you functioning."

Sometimes, I smirk. This would be a prime example of when. "I think I got up and functioned just fine for you last night."

"Oh, my lord. Do I need to call a rideshare?"

Flipping the covers off, I reply, "Fine. I'm up. I'm up." Grabbing that fine ass of hers when I walk by, I add, "And I'm hoping to be up, so far up in you later."

"If you weren't so hot, that'd be gross."

From inside the bathroom, I ask, "But since I am so hot?"

"You sound like Tulsa."

"Please don't bring up my brother when I'm holding my dick," I say, about to take a piss.

"Okay. Fine. It's hot when you talk about being inside me. Hot, just like you." She stands in the doorway dressed, leaning against it. In so many ways, this feels like old times. Natural. Comfortable around each other. Almost as if time hasn't passed. Other than using the bathroom, there were never closed doors between us when we lived together. Since she's still staring at me, I'm thinking there won't be any at all this time around.

She moves her gaze to the mirror in front of her and scrunches her face. "I look awful. I'm not going to have time to fix my hair either. Shit. Shake the snake and come on." Turning on her heels, she's out the door, her flowing hair hitting the doorframe when she leaves.

Stella's standing next to the 4Runner when I rush outside after getting dressed. I open her door and then hit the driver's seat, knowing she's panicked. "How late will you be?"

"If we don't hit much traffic on the way, maybe ten minutes. Take a left up here."

I've never been to where she currently lives. Although we're late and she's stressed about it, she doesn't seem to mind letting me see her place. "How far are we driving?"

"Fifteen minutes." She sighs. "I won't even have time for a cup of coffee. Just a quick shower and time to get dressed. Take a right at the light and then the first right to cut through to West Avenue and across 15th."

"Tarrytown?"

"Sort of on the edge. I rent a guesthouse in a friend's backyard."

"Really? How long have you lived there?"

"A few months." She stares out the side window. "A friend helped me get Meadow into some cheap apartment through school housing. They only had a one bedroom. The landlord found out I had been sleeping on her couch for a month or more and sent an eviction notice for me or have me sign onto the lease, which doubled the rent. He was a real asshole."

"A friend at work overheard me talking to another teacher about my back hurting and needing a place. He had this place sitting empty after a long-term tenant moved out months prior. Offered me a deal I couldn't pass up and here I am. Second driveway on the left. You can pull all the way to the back."

"He?"

"Don't get jealous." She laughs. "Yes, a he. He's the principal at my school."

"The principal? Shit. He won't like me."

I park the SUV in front of the sunny yellow converted garage. The small building has white trim, and she has a flower box hanging under a window. She rushes to hop out and says, "I hate to dash—"

"I could make you a cup of coffee while you get dressed." I wonder if I'm overstepping by inviting myself in. I don't want push her for more than she's ready for. I'm still processing the fact she was homeless at one point after an asshole landlord threw her out. What the fuck? I take a deep breath, realizing this is another challenge she had to deal with on her own because of our past. She faced it head-on and survived. She's so incredible. It's no wonder I love her so much.

"You'd do that for me, Rivers Crow?" she asks with all the sass of her teenage years.

Coming around, I steal a kiss, and reply, "Don't you know, baby? I'd do anything for you."

My ass is slapped, and she scurries to the door. "That's an offer I can't refuse."

I walk inside as she drops her purse on the small couch in the living room and goes into the bedroom. Her place isn't much bigger than a matchbox, but it's decorated with touches of her—flowers in a vase, candles that get burned regularly by the looks of how low the wax is in the jar, and a blanket tossed on the couch.

When I hear the shower start, I pick up the blanket and hold it to my nose, closing my eyes and savoring her scent, wishing I could still find mine mingling with hers. I remember taking so many naps with this blanket and her falling asleep while studying at night under it. We would drag it out onto our balcony and make love under the stars.

For some reason, it feels good to see something of ours in her place.

Going into the kitchen, I find the little coffeepot in the corner tucked next to the small fridge. I add water and the grounds I find in the freezer, which is where she always kept them. While it percolates, I look for a mug and pull out the creamer from the fridge. I note how so many of her habits have remained the same. With my absence from her life, I realize that I'm the change she made.

I pour the freshly brewed coffee into the mug, add some creamer, and stand by the door to her bedroom. Knocking, I turn my back and wait.

When it opens, she asks, "What are you doing?"

"Waiting for you to answer," I reply, looking over my shoulder at the beauty wrapped in a towel.

The towel is dropped, and she goes to the closet in the room while showing off that fine ass of hers. "We made love, Rivers. I don't have anything you haven't now seen." Turning back, she taps her chin. "Come to think of it, I didn't have anything to hide from you prior either."

I walk in and set the coffee down on the nightstand. Sitting on her bed, I take inventory of furniture and décor. She slips on a thong and fastens her bra before eyeing the coffee. "Is that for me?"

"It is."

"Thank you." She hurries over and takes a few sips. "You're the best, and it seems you remembered how I take it."

"You trained me well back in the day."

Running into the bathroom, she starts brushing her hair and then her teeth before dashing back out and pulling a silky looking shirt from a hanger. I rest back on the headboard and watch her get dressed. Other than last night when she did that thing with her hand, this is the best show in town.

She says, "I don't have time to put on makeup. Ugh. I'll just take it and try to sneak putting some on."

"I could drive you to school. You could have your coffee and put on your makeup on the way."

"Really?" She seems to actually be considering the offer.

"Really. I don't mind. I can pick you up too since you won't have your car."

"Thank you, but the ride to school will be enough. I can catch a ride home."

"Ah, that's right. The principal landlord friend is around."

After she slips into pants, she puts on a pair of flat shoes and then comes over to me. Kissing my head, she says, "Be careful with your jealousy, handsome. Some things aren't worth wasting a second over. My friend being one of them."

Less than five minutes later, we're back on the road. She's applying makeup in the visor mirror but stops when we're stuck at a light. She says, "I've been meaning to ask you about the banquet. You said you'd go, but just in case, are you free tomorrow night?"

"Free as can be and all yours."

A playful glint lights up her eyes just as I turn into the parking lot. She says, "Tomorrow night then."

"Unless you're free tonight too?"

"I am." Before she can hop out of the SUV, she straightens her shirt and pucker pops her lips. She slides out of the vehicle and leans back in. "I had a good time last night."

"It was pretty spectacular. Care for a repeat tonight?"

That warrants a good laugh. Despite being late, she reaches her hand in and across the seat. When I take it, she says, "Can't wait. I'll text you later." She steps back and shuts the door.

I roll down the window and catcall her because all those naughty teacher fantasies start occupying my mind, and hot damn, she looks fine. When she turns back laughing, I wave. "Have a nice day, Ms. Fellowes."

Walking backward, she gives me a wink. "You too, Mr. Crow."

22

Stella

I RUN down the empty hallway to my classroom and skid to a stop. With my hand on the doorknob, I take a quick breath and exhale before turning. The door is opened, and my eyes meet Brian's.

He's standing at the chalkboard pointing at a stick figure with a speech bubble that has the words I cannot tell a lie inside. Basically, he's teaching my junior and senior students first grade history. False history at that.

"My apologies, class, for being late." I march straight to him. "Mr. Teller, thank you for stepping in."

Irritation burns like fire in his eyes. It's an expression I've never seen before especially not one directed at me. "Ms. Fellowes, may I speak with you in the hall?"

I set my bag down on my desk and turn to follow Brian back out of the classroom. I instruct my students to turn to chapter ten and start reading silently. The door is shut, and Brian stands before me, fuming. "Why are you late?"

"Traffic?"

Narrowing his eyes, his temper flares. "Are you asking me?"

"No. I'm sorry. I've never been lat—"

"It doesn't matter if you've never been late before. It matters that you left students unattended. If I hadn't gotten wind that you weren't here, who knows what trouble they would have caused."

"I'm sorry. I overslept and—"

"Why weren't you home last night? Where were you?"

Surprised by this personal interrogation, my head jolts back. "Excuse me? That is none of your business."

"It is when it directly affects my business, and this school is my business."

How dare he talk to me like that! My fury erupts in my whispering yell, "You are not my parent, so do not speak to me like you are. You're my principal, so if you feel the need to write me up, then do it. I take full responsibility for being late. But to get these kids back on track with their day, I'll be returning to my classroom now."

As soon as I turn, my arm is grabbed, his hold tight, and strong enough to physically angle me so I looking him in the eyes again. "What are you doing?"

"Shut your mouth and you listen to me."

Pain shoots through my arm and red flags fly up. My fight or flight instincts kick in. *Flight.* I try to yank my arm away, but he digs his fingers into my muscle. My eyes water as he leans down, getting even closer. Through gritted teeth, he warns, "Don't screw up again or there will consequences and I'll have no choice but to punish you."

"Principal Teller?" a voice asks, echoing down the hall.

His hand immediately drops to his side, and we both look down the hall at the same time. A fake ease fills the space between us when Brian replies, "Mrs. Warner. How can I help you?"

"Is everything all right?" Her gaze slides from his to mine. "Ms. Fellowes?"

Another warning shot is fired when Brian quietly clears his throat.

I reply, "Fine. I'm just returning to class." When I take hold of the doorknob this time, the metal rattles in my shaking hand. I briefly squeeze my eyes closed because I know they both heard it. Opening the door, I step inside. I keep my eyes focused forward on my desk.

When I sit, I tuck my hands under the desk and hold them together, hoping to stop the nerves from exposing the fear that's bubbled inside me.

"Ms. Fellowes?" I look up at my students who, judging by their expressions, seem concerned. My gaze lands on a studious girl in the front row. "We're done reading. It was a short chapter. Are we going to discuss it like we usually do?"

"Yes. That would be good. Let's break into small groups and discuss the chapter among yourselves."

The sound of chairs skidding against the linoleum hides the hiccup that frees itself from my chest. I want to sob, but watching the students, I know I can't. I pull my laptop from my bag and go about setting up for the day, busying my mind to stifle the fear I feel inside.

My hands shake from the encounter. What the hell was that out there? I've never seen Brian like that. I've only been more frightened one other time . . . *shit.* That's not a memory I ever want to relive. Ever.

My thoughts drift back to Rivers in his old 4Runner giving me a wave and making me feel beautiful. I hold that visual tighter and the knowledge that I'll be seeing him again for a repeat will help me survive the day.

I skipped lunch today for two reasons.

1. I forgot to make one in my rush out the door.
2. I don't have a car to leave to go buy anything.

I'll get by. It's just a growling stomach. I can manage a little longer since it's the last class of the day. Anyway, it's not my hunger that's been on my mind. I lost my appetite this morning in the hall, and it seems I suddenly have bigger problems on my hands than being five minutes late to class.

This sudden turn in Brian's behavior is shocking. I fully expected to be written up. I never do anything wrong, so it's not like I have a record or would be fired. But the anger in his eyes keeps flashing before mine. Do I talk to him after school about what happened or pretend it never did?

With no idea how to handle the situation, I turn my attention back on another growing issue—Josh Baird. I can usually handle rowdy students or rude students. I've never had a fight with one or even had two students get physical with each other in my classroom.

This private school is one of the best in the city and in the state of Texas, and a lot of money flows through these halls. Even though most students don't fear the staff here, they do fear their parents and the threat of losing their hefty allowances. So we generally have well-behaved kids. But Josh has been getting bolder as the year has progressed.

While the other students read the chapter in front of them, his eyes are burning holes into me. When I look up, he doesn't even have the courtesy of looking away. No, while slumped in his chair, he holds my stare while tapping his pen against his lip.

It's not the stare that bothers me. It's his arrogance that he has the right to look at me like he's undressing me with his eyes. The top of the pen dips into his mouth and pokes the inside of his cheek a few times before he blows me a kiss.

"Josh, tell me about the battle discussed in the chapter you just read?"

"No please?"

"No please or thank you, Stella?" The sound of my name mixes with the metal teeth of his zipper. It's over. "I just gave your father his life back. A little gratitude would be nice."

"Why don't *you* tell me, Stella."

I don't blink, and I don't find him amusing, though some of his classmates do. "If you call me anything other than Ms. Fellowes for the rest of the year, you'll be spending your free period with Principal Teller. Do you understand me?"

"I understand you, Ms. Fellowes." He sits up and raises his hand.

"What is it?"

"Where are your glasses?"

Shoot. I forgot them in my car. That's when I realize my hair is down as well. *Shit.* What is going on today? And how on earth did I not put my glasses on or even do my hair? I never leave for work unless I have on my full armor. *Because I hate the attention on my looks.* My appearance has never been anything more than a nuisance that makes men want to belittle me. My mother was beautiful and made it clear that we should use our looks to get what we want or be used.

She chose to use hers, but I refuse to use mine. Appearances can be a blessing and a curse. I have no doubt that "the boss" gave me that ultimatum once he saw Meadow and me. There is no silver lining when it comes to that situation. He took my integrity away when he bent me face down over his desk while his lackeys watched. I guess he could have let them have a turn right after him. *Should I be grateful he didn't?*

"Sasha, will you fill us in on the battle?"

She answers my question, and then I instruct them to discuss the chapters as I've done with every other class today. When the bell rings, I call Josh to my desk. He slings his backpack over his shoulder and high fives his friend like he's about to get laid. Spoiled little shit.

I stand, not wanting him looking down on me, and watch as he takes his sweet-ass time. Rude. I'm still not eye level with the eighteen-year-old football player, but I intend to hold my own. "Your behavior has progressively gotten worse. You're disrespectful and not working to your potential. I wanted to get your thoughts on a parent conference where we can all openly discuss the issues."

He taps my desk as if he's in control of this conversation. "That would be an unwise decision on your part."

Crossing my arms over my chest, I glare straight into bratty eyes. "Are you threatening me, Mr. Baird?"

"I don't need to."

"What does that mean?"

"Good day, *Stella*."

A shiver runs the length of my spine as I watch him walk away. What the hell just happened? He shuts the door, and the loud conversations on the other side are cut off. Standing there, I continue to stare at the light wood door as if it will give me the answers I'm searching for. Did he just threaten me?

I try to gather myself together, though I'm not sure what I'm supposed to think or feel after that encounter. Today is fucked-up, and I'm ready for it to end.

Damn it. I don't have my car here, and I don't want to drag Rivers across town to pick me up. I want to go home and have a long relaxing bath to wash off the day before I head to see him. That doesn't seem possible unless I can check in on Brian and hope he's cooled off. I can't relax with the discourse from today.

We need to talk about what happened this morning anyway. There's no way I'm going to allow him to treat me in anyway less than professional. Adding Josh Baird's unacceptable behavior to that list, I head for the office as soon as the final bell rings.

Judy, our school secretary, says, "Hi, Stella."

"Hi. How are you?"

"Swamped, but nothing new with that. How can I help you?"

"Is Principal Teller available?"

She leans back in her chair and spies on him through the window next to his door. "He should be. Go on in. I know he's always happy to see you."

I know what she's hinting at, and it's something that needs to be put to a stop. "Thanks." Instead of going in like she said because "he's always happy to see me" I knock to keep it professional.

"Come in." When I open the door, he looks up from the paperwork littering his desk. "Ms. Fellowes."

I can play that game too. "Principal Teller."

"Have a seat." I set my bag on one chair and sit in the other facing his desk. He steeples his fingers and a bad memory of "the boss" steepling his before . . . I try to shake off the memory, not wanting to ever think of it again. "I was disappointed this morning."

"I understand. You had every right to be. I was disappointed that I was late as well. But you had no right to touch me in the manner you did. You hurt me. On purpose."

"I felt disrespected."

"I felt disrespected," I counter.

"I think you've forgotten your place."

Am I in a world gone mad today? What the hell is wrong with everyone? "My place?"

"When you were falling apart last year, I was the one who let you keep your job. I gave you a roof over your head and helped you find a reliable car. Now you repay me by pulling this shit."

Shocked by his swearing, I shift and grab my bag. I'd rather call a ride share than fight with him. I stand. "I'll be moving out soon. I thought I'd give you notice."

Brian stands abruptly. "You're leaving?"

Keeping my tone even, I say, "I appreciate everything you've done, but it's time I move on." He comes around the desk, but when he gets close, I take a step back.

"We're friends."

"I thought we were too. Yet you manhandled me and you're out of line in the way you're talking to me."

"I'm sorry. I'm sorry for this morning."

"I think it's best if we keep our relationship on a strictly professional level."

My words seem to slap him. His head drops, and he reaches for the desk to steady himself. "I said I'm sorry."

"I appreciate that." I walk to the door, but before I open it, I add, "Thank you for all you've done for me. I'll remember it." I walk out and don't look back. I don't think he'll fire me. There's no cause. As for our friendship, he damaged it beyond repair. "Have a good night, Judy."

"You too," she replies.

It's earlier than I usually leave, but I've had enough of

this day, and I'm ready for it to end. I pull my phone from my bag and order a car. Since it's only a few minutes away, I walk outside and down the sidewalk. I reach the edge of the parking lot ready to wait, but when I look up, it's not a rideshare I see.

Rivers stands in front of his SUV with a handful of wild daisies. *Oh, thank God. How I need him right now.* "How was your day, Ms. Fellowes?"

It was awful, confusing, and a big mess.

"Better now." *Much better.*

23

Rivers

Seven hours earlier ...

Tossing the trash from the breakfast tacos I just devoured, a knock drags my ass off the couch. When I answer the door, Meadow is standing there looking every bit the spitting image of her older sister. In my mind, I still see the little kid she once was, just sixteen when I was effectively shut out of their lives. Another example of life moving on when I wasn't looking.

Ridge honks from the curb, salutes us, and drives away.

Asshole. There's no way I'm not going to have a talk with him about dumping her off without so much as walking her up to the door. I still see her as my little sis even if she is old enough to hookup with guys without giving Stella or me a say in the matter. Maybe I'm still a little protective. Or more than a little when it comes to the Fellowes sisters.

It's amazing how all those old feelings are back like they

never left. I guess they didn't. I just didn't have a right to say anything.

I kick the door wide open for her. "Good morning. Did you come for the keys?"

"Sure did," she replies in a chipper voice, walking right past me. It's good to see some things don't change. She's always had a sunny outlook on life. "Did my sister get home safely last night?"

I pause, careful with my words. I think Stella should tell her sister. Personally, I think Meadow's onto us already. "She was safe last night." I toss her the keys to her car, but she stands by the door, not making a move to leave. I'm quick to realize I've been set up. "Something on your mind that you'd like to discuss, Meadow?"

"My sister likes you."

Ah. Here we go. I'd expect nothing less from her. Rubbing the back of my neck, I look up to see her eyes analyzing me. "I like your sister."

"Do you still love her, Rivers? Because if you don't, then let her be. She's been through a lot over the years, and she deserves to be happy."

"Do you think she'll be happier without me?"

"No. That's why I'm making sure if you're coming back into her life, which it looks like you are, then it has to be for the right reasons."

"She's the only reason I came back. I love her, Meadow."

Her smile is as bright as I remember in happier times. "You know, if you play your cards right, she'll be putty in your hands."

Putty, like last night when I replaced her hand with mine . . . so hot. "I intend to win her heart, Mead. Any insider tips?"

"Treat her kind. She deserves it."

The ways she speaks of Stella makes me wonder if she knows more about what's happened to her than she lets on. "Are you in a hurry?"

"I have a few minutes."

"Coffee? Juice?"

"Ridge and I just got back from breakfast, so I'm good." She sits on the couch and drops her bag on the coffee table.

"That's something else we need to talk about."

She rolls her eyes just like Stella. "I don't have *that* much time."

"I'll guess I'll save that lecture for another day then," I say, chuckling.

"I'm not a kid anymore. I'm older than you were when you knew me."

I rest back and think about that. It's true. She's a year older than I was, but does that mean I don't know her anymore? "I'm not your dad—"

"Thank God."

Her and Stella definitely have that in common. "I'm not coming back into the picture to pick up where I left off. I was a fucking mess back then."

"Only at the end," she says, fidgeting with her keys. I'm not sure if she's nervous, bored, or uncomfortable. She's hard to read, holding her emotions closer to her chest than she used to do. When she tilts her gaze back up at me, she asks, "Are you better now?"

"I'm better with her."

"That's not what I asked. Are you better in life?"

"Yes."

"Do you do drugs?"

A laugh comes out, maybe even a scoff. "Who's the parent now?"

"We don't have parents who give a shit about us, so we look out for each other."

She never used to swear. Neither did Stella. Life has a way of hitting you sideways. If swearing is the worst they're doing, they're winning. "I don't do drugs. I drink. You've seen that. I talked to a therapist some years back for a time. Therapy's expensive when you don't have insurance."

"So you went a couple of times?"

"I went for a few months." I respect that she's holding me accountable. *She should.* She should make any man toe the line if he wants to be in her sister's life. "I'm sorry for what I did, for not being the man you and your sister deserved."

"Are you now?"

Unwavering, I answer, "I am."

"How have you changed?" *Perhaps the question should be how haven't I changed?* Deep down, I'm not sure I've changed as much as grown back to who I was. I *was* someone who had solid footing in the world. I *was* someone who had the love of a great woman—well, *women* when my mom was still alive. I *had* dreams and visions of an awesome future.

"I know what I lost. I can see how much hurting and consequently losing Stella stopped my heart from functioning properly. I know what I had, and I want it back."

"My sister." Not a question, just a statement she's mulling over.

"My family."

Her eyes return to mine, and some of the embattled territory this conversation has detoured into lifts from her expression, and she smiles. "I missed you. You were my brother. You were my family."

"I missed you, Mead. My brothers still talk about you and Stella as if you're Crows. You were to us back then."

Her eyebrow quirks. "Maybe Stella will be one day."

"It's a thought I've had often."

"Rivers, let me ask you something." She leans forward, her tone turning from fun to serious. "She knows where I stand when it comes to you. I'm a big believer in giving second chances and believing people can change. From what I've seen of you over the past couple of days and the time we've spent together, I think you have. I believe you when you say you recognize what you had and what you lost. But does Stella? Have you told her what you're telling me? Have you apologized to her? At the end of the day, how I feel about you, no matter how I think you've changed, I'm team Stella."

"I've apologized. I told her I didn't cheat."

"Despite her toughened exterior, she's soft-hearted. She wants to see the good in everyone, but she's seen a lot of bad. I owe her more than the loyalty of a sister. I owe her more than I can repay her."

"You're repaying her by finishing school and keeping your life on track. She worries about you more than she ever worries about herself."

"I know. I don't think she'll ever change in that regard. I probably shouldn't tell you this, but I could really use an ear and an opinion." She stands and walks to the front window, opening the blinds and letting the sunshine in. "Something happened, a change about six months ago. I don't know what." Turning back to me, she rests against the windowsill. "She won't tell me, says there's nothing to tell."

My stomach tightens along with my fists thinking about her being used to pay off a debt, raped . . . my star, my whole fucking life . . . I try to keep the anger, the pain, the sickness I feel inside, hidden from Meadow. She doesn't know her sister carries the burden of making a choice, as if she really had one. *She didn't.*

Clamping my mouth shut, I can't say anything. I already have my own plans to find these fuckers, and there's no way I'm involving Meadow. Her bravado is admirable, but it can get her in trouble that she might not recover from.

I stand, unable to hide my growing anger. Walking into the kitchen, I start the coffeepot as a distraction. "You should talk to her. Maybe she'll open up."

Silence fills the space between us and the house is too small to hide the truth. She says, "You know, don't you?"

Sticking the mug under the spout, I shove a K-Cup into the holster and start the machine, keeping my back firmly to her, blocking her from reading the feelings I know are written all over my face. "You need to talk to your sister."

She's quick and standing next to me before I have time to pretend I'm tired and disappear down the hall to hide in the bedroom until she leaves. Poking my arm, she says, "I'm talking to you."

I look to my side and straight into a darker shade of Stella's green eyes. "Mead, I came back because I want Stella. I want you both in our lives again." Though these "loan sharks" have solidified a reason beyond my star to be back here. "We've talked about a lot of things, and I'm not sure what she's shared with you. If she hasn't shared something with you, I'm sure has her reasons. I leave in two days for LA, and more than anything, I want things fixed with your sister. Okay?"

Leaning against the sink, she stares across the living room. "Yeah, I get that, Rivers, but she pretends there's nothing wrong, and for once, I want to be able to take care of her." She sighs her frustration and pushes off the counter. "I need to go. I have class and then a late shift at work."

I follow her through the house and walk her out. Out on the porch, she stops and then runs into my arms, wrapping hers around my body so tight that she doesn't need words. I hold her, and say, "I missed you, too."

She nods her head against my chest, and I know from the lack of words that she's feeling a lot. I get it. I do too when it comes to these two women. I love them each in different ways, but both are my family. With her head down, she takes a step back and pretends to get something out of her eye. "Stupid allergies."

"Hey, Meadow?" When she looks back up at me, her eyes are glassy and her nose a little pink. I say, "I trust Ridge, but if he fucks with you or hurts you, all bets are off."

That brings her sunny smile back. "Good." Poking me once more, this time in the chest, she says, "Same goes for you and my sister."

"I'd expect no less."

She gallops down the stairs and races to her car. "Gotta run. I'm late."

"Take care of yourself."

Tilting her head to the side, she stands at the curb with her door open. "I always do, and if I don't, Stella does."

"I think Tulsa resembles that remark."

"How is that wild child hot brother of yours?"

"Married."

Her face scrunches like she sucked a lemon. "So I heard."

"Hey, what about Ridge?"

Wiggling her fingers in the air, she laughs. "I don't see a ring on my finger."

"You're bad for my blood pressure."

"At least you're alive again." She gets in and shuts the door before I can reply.

The truth of the matter is I don't have a comeback to that. She's right. Stella lived through the worst of me. She now deserves the best.

I go inside and start my planning.

The flowers are bundled in glowing green paper. I watch as the florist starts tying the string around and telling me how much she loves my music. She picked out the flowers, insisting I had to get them. "Any lady would be lucky to receive these . . . best in the store . . . spare no expense when it comes to love . . ."

"Wait." The woman with flowers in her pink and silver hair looks up with two loops in her hands. I say, "They're very pretty flowers, but they're not the right ones."

Unwinding the bundle without missing a beat, she says, "We'll find the right ones then. I have lilacs in the back. Let me go grab those real quick."

"No, it's okay. I shouldn't be here." I pull my wallet out and give her a handful of twenties not sure how much those fancy flowers cost. "Thank you for the assistance and I'm sorry for the trouble."

I turn to leave, and when I push open the door and the bell chimes, she holds up the money, and says, "But you didn't buy anything."

"It's fine. Keep it." I walk out into the sun, pull my shades from my shirt, and cover my eyes. Stella never needed fancy. She just needed me like I needed her.

I know what to do and where to go, so I get in my SUV and drive out Highway 290 until I find the perfect field. I pull over to the side of the road and carefully climb over the barbed wire fence. The beauty of Texas is like Stella. It never ceases to amaze me.

But since I'm trespassing on somebody's property, I start picking the prettiest daisies I can find, ignoring the cows grazing peacefully twenty yards away. Daisies were my mom's favorite flower. I used to pick them on our walks. She would kneel and have me put them in her hair.

I smile from the memory. With three boys who loved their mama, she would be covered in flowers by the time we got home. As we got bigger, she would leave little vases around the house. While we were outside shooting BB guns or playing hoops, we'd pick a handful on our way home and plunk them in there.

Standing in the middle of a field of wildflowers, I feel sick. When did we stop picking flowers for her? When did she stop putting vases out?

Why was she taken from us?

From me?

The pain is crippling. My heart hurts as much today as it did the day I lost her. I look up into the fall blue sky, only finding clouds floating by as life carries on without her. It doesn't. My life doesn't. Jet's nor Tulsa's. Stella and Meadow's life was touched, irrevocably touched by the woman who loved us so much that it doesn't seem blue skies should exist without her here to see them.

She was buried under endless blue with not a cloud in the sky and a cool breeze. Novembers in Texas are supposed to be overcast and dreary, the weather turning from fall to winter.

Not that day.

It's as if heaven rolled out the perfect blue to whisk her away. I couldn't understand how there could still be happiness or laughter heard in the world when the woman who made our days incredible was no longer with us. I miss her so much. Eight years later and I still miss her so fucking much. *Tell me you love me, Mom. Just one more time so I can hear your voice. Please.* Holding the flowers in the air while tears fall down my face, I beg, *"I'll be the man you always said I'd be, Mom. For you. For Stella. But can I just hear your voice again? Please?"*

Like every other time, I don't hear her voice. I can barely remember what she sounded like when she sang, but I do remember that she had the voice of an angel. *"Maybe God wanted His angel to be with Him in Heaven, Riv."* Meadow said that to me at the funeral. I was so angry that I probably said something horrible back to her. Stella had held us both tight despite my anger and pain. Then she'd moved on to Jet and finally Tulsa. They had both melted into her hug, knowing she was mourning just as much as they were. I felt so guilty, as if it was because of me.

The sound of an eighteen-wheeler driving by brings me back to reality. A reality where my mother no longer exists. I look at the flowers in my hand and remember why I'm here.

Stella.

Stella is so much like my mom. They both loved these wildflowers, and somehow, they fit both of their personalities. Luxuries are nice, but they don't fill the soul. It's never been about money; it's about the thought. It's about moments. Memories. I keep searching for the perfect flowers to pick, remembering when Stella told me we didn't need things because we had love. Our love would always be enough.

She's forgotten, but I'm going to prove to her she was right.

24

Rivers

MOST OF THE students cleared campus thirty minutes earlier with a few stragglers still hanging around. I stayed in my car to keep a low profile until I felt the coast was clear. Fortunately, the teacher's parking lot is separate from the other lot, but I didn't want to draw any unwanted attention to Stella. *She'd hate that.*

I know she said she'd catch a ride, but screw this dude, friend, principal, landlord whatever the fuck guy. Something smells fishy. I haven't even met him, but I know how guys operate, and I sure as fuck know how they think. Stella is too trusting when it comes to strangers. She always did think the best until she was screwed over.

Naomi did a job on her, which blew up in my face.

I've learned the hard way not to trust anyone if your last name isn't Crow or Fellowes. I'm letting Ridge into my close-knit circle of family and friends by the skin of his teeth, though I still need to have a talk with him about Meadow.

Whoa. Is that Stella?

Expecting a longer wait, maybe even a few hours even, I'm surprised to see her. I grab the flowers from the 7-Eleven cup of water I bought to keep them alive and hop out of the vehicle.

She hasn't seen me, her eyes cast down, glued to her phone. But when she does, it's better than I ever hoped for. Her feet have stopped but a smile moves into place as if I'm the best part of her day.

Please let me be the best part of her day.

When she comes toward me, I start walking to meet her in the middle. "How was your day, Ms. Fellowes?"

"Better now."

I hold out the bouquet. "Picked you some flowers."

She drops her phone into her bag. "You sure did," she replies, taking them in hand. Standing there, looking down at the flowers, her shoulders shake with the quietest of sobs. "Thank you."

"Are you crying?" *Why is she crying?*

"I had a terrible day, and here you are looking incredibly sexy with flowers that you picked just for me and after you were so sweet to remember how much creamer I like in my coffee."

Opening my arms to her, I match her happiness without the tears. "Aww. C'mere." I embrace her from the awful day, wishing I could give her only the best from this day forward.

"So what you're saying is I'm looking sexier than usual?"

My chest is whacked as she pushes out of my hold. "Ugh. You're ridiculous." She walks around me to the car, but I beat her to the door and open it.

"But incredibly sexy. Not *just* sexy. You said the word incredibly."

"Yes. Yes. Incredibly, you annoying beast of a man."

I shut the door, laughing while I move around the back

of the SUV. The smile on her face was worth being ridiculous at my own expense to earn it. Hopping into the driver's seat, I start the vehicle. "Your place?"

The question makes her ponder, worrying her forehead as she stares back at the school. "Yeah, I need to change clothes."

She has me park behind her car to leave the other side of the driveway free for this landlord guy. We go inside, and I sit in the living room while she changes clothes. I want to pounce her and have our repeat sooner than later, but she's had a rough day, and I want her to feel safe to keep some space if that's how she likes to unwind after a rough day. "What happened today? You said it was terrible."

She comes out of the bedroom, and my dick gets hard just looking at her. Full tits I can see through a tight white little tank top over a dark pair of even shorter cutoffs than the other day exposes her tan stomach and long legs. "Fuck me, woman. Are you trying to kill me?"

"What?" she asks while reaching into the fridge, showing off that fine ass of hers.

"Uh-huh. Sure." She totally knows what she's doing.

She pops up with two bottles in hand. "Beer?"

"Yep. A beer and you. Get over here, sexy thing."

With bouncing tits, she comes to me and straddles my lap. The tease. While she twists the caps off, which is sexy in and of itself, I hold her hips down so she can feel my pain. She wriggles around, making it evident she knows and making my hard-on worse. The vixen doesn't even kiss me before grinding on me and sipping her beer like I'm just here for her amusement. "Damn. You really don't play fair."

"Is sex fair?" she asks, her hair flowing over her shoulders and covering that neck I love to kiss.

"Fun and fair. Want me to show you?"

"Did you bring protection?" Stretching back, she sets her beer on the table behind her.

"I'll be ready anytime and anywhere when it comes to you." I take a long pull of my beer before wrapping one arm around her to hold her in place, leaning forward, and setting it on the table behind her. I dig out my wallet and toss the foil packet on the couch next to us. Running my hand from the nape of her neck into her hair, I bring her in so I can kiss her. All the tentativeness of the previous few days is gone.

Although she's had a rough day, she bends toward me, comfortable on my lap. The bad starts fading away from her shoulders, and she kisses me like we do it every day. If I have my way, we will.

I lift her tank top up from the hem. When she raises her arms straight up, I remove it and put it next to me on the couch while admiring the pink pert nipples of her bare tits. I adjust her on my lap so she moves one to my mouth while her arms leverage my shoulders for balance. I hold the weight of her tit in my hand.

Taking the soft nub between my teeth, I put gentle pressure eliciting little moans. Her hips start moving again as her head goes back. I swathe with my lips and lick before moving to the other not wanting to leave any part of her body not attended to properly.

The way she moves on top of me urges me on, and I run my other hand down the curve of her waist and to the front, popping the snap on her shorts. "I want in."

"My shorts?" She starts to lift on her knees, but I take her hips and lift her to her feet.

"You. Take everything off."

The sly grin that appears is tantalizing. "You take everything off too."

I stand, invading all her space like I want to invade her. Reaching over my shoulders, I pull my T-shirt off and then start on my jeans and boxers while kicking off my shoes. Her shorts are dropped, and my girl didn't bother with underwear either. I'm liking this old side of her that seems to be coming back so naturally.

Pushing me back on the couch when my clothes are off, she slinks to her knees in front of me and takes my cock in hand at the base. "What are you going to do with that?"

"Taste it. Taste *you*. Reward myself after a long day."

I shouldn't feel so smug over her stroking my ego, but damn, she knows how to stroke . . . *my ego*. "Yeah, just like that, baby." *This is her reward? Surely, it's mine alone.*

Lifting higher on her knees, there's nothing shy about how she takes me in her mouth and sucks, sending my head to the back of the couch. No way am I missing this show, though. I lift to find her eyes closed as she slides down, savoring me like the reward she called me.

Her mouth is hot, wet, and—"Oh fuck."

Just when I think it can't get better, she changes her speed or suction, touching me just right with her teeth or tongue to keep the nerves on end. I touch the side of her head and watch until I can't take it any longer. "I'm gonna come." The pace picks up, but I sit up and lift her chin. "Inside you."

The pink lips I like kissing are red and swollen, tempting me to fuck them some more, but my carnal cravings want to stake my claim deep inside her again. I take the condom and hand it to her. The package is ripped open, and she slides the rubber down my slick length.

She doesn't wait for an invitation. She just takes what she wants by getting up and moving over me. I position myself at her entrance, and she slides down, her palms pressing into my shoulders, nails digging into my back, desire seen in her eyes. She kisses me when she comes to rest in my lap.

I like this. I like her too much to let her slip away again, so I hold her there and keep kissing her. The connection extends more than physically. My heart attached to hers while words I shouldn't say hang on the tip of my tongue as she swallows them, and me. My soul. Wholly owning me again. "Stella?"

Our lips part and her eyes slowly open, glazed as if woken from a dream. She caresses my face and leans her head against mine, then whispers, "What is it?"

It's too soon. I know it is, but how do I hold in what I've always felt for her. Do I say it and potentially scare her off, or take it slow and wait like I'm supposed to? *Fuck.* "I love you."

Her head goes back, and eyebrows shoot straight up. Her lips part, but just as regret starts to filter into my head, a curve to her mouth turns into a smile and her whole expression softens. Still cupping my face, she says, "Your words are music to my heart."

"You feel them? Do you feel how much I love you?"

"Rivers, I feel so much of everything when I'm with you. It's as though we were never apart but excited being reunited."

She doesn't have to say the words. I don't need the words. I only need her. "It just fucking bubbled up inside me and came out. I don't care if it's too soon—"

"It's not too soon. It's perfect. You're perfect." I'm attacked with her mouth on mine. Close to tossing her down on the couch, I want to fuck her senseless, but she's gotten the best of me. Her moans aren't quiet but loud reverberating through my body as she starts moving on top of me, making my mind go hazy as we fuck our way to a release.

My name is called as her tits move in opposition to the rhythm we've found. I'm so close to coming again that I start to buck, my thrusts getting harder as she rises and lands on top of me. Her mouth wide open and her head back, she calls my name like a curse word ripping through her, and her body tenses, squeezing my release from me. My arms looped around her and holding her down on top of me by the shoulders, I rest my head against her chest as the last of my orgasm is thrust from me.

I lift my head and look up at her still seated on my lap. She says, "I love you, too."

"You do?"

"I never stopped." Her shoulders sag. I know the feeling.

I caress her neck and make sure her eyes are on me. "I've spent years denying that I still loved you, but when I'm with you, especially like this, I can't lie to myself and won't lie to you. I love you, Stella Lilith, and always have."

"I love you, Rivers East. She kisses my lips, and then whispers, "We're quite the pair, aren't we?"

"We always were." *And hopefully, we always will be.*

25

Stella

WITH MY FEET kicked up on the arm of the couch and my legs tangled with Rivers, I'd fallen asleep in his arms on the loveseat. It felt too good to leave where we fell—fell into each other and fell in love. *Again.*

He loves me.

He told me.

He told me first, offering his heart to me again.

I felt it, though I denied it to myself worried that this was some elaborate ruse I wasn't in on. But he said it, spoken from the heart as if he couldn't contain it any longer. My sweet man.

Rivers is a big guy with an even bigger heart. I run the tip of my finger over the star on his chest, light enough not to wake him. I hope. Thinking about the stuff that went down with Naomi and what followed.

We haven't gone into details about that night or any that followed, but where I was once confident I was right and he was a liar, I now feel in my gut, or maybe it's felt in my soul that he was always telling me the truth. I was just too upset to see through the blurry red of my anger. I was young, so young. Twenty feels like more than five years ago. It feels like a lifetime of innocence swept away in the blink of an eye.

Rivers's hand covers mine, and he brings it to his mouth, kissing the tips of my fingers one by one. Although I smile, he doesn't see because his eyes are still closed. Placing my palm over his heart, he holds it there, and peeks one eye and then the other open at me, greeting me with a smile. "How long were we asleep?"

"Almost two hours."

"Hungry?"

"Starving."

A knock on the door startles me. I look up to see Brian through the blinds standing on the porch. *Shoot.* Scrambling to my feet, I say, "Go to the bedroom."

"What?" he asks, sitting up but not hustling to hide. "Why?"

"Because I need you to. I don't want to introduce you while you're naked."

Rivers finally stands. "You're naked. I'm not letting you answer the door dressed in nothing, that's for damn sure."

"Stella?" Brian calls. "Do you know whose car that is in the driveway?"

When he looks toward the door, I shoo him into the bedroom. "Please. And get dressed."

Picking up his jeans and shirt, I throw them, accidentally hitting him in the face. "Jeez, thanks."

Brian calls louder, "Stella? Are you in there?"

I pull on my top and yank up my shorts. "Coming."

Rivers is pissed. Standing just inside the bedroom, he says, "It better be a good fucking reason for bothering you."

"He was my friend."

"Was?" he asks, zipping up his jeans and stepping out into the living room.

I hurry for the door so Brian doesn't knock again. Checking Rivers one last time, I whisper, "Stay in the bedroom and let me handle this."

He crosses his arms and then turns to go back inside. "Make it fast."

I open the door just enough to peek out. "Hey. What's up?"

Brian points at the car. "Is someone here?"

"Yes, I have company."

"Who?" he asks, trying to look behind me.

Now I'm as annoyed as Rivers. "A friend. Do you need anything else?"

His eyes return to mine. "Yes. I was hoping we could talk about today. I wanted to apologize. I've been under a lot of stress."

"No need. Enough was said. I gave my notice, and I think it's best if I just give you a final date now. I'm thinking three weeks to finish out the month."

"I don't want you to go. You can stay for as long as you nee—"

"I think it's best. Thank you again for all you have done. I'll be out of your place by the end of the month."

When I start to shut the door, his hand goes flat against the metal. "Can we at least talk about it?"

"No."

"That's not fair."

What is he? Twelve and not getting his way? "What's not fair?"

"You can't just leave—"

"Brian is it?" Rivers. *Shit.* He stands behind me.

Brian looks at him as if he recognizes him but can't place his face. Crossing his arms over his chest, he replies. "Yes, Brian Teller. And you are?"

"Her boyfriend."

And the gauntlet is thrown down. *Men.* And boyfriend? I smile, though it's probably the wrong time to do so.

"Boyfriend?" Brian looks at me, and asks, "I thought you said you had a friend in town?"

"Yes—"

"Yes, a boy*friend*," Rivers says. "Now, if you don't mind, you caught us at a bad time. We're just leaving."

"Oh?" he asks, keeping his eyes on me. "Well, guess that notice came at a good time."

"Yes, I guess it did." I start to close the door, but add, "Thanks for stopping by."

I close the door and lock it. When I turn around, Rivers sits down and starts to put on his shoes. "He's a fucking creeper."

"Well, that did not go as planned."

"You had a plan?"

"No, but it didn't adhere to any either."

"I don't like the way he looked at you. Let's cruise out of here and go to mine."

Slipping on my flip-flops, I go into the bedroom to pack a bag. "I have a feeling you won't like the way any guy looks at me."

"This is true."

I come out with my bag that he promptly takes from me, and asks, "You ready?"

Grabbing my keys, I hold them up. "Ready."

We walk out and find Brian in work-out clothes doing stretches like he does before a jog. Rivers has to push those buttons, and say, "We'll see you around, *Bri.*"

He doesn't say anything but watches me as I get into my car. Rivers reverses, and I back out right after. I plan on spending the night again, but this time, I'll have my car so I can get to work on time tomorrow. I'm still feeling a little shaky from Brian's . . . hostility. Cruelty. Every interaction today with him has just been so weird. If only I could move out earlier . . .

"So you don't go out much?" I ask, sitting next to Rivers while watching a travel show.

"Not as much as I used to. Fame sounds fun until you're in the middle of it."

"But you said yes to my event."

The back of his hand taps my leg, drawing my attention. "I'll go for you."

"It's tomorrow night, but if you really don't want to, I'll understand."

His hand slides up my leg and covers my entire knee and more. I love it. "I want to support you. I'll be there."

"Because you love me," I tease.

"Exactly," he replies, not teasing at all. "Did you get enough to eat?"

I eye the paper plate on the coffee table. Only crumbs are left of the pizza. "Too much. I'm stuffed."

"I like all these *toos* with you." Resting his arm across the back of the couch, he turns sideways to face me. "Meadow came over this morning."

"She got her car all right?"

"Yeah, but she stayed a few minutes, and we talked."

That gets my full attention. Adjusting my back against the armrest, I stretch my legs out. "About?"

He starts rubbing my feet, and it feels so good I won't argue. "You mostly."

"Me?"

"I didn't tell her anything, but should you?"

"No."

"She knows something happened, that something affected you deeply enough to change parts of you."

Lying back, I stare at the ceiling. "She knows I was dealing with my father's problems."

When he stops rubbing, my gaze makes its way back to him. "She knows I know."

"How?" I sit up and swing my legs down. Standing up, I walk to the front window and look out.

"Well, despite you thinking I'm the best liar in the world, I'm really not. She could read my face."

I turn around and swirl my finger in front of my face. "Well, don't let your face tell her anything. She can never know. I don't want her to feel guilty or worry. I'll be fine."

"Will be?"

I roll my eyes. "You're picking apart my words. Let's just drop it."

"Have you talked to a therapist before?"

"Stop it!" I hate myself for raising my voice the second the words rage from my throat. Trying to even my tone, I struggle not to grit my teeth. "I don't want to talk about it. I don't want to think about it." My anger pushes tears into my eyes. "I don't want to relive it right now, not with you. I do it every other night. Please let me have a reprieve."

He pushes off the couch and comes to me. Holding me so gently by the face. "I want to give you that. I want to be that place of comfort for you."

"But?"

His hands go back to his sides, and he looks away.

"There are no buts." Walking into the kitchen, he stops on the other side of the bar, and says, "You don't see it, but I do. I've been there, Stella. You'll be your downfall, but it won't be just yourself you take with you. It will be everything you care about—Meadow. Me. Your career."

Crossing my arms defensively over my chest, I ask, "What do you want from me?"

"It's not about what I want. You're here. I have everything I need. It's about what will heal you. Have you talked to your dad?"

"It's getting late. I have to get up early."

"It's eight fifteen."

"This is messing with my routine."

"I thought I was worth breaking your routine."

"Stop turning this around on me, Rivers, or I'm going home."

His stare is steady as he measures me. The extended pause is purposely long. I'm tempted to fill the empty space, the silence, but I hold my tongue, forcing him to make the next move. He takes a dishtowel and starts mindlessly wiping the bar while still watching me. His hand stops, and he leans forward on his palms. "If you'd prefer to go home, then you should do what feels right."

"Why are you doing this? We were having a good time."

"Was that all, Stella? A good time?"

"What do you want from me?"

"I want you to stay and break your routine. For me. I want you to answer questions that, as someone who loves you, I have a right to know. I want you to let me in all the way so we can move forward together or we're no better off than we were a few days ago."

"That's a lot to ask of me."

"And less than I want." He comes around the bar and

rubs my upper arms. "I don't want fragments of you. I want all of you, but I want you whole." Tilting his head to the side, he comes even closer. "When I said I love you, I meant it. Not just because of the sex, but because you are a part of me. I've said it before. You're in my blood, baby. I'll take you however I can get you, but you'll never be happy until you release some of the pain you're holding so tightly. I'm yours, Stella, so please allow me to carry your heart as well."

I don't turn and leave. I don't run away, though my flight instinct is kicking in more than my fight. I stand there feeling exposed in ways that make me uncomfortable. But when I look into his eyes, I know he's right, so I don't hide. I don't put up walls. I show him all of me, all of the ugly parts. Moving into his arms, I let him embrace all the broken pieces of me.

26

Stella

MY PASSION for teaching has faded. The days are long, and the tension is growing between Brian and me. I feel it filling the halls I once loved walking down. I see it in his eyes when we're in the same vicinity.

Although I'm tired after spending the night with Rivers, I take the long way to the teacher's lounge to avoid the administration office when I need coffee during my free period. I ate my lunch in my car, needing the peace of this little haven.

Sasha has been a great help, sending me the dance committee theme idea list, which I nixed burlesque from immediately, and gave my approval to masquerade and dress as your favorite celebrity. I'll let them decide from there.

Josh Baird, on the other hand, has been staring at me all period. I'm not sure how to handle him. His parents practically own this school, and he knows how to lie through his teeth to suck up to authority. Except me. I'm not sure why he feels so emboldened, but I need to end his disrespect or have him removed from my class.

The bell rings, and the class shuffles out. Since the banquet is tonight, I worked while eating lunch and through my free period so I have time to go home and get dressed. I wish I could blow this off to spend time with Rivers.

His words may have felt harsh last night, but I needed to hear them. They came from a place of care and concern, something I haven't had anyone do for me since him. I hadn't realized just how much I missed him until that moment when he took me into his arms and held me close. *I'll take you however I can get you, but you'll never be happy until you release some of the pain you're holding on to so tightly. I'm all yours, Stella, so please allow me to carry your heart as well.* I felt cushioned. Embraced. *Held.*

Not to discount Meadow, but I don't want her view of the world tainted by my experiences. She has too much potential to waste it worrying about me.

I stand and shove my laptop into my bag when I notice my latest nuisance standing on the other side of the desk. I look up and give Josh a death glare. He's getting a warning, but I'm not afraid to follow through. "What is it?"

His hands go up like he's an innocent caught in my wrath. "Whoa, Ms. Fellowes."

"I don't have time to deal with your antics. What do you want?"

I regret it the second I say it.

His posture is bold. He's big as he stands before me, using every inch of his body to intimidate me. "What do I want? Hmm." His devious grin rattles me, but I won't give him the satisfaction of seeing me scared.

"Leave my classroom." I point toward the door. "And shut the door behind you."

"Wow." He struts toward the door, and mutters under his breath, "Not even a please or thank you. Ungrateful bitch."

The earth shifts under my feet, and I grab the desk to steady me. "What did you say?"

He stops and looks back over his shoulder. "Have fun tonight."

"What does that mean?"

When he steps into the hallway, I almost run after him, shake him, and force him to talk to me, but I'm smart enough to know to let him go. For my own safety and his.

Taking my bag, I swing it onto my shoulder and head to my car. As soon as I'm inside, I lock the doors, start the car, and turn the music on so loud that no one can hear me scream. My throat hurts, and my water bottle is empty, but the scratchy ache blocks the edge of fear I felt.

I look up and see one of the science teachers staring at me from inside her car, which is parked in front of mine. I wave and then reverse my car to get the hell out of here.

Am I losing my mind?

Is my mind playing tricks on me?

Have fun tonight. Why would he say that?

I stop at a light and look down to discover my skirt and shirt are wet. Pulling the visor down, I pop open the mirror and my face is streaked from tears.

How did I not feel it?

How did I not know?

I touch my cheek but feel nothing.

Numb.

Thinking about Rivers and what we talked about last night, I realize I'm so used to safeguarding myself from the memory that it lives in the recesses inside me. The events that took place still exist. They're just usually buried in my nightmares.

I scroll to find Rivers's number in my recent calls but am honked at before I have a chance to call. When I start driving I bear down on the pedal ready to be home. It only takes a few minutes, but it feels like forever being trapped in this car, withering in the stifling turmoil.

My thoughts are crazed, my hands shaking. I pull up to my place and throw my car into park. Running inside, I shut the door and lean against it. I haven't told Rivers how I was treated once I'd given my body to pay off the debt. I couldn't tell him how I was slapped across the mouth, and I told him to fuck off. The utter helplessness and shame of having three men watch as I took off my underwear and was forced to spin so they got the full view. *He can't know. He'd never love me the same.*

I reach under my arm and lock the door before shoving off and forcing my feet forward. My body is heavy as though lead weights are wrapped around my ankles. I fall to my bed, lying on my back with my feet hanging off.

My phone rings in the other room, but I can't be tasked to move. I tug my covers on either side of me and wrap myself up. Closing my eyes, I want to forget, keep the secret buried like it had been before Rivers showed up. I didn't have to answer to anyone or field questions. I could work, sleep . . . work and sleep without being seen.

I had become invisible in my life, all because of a choice I made.

I expected a black car with tinted windows so dark no one could see inside. What I got is a green Toyota Camry with car seats in the back. Brown rolls down the driver's window, and says, "Sorry, the other car's in the shop. Sit between the seats. They're a bitch to get back in, so leave them where they are."

There are no guns aimed at me or pomp and circumstance. Yellow is in the passenger's seat violating me with his eyes. Both men are dressed casually. I don't know why I expected more of a movie scenario when my life feels on the line. "Get in," Brown says, this time with less patience than before. "Or we'll be late, and it won't be me who pays the price for keeping the boss waiting."

I'm not sure how it can get worse, but I get in, not willing to test them. I open the door and climb over the one seat before falling into the small space between the car seats. I'm wearing the thin, stretchy dress and high-heeled shoes that were delivered. While getting dressed, I pretended I was reenacting a scene from Pretty Woman, *but my story won't have a fairy-tale ending.*

A pink stuffed bunny is sticking out from under the seat. I reach down and pull it out, holding it in my lap. Yellow watches me in the mirror of his visor. The color of his teeth makes me think that's how he got his name. My heart starts beating harder in my chest when I realize their boss didn't specify who was going to have sex with me or how many.

My grip on the rabbit tightens, and my mind flits through every possible scenario to prepare myself for the worst case. There is no preparing for the unknown.

I look out the window and see a billboard along the highway.

The Crow Brothers – Austin's Own: Opening for The Resistance. LIVE in Houston and San Antonio.

They look good. Healthy. Happy. The promo photo is so professional. My Rivers looks handsome . . . I catch myself and rethink the thought.

He's not mine to claim.

Time has treated him well, by all appearances. No doubt I'm just a long-forgotten face amongst a sea of many women. Just a girl before Naomi and never to be touched again.

The billboard is long gone, but the image is burned into my mind. Even though he left, threw us away, he was wise to get out when he did. Imagine if he had to live through what I'm about to do. I'd lose him anyway.

We turn off just north of downtown and pull into a gas station. Yellow throws a blindfold at me. "Put it on," he grunts.

I glare for a moment before he raises the back of his hand at me. The red bandanna won't hide the skyline from me. I know this city like the back of my hand, but I am not willing to risk getting Meadow or my father hurt. They're why I'm doing this.

I tie the scarf around my eyes and pull it tight to show them it's secure before sitting back and holding the bunny again. The brightness of the sun is eclipsed minutes later, and darkness fills the back of my lids. It sounds like a parking garage.

The tires squeal as Brown makes a sharp turn, and then the car comes to a stop. The bandanna is yanked off my head and sunglasses are handed to me. "Put these on and do not look anywhere other than down."

The sunglass lenses are pure black. No light can be seen through them or anything else. Brown takes my arm and pulls a little too hard when I stumble over the car seat and onto the cement garage floor.

I'm led by the elbow to an elevator. When it dings, we step inside. Through the sides of the glasses, there are only five buttons for floors—twenty-five to thirty. Penthouses. Money. Dirty money.

A card is pressed to a black pad, and the button for the top floor lights up. My head is pet from behind, and I jump. I know from the proximity of his shoes it's Yellow, which I'm coming to realize matches his chicken-bellied soul.

The door slides open, and I'm guided straight into a living room. The glasses are pulled from my face. I don't have time to *appreciate the vast view of the city and the Lady Bird Lake before Brown says, "The bathroom is down there."*

"I don't need the bathroom."

"Go to the bathroom, clean your body in the shower, and put on the robe and nothing else. Do not get your hair wet and leave it down when you come out. You have five minutes before we come in there and do it for you."

I should be scared, but I'm struggling to pull the fear forth with so much anger coursing through me. Before I say something I'll regret, I walk toward the hall and find the bathroom on the left. The plush peach robe hangs from a modern brass hook on what looks to be very expensive teak walls. The glass enclosed shower takes up a large portion of the bathroom, which is odd, considering it's not attached to a bedroom. Custom job, I assume. Fit for a scumbag who insists his victims shower before fucking them. Dual showerheads hang high on the ceiling ready to rain down. It's going to be hard to keep my hair dry.

Looking around, I find a clip for my hair and use it after getting undressed. The billboard comes to mind as I lather the perfumed shower gel over my body. What would Rivers think of me now? Would he feel sorry for me, think I'm pathetic, or would he rush in to save the day? My gut says the latter.

Could I have called him and asked for the money? He's famous now with a hit record. He might have the money, or he might not.

I pat my body off quickly and slip on the robe. The clip is removed and my hair tumbles down over my shoulders. I pull my underwear back on because fuck them. The door is opened when I reach for it and Yellow licks the front of his teeth as he gawks at me. "Put the shoes on. He's ready."

"Who?"

"None of your fucking business. Stop asking questions or you'll get answers you're not wanting."

I don't know what that means, but that fear I didn't have earlier now fills every ounce of my being as I slip on the heels again. I'm in over my head, and I know it. At one time in my life, I would have called him to help me. But he left and isn't here to shoulder any stupidity of mine. Or my father's.

But maybe he'd answer.

If his number is the same ...

If he's available ...

If he's not seeing someone else ...

I'm led to an office, not a bedroom. I don't know why I feel relieved, but I suddenly feel I might be given a chance to make a deal, to change my fate, to repent and be given an opportunity to get the money. To make a phone call. Just one. He'd take my call, wouldn't he?

My hope sinks to my feet when I'm brought around to the other side of the desk and the leather wingback is rolled out of the way. Brown points to an X marked with masking tape on the wood floors. "Stand there and hand me the robe."

"What?"

His expression reminds me of what Yellow said—no questions. I release a shaky breath and remove the robe. Brown's mouth purses as agitation sets in when he sees my panties. "Why'd you have to go and do that?"

Regret rushes my veins, and I reach down to try to remove them, but a door in the corner opens and a man walks in. "It's fine. Leave them."

If I were in any other situation, the man who enters the room would be described as distinguished or even handsome. His gray hair is full and styled, his suit tailored to a body he takes care of by the flat stomach and muscles that wield the fine light fabric.

But we're not in another situation.

His tan highlights his white teeth when he smiles, and his eyes are clear blue. The gold band on his left hand shines as if polished regularly. My body folds in on itself as he takes me in from the other side of the desk. In these surreal circumstances, I'd almost forgotten I was naked, but now I feel exposed.

Making me feel every second of vulnerability as though I'm a lamb headed to the slaughter. The smile doesn't stay when his gaze lands on my chest. "Tattoos are so unseemly. I was wrong with my first assessment of you."

When his eyes trail lower, his jaw goes taut and tics twice, revealing his displeasure. "Come around the desk."

My legs are shaky, and I'm sure the sound of my teeth can be heard chattering. My body feels less my own with every step I take. When I reach the other side of the desk, his voice matches the firmness of his face. "Take them off." I pull down the white cotton underwear and step out of them. "Spin."

I do, giving everyone in the room a good view. A million questions cross my mind, but I silence them like I was told and wait for the next direction.

"Has your sister been with a man before?"

"Fuck you." I'm backhanded so fast that I never saw it coming, but the taste of copper seeps into my mouth.

The back of my head is grabbed before I recover, a handful of my hair yanked so hard pain spikes across my scalp. "Fuck me? No, honey, I'll be fucking you." I'm dragged backward in the heels, and my ankle twists. My stumble doesn't stop him from returning me to the X on the floor and then shoving my head against the desk.

I will not let this destroy me. I will not let him win. With my cheek pressed to the hard wood of the desk, I close my eyes and let my mind drift to happier times.

27

Stella

Wiping my brow, I ask, "Is it hot in here?"

Sasha's mother glances between the water glass in my hand and my forehead. "I'm comfortable, but I can see if someone can turn down the air."

"Thank you." I look toward the entrance of the cafeteria, but there's no sign of Rivers yet. He's not late, but I was hoping he'd rescue me sooner.

After Brian accepted his award, I got stuck in what felt like an endless brag session with Josh Baird's mother. I wanted to tell her she's raising a psychopath, but I kept my mouth zipped.

I'm on edge. After the confrontation at school and then the nightmare I had when I got home, I haven't been able to shake it off. I never can, but I always hope that changes. It never does.

I hate to quit something I used to love, but there's no love if anxiety fills my day. Brian moseys over, and I roll my eyes. I don't have patience for him anymore either. Standing next to me, he takes a sip of his tea and then looks around. "Where's your boyfriend?"

I don't bother responding. I just smile at the parents and pretend they aren't raising spoiled little shits.

Surprised by my silence, he steps in front of me, and says, "I'm sorry. What more do you want me to say?"

"Sorry for what?"

"Whatever you're mad at."

Scoffing, I walk away without saying a word. I pick at the veggie platter, finally settling on a carrot. I shove it in my mouth just as someone leans against my back. "Ms. Fellowes."

With a full mouth, it's hard to smile like I want, like how he makes me feel. When I turn around, I push my glasses up the bridge of my nose and take a step back to appreciate him properly.

I was right having him come later. He's a showstopper. Rivers is looking every bit the bad boy gone good for a night —wearing black from head to toe. His button-up shirt fits his frame, showing off what I'll be licking later. With his sleeves rolled up, it's easy to see the strength he's built in his forearms and hands, the veins ever present. I love the way he uses his hands—on me and when playing music.

The black pants are tailored in length and the flat front brags of those six-pack abs beneath.

The matte black leather shoes look brand new without a scuff in sight and match his belt. A large face silver watch that looks more expensive than my car wraps around his wrist, and for a split second, I imagine a matching ring around his finger.

"Wow."

He tilts his head to the side with a smirk on his face. It should be illegal that I get this wet when he licks his lips while looking at mine. When our eyes meet, he says, "You like?"

"I like very much. You look like a movie star." I laugh at myself. "You look like a rock star."

That brings a lighter smile to his face. "I wanted to blend in for you. This was the best I could do."

"I never want less than your best," I say, winking at him. "Anyway, there's no way for you to blend in. You never did. It's one of the things I love about you."

"I'm really digging this naughty teacher look. I like the addition of pearls tonight."

"First of all, I'm not dressing naughty. That's just all in your fantasy." Clasping the pearl necklace between my fingers, I say, "And don't be too impressed, the pearls aren't real."

"You think no one notices you, that no one sees the real you, but I do. I see you." Stepping into my space, he leans down and kisses my cheeks, then whispers, "You can wear baggy clothes, glasses, and tie your hair up in a messy ball at the back of your head, but your beauty can't be hidden." I feel the brush of his fingers across the bare skin of the back of my neck and then a little tug. My hair falls down, around my shoulders and past.

He leans back and takes the glasses gently from my face, folds the arms, and tucks them in his shirt pocket. "I think you're beautiful with or without those, but wear them because you need them, not because you're trying to hide who you are behind them."

I want to fall into his arms and deeper into him, lose myself in his lyrics, and listen to his heartbeat as it plays our melody. Rivers Crow was different from the moment I saw him in the music room when we were fifteen, but it's what I heard that set him apart.

Music.

I hear music. Whoever is playing the guitar isn't missing a note of "Blackbird." I hum along, the song speaking to me in ways I sometimes don't like to think about. It's a song I only know because when I'm home, I let my mind slip inside the lyrics of old bands. I seem to relate better to those than the pop songs on the radio.

I'm supposed to be going to the library to return these books for Mrs. Johnston, but my feet slow as I reach the far end of the hall. The song ends, and the musician strums another song that I know by heart. When my parents fight, and I'm made to feel less of what they want and the reason for their problems, I put on my headphones, praying one day I won't be the one they blame. Maybe one day, I'll fix their problems, help them in a way that no one else will be able to save the day, but me.

Or maybe one day, someone will come along who can fix me. I'm good at hiding behind a façade of the studious student, the one who gets along with everyone. I could spend my lunch period hanging out at the cool kids table or date the junior varsity quarterback. But even when he used his suave tone, I knew I was just someone he wanted to bang and brag about later.

If someone really cared, they'd realize I'm not breaking down from reading a sad book. I'm crying because it's the only way my insides know how to cope.

Leaning my back against the painted wall, I hold the books to my chest and close my eyes, letting the song save me. When it ends, I look both ways. The hall is still clear.

A different sound—richer, deeper—another guitar is played effortlessly from the way the notes link together. I don't know this song, but it pulls my heartstrings so naturally that I bend around and steal a peek at the person who seems to know me better than I do.

I spy the familiar face of the middle Crow brother. Everyone *knows who they are. As an eighth grader, his youngest brother earned a reputation for getting tenth grade girlfriends last year. His older brother, is known to charm not just cheerleaders, but any girl who walked in his vicinity. Rivers Crow is the quietest of the three, though his personality draws everyone into his orbit.*

What intrigued me most about them was that they didn't come off as players. Rumor had it that they never kissed and told anyone. So whether they did or not has not actually been proven.

Now the girls, on the other hand, loved to talk about landing a Crow.

Handsome.

Charming.

Smart.

They think people didn't notice that they had frequented the honor roll over the years just as I had. The difference is they didn't seem to have to study their butt off to do it.

They were anomalies—fitting in with the jocks who staked claim to the picnic tables, the stoners who hung out behind the trash bins, and friendly to people they didn't even know. Some judged them by their bare-thread flannel shirts and faded old jeans. But those kids judge everyone, so that's not news.

As for me, I've seen Rivers around, typed his name a few times to get a feel for the right font for the letters, and I might have once dreamed of a kiss under an oak tree, but that was just a Mr. Darcy fantasy.

I spin back, glued to the wall and hoping he didn't see me when his gaze traveled across the music room to the cracked open door. "Is anyone there?" he calls out.

With the books cradled in my arms, I hurry in the direction I came, taking the other stairs to the library. That night I ask my dad about the different guitars there are and played "Blackbird" on repeat until I fell asleep.

. . . My heart is beating as fast as it was that day, the

memory reminding me of how Rivers has always had a gentle soul. "The first time I heard you play a guitar, you were playing 'Blackbird' by The Beatles."

Rivers touches my neck and runs his thumb down the slope onto my shoulders. "Yeah?"

"The awards ceremony is over. What do you think about taking off?"

He gives the ruffle of my sleeve a little tug. "I'd rather be taking this off."

"That can be arranged."

"Ah, the boyfriend has finally arrived, making his grand entrance." Brian steps up from behind Rivers, popping our happy bubble. "Thanks for showing up to celebrate my award." He pats Rivers on the arm. "I appreciate the support."

Eyeing Brian's hand, Rivers says, "Don't ever fucking touch me again."

I clap once like we're tapping out of a wrestling match . . . or trying to avoid one more like it. "Okay. On that note, I think it's time for us to go."

Brian's hands are shoved into his pockets, but his mouth is still loose. "So soon. The parents made time for us. It would be nice if you made time for them, Stella."

"I helped set up. I think they'll understand if I leave since most of the banquet is over."

Brian throws on a fake smile and his arms go out as the president of the PTA joins our little party of three. "Mrs. Baird, how can I thank you enough for such an amazing night?"

She straightens his tie, causing me to roll my eyes. That is totally inappropriate, but more so is what she does next. Smiling at me, she says, "I want to have you and Ms. Fellowes over for dinner this next week. We have a special dinner for one of our future state representatives, and we'd love to have our most respected administrator and our son's favorite teacher join us."

Holding my finger up armed with an excuse, I say, "Unfor—"

"I absolutely will not take no for an answer," she says, lowering my hand. "Mr. Baird will also be there to present the school with this year's donation. He would like to personally thank you for all you've done for our sweet Joshua."

Brian says, "It will be our pleasure to be there."

Looking Rivers up and down, she conspiratorially whispers, "Will this gentleman be joining us as your plus one?"

Rivers takes my hand and kisses it, making me swoon inside from the sweetness. I don't care if he is territorially marking me. I'm his, so mark away. He says, "I have business out of town this Thursday to tend to, but if the invitation still stands, maybe another time?"

And she blushes and giggles like a schoolgirl. "That would be delightful. I'm Margery Baird. I didn't catch your name."

"Rivers Crow."

"And you do?" she asks.

"I'm in the music industry."

"How exciting. Well, you must come for dinner when you're back in town. Our son would love to hear all about it, as would I." Turning back to me, she adds, "We'll see you and Mr. Teller this Thursday."

When she walks away, my smile falls flat on the floor as I grind my teeth. "You had no right to obligate me to a dinner with you."

"If it's best for the school, it's best for you, Stella. Or do you not care to keep your position?" His hand makes contact with my arm for .02 seconds before it's knocked away by Rivers.

Rivers is ready to bear down on him by the way his jaw ticks. "What goes for me stands for Stella. You touch her again, and I'll annihilate you right here in front of everybody without a second thought. *Bri.*"

A sleazy grin points up at the ends. "You're in The Crow Brothers." His eyes find mine. "Things are making a lot more sense now. The shirts. The music. Had I known we had a celebrity coming to the party, I could have arranged for you to perform for me." *What is happening here?* It's as if I am in the presence of a completely different Brian Teller. Surely, this isn't just about a crush. I have enough on my plate. This has to end.

Closing my eyes, I rub the bridge of my nose. I sigh and then open my eyes. Rivers is about to say something, but I touch his chest, and instead say, "I don't know what's happened to you. Why you've turned so hateful toward me, and thus toward my guest. It's sad and really pathetic, but worst of all, it's disappointing that my friendship meant so little to you."

I take Rivers by the hand and lead him through the mingling PTA members and school staff and straight out the double doors into the fresh night air. Walking toward the cars, I ask, "What do you want to do?"

"Get down and dirty with the naughty teacher."

Laughing, I roll my eyes. "You are so ridiculous."

"C'mon," he says, taking my hand. "I'm going to show you how ridiculous I can be."

28

Rivers

"I'm gonna rip it."

"No."

"Let me fucking rip it. Rip it right the fuck—fuck, you taste amazing. I'm going to fucking shred it."

"No."

I look up, trapped between annoyed and amused by her. Swiping the back of my hand across my mouth, I ask, "Why not?"

Stella releases her hold on the top of the hood near the windshield wipers and lifts up on her elbows. "Because I'm not made of money. You don't see me going around ripping clothes off you because I don't want to take the time to undress you."

Money. *Fucking money.* "I'll buy you a whole new wardrobe if you'll let me rip this scratchy skirt off you."

"You said you're not that rich, so why do you want to blow money for no good reason."

"Oh trust me, baby." I wink and pretend to rip this cheap

fabric. "This is a damn good reason. Anyway, I didn't lie. I'm not *that* rich, but I'm really fucking rich."

"You didn't have to tell me that. That's your personal business, Rivers."

Running my hands up the inside of her thighs, I let the tips of my fingers trace circles in the wet. I really love how her body entices me. "You are my personal business, now and always. You're not shaking me, and so we're clear, I have a lot of money now. That means I can take care of some of your worries, including this fucking skirt."

"How is that possible?"

Shrugging, I reply, "The ladies and dudes love us. Well, the music."

Lying back, her hand rolls in the air for me to carry on, but I decide I'm tired of this bullshit wooly skirt against my ears and neck. "Can I rip it?"

She lifts her ass in the air as if I'll ever use the zipper to take the skirt off her. "No."

Pushing her middle back down on the hood of the car, I try one more tactic. "Let me put it to you this way. Financially speaking, on a scale of one to Johnny Outlaw, I'm currently a five, moving into a seven within the year."

Lifting her head, she purses her lips to the side and then lies back again. "Fine. Rip it."

I gather the shreds of what's left of the skirt and toss the pieces in through the open window of the back seat of her car. She fell asleep lying back on the passenger's seat after we had sex on the hood of the car overlooking the whole city from miles away.

When I get in the car, I don't rush to start it. I quite like looking at her sleeping. She's restless most nights, kicking me in the shins a few times and almost kneeing my balls on another. But right after we make love, she finds peace.

So I stare through the windshield for a few minutes, taking in the view of the city where I once belonged. With my brothers in Los Angeles and my career based there, Stella is the only reason I'm here. And come tomorrow, I won't be.

She stirs, slowly opening her eyes. Her troubles return as her mind wakes up. Resting my head back on my seat, I try to give her what she wants and smile. It's not good enough to tempt one from her because she knows with each passing hour, we're closer to the unknown.

I know.

She's just not fully there yet. I get it. I do. I don't like it, but I understand. She's been through the unimaginable and had no one to rely on but herself and her sister when she couldn't afford to confer with her.

No, she's not the same girl I once knew.

She's better.

So fucking strong.

Brave.

And she managed to hang on to care and concern for others.

"Will you let me care for you?"

Turning on her side, her hands are pressed together in prayer and tucked under her head. "I thought you already did care for me?"

"Will you let me take care of you?"

"What does that mean, Rivers?"

I run my palm over her bare thigh and back again. "I was bragging about my money to impress you." I chuckle under my breath. "I should have known it wouldn't."

Her hand covers mine, and we still together on the peak of her hipbone. "Money will never impress me because I've seen what it does to people. What it turns them into. But you, my love, *my Rivers*, will always impress me because your heart will always be pure." She sits up and adjusts her seat. "You came back for me."

"You believe me." It's hard to see the protective shell she built around her heart when she's become so soft with me. That's the girl she used to be. I like the contradiction. I love all sides of her when she's with me.

Facing forward, her eyes are directed on the night before us. "What becomes of us?"

"It's good for us to talk about this, but my feelings for you won't change if that's what you're worried about."

She nods as moonlight reflects in her glassy eyes. When her gaze finds its way back to me, she confesses, "What becomes of me once you leave?"

There is no answer for me to give that will reassure her. I know my heart. I hope what we've shared in this week means she knows my heart as well. "I don't have the answers. I'll fly you out whenever you can come visit me. Every weekend, if you want. I'll fly back anytime I have time off. I'll be here when you need me, but it might not be physically."

"You've given me so much to think about. It's probably best you're leaving. I can't seem to think straight when you're around. I look at you, and you're just so hot." She laughs lightly. "You're very distracting." Then a heavy sigh comes out. "I wish I could beg you to stay even though it won't make a difference. But know that I'll miss you when you're gone."

Leaning over, I kiss her cheek. "I'll miss you when I'm gone too."

Her arms wrap around me, and she holds me to her, tucking her head into the crook of my neck. Through tears falling on my shoulder, she says, "Why did you have to make me fall in love with you if you're just going to leave me again?"

I'm careful not to scratch my scruff against the soft skin of her face when I lift enough to kiss right in front of her ear, and then whisper, "Falling in love was never the problem. Never falling out of love is what hurt."

"I love you, Rivers Crow. I love you so much. Don't go falling out of love with me once you're back in the city of lost angels."

"I'm only lost when I'm not with you." I lean back and tilt her chin up. "Listen to me, baby. We may not always be in the same city, but my heart will always be yours. You understand that? Yours. No one else's. My whole world is wrapped inside you, so you take care of yourself and my soul."

She rests a hand on my cheek. "And when you return to me?"

"We're going to talk about our future, so be thinking about it while I'm gone," I say, then tease, "since you can't think straight when I'm here."

"I will."

I kiss her because I can't be this close to this woman and not kiss her. "I love you."

As much as I don't want to ruin our last night before I leave town, I owe Stella a lot more than promises for when I return. I owe her the full truth. My unfinished business has dragged us through hell. There's no way I'm putting this off until I return.

Stella was pissed at first when I told her I wanted to visit Naomi to clear the air, but I won't go unless Stella is okay with it. She told me she's ready for our slates to be cleaned so our future has nothing but blue skies ahead.

I step out on the front porch and sit on the swing with my phone in hand. Ever since we got back, she's been playing Beatles music. "I Want to Hold Your Hand" is heard through the cracked open front door.

I pause because I don't want to hurt Stella after finally getting her back. But will it hurt her more if I can never tell her the full story? Yes.

I'm not sure if Naomi has the same number she did years ago, but I text anyway. *Hey. Long time.*

Not wanting it to sound like a booty call if it's the wrong number, I stop there and stare down at the screen. Nothing.

Then three dots appear and the following message: *Rivers?*

Me: *Yeah. I'm here for a short visit and wanted to see if I can stop by?*

Naomi: *Yes. When?*

Me: *It's late, but tonight?*

Naomi: *Tonight works. I'm out in Buda now.*

Me: *Send me the address and I'll plug it in. How does thirty minutes sound?*

Naomi: *Let me take care of a few things first. Forty-five?*

Me: *See you then.*

I stand with a sick feeling in my stomach and tuck my phone in my back pocket. I've lived under the shadow of this confrontation for five years. Naomi cost me the love of my life. I'm just grateful that I got Stella back. I push open the front door and step back inside.

Stella's in the kitchen with a full glass of wine on the counter in front of her. I shut the door and close the distance. The song changes, and I hold my hands out. She takes one, and I raise it into the air as her other settles on my shoulder. We begin to slow dance to "In My Life." The lyrics feel as if they were written for us.

We've had our moments, from the good to the bad. All are still so vivid in the present, though, when I look into her eyes. "I've loved you longer than I haven't."

Her mouth curves up on one side. "You've known me less time than when you haven't, silly."

"When it comes to us, years don't matter. Only heartbeats and I don't remember a time when mine didn't beat solely for you."

Coming closer, she rests her head on my chest, and says, "Think of me, okay?"

"Always."

29

Rivers

THE GRAVEL GRINDS under my tires as I drive down the street. My headlights flood the front of my SUV and lamps inside houses make the windows glow in the dark of the run-down neighborhood. I turn onto a dirt driveway carved through the front yard, my tires kicking up dirt when I brake and shift into park.

I'm only here for one reason—to end an agreement I should have never made. I'd love a cure for the side effects of healing the sickness that has diseased my heart ever since that fateful night five years earlier.

When I cut the engine, the screen door opens, the hiss of the squeaky hinges alerting me to look up. I get out. Naomi leans against the chipped railing of the front porch. I can't make out her face in the dim light, but I hear her say, "Good to see you, stranger."

"Yeah, good . . ." It's not, and my tongue sticks to the roof of my mouth in protest for even attempting the lie.

I shove my keys and hands into my pockets and walk to

the house, stepping around a pile of rocks and a few dead plants in their pots. There's an old Toyota truck up on blocks on the side of the house and a rusty kids bike on the porch.

The lights are brighter as I near the door, causing me to squint when I first see her again. Naomi opens her arms and hugs me tight. "Wow. Rivers Crow right here at my house. I've missed you."

She feels as wrong as those words feel foreign when it comes to her. Her Southern accent is stronger than I remember, but to me, she was another chick in our group of friends. Her and Stella were close enough at that time not to fuck each other over, or so I thought. I don't remember much about Naomi back then. I'm not sure I really knew her that well at all. I knew her enough to know she'd gotten herself in trouble—dating a guy who liked to take his life's disappointments out on her.

John Cables was older than us but wanted to relive his youth. He trolled the high school parking lot even though he had long since graduated. Met Naomi when she was seventeen and they were a couple from that point on. No idea what happened after I left.

He supplied a lot of the alcohol and popped pills like Tic Tacs. If he wasn't drunk, he was high. If he wasn't high, he was low. If he was low, he hit Naomi. Everyone knew it except Stella. She could hang in a party scene, but she always kept an innocence about her that I tried hard to protect. I may have hit bottom, but I didn't intend to drag her down with me.

I scan the area, but there's not much to see. Without streetlights, it's hard to see jack shit in the country. She once told me she had big dreams. If I helped her, she'd make sure they came true. I don't have to ask her how that worked out.

I have a feeling a house that leans to the left with foundation problems and a car in the yard missing its tires aren't the dreams she had in mind. But sometimes life fucks your plans up before you have a say in the matter.

Naomi's taller than the average girl and was born into good genes. From what I remember, she liked attention from the opposite sex even though she was taken. I couldn't tell her the differences I see in her from then and now. I never paid that much attention to her. I remember her confidence and strong will. She could drink most guys under the table when it came to cheap tequila. Back then, holding one's liquor earned instant respect.

She leans against the siding of the house and twirls a few strands of dark blond hair that looks like she took the time to curl. She's not the ingénue she likes to pretend to be, and I'm not looking for a hookup, so I avoid her batting eyelashes and just come out with my business. "I once made you a promise."

"I remember."

"I need you to free me from my word."

"Free you? Were you shackled to them?"

"Yes, pretty much."

She smiles as she opens the screen door. "Let's go inside and talk about it."

"No. I'm good."

"It's a nice night, but I'm cold." She walks inside the house.

Although this wasn't a part of the plan, I want to end it, and the winds have picked up outside. I go inside and let the door slam shut. She turns back with her finger to her lips. "Shh. I've got littles sleeping down the hall."

I stop just inside the living room. Wood blocks are bumped up to the toe of my shoes, cars abandoned on a broken track, dolls that are half dressed and other toys are scattered around the room. "Littles?"

"Kids, Rivers."

Plural.

Wait a minute. I give my head a shake. "You have kids?"

"I've also got cold beers. Pabst Blue or Milwaukee's Best?"

Beer? "No. Kids? With?"

"Well, that's rude."

"I don't mean to be. But you didn't want kids. Wasn't that one of the reasons you needed my help?"

"It's true. I didn't, but since I had the first one, I figured what did it matter after that. Know what I mean?"

"No, I don't. I don't have kids. I don't have anything because I gave you my word not to tell a soul your secret."

Her head pops up from behind the fridge. "You kept your word?"

"Yes. Why wouldn't I?"

The fridge door is closed, and she says, "Because it's just a word. It's not like you were going to hell if you told someone." *What the fuck*?

"That's just it, Naomi. I did go to hell because I couldn't tell anyone."

"Oh, no no. You're not going to blame me for your unhappiness." Waggling her finger at me, she looks at me sideways. "What do you have to complain about? You have money. All the fame a girl could only dream about—"

"I never wanted fame. I didn't even wish for money. I wanted two things. To be able to play music for a living and Stella."

"It's been years, and I'm still listening to the same broken record. Poor Stella." Her upper lip curls into a snarl. "Is this really about Stella?"

"Of course, it's about Stella. It's always about Stella for me."

She pushes her hair behind her shoulders in contempt. Disappointment or hurt feelings crash into her expression. She's hard to read. "I thought—"

"You thought what?"

"I thought you wanted to see me. That maybe you missed me like I've missed you." *Missed her? I barely knew her.*

"Why? We weren't that close, but you still dragged me down into your hell and then abused the little friendship we did have."

"You chose to help, Rivers. If you didn't want to, you could have looked the other way like everyone else."

What the fuck?

I'm not frustrated. I'm angry. At myself for letting this happen. She's right. I should have looked the other way if my help meant so little. But I couldn't. My mother. Stella. My brothers. Myself. Looking the other way would have meant disappointing them in another way. Looking the other way when someone needs help is not how I was raised.

I'm struggling to understand how little she valued me and her friendship with Stella. I stepped in when she had no one else looking out for her. I helped so she could have a better chance at that life she dreamed about. "You confided in me that John would hurt you when he found out you were pregnant. That you didn't want that connection to him and had tried to leave."

"I didn't confide in you, Rivers. You're just the only one who took the bait."

My stomach churns like a hurricane gaining strength. "The bait?"

"Shh. Keep it down." She picks up a blanket from the floor and starts folding it. "I thought you wanted to sleep with me, and I wanted John to settle down and commit to me."

"He hit you."

"Only a couple of times. He's gotten better."

I'm too stunned for words. I can't believe what I'm hearing, and the lack of any sane emotion coming from her. She's fucking whacked out of her mind, but that doesn't change the fact that my life was fucked because of her. "I protected this fucking secret. I lost everything because of it."

Angling her head, she smiles. "I knew you were noble."

"Noble? A fucking idiot is more like it. This was all to make your abusive boyfriend jealous? Cables fucked half your friends. That didn't matter? All that mattered was trying to convince someone who never cared enough about you to give a shit for two seconds? Fuck me." I turn to leave, but she grabs me.

My head whips to the side, and a hard glare lands on her hand that's attached to my bicep. "Step back, Naomi."

With a pound of arrogance in her eyes, she still backs away "Ohh, how the mighty have fallen. Are you going to hit me?"

"That thought right there shows how little you know me. Let's keep it that way."

I head for the door, but before I reach it, she says, "You're no better than John. You just have more money."

Money.

Money.

Money.

Fucking money.

Looking down, I see the band on her finger and the green line beneath it that has seeped into her skin. "You know what money can't buy me? Morals. A clear conscience. Happiness. Guess what? It won't buy it for you either."

"Go ride your high horse on out of here, Rivers. I don't need your judgment wasted on me."

"I'm not judging you, Naomi. I feel sorry for you. All your dreams have come true. Be careful what you wish for and all that."

When I step out onto the porch, I close the screen door so it doesn't bang against the frame. Like her, I feel sorry for these kids who will grow up with a mother who has nothing but herself to blame for the life she hates so much. I glance back once, seeing her stand in the doorway behind the screen with her arms crossed and her chin raised. The desperation in her eyes is seen on the other side of her pride.

I almost can't be mad at her. It's my own fault for throwing her a life ring. She did what she learned to do way before I met her. She used her survival skills. I was just too dumb to realize she was surviving while drowning me.

Speak of the devil.

I don't bother to catch up with John, who's leaning against my SUV, but after unlocking the door, I turn and look him in the eyes. "You knew, didn't you?"

He shrugs and kicks up some dirt with the heel of his worn in boot. "I always liked you, Rivers."

"Apparently."

"Maybe next time you're in town, we can grab a beer," he says with a laugh that seems to indicate he doesn't understand how this is going down. "Or maybe you can hook us up with some tickets to a show."

I have to force my gaze away from the blind nerve he has, but I manage. I open the door and don't waste time where I should have never spent it in the first place.

30

Rivers

DROPPING the towel to the floor, I go quietly back into the bedroom after taking a shower. I needed to clear my head and wash away the anger I held on to during the drive back. That's not what I wanted for my last night with Stella. And if I've learned anything over the years, holding so tight to something so negative is destructive to the potential of what could be.

Stella went to bed while I was gone. Even though I wasn't gone long, I'm glad she put her worries to rest instead of sitting here alone thinking about what's going on.

The room is dark, but she left the blinds open. I use that light to guide me. I'm not sure what's clean in my suitcase at this point, but I have a few hours left to wash my clothes before I leave again. I walk to the open suitcase that was dumped on the floor a week ago and stop, standing over it.

There are four short and neat stacks of folded clothes, packed and ready to go. I look back at my sleeping beauty, realizing she washed, dried, and folded my clothes. I was only traveling with a week's worth of clothes, one load, but still. Warmth spreads through my chest as I stare at her in awe.

There wasn't an expectation for her to do this. It's a load of clothes. Not monumental in the scheme of life, but it's a big deal to me. It's not words she's saying. It's her love in action. I squat down and pull a pair of boxers from a pile, knowing every time I do for the next few days, I'll think of Stella. Maybe that's what she wants, but deep down, I know it's not a selfish act on her part. This was for me. This was telling me the things she can't always say. Yet.

I put the underwear on and carefully slip into bed behind her. It's not the side of the bed I normally sleep on, but with her body partially in the middle and taking up space on my side, I want her to know that she doesn't just own my heart. She owns every part of my life, including the bed.

When I wrap my arm over her, she moves back into my body, and whispers, "Are you okay?"

I destroyed our lives by protecting a secret that caused her pain she should have never felt, and she's checking on me. God, I love this woman. "I'm okay. Are you?"

She turns in my arms. Her eyelids are heavy but open as she searches my eyes. Her hand finds the side of my neck and rests the tips of her fingers on my pulse. "Is it over? Did she give you the permission you were seeking?"

She has a right to be upset and ask questions. I don't think my answers are going to be as satisfying as she hoped. *Because it's just a word. It's not like you were going to hell if you told someone.* How can someone think like that? Live like that? Lie like that? I still feel shafted from Naomi's ploy. But how I feel doesn't matter right now. All that matters is Stella. "Do you want to talk about it now or in the morning?"

"I have work tomorrow, and I don't think having this conversation at six in the morning will work out well for either of us since we'll be tired."

When her hand leaves my skin, I take hold of it again, wanting the contact. "She used me to make John Cables jealous."

"Oh God, Rivers," she says, pulling her hands away and dropping her head into them.

"I take full responsibility. I'm to blame."

Looking up, she touches my cheek. "Your heart is so big."

I cover her hand and keep it there, loving the feel of her touch on my skin again.

Although her voice is quieter, more contemplative, she asks, "What happened?"

I tell her about the house and car in the yard, how Naomi looked, and about her sleeping kids. I'm not going to lose Stella by leaving out the details. "She told me I was the only one who took the bait."

"She took advantage of you?"

"I'm the one who fell for it."

"You fell for it because she knew what kind of man you are—honorable and caring. That's the man I fell in love with. The man she wishes she had then and now. You're still that man, Rivers. I hate that I lost sight of that. I'm sorry."

"I was nothing more than a tool she used to make John jealous. But I'm the one who fucked-up by helping her."

"I just can't believe the lengths she went to, and how she threw our friendship away for temporary gain." Again, she sighs. "It worked too. I hate her. I hate her so much, and then I hate that I have to hate anyone. I used to trust everyone first. Now I'm . . . I fell for it too. She spread the rumors about you and then never denied it when asked. She could have ended the speculation but chose not to."

Exhaling loudly, I say, "It didn't matter that John hit her; she just wanted him to commit to her. Her plan was to target me to make him jealous. She laid down some story about him hitting her if he found out she was pregnant, so she needed money and help. It was a fucking ploy to make him want her more by thinking I liked her."

"Did her plan work for her?"

"Guess so. He was hanging around my 4Runner when I was leaving."

"What did she have to say about us?" Her anger pitches in her voice, and she sits up.

Remembering how Naomi shrugged, how she practically spit when she spoke Stella's name, I roll onto my back, and reply, "She wasn't too concerned."

"She's the reason we broke up. Her games to win John destroyed us, and she didn't seem concerned?"

I was the fool. "I'm sorry." Sliding down, I can't find comfort in a bed I usually sleep well in. I close my eyes, wanting to turn back time, and feel like a failure that I can't make this better for her. Stella deserves better than a fucking fool who falls for a jealousy ploy. "I gave her money to leave him. Money I didn't have to pay my electric bill that month. She took it with fake tears in her eyes, telling me that money would allow her to leave him. I helped her fucking pack a bag and drove her to her mother's house. Stella, I'm sorry. So fucking sorry."

Feeling all the guilt I've carried with me for years come back, I close my eyes, wishing I could change the past and do it right the second time around. When she rests her palms on my chest, she gives me hope that maybe I can, maybe we can together.

She slides back down in front of me and caresses my face with a firm hold in a silent request to open my eyes. When I do, she says, "After your mom's accident, you were always making sure your brothers we're okay, and the band kept working, even through the pain. You managed them, your career, paid the bills, and kept going to school. You, my love, took care of my sister and me. Don't you see? You took care of everyone except yourself." A tear falls down her cheek as she looks at me. "You're so much like your mother with your heart of gold and good intentions. Your mother is so proud of the man you are. She may not be here to tell you, but she knows your heart."

Reaching up, she wipes a tear from my face I didn't realize had leaked. Her forgiveness is spoken in the weight of her words. We don't need apologies. We just need each other.

"Naomi took advantage of your generous heart. You weren't gullible. You just can't bear to see someone hurting."

"I hurt you."

"Let me ask you something about that night. When you came to talk to me, would you have told me everything?"

I taste the pain as if it were yesterday on the edge of my tongue. "I would have told you what I could. I wouldn't have broken the promise I made to her. I believed she was in danger."

"That's why she targeted you. She made you give your word because she knew what your word meant to you. Her lies were safe with you." The heaviest parts of the conversation are exhaled.

"Picking my stuff up—"

"God, yes. Off the lawn. I'm so ashamed, Rivers. When I look back now, I can't believe I was so callous with you." I nod because I'm feeling so choked up about this fucked-up situation. *So many wasted years.*

"It hurt so much that you didn't believe me or have more faith in me, Stel. I got angry after that. Out of everyone who knew me, you knew me best. When you forgot who I was, how my heart bled for you, I stopped fighting, too hurt to keep trying."

"You're right. And now, older and hopefully a little wiser, I can see what you're saying is true. But at the time? I think I was already hurting. I was already feeling a little unsteady. And that's not all on you, but the partying and drugs . . . it was taking a toll. On us. On me."

"I know. Now. I had nothing left. I just . . . I really didn't consider that you'd believe the lies."

"And I got mad at you for giving up on us so easily. Rivers, I'm sorry—"

"No. I don't think we need to keep saying that, Stella. I should have contradicted the rumors."

"Yes, I think that's what I needed. *But now?* I can see that we were caught up in a vicious circle. I thought I knew everything. We were only twenty. I thought because we pretended to be adults and lived like them, that I was smart enough to see the truth."

"I had no clue. I had no clue that trying to help her would destroy you or destroy us."

"I know. I know that now. And I'm glad you went to her so we could both process the truth together. We needed that."

"I love you so much."

Just when I think we'll be spending hours confessing our sins and mistakes, Stella climbs on top of me. Pressing down on my chest, she hovers over my face. "Hey?"

"What?"

A bright smile lights up her face. "I'm so fortunate."

"How so?"

Leaning down, she kisses me once, twice, five times before lifting up enough to reply, "Because you defied our fate and were brave enough to talk to me that day under the oak tree."

"It wasn't me who defied it. Our love was strong enough to change our fate."

Thinking of Naomi and John, I contemplate how little has changed with them. They're more set in their ways, stuck in the life they chose. I realize how fortunate I am. Back then, we were young and stupid. We both lost five years with each other, but here she is sitting on top of me smiling because we changed our fate and created our own destiny. *Together.*

Turbulence wakes me from the sweet dream I was having of my woman—her mouth on me, my mouth on her, fucking, loving, cuddling because damn it she likes to cuddle with me.

Last night we didn't just talk about the past, but I made sure she had plenty to remember me by in the immediate future. I gave her every ounce of my all before we fell asleep for the few remaining hours we had together. It was cathartic. And I felt as though a large hole in my heart was finally starting to heal. On the front porch of the house, she gave me a long hello kiss because she still insists we're not allowed to tell each other goodbye. In return, I gave her the keys to Jet's house.

I don't want her staying on the creeper's property even if she has locks on the door. I don't trust that asshole. Not one bit. She was thrilled about the idea, so it's a win all around.

Ridge stands as soon as the plane lands. "Go."

By the time we walk into the sunshine of California, a red Ferrari honks as it pulls up to the curb. Tulsa Crow and his wife, Nikki, and their newlywed smiles greet us. Tulsa shifts into park and stands on the seat of his convertible. His arms go wide and with Ray-Bans covering his eyes, he yells, "Welcome home, brother."

"Fucking hell, Tulsa."

Nikki laughs, then asks, "Did you expect less from him?"

The paparazzi were already on our trail, snapping photos. Even with security by our sides, this scene is too Hollywood for me. I laugh at the "too" addition. Stella's rubbing off on me, and I like it. "Alert the paps, why don't you."

"Seems you already did, Riv?" Tulsa holds his phone for me to see.

"What is that?"

"You tell us."

An officer blows his whistle and thumbs for Tulsa to keep moving.

I drag my suitcase up to the side of the car, but I'm stumped how this is going to work. "Hey, this is a fucking two-seater. How are you planning on fitting us in there?"

Tulsa drops to his ass and fastens his seat belt. "I'm not." Signaling to the Range Rover behind us, he adds, "You're catching a ride with Jet. See you later, fuckers."

As he whips into traffic, Ridge and I head for the Rover. A tinted passenger window rolls down, and he says, "Curbside service, but I'm not carrying your suitcase, so throw it in the back and let's get out of here."

"Good to see you too, big brother."

I load our carry-ons into the back and settle into the front seat. Jet reaches over and as we shake hands, we bring it in and pat each other's back. My oldest brother is most like me visually with his dark hair and a small cowlick my mother could never keep down with her spit-hand attempt. Brown eyes and olive skin. Personality wise, I'm more reserved than either of my brothers, but we all have a few traits that define us as brothers.

"You look good, Rivers. Healthy."

Happy.

Stella.

We have time to go over that without hitting him over the head with it the second I get in the car, but I feel her with me even though we're miles apart. "You missing me?"

He laughs. A little too much.

Then I remember Tulsa's phone. "Tulsa flashed a gossip piece."

"I was going to let you get in the car before bombarding you with it. Leave it to Tulsa to hit you with it the second you arrive."

"What is it?"

"Guess you went to see Naomi while you were in Austin."

Fuck. "Don't tell me she sold a story?"

"Rochelle said the piece is hearsay at best, and the photos are weak. Not much details. She said to let it ride. No one will care in two days."

"Photos?" *Stella.* I grab my phone and plug in the site. *Fuck!* "This looks bad."

"Nah, but it sucks she made a few dollars off you." Jet's presence carries weight, an authoritative tone that makes you want to hear what he wants to say. So when he speaks, we listen. "Let it roll right off. There's nothing you can do."

"I need to call Stella." I dial the number and wait three torturous rings and then I'm tortured some more by getting voicemail. "Hey, I landed. Call me when you can."

I hang up and turn the phone over in my hand several times.

"Sucks, but it will be fine, Rivers. Don't stress. Anyway, we have a lot to go over now that you're back, but first we eat. You guys hungry? Hannah's cooked a feast. She knows how we like to eat."

Ridge says, "I'm ready for a home-cooked meal. I think I ate enough tacos to fill me up for a year."

"Starved," I reply. Content in where Stella and I left our relationship, I watch the world fly by, feeling lighter than I have in years.

Guess Jet notices. "Going back to Austin was good for you."

"Going back for Stella was even better." *I feel like myself again. No longer . . . incomplete.*

31

Rivers

"THIS IS QUITE THE TURNABOUT," Hannah says when I set a cold glass of water in front of her since hers is empty.

"It's water. I was going inside anyway," I downplay. The truth is, I'd do anything to help her out. She became family well before she exchanged I do's with Jet last year.

My oldest brother is the one who sacrificed his own ambitions for ours. If one of us had to go without, he always chose himself. He and Stella are similar that way. What they don't realize is we're all in this life together. We can row the boat when they are tired. We can man it when they feel weak. We can step up and let them recover.

Unless we don't know. They hold their cards close to their chest until you get close enough to sneak glimpses of the burden they carry. The moment Stella allowed me in, to let me share her pain, she blossomed like a flower seeking the sun for me. And it is a beautiful sight to see.

Hannah went a different route, bringing a son Jet never knew he had into the picture, into all our lives. Alfie dashed from the table as soon as he was excused to return to playing a video game he's obsessed with. Jet's family went from us to six in less than two years. Nikki made seven. And Ridge, former sufferer of cool name envy when he used his birth name of Dave, feels right at home sitting at the large Crow family table. Whether he's Dave or Ridge, he's part of the family.

Hannah laughs but then leans over the side of a little portable baby bed when Violet, their three-month old, stirs. The baby grabs her finger and falls back asleep. Lowering her voice, Hannah says, "I mean you and Stella. Thank you for the water, though, too."

"Oh." I chuckle. My own unburdening in Austin has allowed me to sit back and enjoy being around my family again and not harbor any envy or sadness that I was slowly becoming the odd brother out. I don't want Stella in my life because of being lonely, though. I want her because she should have been here all along. She should be sitting here now. She's the half of my being I've been missing. It feels good to spend time with these couples, these amazing people, and feel whole.

I knock the top of my bottle against Ridge's, and ask, "We didn't have a chance to talk back in Austin—"

"Not my fault. You were a bit preoccupied at the time."

I can't deny I was utterly distracted in every minute of every day—happily distracted. "Nice try. What's up with you and Meadow?"

Tulsa practically spews his beer, causing Nikki to jump up from the chair next to him. "What the hell?" she asks, making sure she's clean from the scene. Then Violet garbles, and she says, "Sorry."

Hannah smiles, waving her off. "She's fine. Don't worry."

He says, "Man, I haven't thought about her in a while.

How's she doing?" I'd almost forgotten Tulsa used to have a crush on Meadow. With a constant threat of me kicking his ass hanging over his head, he was wise enough not to go near her . . . *At least I think he didn't.*

When Nikki sits in his lap, he wraps his arm around her without missing a beat. They're good for each other and uniquely them—full of love for each other and for life. They soak in everything life has to offer and laugh with each other. A lot.

Being a lead singer of her own band gives Nikki a perspective that not many other people understand. Not only does she understand what we go through to make our music, but she also gets Tulsa like no one else ever has. She has a freer spirit—a cool calmness—about her.

I once said how incredible it is that Tulsa found his perfect match, and I meant it. He's never looked better. He's never been more focused when he's hitting the drums, and although the Ferrari surprised me at the airport, his rowdier ways seem to be settling down.

I set my bottle on the table, and say, "She's good. Right, Ridge?"

Ridge laughs and hits my upper arm. "You're an asshole."

Jet starts laughing. "Do I want to know what that's about?"

Taking a long gulp of avoidance with his beer, he finally just says, "We messed around a little. Nothing serious."

A feeling of protection zips through me. "Does she know that?"

He's already shaking his head by the time I finish the question. "She's the one who said it."

"Shot down?" Tulsa cringes. "Man, that's rough."

Nikki asks Tulsa, "Did you date her?"

Tulsa shakes his head. "Nah. She's like a little sister to me." Eyeing Ridge, he nods, and adds, "Like a hot little sister." That earns him an elbow to the ribs.

"How do you put up with his shit, Nik?" I ask, sitting back in the patio chair, stuffed from the food that still covers the table.

"As long as it's in the past, it's ancient history. If it invades my present, that's another story altogether." She turns to me. "My brother said to give 'em a call when you and Ridge got back to LA."

After touring all summer with her band, Faris Wheel, all of us became friends. Her cousin and brother round out their sound, and the guys are free to mingle. I wouldn't mind hanging out with them and grabbing some beers, but the status quo has changed. I'm not going to do one damn thing to screw up what I'm rebuilding with Stella.

Ridge answers for both of us. "Will do."

Resting my elbows on the table, I look at Jet. "Can we talk? In private?"

His eyes go to his wife's first, and then he nods at me. "Sure. Let's go to the studio. The sound equipment was installed last week. It's sick it's so sweet."

We leave the others, and I follow him down a Saltillo tiled hall. They bought a Spanish style home in Benedict Canyon. I'm not familiar enough with LA to lay down roots yet, but with two kids, Jet and Hannah had other things, like schools, to consider.

Jet shows me the soundboard and the latest in innovations connected to it. Taking over the captain's chair, he rolls the other toward me. "Tell me what's on your mind."

"I told Stella she could stay at the house."

"Of course. We're probably selling it soon, though. Even if we ever wanted to move back, we wouldn't move back into that house." I kick my feet up on the desk, and he promptly knocks them back to the floor. "Respect, man." He's teasing, but he still means it. "What's going on with Stella? Does she need a place to live?"

"Landlord and asshole issues." I rest on my forearms, needing advice. "I want her with me, but that's fast, so I'm not sure how she'll take it. I don't want her to think I don't respect her career or her by asking her to dump her life to be with me. And then there's Meadow. Stella will never leave her behind, and I don't think it's right to either. Unless she wants to stay."

"You said at dinner that they're estranged from their parents. I'm sure there's a story to back that, but do you think they'll want to move across the country and leave everything behind?"

Lowering my head, I rub the back of my neck. "She's been through some shit she never should have been." I look back up. "I don't think she'd mind a fresh start. I just don't want to take away her independence."

"If Stella wants to be with you, that's not taking away her anything. It's adding to her life. Like Hannah, man. For some unknown fucking reason, she loved me enough to allow her life to move in a different direction. But love does that. It doesn't compete with who is more important. True love just gets shit done." He stands and turns a few knobs before leaning against the desk and crossing his ankles. "You guys were kids back then. Reasoning hadn't even kicked in. Mistakes were made. This is a second chance that I can see you want. Now you need to find out what she wants before you move in different directions."

"Yeah," I say when I stand. If there is one thing I truly appreciate about my big brother, it's that he gets the deep stuff . . . and doesn't need many words to communicate it. It's what makes him a good brother, and excellent lyric writer, and a man I admire. *True love just gets shit done.* We walk back down the hall. Before we reach the others, I ask, "Do you remember how Mom used to put vases around the house?"

He stops and looks back with a grin that accompanies that happy memory. "I remember that. We'd pick flowers for her and put them in the jars. She always said the only bad thing about flowers was watching the slow death of something so beautiful."

Instead of the daisies Mom loved coming to mind, my thoughts are on Stella. "That's true."

I claimed the guest room at Jet's while Ridge took off with Tulsa and Nikki to the bungalow they're renting in the Hollywood Hills. There was talk of going down to Sunset and getting drunk, but I want to lie low tonight and check in with my woman. Even more so because of the story that broke.

"Hello?" she answers after the first ring, making me feel victorious.

"I've been wanting to hear your voice all day."

"I was stuck in class all day thinking about you. That's why I missed your call."

"It's okay, but I need to tell something."

"Is it the Naomi story I saw online?"

"You saw?"

A heavy breath like a load off her chest is heard. "I didn't read it. Screw her. She's stolen too much of my time away with you already. I'm not giving her a second more."

My chest still feels tight. I can't have us moving backward after all the work we did to repair our relationship. "I told you everything that happened."

"And I believe you. I do. When I decided to trust you again, it wasn't just for the past but also for the future. I trust you, Rivers. So let her get her thirty seconds of fame and then we never have to think about her again."

"Thank you."

"No thanks needed. As for you being gone, I already miss you. That's not normal, right?"

"It's normal for us because I miss you too. I've been thinking a lot about that."

"Do you want to share those thoughts?" she asks in a low voice, a tone that makes me feel like a voyeur intruding on an intimate moment. So fucking sexy.

"I'll give you a hint. Every thought is about you and me being together."

Her light laughter fills the line between us. "That sounds like more than a hint, babe. Remind me never to play poker with you."

Babe. That's new. I like it. *A lot.* "When we're alone, I won't be wasting time playing cards with you unless it's strip poker."

"We don't have to play cards for you to get me naked." A heavy breath laced with desire is heard. "I probably shouldn't tell you—"

"Tell me. Don't ever hold back."

There's a pause and another breath, but then she says, "I didn't know . . . after what happened to me . . . I put the memory in a box like a bad date so it wasn't as horrific to ruin something I once enjoyed. That box in my mind never closed, though, until I saw you. I didn't know I could feel desire, that I would crave your hands on me in ways that are dirty but never made me *feel* dirty when you touched me. Rivers?"

"Yeah?" My voice lowers to match the desire stirring in me from her confession and the images of her on top of the car as I took her for all the stars in the night sky to see.

"When I said I loved you, those weren't just words to me."

"I'm coming back to you, Stella Lilith. There's no way I'm not."

"Even though you left this morning, I've been smiling all day. You know why?"

"Why?"

"Because when you said that miles are the only thing that will ever be between us, that spoke for my heart as well. It's not a matter of believing. It's a matter of knowing. I know we'll be together, and I can't wait because I suspect that reunion sex with you is going to be pretty spectacular."

"Fireworks spectacular. I promise. So you know, this is new for both of us. When we were together before, I only left town once without you and that was a night of sleeping in the truck since we couldn't afford a motel much less a hotel."

"You had a gig in Nacogdoches right before finals. I couldn't get off work to go with you."

"You remember that?"

"I remember how lost I was without you." *God, I love this woman.*

Holding the phone to my ear, I tighten my fingers around it, and whisper, "Now I'm the one who's lost."

32

Stella

THIRTEEN DAYS HAVE FELT like years. It's a tragedy in the making. I'm a mess because I miss Rivers so much. We talk every night, but it's not the same. I tried to stay at the house —stopping by three times. But every time feels wrong without him there.

Stuck in my work routine, I look out over my classroom while the students are working individually on their history projects. "Five more minutes."

As if he's been waiting for the opening, Brian stops by my classroom and knocks lightly. When I open the door, I don't step out into the hallway. I protect myself instead by just cracking it open. When he holds up a key, he says, "This is a master key. Fits all the locks in the school universally."

"Thanks. I'll make sure to take care of it. We have the dance committee meeting tonight."

"Let me know how it goes."

"I will." I nod inside. "I'm getting back to my class now."

"Sure."

I shut the door and walk back to my desk. Opening a filing drawer, I hide the key in the back and then glance at the door, hoping he's already gone. He hangs out alone for a few minutes before he carries on. Resuming what I was doing, I turn the page in my planner and start the next lesson. *Creepster.*

Sasha sits with her laptop on the gymnasium floor when I walk in from the far corner. She looks up with her lips twisted and scratches her head. "Hi, Ms. Fellowes."

"Hi. Are we the first ones here?" I ask, approaching.

"Yes." When she glances down at her laptop again, she says, "Something's weird with the dance funds account."

"Really? What is it?" I set my purse and bag on the floor while she stands up to show me.

"See the budget balance?"

I see the numbers, but they don't make sense so I hard blink and look again. The number doesn't change. "$250,000? What's the budget supposed to be?"

"Two thousand five hundred."

"Well, something is obviously wrong. I'll look into after our meeting. Stick to the regular budget."

I tried to focus on the meeting, but the thing is, I couldn't just forget about it. That's not the kind of mistake a bank makes. I pull up the account on my phone and screenshot it for reference.

When I get home, I run a hot bath and check the account again out of curiosity, but this time, I get the regular budget balance. Even when I check the activity for the account, it's as if it was never there. *A weird glitch maybe?*

I can sit here all night and let my tub overflow or get in

with a glass of wine and try to get my mind off Rivers being gone by getting lost in a good book.

Anything that helps the time fly until I see him again.

I step out of the bath and dry off before wrapping a towel around me. With my wine glass in hand, I finish the last drops of the pinot noir and walk out of the bedroom to return the glass to the kitchen.

My gasp catches in my throat. The glass falls, shattering at my feet. "What are you doing in my house?"

"It's actually my house."

I tighten my towel around me and look at my feet. Shards of glass stab into my skin, and there's no way to avoid getting more cuts if I move. My gaze flicks back to him. "I know it's your house, Brian, and I'll be out soon. But why are you here now?"

"Inventory. I didn't know you were here."

"So my car out front didn't tell you that?"

"I'm sorry."

"You seem to say that a lot lately. I'm very uncomfortable right now. I want you to leave."

He makes his way to the door, but says, "I wasn't thinking straight. I've had a lot on my mind. I have someone interested in renting this place starting next month."

"I'll start packing."

Silently he leaves, shutting the door behind him. He's smart enough to know when to leave, but I wish he were wise enough to know not to come near me. *Why is he behaving like this?*

Using the wall to stabilize myself, I slowly lift one foot and shake it just enough for the loose pieces of glass to fall. I reach down and dust off the tiny shards stuck in my foot.

I'm not sure if it's the glass, the scare of finding a man in my house, or because Rivers is gone and my whole soul misses him, but I lose it. The tears come hard and fast, and as I step away from the broken glass, I manage to locate a few stray pieces with my feet.

My phone rings, and I rush to answer it, wanting to talk to Rivers all day. But with each step, the glass embeds itself deeper into my foot. "Shit." I hobble over and fall onto the couch, pushing the button when I do. "Hey!"

"Hey," he says, his voice like a bandage to my wounded heart. "Bad time?"

"No, perfect time."

"What's wrong? You seem upset?"

I think about what I should say before I say it because I am upset, but I don't want to upset him. I shouldn't hold back. I can't if we're making this relationship work and there's nothing more I want than to be with him. "I broke a glass and some of the shards hit my foot."

"Are you okay?"

Not in any way. "I'll be fine. I have some micro shards I need to dig out, but . . ." I adjust the towel around me again, and a sniffle slips out.

"Stella? What's going on?"

"Don't freak out, all right?"

"You know as soon as someone says that you're going to freak out."

"I know," I say with a small smile. "It's handled. So before you freak out, remember that."

"Just tell me."

I see a spark of light reflected near my toe and reach down to pull the glass out. It's satisfying to have it out, and I lean forward to set it on the table near the keys to Jet's house. "I came out of my bedroom and found Brian in my house."

"What the fuck?"

"I'm leaving. I'm going to get dressed—"

"Get dressed? He saw you naked?"

"No. I'm in a towel?"

"Fucking creeper. I should've kicked his ass. Stella, get dressed, get the fuck out of there, and call the police." That's the Crow in him. Zero to hellfire in no seconds flat. It's both hot and concerning. Sexy to me. I love how he's always made me feel protected. Worrisome for the person who pisses him off.

"Calm down. He's gone. I'm fine. I'll just pack my clothes and go to Jet's."

"I don't know why you're still there. I've been gone nearly two weeks."

I run my fingers across the bottom of my foot, hoping I don't find any more glass. "I went over the other day, but I stood in front of the bed and it just made my heart ache without you in it."

"Your safety is my only concern right now. You need to call the cops, and you need to get out of there, Stella. If you don't, I will."

"Don't." I stand and hobble to the bedroom, walking a wide berth around the broken glass. "I'm packing now." Slipping on my flip-flops to avoid any more shards, I slip on underwear and a T-shirt, then grab my case from the top of the closet.

"You're not safe at work with that psycho roaming the halls."

"I can't quit. I need the money."

He growls. "I can fucking afford for you to quit. Take the money, Stella. Whatever you want, whatever you need. You can take all of it if I get you."

I toss a few shirts in the bag and grab shorts. "That's your money, Rivers. You earned that. You deserve it. Let's not jump so far ahead that one day you'll look at me with regret for sponging off you."

"A spouse doesn't sponge. Marriage is about equality—" He stops speaking as soon as he realizes what he said.

I'm standing in the middle of my closet holding a skirt and stunned to the spot. "Marriage?"

He releases an audible breath. "We should have been married already. Years ago. That's where we were headed. We both knew it then. I know it now." He doesn't make up some elaborate excuse or call it a slip-up. He owns his words and he means what he says. *I love him even more at this moment.*

Walking out of the closet, I sink to the mattress with little pink hearts floating in the air as my own heart beats rapidly in my chest. "I know it too."

"I didn't want to have this conversation over the phone."

"But we are."

"Yes," he says, a lighter tone than the one before. "Look, Stella, I love you. You love me. We've wasted a lot of time not being together. I don't want to waste any more. I'm not asking you to marry me over the phone, but one day I will ask because I'll love you till my dying day."

"Well, crap. How am I supposed to have a pity party when you're being all sweet like that?"

"No pity parties. Be strong. Be brave, like the woman I know you are. Pack your bag and leave right away. I'll send movers to get the rest of your stuff. As soon as you're at the house, call the cops and report it. If you let him get away with it this time, he'll do it again."

"There will be a fallout. He's my boss."

"Promise me, Stella, or I'll fly in and take care of him myself."

I don't doubt his conviction on the matter. I feel the

same, but I'm trying to handle this the right way—delicately. "I promise. It won't be easy, but I'll do it." Looking around the little cottage, I realize this might be the last time I'm here. I'll take him up on the moving offer, so I don't have to return. "I'll go home to the house after the dinner tonight."

"What do you mean?"

I rub my fingers across my forehead to ease the tension I have built up over this dinner. "I have that dinner at the Baird's tonight, the one she gave us no out at the banquet."

"Asshole will be there, though."

"Dinner will be fine."

"I don't like this. Not one bit. Don't go. It feels wrong."

"He's not going to risk that donation check."

"I don't care about the check. I only care about you. I meant what I said about the money. You can take what you need. You don't have to work a shitty job that puts you at risk just to make a buck."

I stand back up and throw a few more items into the bag. "I appreciate everything you're saying and willing to do, but I need to quit once I have another job. I don't feel right about living off you. Not at this point at least," I joke, trying to lighten the mood.

"You're not scared, are you?"

"There are plenty of monsters in the world to be scared of. I don't think Brian is one of them. Though all signs are leading to creepy perv."

"Don't ignore the signs. I have to run. Our break is over but call the cops, okay?"

"I will. Love you."

"Love you more."

Grabbing everything I need for the rest of the week, I get dressed, and load the car. I hop in the car and spy Brian coming out of the house. Shifting into reverse, I back down the driveway before he has a chance to feed me another meaningless apology.

When I get to the house, I grab my bag from the back seat and let myself in. I'm hit with the faint smell of Rivers warming the air. Comfort and love fill me as I drag my bag to the bedroom. Sitting on the edge of the bed, I feel his absence, but he's right. I should have been staying here all along. I'm safe here.

Fulfilling my promise, I call the police and report what happened. It's more complicated since he's the landlord, but they'll send someone out to follow up in the next couple of days. Not reassuring at all, but at least I don't have to live there anymore.

Once I hang up, I get ready for the dinner. I didn't tell Rivers because he was already worried about me, but that feeling he has about tonight is trifold for me. I never want him to see me as less than brave and strong.

It's only dinner.

A few hours of meaningless chitchat. That's it. If Josh tries anything, I'll tell his parents. He may be eighteen, but I know he's scared of his parents.

On the drive over, I play my favorite band—The Crow Brothers—and let them rock my world while keeping me company.

A valet drives my car away when I arrive to the palatial property, so I make my way up the front steps and ring the bell. When the door opens, Mrs. Baird greets me with friends and family mingling in the great room behind her and welcomes me inside.

I follow her to the sitting room and take a glass of wine from a silver platter as an employee passes by. Brian arrives shortly after me but keeps busy with other guests. Josh is wearing a suit and looks every ounce the man of the house.

Asshole. His father is a mystery. I've never met him or seen him, but everyone speaks very highly of him, which surprises me, considering his son is an asshole.

Mrs. Baird comes back into the room, and says, "Dinner is ready, and my husband is finally joining us. Coincidence?"

She teases and smiles just as her husband comes up behind her and kisses her cheek, "Honey." In front of a room full of people, his clear blue eyes and white smile find me. Without faltering, he says, "Let's eat."

33

Stella

MY BREATH IS TRAPPED SOMEWHERE beyond survival.

My heart sunk to the bottom of my stomach.

My feet won't walk.

I'm unable to move at all or think . . . *flight*.

What feels like hours since Josh's father entered the room has been seconds at best. The room is still full with guests slowly filing out and moving down the hall to feed into the dining room. Like a leaf floating on the surface of a mightier river, my body flows with the tide.

Can I blend in?

Can I leave?

The front door is farther away than before as we're led into the large room with the crystal chandelier and seating for twenty. At the edge of the entrance, I turn before I'm seen.

"Ms. Fellowes, please join us." Hearing him speak reminds me of how little he did before he slammed me to the desk. "I've made sure you were sitting next to me, so we can get to know each other better."

I pretend not to hear him and take a step, but an arm loops through mine, and Mrs. Baird says, "Are you looking for the restroom? I need the powder room myself. Right this way."

Glancing back before I'm dragged away, I find "the boss" is not pleased. Mrs. Baird is talking about the wallpaper that decorates the hall as we walk down to the bathroom. We enter a small sitting area where she lifts a tissue canister and pulls out a lipstick. "I hide my lipsticks around the house so I can freshen up quickly, but they're hidden from view." Looking at me in the reflection of the mirror, she offers, "You're welcome to use my red, but the shade you're wearing is so lovely. What's the brand?"

"I don't know. It's from the grocery store."

"Oh. Well, if we can save money and get a pretty shade, I'm all for it." Pointing behind me, she adds, "The water closet is that door."

I set my clutch down and turn around as if instructed to go into the room that has enough space not to feel crammed. As I attempt to pee, though I didn't need to, I hope she can't hear me. I hope she leaves. Should I stay in here long enough for her to return to her guests? If I do, I can slip out the front door.

The wood door is solid. I can still hear her voice but don't understand what she's saying. I listen hard to the silence and start counting in my head. She can't leave her guests for long. I decide to wait her out.

Long minutes pass and I think the coast is clear. I flush the toilet to finish the act I'm performing and open the door. Relieved to see the coast is clear, I close the door and jump when I find her sitting on the pink padded bench. She stands. "I was worried about you. Do you have an upset stomach? I can get you something."

Tears well in my eyes as I realize there's no getting away. Unless I plan to tell her about her psychotic husband, which will put me, Meadow, and my father in harm's way, I have to play along with this charade. "Yes, I have an upset stomach. My apologies. I think I should go—"

"Oh no. Please. We have a lovely meal. The soup might settle it."

I move to the sink and start washing my hands as she stands with worry drawing her eyes to the door. Then her eyes go wide, and she smiles. "I have just the thing. It's a little concoction my butler whips up for me sometimes. It's a shot of goodness for your intestinal tract. That's such an awful name, but let's get you a little shot and join the party. Soup should be served, and I have it on good authority that it's delicious."

Moments later, I down a shot glass of dark brown liquid. I don't even care what it is at this point. It can't hurt me ... unlike her husband. We enter the dining room to some quip she's come up with to amuse her guests as she takes her seat at the other end of the table. Among the laughter, I walk the dreaded mile to my seat next to Mr. Baird, *and oh joy*, across from Josh.

"The boss" stands and pulls my chair out for me. I go through the motions though I'm feeling less in my body by the ticking second. When he scoots me forward, he whispers, "Your hair is lovely when worn down."

My head spins, and my eyes close as I try to erase the memory of his hands on me and that night completely.

Brown doesn't open the door. He doesn't even bother to get out of the Camry. I reach over the car seat and pull the handle to release the door. Pushing it open, I try to steady myself, but my legs are wobbly, so I take off my shoes and work my way out of the car on my own. I'm unsure of the state of my mind, not knowing what to think, what to say, if anything.

As I stand in front of my car in the school parking lot, I realize too late that I didn't catch the license plate before they left. I open my car and sink into the seat, locking myself in. Starting the engine, I push the radio button, and turn up the music so loud that no one else can hear me scream. So loud that I lose my voice in the metal that's blaring through the speakers. It's the only thing that drowns out the many voices on repeat in my head. It's my escape. The only escape I know.

I return to the apartment and am glad Meadow is working a late shift tonight, which is one of the reasons I chose tonight to fulfill the deal.

Under the hot water, I scrub my body inside and out, and then again. My skin is raw and red, inflamed and sore between my legs. I don't realize how hard I've scrubbed since my skin is numb until drops of blood hit the base of the tub and slide down the drain.

When I get out, lotion stings so I skip my normal routine and slip on a pair of loose fitting boxer shorts so they don't cling. I've had these forever. They're my favorite pair, and when I see the pattern, I remember how good they once looked on the original owner. I shouldn't think of him. I don't have that right anymore.

He got everything he ever wanted once he left me, but I fell apart without him. I'm not bitter about his success. In some twist of fate, his success brings me happiness, as if I still hold a small part of his heart with me. I hold more, but it's not healthy for me to think about it.

Sliding on a T-shirt and flip-flops, I grab the trash and walk to the dumpster behind the apartment building. I throw the dress and shoes inside and toss a full trash bag from the kitchen on top to bury them hopefully forever. I stand there staring at the flies that nest on the metal edge, but the stench is lost on my senses. Numb. I'm numb to the experience, feeling more like I belong here than the fairy tale I once lived.

Rivers and I never needed more money than we had. We got by, and we loved. With our whole hearts, we loved so hard. Sometimes, I forget what caused our pain. Sometimes, I relive it. Everyday, I wish I would have done things differently, let him plead his case, and let him back in. My heart is resilient, but that day never came. Once he tried and then he didn't again.

I walk back to the apartment and lie on the couch, hoping to put this night behind me like a bad dream. Aches and pains are felt from my heart on the inside to my skin that feels raw on the outside. I thought I was doing what was best, but I struggle to find a silver lining in the destructive choice I was given. There's nothing to feel proud about other than I left with my soul intact despite that monster's best efforts to steal it.

Tomorrow I'll tell my dad I negotiated so the interest rate and the balance were dropped. That I saved him from a fate that would have taken him from us forever. He'll see the error of his ways. He'll get sober and clean up his life. He'll love me because I gave him a second chance. And hopefully, we'll get our father back.

My heart starts beating after a long night of stillness. This was the right thing to do. Feeling like maybe we might be okay, I pick up the phone and take another gamble. He's been on my mind so much lately. I wonder if five years later he ever thinks of me.

The name sits proudly at the top of my screen. With my finger hovering over the call button, the front door opens, and Meadow walks in. "Tonight sucked big time."

I lower the phone to my side, hiding who I was about to call as she strolls past me being her dramatic self. "The tips were horrible, and some asshole came in right before I was about to get off and requested my section." She rolls her eyes. "Perv. He sat there drinking a coffee and staring at me. Told me I should wear my hair down, using a line about how lovely it is when worn down." She kicks off her shoes and puts her hands on her hips. "Know what I told him?"

The beats of my heart fade away as my mind connects the dots. I sit in stunned silence while she says, "How would you know? I tightened my topknot in a fuck you manner if that's even possible and clocked out." Going into the kitchen, she pulls out a can of cream soda and pops the top, causing me to jump. "On edge much?" She takes a drink, and then asks, "What'd you get up to tonight?"

"Nothing. Trash," I mumble. I achieved nothing tonight. And he has made sure I know that. How had I been so naïve? I try to muster the anger I held on to for years and hate Rivers for hurting me. I was stronger that way, not weak like I feel now. He deserves someone better than a girl who's not better than another man's trash.

"What?"

I clear my phone and turn it off. "I took the trash out."

"Wow. That sounds eventful," she replies sarcastically. Then she adds, "Sorry about Rivers."

Sitting straight up, I ask, "What? What do you mean? What happened?"

"Well, I know you have a silence pact when it comes to hearing news about him, but it broke my heart to see him with that model."

Oh. At first, I was relieved she couldn't read my mind, but now I feel my own heart severing from the news. "Model?"

"Yeah, she was walking in the Victoria's Secret runway show last night. Rivers was there."

I rush to the bathroom and vomit, my body also pushing out the tears I should have cried while being violated. I had more to *be concerned about than my heart at the time. Of course, he's with a model. Someone beautiful. Someone pure. Now the broken heart I've nursed for years has become the least of my concerns. The man I thought would be my forever is most definitely gone now. Everything is gone. My heart. My pride. My soul.*

. . ."Do you not like the soup, Ms. Fellowes?"

My gaze lifts to find Mr. Baird staring at me with a spoon in front of his mouth. My spoon still rests to the side of the bowl, untouched. I don't respond but keep my eyes down.

Brian, who is sitting in the middle of the table, says, "Ms. Fellowes." I look his way, struggling to hide the contempt I have for him. He adds, "Has been a wonderful addition to the Rostinal team. Although I've only been there four years and her two, we've worked hard to make the best environment for your future CEOs."

The last part earns him a laugh. He goes on to say, "We would like to thank you on the behalf of the school not only for hosting us tonight but also for the significant donation."

Mr. Baird says, "Is that a subtle hint to hand over the check, Teller?" Another round of laughs. He stands, placing his napkin beside his plate. "Ms. Fellowes will accompany me to the office, and we'll take care of business now so we can enjoy the rest of the night." I want to suggest he take Brian with him, but I'm still in shock. I have no words. *How is this real?*

Baird points at the man he intends to put into office and teases, "Don't delve too deep into politics while I'm gone." The future state representative, as well as the sheep around this table, start clapping after the entertainment by their host.

He pulls my chair back and then stands with his elbow out, waiting on me to take it. "Josh, join us."

I shouldn't have had that GI cocktail. My stomach

churns as everyone stares, waiting for me to take the arm of my enemy. I have to leave.

As we round the corner, my hand falls to my side, my clutch held tightly in the other. We walk toward the front door with his son behind us. I stay straight, walking to the door when he turns to go to his office. I know he won't make a scene, and there's nothing he can say to keep me here.

"Your father has racked up another large debt."

Except that.

Shit.

34

Stella

JOSH BAIRD TAKES a remote and sits on the couch, kicking his ankle to rest across his knee. It's incredible to watch how emboldened he is when his father has the upper hand.

Conrad Baird sits in his leather chair with his fingers steepled in front of him as if there's some great mystery he's trying to solve.

I took a seat on the other side of the desk when I had the rug pulled out from under me. The mention of the debt my father has accrued is news to me. "I don't speak to him any longer. I haven't seen him in months."

Mr. Baird's eyes shift to mine, and he nods. "I can imagine selling yourself for his financial problems can cause quite the rift in a father-daughter relationship."

I'll tell him nothing that feels too close to reveal. If I can get out of here in the same condition I arrived, I'll deal with the issue of my father's debt directly with him. I can't help him this time. I won't. If he knew what I gave of myself, the sacrifice I made last time, would he have kept gambling me away? That's what he's done. With every hand of cards, every roll of the dice, he anteed me up like a dollar chip.

Do I mean nothing to my dad? Does my life not matter to him at all?

"Turn your chair around, Ms. Fellowes." I don't want to do this. I don't want to be here. Will they let me get up and walk out of here without consequences? "Play the recording, Josh."

From behind me, I hear Meadow's voice and turn around to see they filmed her at work with a hidden camera. My sister—so young and beautiful, nothing tainting her bright green eyes. She laughs as the person filming makes some comment about the food. Josh says, "Dad promised I could have her if I got straight As this quarter."

I brace myself on the arms of the chair, my hands turning white from holding it too tight. "What? No," I reply, shaking my head. "No. That's not how this works. I paid the debt. Me. Me. I did. She has nothing to do with this."

"Are you asking me to deny my son his rightful reward?"

Panic sets in, and I can't think straight. Only nonsense I pray will work. "He has a B in my class, not an A."

Josh rubs over his crotch as he stares at the screen, as he ogles my sister like she's prey. "I need an A." When he looks at me, he asks, "How about some extra credit to earn that A?"

His father says, "Yes, I was so impressed with your skills that I think my son could really benefit from them." I turn to stare at him, in shock.

What fucked-up world am I living in?

I hear it before I see it. The slap of skin. My pain grunted quietly. His moans while he's getting off. Yellow whispering in the background. I didn't hear any of it when it was happening, but now as the video is played, I hear and see it all on the big screen when I turn back around.

Josh stands and walks closer. "This is my favorite part. I blow every time." *Oh my God. He's a monster just like his father.*

"You get off to your father?" I have nothing left to lose.

Glaring back at me, the video of my violation, *my rape*, because that's what it is, is paused. "Don't be a bitch." It starts playing again, but it's paused when I look up. "That right there. That look in your eyes. So fucked. So hot."

"That look only proves to show how dead I am on the inside."

"You felt quite alive to me. Anyway, we have dinner guests waiting on us. I have the check ready to hand over, and you'll be contacted by my associates to start on the debt repayment plan." He comes around and yanks me by the hair at the back of my head. Tilting my head back so I'm forced to look at him, I grind my teeth, holding the last shred of my pride. He says, "Make sure my son gets his A, or we'll be having an entirely different conversation."

He walks out of the room and his son follows, and from the hall, I'm summoned. I push up out of the chair and walk to the doorway, still too shaken to digest the confrontation. Josh is gone, but "the boss" stands there with a check in his hands. I look at the writing and the dollar amount. Brian Teller. Two hundred fifty thousand dollars. That's a lot of money, but why is it made out to Brian instead of the school? He says, "I'll tell our guests you weren't feeling well. Good night, Ms. Fellowes."

When I'm left alone, I race to the front door, swing it open, and run for my car. Valet. *Fuck.*

I walk with him, looking back over my shoulder

expecting to be hunted like the prey he believes me to be. The valet asks, "Is everything all right?"

"No."

I refuse to support the lies that remain in the shadows of that mansion, to pretend the residents aren't demented. I feel sorry for Mrs. Baird. Does she not realize who she's married to, who she's raising? Are they that good at lying and hiding their sickness that she can't see beyond the shiny façade?

She can't, I determine. There's no way. But if she doesn't know the real monsters they are, she's chosen to look the other way.

He hands me the keys, and says, "Drive safe, ma'am."

I don't. I drive as fast as I can until I'm miles away. Being alone in the car reminds me that for the first time in years, I'm not actually alone in life. I have my sister, but when it came to the bad stuff, I tried to shield her. Those sick fuckers better not go near her. I'll make sure they don't any way I can.

I make the call I should have made years before.

"Hey baby," Rivers answers. "How'd it go?"

"I need you."

"I'll find a way, Meadow."

"I need the money. Anyway, I can't just walk out after all these years. I have to give notice."

"Please just listen to me—"

"You haven't told me anything, but you show up demanding I quit my job and go with you. I'm not leaving until you tell me what's going on?"

I pull her by the arm around to the coffee station. "Our father has found himself deeper in debt than before."

"Let him worry about it this time," she says, crossing her arms defiantly.

My hands are sweating as a bead rolls down the back of my neck. "They don't want him to pay. They want us."

"What are you talking about? He didn't care about us when we helped him before, so we're damn sure not helping him out this time. We have nothing to do with him anymore."

"They're bad people, Meadow."

A cook calls from the kitchen, "You covering your tables or what?"

She takes a step forward but stops and looks me in the eyes. Maybe I can't lie as well as I used to or maybe she just never looked deep enough to see the truth, but something keeps her from leaving. "You said they want us, not they want us to pay back the money. *Us.*"

I let her come to terms with her conclusion. "What did you do, Stella? Why would they offer you mercy when they wouldn't give it to our dad?"

"They showed me no mercy."

A steady pause hums between us as she absorbs my words. When another waitress walks by with an empty tray, Meadow taps her on the shoulder, and asks, "Can you cover my tables tonight. I have an emergency."

"Sure, but are you splitting tips?"

"No, they're yours. Thanks, Cammie."

"I'm stuck here anyway, so it's no problem."

"I'll tell the manager." When Meadow turns to me, she says, "I'm parked out back."

"I'll drive around and tail you to the house."

We move around Jet's house in silence. Too worried to go back to Meadow's for any of her belongings, we drove straight here. She's stuck in the T-shirt and shorts she wears to work, has her apron with the tips she made on the shift, and her purse. I don't have much else. My bag that I threw a few things in, but not most of the possessions I care about.

Stuff doesn't matter. It's replaceable . . . well, most of it. For the time being, Meadow is safe and I'm safe. I'm good with that.

I've set the alarm on the house and shut all the blinds, checked the windows, and come back to the kitchen where Meadow leans against the counter with a glass of water in her hands. "Do I want to know, Stel?"

"No."

Opening the fridge, I find a bag of grapes and put them on the counter. My stomach is too upset to eat, but I feel like she needs the option.

The bag is opened, and she's dipping into it. I'm not sure if she's hungry or looking for something to do with her hands. I start thinking about our next move and what our options are, but she interrupts my thoughts. "Rivers knows, doesn't he?"

"Yes."

"You told him?"

"Yes."

"But not me?" She huffs and looks put out. "I don't know what to say or ask or even what to do, Stella. You have to give me something here. I might have lost a job I need based on some unknown that apparently I'm supposed to be afraid of."

"Truthfully, I don't know how to tell you. I can blurt it

out and wait for the judgment or the shock value to wear off or you can try to trust that I know what's best right now." I walk into the living room and sit on the couch. I'm tempted to turn on the TV to be reminded that the world is still functioning normally when ours has been changed forever. "What do you want me to do?"

"I want you to be honest with me. I'm not a kid you need to protect anymore or take care of. I take care of my own life now. Are you in trouble with these people?"

"They're not people, Mead. They're monsters."

"Okaaaaay. They're monsters. So now what? We hide out here for days on end until what? What happens now?"

"I don't know. We call the police? We wait for Rivers to call back?" I stand and start pacing.

"Stella? Are we safe here?"

I hear the wobble in her voice, and when I turn around, I see the tears in her eyes. "I don't know." Reaching into my purse, I find the slip of paper with Rivers's credit card number scribbled down. "And if I don't know, we should go. We can get a room somewhere or leave. We can go to LA."

"I have school tomorrow. Midterms are next month. If I miss two classes, I'll fail." She picks up her purse. "Are you going to work tomorrow?"

"No. I'm not."

"How will we pay for anything?"

I hold up the piece of paper. "Rivers."

With my bag in the trunk and whatever we had on us, we get in the 4Runner and leave our cars behind.

At a stop sign at the exit of the neighborhood, she asks, "Which way?"

"The police. We can't run forever, so we need to go to the police."

"Are you sure?"

Rivers's words from our call earlier come back. *The only safe place is with the police until I can get there. Don't be the hero, Stella. I just got you back. I can't lose you forever.*

"Yes."

Sitting in a room with a table and four chairs isn't as intimidating as the movies make it out to be. Maybe it's because we're not the criminals here. The shortened version of our story warrants a detective to be assigned to the case. So we sit in the pale green room and wait.

Meadow has been pacing and chewing on her thumbnail for the good part of an hour when the door opens. A balding man in a brown suit with a file in his hand enters the room. He references the file before he looks up and smiles. "Sorry to keep you waiting. We're backed up with calls tonight. A full moon always brings out the crazies."

"I can imagine," Meadow says, taking a seat next to me.

He chuckles. "I'm Detective Suthers. I've been assigned to the case. We have someone else already working on this case, so I also wanted him here. He's more familiar with some of the alleged suspects."

The door starts to close behind him when he moves toward the table, but a hand lands on the metal before it can slam shut. I look at the man filling the doorway and jump to my feet. "Brian?" *What the hell is happening here?*

35

Rivers

THE LANDING GEAR touches down in Austin and everyone onboard starts to stir. When we signed with Outlaw Records a year and a half ago, we were welcomed to the family. And when the members of The Resistance say it, they mean it.

The Johnny Outlaw, their infamous drummer, Dex, and the band manager that became ours, Tommy, packed a bag and were on the tarmac before my brothers, Ridge, and I made it to the airport in Burbank. Derrick and Kaz are covering for the band by sticking to an interview in the morning that the band had already committed to.

I have a theory about Johnny and Dex. When they hang with us, they get to relive the wilder side of their youth. They're not old, not at all, but they're old enough to know better. Yet with us, they get to take down a bad guy or two. Other than my brothers, they're my idols and they live up to the title.

A slick black custom van with dark tinted windows is waiting when the private plane comes to a stop. The door rolls down, and I take the lead anxious to get to Stella. We've been in contact, but since she's been talking to the detectives assigned to the case I haven't wanted to disturb her. Fuck, hearing her voice. *I need you.* I hated hearing her fear, knowing I was hours away from her. The bastard has come after her again. *Fuck.*

Once we're settled in the van with Jet sitting upfront, Ridge and me in the second row, Johnny and Dex in the third, and Tulsa and Tommy in the back, we take off. It's after three in the morning, and the hour is wearing on everyone's face. Silence seems to be golden until Ridge asks, "Are we going to the station or the house?"

"The station." My reply is clipped. My thoughts are on Stella. I text her: *Landed in Austin. On the way to you.*

She texts: *Thank you.*

Grateful, as if I'm doing her a favor.

I'm not. She's doing me the favor by keeping that heart of hers safe, that pretty face protected, that soul whole for me. I shift, anxious to get there.

The Crow Brothers aren't strangers to a being arrested, but I think she's managed to find the only police station we haven't been thrown into. When we're buzzed in behind the counter, the female officer's mouth starts catching flies by how low it's hanging. I look back and am suddenly very aware of what this must look like to the outside world. We don't normally travel in a pack like this.

Pointing, she stumbles over her words, "You're Johnny Outlaw, and you're . . . Oh my God, The Crow Brothers. Like, all of them."

I step up to the counter and not wanting to draw more attention than necessary, and whisper, "We're here for Stella and Meadow Fellowes."

She stares at me, and then smiles, wide eyes following.

"You're The Crow Brothers. I've seen you more than a few times."

"Thank you. We appreciate it."

"You play that thing." She starts snapping her fingers as if that will recall what she's searching for.

"A bass guitar."

"Yes!" She points at me. "A guitar."

I'm not sure how to get her back on track, so I repeat, "Stella Fellowes," and hope she knows what I mean.

"Yes." A buzzer sounds. "Come to me. I mean, come on back." Everyone files through the unlocked door, and the other guys take the seats by the front desk. To everyone else, she says, "Don't leave. I'm coming back for you."

Johnny winks. "I'll be waiting."

I see her shiver with giddiness as she squeezes her fists with glee. She stops at the second door down the hall and knocks before pushing a code on the keypad and opening the door. My eyes find Stella, and she flies from the chair. Landing against me with an umf, I hold her as tight as I can without squeezing the life from her. "I love you," I whisper into her hair. Inhaling everything about her scent—oranges and love. I take in the feel of her body, making sure to appreciate that she's here, safe, and in one piece.

Dropping my head to her shoulder, I turn to kiss her neck as soft cries cover my shoulder. I say, "You're okay, baby."

"Now that you're here." Raindrop tears gather at the top of her bottom lids when she looks up at me. As they roll over and run down her cheeks, she caresses my face. "Thank you."

"You don't have to thank me."

"I'm grateful for you."

I catch movement from my peripheral and turn. "What the fuck?"

Brian comes forward cautiously, holding his hand out. "Mr. Crow."

Damn right he knows to address me with respect, but there's no way in fuck I'm shaking his hand. Stella latches onto my arm when my body tenses, and I jut forward. "No, Rivers. He's a good guy."

One arm goes around her waist, and I move her behind me. "A fucking creep stalker is what the fuck he is."

Brian's hands go up in surrender. "I apologize for how I had to act. I've been undercover on this case. I'm Detective Teller."

I'm not sure how to process what he's saying. His words don't feel right. Not when it comes to him. "You broke into her place. Is that a part of the job description?"

"I can explain. You're safe in here. She's safe. Please have a seat and we'll go over everything."

Stella moves in front of me, and whispers, "It's all right. We're all right. Let's just sit down. Please."

Another chair is brought in and set at the end of the small table dividing the two sides. *My girls versus them.* I grab the chair and move it next to Stella's chair. Always on her side. Before I sit down, I walk around to Meadow, who stands and hugs me. I give my little sis a hug and make sure there's not a scratch on her either or I'll take my rage out on *Bri* over there. "You okay?"

"I'm fine. A little shaken and tired, but fine."

The other guy leans forward, offering his hand. "I'm Detective Suthers. I'll be the contact for this case."

Shaking his hand, I say, "Rivers Crow." I sit down and eye Brian. "So he's a cop."

Teller's quick to correct me. "Detective. I was assigned to

this case just over four years ago, put in place at the Rostinal Academy—"

"For?"

He pushes a file forward and opens it. There is an eight by ten of some business guy and two smaller mug shots of different guys. I glance at Stella, who's staring at her lap as her fingers tug at the loose strings of her cut-off shorts. "Who are these guys? What am I missing?"

Brian laughs humorlessly under his breath. "We're really not in a position to fill you in on the details of an ongoing case that has nothing to do with you." Angling his gaze to Stella, he adds, "But Stella said she wouldn't speak unless we included you, and since by law, she doesn't have to, here we are." He taps his middle and index fingers on the two mug shots.

Hearing him utter Stella's name sends waves of rage through me, but seeing how she's folding in on herself, the bright light being snuffed out breaks my heart. When she doesn't say anything, Teller says, "These are the two men who work for Conrad Baird—CEO of a Fortune 500, Austin elite and philanthropist."

"Okay. And?"

"The two men shown here are the ones who do most of the dirty work for Baird. Loan sharks, debt collection, bookie activity, and online gambling. That sort of thing. Some of it legal, most of it not. But that's just the tip of our investigation. He doesn't generally get involved in low-level activity. The practices are in place, and his lackeys run on automation now," he adds and looks at Stella again. *What the fuck?*

"Why do you keep looking at her?" Stella's eyes meet mine, and there's a silent plea I can't read. I cover her thigh with my hand and whisper between us, "What is it? What's wrong?"

Teller inserts himself before she has a chance to answer. "Baird is the one who collected her debt."

Meadow snaps, "Our father's debt."

His eyes shift to her, but I continue to stare at Brian a long second before Meadow's words makes sense. My gaze drops to the large photo as my stomach clenches, firing all cylinders of my blood pressure and shooting it sky high full of anger. The chair skids and falls back on the tiled floor, echoing in the small room. "That's the man who raped her?"

Brian replies, "Allegedly."

"Fuck you, Teller, and your alleged bullshit." I look at Stella who has her eyes closed tight. Meadow takes her hand and holds it between both of hers. "Is this the mother-fucker who raped you, Stella?"

When her eyes open, her gaze darts from the photo, and she nods. Then she turns to look at me. "I'm sorry. I'm so sorry."

"For what?"

"You're upset. I don't want you to be upset."

Kneeling beside her, I say, "I'm not upset with you. I'm upset because you were hurt. Brutally attacked. I'm upset because I wasn't there to help you or stop it from happening. I'm upset because that motherfucker sitting across from you hasn't wiped that smug fucking smarmy grin off his face since I walked in." I shoot Brian a death glare when I stand back up. "Why the fuck are you so happy anyway?"

Detective Suthers stands. "You need to calm down. We understand the distress she's under. We understand you are upset, but you will not threaten us in language or behavior or we'll throw you in a holding cell. Please calmly sit down or leave."

"Do you understand? Have you been raped?"

Teller stands. "You're out of line—"

"I'm out of line? Me?" I turn my hand from my chest to pointing it at his fucking face. "You're fucking out of line, you fucking pervert. You should be in jail for—"

He comes around the table feeling all fucking mighty with that badge hanging around his neck. "Feeling brave, Crow?"

While Suthers stands on guard, Stella stands between us. Pressing her hands against me, the featherweight pressure can't stop me if I want to knock him out, and man, do I ever want to knock him the fuck out. "Please don't do this, Rivers. You have to calm down, or they'll arrest you."

Brian stands with his arms crossed over his puffed-out chest and that shit-eating smug grin. "Yeah, Crow, calm down. And while you're at it, sit the fuck down and learn to listen."

"I should punch your fucking lights out."

He rolls his eyes, and says, "Do it."

"Crow," the guard says, unlocking the cell, "you're free to leave."

36

Rivers

THE HANDCUFFS ARE REMOVED, and I rub my wrists as the door to the seating area is buzzed open. Teller insisted on keeping my hands confined . . . *once he woke up.*

Jet, Tulsa, and Tommy stand while Stella runs to me and throws her arms around my neck. She says, "This is not how I expected our reunion to go."

"Me either," I reply, my blood still boiling. "I think it's best if Teller keeps his distance from me."

"Best for him." Jet chuckles. "Let's get the fuck out of here, ya punk ass."

"In my defense, he told me to do it."

Tulsa shakes his head, but he's chuckling. "Save it for the judge. But a little heads-up, they don't like people hitting cops."

"He's a dirty fucking cop."

Pushing the door open, Tommy says, "Can we get out of here? Everything in here will be used against us."

The van that drove us here is waiting in front of the

station. We pile inside and I lean my back against the window. "Where's Meadow?"

Stella slides across the bench closer to me. "With Ridge at the hotel."

"So this is just going to be their thing when he's in town."

She shrugs. "Meadow claims it's nothing serious."

"So I hear."

The van leaves the lot, and Tommy says, "The guys are sleeping. You'll be happy to know that Teller isn't pressing charges, and the whole event is being suppressed due to the case they're working on with Stella."

I turn to her for answers without asking the questions that fill my brain and make me ragey. Before I have a chance to voice any of them, she rests her hand on my leg. "Don't worry. I'm fine. I only told them I wouldn't work with them if anything happened to you."

"You shouldn't have done that. I can take care of myself."

"You can." She nods, placating me. "But I can too."

"They're using you, Stella."

"If it gets those monsters put behind bars, then I'm okay with sharing my story with the police."

"What else will you have to share?" I shouldn't have said it, but it's out there now.

She says, "We've come this far, but I need your support to go the distance."

"You have me for whatever you need. I just don't want you hurt."

Laughing, she leans her head on my shoulder. "Me either."

"Fuck." I rub my eyes. "I'm exhausted."

Tulsa pipes up from the back seat. "Silver lining—"

"There's a silver lining?" I stretch my arm across the seat

behind Stella and look back at my brother.

"You landed a solid on that asshole's face."

Jet jokes, "We would have disowned you if you didn't."

Reaching over the seat, I hold my fist out. Jet hits it, and Tulsa stretches from behind him to bump. Brothers don't leave brothers hanging.

Tommy groans. "I'm getting too old for this shit."

I lean forward and squeeze his shoulder. "We'll keep you young forever, old man."

"Yeah, yeah."

Covering Stella's hand that's resting on my leg, I angle and wrap my arm around her shoulders. "Sorry about this mess."

Her head rests on my shoulder. "He deserved it."

I chuckle. "Yeah, he did, but I was talking about you having to deal with my arrest when you should be resting."

"I called in, so a substitute could be brought in to cover my classes."

"Good. We need to talk about your job."

"Can we talk after getting some sleep? I don't think I can keep my eyes open much longer."

I hold her even closer and kiss the top of her head. "I think that's best."

With the blinds closed to keep out the day, Stella and I have been lying in this hotel room in downtown Austin for over an hour. I like listening to her sleep except when she whimpers, and then I hold her a little tighter until her breath evens and her heart goes back to steady.

My body is beyond exhausted, but my mind won't rest. I can't get Baird's face out of my head. A bigwig about town raping innocent girls for his own sick pleasure. Fucking hell. That's a front-page headline if I've ever read one. Since I don't know what was discussed after I KO'd Teller, I'm not in on the plan in play.

I'm still trying to figure out how Brian's a cop, yet he treated Stella like he did. He's violated her rights on several occasions. Are we supposed to just accept it, like oh, he was doing his job? How is harassing her and walking in on her while she's naked doing his job?

Fucker.

"You need sleep, Rivers."

"Did I wake you?"

"You're holding me too tight."

I chuckle. "There are worse things, I suppose."

"Yes," she says, lifting up to see me in the dark. "Like getting tossed in a cell for hitting a cop."

"He had it coming, and technically, he told me to—"

"I know. I know. He told you to do it." I like the feel of her body when she's laughing. Beats the crying any day. I like that I'm the one who made her laugh even more. "While you were in the clinker," she starts, "doing time for your unruly and extremely sexy behavior, I was thinking."

Now it's my turn to laugh. "About?"

"What to do next." She pushes up and leans against the headboard. She's still next to me, so I give her the space she seems to need right now.

My eyes have adjusted to the dark since I've been awake the whole time, and enough light peeks through the cracks at the sides of the drapes to see her, watch her, admire her. "What are you thinking?"

She's not fidgeting or nervous. She is contemplative, though, and her words feel measured. "I'm quitting my job. I've been saving every spare penny to put toward a deposit on an apartment with Meadow. She has more than a month left on her lease. Without rent or house bills, I can take the money I've saved and live off it for two months."

Resting on my elbow, I say, "I think—"

"No, please. Let me finish first because you're going to swoop in here and say something chivalrous, and although I love it and you, this is my mess, and I should be the one to fix it. I will still have to pay for my phone and my car and insurance. I'm letting my healthcare lapse because there's no way I can pay for that. I'm selling my furniture and getting rid of most of my stuff, but I also don't want Meadow living alone right now." She turns away from me, toying with her bottom lip.

She's truly amazing, but I can tell this weighs heavily on her, and she's right about me. I do want to swoop in and make things better, easier on her. But she's stubborn. I can offer to help all day long, but she needs to want that help before she'll ever take it. "It's a lot to ask, and I'll make sure to ask your brother as well, but I was wondering if Meadow and I could stay at Jet's house while we figure out our next step."

Next step? *Fuck.* "I thought I would be your next step?"

She slides back down under the covers and faces me with her head on the pillow. "When you think of us, what do you envision?"

"You know what I see. I want to be with you, but I don't know what you see for our future."

"The truth is, I'm scared." Looking at my chest, she traces the star tattoo. "I'm scared of how easily we fell back into us. I'm scared of how I fit into your new life. I'm scared to move to LA. I'm scared to leave my sister while she finishes school. Rivers, the only thing I'm not scared of is loving you."

"You don't have to be scared. I don't want that. I'll be there for you. My brothers are there. Once you get to know Hannah, I know you'll like her, and she went through a similar transition. I know she'll be there for you as well. And Nikki. She's from California. You have all of us to lean on. You have us for support."

"But Meadow—"

"I will help Meadow however she needs or, should I say, lets me. She's pretty independent. She's not going to quit school to move to LA, and she shouldn't. She needs to finish."

"She'll be alone."

"I'm not settled in LA, but it's becoming evident I need to be there. I need you to tell me what you want. If that's me traveling back and forth to be with you, I'll do it."

I watch as she seems to take in my words. "I don't want to lose you again."

"You won't, but I also don't want you moving out of fear or making changes you're not comfortable with right now. I just want to be with you. However that may be. I'll wait until you know what you want, and then we can move forward together."

"You'll wait for me?"

"As long as it takes. You and I, we're what Romeo and Juliet only wished they could be."

"Alive?"

"Wow. Spoiler alert," I tease. "But yes. We have what they were willing to sacrifice everything for." I lean down and kiss the Crow that lies directly over her heart. "Remember that book you told me about under the oak tree?"

She smiles, not just brightening the dark room a little more, but lighting up my life. "Yes. *Until I Met You.*"

"I read it."

"You did? Why?"

"Because you loved it, and I wanted to see what moved you when you spoke of the story." Through whispers and kisses across her soft skin, I recite the lines I memorized for her. "Despite all the water that had passed under their decaying bridge, they stood there, their hearts still beating only for the other. My heart only beats for you, Stella Lilith."

Her lips find mine, and we kiss between more lines from the book that struck my heart and made me think of Stella when I read them. My hand covers her lower back, bringing her closer, and I whisper, "You're beautiful like the stars. You're beautiful like the ocean. You're beautiful like the love I feel for you."

But I stop before we fall deeper into feeling and wrap my hand around the back of her neck, caressing her so she looks up at me. "What is it?" she asks with wide doe eyes. "Where do you see us beyond today or next week?"

Her body molds against mine, and she rests her head on my shoulder. "Right here in your arms. Always."

Before my eyes open, my arms fly wide to the sides only to find the mattress empty beside me. I sit up. "Stella?"

"In here," she calls from the living room. Walking into the bedroom of the suite, she leans against the opening of the door, looking every bit the angel, and smiles. "Good afternoon, sleepyhead." She runs and pounces on the bed before climbing over and looking down on me. "You, sir, have slept a solid six hours. You must have been tired."

Her ponytail swings over to the side and tickles my nose. "We've had twelve fourteen-hour days rehearsing to get the

songs down. And traveling always wears me down." Taking
her by the hips, I roll her to the side until I'm on top. "You're
happy today."

"We got news."

"Really?" I move to the side, the thought of Brian and
this Baird guy ruining my good mood. Sitting up, I plant my
feet on the floor and scrub my hands over my face, trying to
wake all the way up.

"Suthers called to tell me they're closing in on Brown."

"Brown?"

"One of Baird's guys, the one who drove me . . ." Her
good mood seems to fade as she turns her gaze to the ceiling
and then closes her eyes altogether. I want to take every bad
memory she has and destroy it, but I know I can't do that.
God, what she has survived . . .

"Hey, baby, I know you don't want to talk about it, but I
need to know what happened."

"You know what happened. Do the details matter?"

"No, not all of them, but some do."

Moving higher on the bed, she looks at me, and
says, "Okay."

"Are you sure?"

"No, but it's got to be better than living with this alone."
When she filed the report with the police last night, she told
them the story, but I know she left out the gory details. She's
supposed to go back to discuss with a female officer today,
so maybe this will help her clear the way to talk about it
later.

I lie on my side, resting my head on her lap, and take
over staring at the ceiling so she doesn't feel like she's in a
spotlight or under interrogation.

Delving inward, the window to her soul closes, her eyes
losing the smile she had moments earlier, as she shares her

story. "Car seats . . . Toyota Camry . . . Shower and hair clip . .
. Brown. Yellow. Boss . . . I was standing there while they
stared at me. Slapped for smarting back and then . . . X
marks the spot . . . When it was over, my hair was yanked
until I was standing, my head tilted back farther than I
thought it should go. He," she stammers, then swallows
hard. "He said if I told anyone that he would cut the crow
from my chest before killing me."

I thought I was prepared.

I wasn't.

I want to throw up. I want to kill. I want to obliterate
anything that monster has ever touched.

Stella takes my hand and tries to unfurl my fisted
fingers. "I love you, Rivers." Under her soft confession, my
eyes find hers, and she says, "I remember thinking I could
handle death because it had to be easier than living without
you." Holding her hand over the top of the shirt where her
tattoo is on her skin, she adds, "You were always with me.
You have always been the inner strength I couldn't see but
felt. I felt you at that moment, that moment when I realized
I never listened. I assumed the worst of the best person
I knew."

"You were so angry when I showed up. You said you
were caught off guard, but something between then and
now changed."

"When I was dropped off at my car, all my will to survive
drained away. I realized it wouldn't matter if he killed me or
not. Either way, I lost you." Her fingers run through my hair,
soothing my head. "All it took was you showing back up to
make me realize I was never going to be whole without you.
So you see? You're not just my next step, Rivers. You're the
only step worth taking."

37

Rivers

"You'll be mic'd the whole time." Brian points at an open file on the table. "It will have a wire that will run from between your breasts—"

A warning growl rumbles through my chest, causing him to sit back in his chair. I'm tempted to give him a matching shiner to the one he's sporting today.

After clearing his throat, he continues, "To a small pack under the waist of your pants."

When he glances at me, I put a stop to this insanity. "You're not doing this, Stella. No way."

"I have to."

"If he was doing his job, you wouldn't have to." Leaning forward, I ask, "This is all conveniently putting the focus on one monster, but what happened to the report she filed against you?"

Suthers steps up to the desk and leans his palms down a short distance in front of me. "Listen to me, Crow. We don't have to answer to you. That you're even sitting here is by the grace of Detective Teller's mercy. So you should be a little more grateful."

"Picture this." Verifying he's wearing a ring, I look down at his hand. Yup, a scratched gold band too dull to shine is squeezing his sausage finger. "Your wife is taking a bath, reading a book while relaxing. Maybe even having a glass of wine after a rough day. She gets out after soaking and wraps a towel around her body while going to return the wine glass to the kitchen. When your wife walks into the living room, she finds an intruder standing there staring at her. What would you advise your wife to do?"

Turning to Teller, I can see the look exchanged—the one where Suthers knows what Brian did was crossing a line and creepy as fuck, even if it was legal through a bullshit lease. Standing up, Suthers says, "He has a rental agreement that gives him the right to enter the premises at any time. Since Ms. Fellowes gave her notice to evacuate the premises by the end of the month, the landlord has a right to take inventory of what needs to be fixed or charged before returning the deposit. Also, to prepare the space for the next renter."

I slow clap him as he walks to a tall dented gray filing cabinet in the corner. "Textbook memorization. Bravo. But again, imagine if that had been your wife. Would you be defending her *or* the fucker who broke in to catch her naked?"

Brian stands abruptly. "I was not breaking in to catch her naked. I had no idea she was even home."

Stella scoffs. "So my car out front gave you no warning before you took your master key and walked inside? Why didn't you knock? I would have heard it. I was reading. I wasn't listening to music, and the TV wasn't on."

Suthers slams a filing cabinet shut. "Enough. We're not here to discuss that. Stick to this investigation."

Standing up, I hold my hand out for Stella. "I think we're done here."

She's hesitant but takes my hand and stands. Holding me in place, she says, "I have a chance to put a monster away for good."

"Baird?" She nods, so I say, "I'm not convinced one testimony will do anything other than make you a target for revenge."

Her face goes pale, and she moves closer. Lowering her voice, she says, "I'm not the only one."

"What are you saying? Have others come forward?"

"No, but it was too planned out. Steps to follow. A routine in place before I got there. Those men had done that before, telling me to shower, not to get my hair wet, wear the robe, and put my shoes back on. Everything had a place—the robe, the hair clip, the perfumed body gel. Me, standing on the X."

The fucking X. *Sick fucks.*

"What do you want me to say, Stella? You want my permission? I think it's bullshit Teller would even put you in this position. Secondly, he's not a good guy. He's an asshole hiding behind a badge." I step closer and lean in to add, "I don't trust him any more than he trusts me. The difference is he knows I would never put you in danger to get something I want. He's using . . . no, he's been using you for over two years now. He's been undercover and has jack shit on Baird. You fall right into his lap as if . . ." My gaze rises over her head to meet Brian's. *What the . . . No way. Surely, he didn't seek her out. Fucking hell. I don't believe it.*

"You knew. You set her up. You let her get tangled in this mess to save your ass because you had nothing else on him."

Stella holds my sides. When I look down, she narrows her eyes, and asks, "What are you talking about?"

"These 'loan sharks,' how'd your father first come into contact with them? How'd he find them?"

"I don't know."

When I look back at Teller, Stella turns to look over her shoulder. To him, I ask, "Why do I get the feeling you know the answers to these questions?"

Stella's arms wrap around her waist, and I reach for her when she seems unsteady. Her mouth is open before she asks, "Brian? Please tell me Rivers's theory is wrong. Please tell me it's crazy, and he's grasping at straws." When Brian looks away from her, I see the first semblance of regret working its way onto his face. He's about to shatter her world, and there's nothing I can do to hold her together.

I wrap my arms around her from behind in a bad attempt to keep her together, but her body tenses. The meek girl is gone, and the strong woman emerges. When she steps forward, I let her go, finger pointing until she's toe to toe with him. "Tell me Rivers is wrong." Demanding fists hammer down to her sides, and she yells, "Tell me!"

"I can't—"

The slap comes so fast that none of us saw it coming. Brian's eyes open, and he turns back to her with a red handprint emblazoned on his face under the black eye I gave him.

Suthers seems so stunned that he's slow to react but finally does. "You just hit an officer of the law, Ms. Fellowes. I'm going to have to take you into custod—"

"No!" I shout, moving to block his path to her.

"Move aside, Crow, or I'll throw you back in."

I'm ready to defend her however I can. If it means going down again in place of her, I will.

Brian's hands come up, halting Suthers in place. "No. I'm not an officer right now. I'm a friend."

"What the fuck, Teller? A *friend* sets up a female he works with and respects to be vulnerable before a monster? A fucking *friend* does that?" I stand my ground right before her. I see him swallowing heavily, probably trying to come up with some other bullshit comment. If he so much as touches her, I'll take him down again. I don't care if I'm fucking arrested. He'll never so much as touch a flyaway strand of her hair, or he'll be paying the fucking piper.

With his eyes still on Stella, remorse seeps into his tone. "I'm sorry, Stella."

"Sorry?" The word is strangled as she struggles with the truth. "You're sorry?" She takes a step back and lands against me. "I was raped, but before and after that, I was mentally tortured by the thought of what they would do to my little sister. Two days ago, that monster told me not only would his son have my sister as a reward for straight As, but that I would be his extra credit because of my 'skills' of being fucked over a desk while two other men watched."

They want to go after Meadow too? Fuck. This isn't about me, so I focus inward, remembering how my heart beat strong this morning when she looked down at me with light, life, joy, and possibility in her eyes. She looked at me like I was everything she ever wanted and everything she ever needed.

The sage green of her soul is calming, but the raging, choppy waters of her sea can be deadly. Her breath is ragged, and she turns to walk around me. Pacing the office of Detective Suthers, she stops, and says to him, "An eighteen-year-old student of mine, taking after his deranged father, grabbed his crotch and told me that his favorite part of the video always makes him blow his load."

A video? Fury rushes my veins. My heart goes cold, no beats left to be found. Hearing that my everything was treated like she's nothing destroys what little good I had left. I will destroy him like he tried to destroy Stella. Whatever it takes. All my money, my brothers, The Resistance—every connection I have, I will use to help me take him down for good.

Her voice shakes, and with a barely repressed sob, she says, "Want to know which part? It's when I look up. He even froze the frame so I could see the pain on my face. That's the part he gets off to on the regular. What he doesn't realize is that look in my eyes was death. Death consumed my thoughts as I prayed to be free from my body forever." She spins and walks toward the door.

Seeming to come back into herself, she puts a hand on her hip. "I survived, but I live with that torment every day of my life. We're not friends, Brian. And if Rivers is right, I have a feeling you've broken a few laws yourself. This is your chance to take me down because once I walk out that door, you are a mortal enemy to me, and I will do everything in my power to bring *you* down."

Holding out her wrists as if they're going to slap handcuffs on her is a nice touch, but we all know it's not going to happen. He needs her help on this case too much. With my eyes back on Brian, I nod toward Stella. "She pretty much covered everything for me as well. Last chance, Bri. Take us or leave us, but you'll never be rid of us."

Suthers sighs, and as if he's tired of defending the indefensible, he mumbles, "Making a threat against an officer breaks code—"

Teller stops him once again. "It's fine. She has a right to say that to me." Holding eye contact with Stella, he adds, "I was your friend even if you don't believe it."

"I *don't* believe it," she replies, turning curtly, then she opens the door and walks out.

"That's too bad, Stella. We could have made things happen together."

Suthers says, "Detective Teller, I'd advise you to keep this investigation on track by keeping your personal opinions to yourself."

"I don't think Detective Teller can hide his bias toward my girlfriend to himself." I walk to the door.

"Fuck you, Crow."

My back is still to him, but I'm tempted to flip the bird and leave on that gracious note. I just can't seem to make my feet move forward. Instead, I find myself turning around. "Ya know, *Bri*. I was taught to respect my elders, but you're making it really fucking hard to walk away right now."

"I'm not your elder, fucking scum. I'm thirty-five."

"Whoa," I say, nodding my head. "You have some fucking nerve. You set Stella up and call *me* the scum?"

Stella tugs at my belt. "He's not worth your breath, Rivers."

I'm about to leave but go for one last dig. "Also, I took you for older, you fucking troll."

This time, when I turn around to leave, Stella not a foot in front of me, Brian calls from the office behind us, "You're fucking lucky I didn't press charges."

"Fuck you."

"What?" Brian yells when he steps into the corridor. "No please or thank you?"

Stella stops so fast that I run into the back of her. Catching her by the hips, I ask, "What?"

With her back to me, she tilts her head to the side as if she heard wrong. "What did he say?"

"Fucking hell, just bullshit."

"No, Rivers. Tell me. Tell me exactly what he just said."

"I don't know. Um, I'm lucky he didn't press charges, blah. Blah. Not grateful."

"No please or thank you?"

"Yeah, that."

"We have to go. Now."

38

Stella

I RIP the page from last year's yearbook and toss the book to the back seat. With my hand on the door handle, I stare at the apartment building in front of me. It's worse than I expected, and I thought my expectations were pretty low. Nothing about this place has meaning to me. Not even the man inside.

Rivers asks, "Are you sure you want to do this?"

"I am. But please wait here."

Running his hand through his hair, he swallows his natural reaction, too controlled when he turns to me. "You're asking me to let him get away with hurting you. That's impossible."

"He doesn't know what happened to me."

"He should!" he shouts, hitting the steering wheel.

I reach over and touch his forearm with care before I shift closer, the cup holder and console under my hip. "Kiss me, Rivers." I set the paper down and touch his chin, encouraging him to turn my way. "Please. Kiss me."

His gaze finds mine just before our lips caress in a soul-searing kiss. It would be easy to forget this mess and fall into our bubble of love again. But we can't, and we both know it. Until it's settled, we will never feel safe. So when we part, I don't move away quickly. I stay, our lips lingering together before he says, "I'll stay here."

I smile, a happy side effect of loving him and feeling how much he loves me. I kiss his cheek before grabbing the paper and getting out of the car.

Knocking twice, I stop and listen to hear if he's home. I hear his grumbling before I see the peephole go dark and the two locks unbolted. The door swings open, and my father says, "Stella? What are you doing here?" He peeks out the door and looks down the breezeway. "Where's Meadow?"

"Hi." I'm suddenly unsure what I should say. "She's not here, Dad. Just me."

"Come in. Come in," he says, shuffling to the side.

I promised Rivers to stay in sight at all times. It was the only way he felt it was safe. "I can't. Can you come outside to talk?"

"Um. Okay." He slips on his flip-flops and follows me to the sidewalk in front of the parking lot. "Is that Rivers?"

"Yes."

His eyes go a bit wide in surprise until he looks back at me with a gentler smile than I remember him having growing up. It's the kind that's been beat down more than a few times in life. "I'm glad to see you're spending time together again." I glance back at Rivers who nods once. "Tell him I see him on the TV sometimes. He's become quite popular."

"Yeah. I'll tell him." Turning so we're standing side by

side, I hold the piece out for him to take a look. "Dad, do you know him?" I point at the principal's photo of Brian.

He does. I can tell by his body language that he recognizes him. He's slow to respond, rubbing his chin as if he's deep in thought. When he looks at me, he says, "He's a principal?"

"Yes. He's my principal."

Scratching his head, he seems lost on this train of thought, so I ask, "How do you know him?"

"Um. Why do I get the feeling you already know the answer?"

"Because I do. I just need to hear you say it."

"Don't go near him. You're too good to get caught up in his world."

"Too late, thanks to you."

Taking a step toward his apartment, he asks, "What does that mean?"

"Tell me how you know him, Dad."

"Poker down at that club in Sequin. The one where I lost the money."

"You lost money. I lost everything."

"I'm sorry, honey."

"So am I. The only way I can fix this is if I know exactly what happened when you met him."

Not five minutes later, I climb into the 4Runner and shut the door, making sure to lock it right after. Rivers asks, "What'd he say?"

"It was a friendly game of poker. Small bills for months. Brian had been watching for over a week before he anteed in. Everyone lost their shirts. They were told to be back the next week to try to win their money back, and they were not given a choice. The houses. The cars. Boats. 401ks were thrown in over the next month. He walked away with five men deep in debt to him."

I stretch my arm to rub the back of his neck as he pulls out of the complex and starts back for the hotel. He reaches over and rubs my thigh. "What are you thinking?"

"I was recruited to Rostinal Academy through the university's placement office."

"Recruited or requested?"

"I don't know. That's the big question."

Besides my sister, I'm most worried about Rivers. Logically, I know he can take care of himself—financially, physical health. But he's a sensitive soul when it comes to the ones he loves, and he loves me. He would give his life for mine, and I for him.

With my feet kicked up on the coffee table of the living room in Johnny's suite, I try to pretend I'm not completely freaking out inside. *I am.* My insides waver between an utter meltdown and surges of anger wanting revenge.

Meadow blends right in with this group of rock stars, even Tommy who has built a fan base of his own from managing living legends and helping others reach the height of fame. I've tried to not freak out that I'm in Johnny Outlaw's hotel room or sitting just a few feet away from one of the most iconic drummers in music today . . . and Tulsa. He's pretty awesome, too.

Jet's come over and checked on me, his character deeper than an old soul's. They're rock stars. Allies. Friends. Brothers. When something happens to one, it affects them all. I've teared up several times over the past twenty-four hours when I see how much Rivers is given. Everyone has come together to be there for him, and he deserves it and more. He extends more kindness than he'll ever expect in return.

While he speaks with Jet and Johnny in hushed voices in the far corner, I catch his eyes on me, checking on me, silently asking if I'm all right.

I am.

When I'm with him. But I worry about another downfall. Not cheating, but the drugs, or drinking himself into a stupor. He's dug himself out from the hole he was once trapped in, but if something happens to me, if I die like his mother did, where will that leave him?

I'm not planning on becoming a vigilante, but what Brian said as we were leaving, the same thing Josh and Conrad Baird said, tells me there's a connection that I can't let go. I didn't trust Brian after the stunts he's pulled with me, but based on Rivers's theory about my father being set up, my gut tells me Brian's working for the wrong side. He's not working for the police. He's working for "the boss." *I'm not sure who I can trust at the police department. Even Suthers could be crooked.*

Turning my attention to Meadow, I watch as she laughs and even flirts with Ridge. She has stars in her eyes even if it's "nothing serious" as she claims. I see the same when he looks at her, which makes me smile on the inside.

I don't know if anything will come of them being together, but it gives me some peace that she's not miserable right now and happily distracted.

Plotting, I think about the first step and how to get out of this room without Rivers being with me. If he knows what I plan to do, he'll be locked away for life for murdering Brian. I don't want Brian dead. I want him to suffer for years to come.

Step one: Get coffee.

Step two: Hop in cab.

Step three: Find Brian.

Step four: Stay alive.

I can't believe I'm doing this. There is nothing smart about this plan or safe, but I sit up anyway, and whisper, "Tulsa?"

He glances up from his phone with curiosity in his eyes.

"I want to get a coffee downstairs."

"Okay." After a quick scan of the room, his gaze settles on Rivers and Jet. "Do you want me to get Rivers?"

"No." I quickly peek at Rivers. "He's busy." Just how I want him. "Anyway, it'll give us a chance to talk."

"Sure."

When we stand and start for the door, Rivers says, "Where you going?"

"Coffee downstairs," I reply, purposely keeping my tone even and on the lighter side.

He does exactly what I knew he would and starts walking with us. "I can go with you."

His concern for me is heart-filling, but I need him to stay. "It's okay. Me and Tulsa will be fine."

Rivers insists, "It's no trouble."

"It's no big thing." Tulsa makes a mistake when he says it. "We'll be right back."

The comment takes him back, hitting him wrong. "No big thing?" He stops where he stands, and the room goes silent.

"It's coffee, bro."

"It's Stella. So it's a big fucking thing to me."

Stepping between them, I say, "It's okay. Calm down. I asked Tulsa to come with me. We haven't had a chance to catch up yet."

Tulsa's entire makeup has always been to react and then

think. Maybe he's maturing or maybe it's his wife, but he doesn't get defensive. It's as if he understands, and says, "I'll make sure she's safe."

Rivers looks at me, then back at his younger brother, and nods. Coming to me, he kisses my forehead, and says, "Be careful."

"I will. I promise."

His eyes search mine a little too long. His hands hold me a few more seconds. He kisses me again as if his whole being knows better than to let me go. "I love you."

"I love you, Rivers."

When he doesn't let me go, I take a step back, pushing out of his embrace. Tulsa opens the door, and everyone in the room watches as I force myself to turn around and leave . . . him and the soul that is begging me to stay.

Raising my chin up, I walk past Tulsa and down the long hall to the bank of elevators. I push the button, and Tulsa shoves his hands in his pockets as he rocks back on his heels. "What are we doing, Stella?"

"Getting coffee," I reply, but I hear the inflection at the end and he does too.

"Are you sure?"

My gaze lowers to the swirly design in the gold, black, and burgundy carpet. "Do you remember the night Rivers and I broke up?"

"It's hard to forget something like that." The elevator arrives, and we step inside. He's testing me every step of the way, and asks, "Lobby?"

"Yes. Starbucks is on the same floor."

Jabbing it, he says, "Just checking."

"I never got to thank you for what you did that night."

"What'd I do?" His blue eyes are full of warmth like I

imagine the deep blues of the Mediterranean Sea, not ice cold like the monsters.

Tulsa Crow always got a bad rap as the wild and carefree playboy. I guess being the youngest of three brothers—not having to be the responsible one and having two older brothers looking out for him all the time—gave him that freedom. After their mom died in the accident, Jet was stuck between being a father figure while fighting to keep his family together and still being a kid at just nineteen. He gave up college and walked away from a full-ride academics scholarship to work full time during the day so he could play music at night.

My Rivers was the lost middle child who carried the blame for his mother's death. In so many ways, that burden still weighs him down. One day, I hope I can give him the carefree spirit of Tulsa and the peace Jet has found. Rivers needs to realize that his family only works because he's a part of it. But today I have to do what only I can.

I reply, "You drove me home."

His signature smile—a little happy, a lot cocky—shows up. "I didn't do anything anybody else wouldn't do."

I laugh to myself, watching the floors end through the glass elevator as we enter the atrium. "You used to call everyone darlin'."

"Now, I only call my wife darlin'."

The elevator stops on the lobby floor, and we walk out, stopping just shy of the front desk. "You were so sweet that night. You let me cry on your shoulder and stayed a few extra minutes until I forced you to leave. I saw who you were then and knew the right woman would see through your act."

"She did. Right through me."

That makes me smile, my heart happy for him. Maybe

because it feels like old times, the two of us falling right back into our brother sister relationship from years ago, but I give him a hug. "I'm so lucky to know you."

He embraces me, and says, "I told her all about you."

The sentiment makes me misty-eyed when I step back. "You did?"

"Of course. There may have been distance and time between, but you've always been a part of the family. Now I just get to see you again."

"You could've always stopped by, but I understand."

The smile softens in the corners, and he looks toward the coffee shop. "Are we getting coffee?" he asks again, knowing we're not.

I shake my head gently.

Taking a deep breath, he looks me over. "I can't just let you leave."

"I'm not asking your permission, Tulsa."

"What am I supposed to tell Rivers?"

"I don't know. I just know what I need to do."

"What do you need to do, Stella?"

"Find the truth."

"Not alone."

Taking another step back and two more, I beg, "Please let me go."

"How determined are you?"

"If I don't leave now, I'll find another way."

He takes a step forward, not to intimidate, but by the look in his eyes, he doesn't want me to leave. "Don't do this. It's not safe, and if anything happens to you, what happens to Rivers? To me and Jet? What happens to Meadow?"

"You'll be there for her. Rivers will make sure she's taken care of. Jet will watch out for her."

"And that's better than you?"

Two more steps toward the door are taken. "No. But I have no choice."

"You have plenty of choices, and you have us to help. That's why we're here."

"Please let me go."

"I can't stop you, but I can follow." When I turn to walk away, not wanting to draw attention as I leave, he says, "I'm right behind you. I'll always have your back."

A loud boom is heard, and I jump, startled as I look up to see Rivers descending in the elevator. I can't hear him, but the look of devastation is enough for me to know that he's yelling no.

"I'm sorry." I run because I know this is the only shot I've got. Tulsa will be there. Rivers on his tail. I'm not doing this alone despite wanting to save them and set Meadow and me free.

I reach the taxi line, and the back door is opened for me. I'm about to duck inside and leave, but I know I can't. *He never stopped loving me. He came back for me. For us. For our future.*

A bad decision on my part could ruin the good Rivers and I have rebuilt. I stand there, staring at the empty back seat because I can't risk my life if it destroys Rivers. "Sorry. I don't need one after all."

When I turn around, Rivers and Tulsa are standing there, right behind me, having my back. And when I move into Rivers's arms, it's not just my back he has covered. It's all of me.

"Going somewhere?" he asks, embracing me in his love.

"Nowhere without you." The top of my head is kissed, and I add, "Brian is working for Conrad Baird."

39

Stella

"Do you know how insane that sounds?" Jet says, walking the length of the couch and then back again. "You can't do this alone, Stella."

"I can't do this with a group of celebrities." Waving my hands around, I'm dumbfounded how they think they'll go unnoticed. "You can't even walk outside without being attacked by groupies. How do you expect to walk into a school unnoticed?" I snort and then begin to stutter as these sex symbols stare at me. "Have you seen you? There's nothing normal about this—visually—like all of you together . . . like this . . . separately or together." I scoff and roll my eyes, muttering under my breath, "I mean, really, you're a band of musicians, not vigilantes." I stand from the couch. "I need to do this alone. I have the key card to get through security, and if Judy's there, she'll let me wait in Brian's office."

"No." Rivers nixes the idea as soon as I say it.

Johnny's large suite is starting to feel small with all these bodies packed in the living room. Somehow, my fate is a group debate. I'm both touched and overwhelmed. Tommy says, "If this Teller guy is the bad cop, maybe Suthers is the good cop. Should we talk to him?"

Dex leans forward. "What if they're both bad? We have security on standby. I'm with Rivers. I think everything that's been suggested is a bad idea. I wouldn't let Rochelle go near danger much less walk into it alone."

Rivers, who is leaning against the windowsill, asks, "Why are we even discussing this like we have options?"

"Because we have options right now," I say, hoping he'll see the only opportunity we have. "If we wait too long, we won't."

Johnny says, "We can't do this. This is dangerous. I've lost one brother. I'm not willing to lose any of you. Let's get on the phone and talk to our attorneys to see what legal options we have."

Dex adds, "Stella is one of us. If she's threatened, we're all threatened." While I become of puddle of goo under his sweetness, he looks at Johnny. "I don't see what a bunch lawyers are going to do about dirty cops."

Standing up, Johnny shakes his head while rubbing his hand through his hair. "If I had a choice, Cory would be alive. If I have to make the same choice regarding any of you, I choose life as well. This isn't some Scooby-Doo caper. This is real shit that can end any of us." He walks toward his room. "Everyone will have security detail until further notice." The bedroom door slams closed, and silence spreads like a fog after his final word.

I don't know who to look at for a follow-up to that. Tommy stands and messes with his phone in his hand, giving Dex a look that only they understand. He then says,

"He's right. We need to keep this legal and more importantly, safe. I'm going to my room."

As soon as he leaves, Dex says, "And people call me the moody one."

Meadow chimes in, giggling, "Johnny's more broody."

When Dex stands up, he says, "I don't know what that means."

She shrugs. "It's a girl thing."

He nods and heads for the door. "I'm catching a flight tonight. One of my kids won their division in the science fair, and I promised him I'd be there for the awards ceremony." Before he walks out, he adds, "We have schools in LA if you're considering moving out west. I'm happy to put in a good word for you." I'm taken aback by his kindness and left speechless while holding my hands over my chest. "If you need anything, Rivers has my number."

"Thank you."

Meadow stands, holding Ridge's hand. "We're going back to our room. Call me later."

Tulsa says, "Guess that's our cue." He comes to me, and when I stand to move toward the door, he gives me a hug. "It may not feel like it, but you made the right decision."

"You're right. It doesn't feel like it."

His low laugh makes me smile. Moving toward the door, he says, "I'd tell you to take care of yourself and Rivers but taking care of yourself is taking care of my brother. Remember that, okay?" He taps my nose. "Boop." Calling over my shoulder, he nods for Jet to go. "We're out of here. Call us later, Riv." He shakes his hand and then pulls him in for a one-armed bro-hug.

We all walk out together, but we turn right to go to our suite as they turn left.

Once we're inside, Rivers says, "We have the entire floor

reserved for our group. Guards at the elevators and exits. You're safe here. I want to keep it that way."

Kicking my flip-flops off, I can't hide my sarcasm, "How long will we be on hotel arrest? One week? A month? Maybe a year or two?"

"You can make fun all you want, but at least you're alive doing it." He moves toward the large windows where the sunset shines in, turning the room a golden hue.

He's a stunning, beautiful man basking in the light. His heart may be heavy, but he's still breathtaking in his anger. He turns around, his face silhouetted in shadow. "Let's get married."

I laugh, not able to take this seriously, not because I don't think he means it, but because it's not the time, and he knows it. "Is this how you always dreamed of asking me?"

"No, but none of that matters. I just want to be your husband and for you to be my wife. I can't care about what others think or will say—"

"They'll say I'm pregnant. I've seen how it plays out. I'll be cast as the villain who trapped you with a child. Is that how you want us to start our marriage?"

Walking to me, he holds me by the arms. "No, but I still want you. Knowing what you've been through, what you endured, and then seeing how you love me so unequivocally despite it all, I'm not deserving. So my motives are selfish. I'm definitely dating above my pay grade."

Slipping into his arms, my most favorite place to be in the whole world, I ask, "How is one of the most famous musicians in the world in love with such a troubled but simple girl?"

"There's nothing simple about you or us. Like our love, you're worth fighting for."

He's worth fighting for too. I was wrong five years ago

when I didn't do that. But now? Now there is only one way I know how to fight, to protect the life I plan to live with Rivers.

But he also makes this so damn hard, almost painful to go through with. I just can't sit around waiting for a lawyer or a hired detective to do their work while these monsters continue to terrorize Meadow, me, and who knows how many countless others. I can't involve these amazing men who are a vital part of Rivers's life. His brothers have families now, and I don't know how far Baird's reach actually is. Will he go after them next?

I won't live my life looking over my shoulder for the boogeyman. He has to be stopped, and I know what I have to do. My mind is made up.

Resting my chin on his chest, I say, "Always remember I love you."

"I don't know what you're planning, but I see the cogs turning in your eyes, and I'm pleading with you, Stella, not only to you as the person who owns me, but as the caretaker of my heart. Don't do anything you know you shouldn't to be the hero. I can't . . . I can't lose you."

I hide my eyes from him and rest my ear to his chest, listening to his usually steady heartbeat quicken. "Always."

———

Rivers fell asleep after mentioning not once or twice, but four times how our floor is a fortress. There's no getting on or off it without security knowing. With that in mind, and wearing black yoga pants and shirt, and sneakers the hotel had sent on request, I check my phone. It's time. I kiss him on the cheek and walk right out of the hotel suite.

Working on a wing and a prayer, I walk straight to the

elevators where three men dressed like secret service sans the sunglasses sit in chairs. One stands when I approach. "Ms. Fellowes."

Interesting. He knows who I am. "Hi." I reach to push the button, but he sidesteps to block it. "I'm sorry. Unless we send someone with you, we've been instructed not to let anyone on or off the floor."

"No biggie. Who's coming with me?"

Another guy, bigger, broader, blonder stands. "I will." Reaching forward, he says, "I'm Looty."

"Looty? That's unique."

"My past caught up to me."

"I don't know what that means, but I know the feeling." The lead takes the vacated seat, and I press the button after he leaves.

"Where are we going, Ms. Fellowes?"

The elevator door opens, and I step inside. When he joins me and the door closes, I press the parking garage level and reply, "On an adventure."

"My apologies, Ms. Fellowes, but I need to make a quick call upstairs to inform our bosses that you're leaving the premises."

"Inform them?"

"Yes, I have to let them know."

"Let them," I say, pitching my tone up an octave until I hit that perfect note of insanity. "I am not anyone's property." I poke him hard in the chest, which actually hurts my fingertip. "You are not my boss and no one owns me."

"Ma'am, I didn't mean to offend you. I wasn't inferring that anyone owns you like property. This is our protoc—"

The door slides open and I see my target, dashing out as soon as he looks down. I practically dive into the car and lock the door. "Go. Go. Go."

The driver hits the gas, leaving skid marks on the parking garage floor. Looty barely hits the car before we're too far-gone. Turning back, he's on his phone with his other hand raised into the air.

The driver makes eye contact through the rearview mirror. "Stella?"

Checking my phone, I see my driver's name and look up again. "Topher?"

"Yes," he says, seeming to relax. "What was that about?"

Rolling my eyes, I wave my hand. "Crazy ex."

"Ugh. I have a few of those." When his car tells him to take a right, he confirms, "Rostinal Academy, right?"

"Yes. Thank you."

"It's a bit early for a school visit."

It's really none of his business what I'm doing no matter if it's three p.m. or three a.m., but since he's mentioned it, it would be suspicious if I didn't say something. "I work there. I'm a teacher. Midterms start tomorrow and my printer at home isn't working. I have to be ready when the students walk in, so it will be a long night, but I refuse not to be prepared."

"That sucks. Do you like teaching?"

"Love it," I lie. Then I pretend to play on my phone, so he leaves me alone.

When he pulls into the parking lot, he asks, "Are you sure you'll be okay?"

The kindness of strangers is never lost on me. "I'll be fine. Thank you." I get out and send a bonus tip and give him the highest rating as I walk to the back door. Digging into the secret pocket of the pants, I pull out my key card and hold it to the security pad. The door unlocks, and I'm in.

The school is highly secure. Every camera in the place

will show I've been here, but I don't care. I'm hoping to be in and out before the alarm company calls. By the time I enter the front office, though, I realize I'm not fast enough. I answer to keep them at bay. "This is Safe Haven Security, can you please identify yourself."

"Sorry for the late-night visit," I start feeding the same midterm lie to this guy. "Stella Fellowes. 569 is my security clearance. I used my card to get in."

"I'm scanning the list. Yes, you're right here. You have clearance. Thank you, Ms. Fellowes, and have a safe night."

I hang up and rush to my classroom to get the universal key I was given last week to meet with the dance committee in the gymnasium at night. Grabbing it out of the back of my filing cabinet, I lock my drawers again and head back to the first floor.

If my suspicions are correct about the money, I need that check as evidence. It will be the key to everything. I'm either right, and this will put them all away, or wrong and back where I started no safer than I was hours ago. It's worth the risk.

After unlocking the door to the front office, I rush to Brian's office. I'm quick to learn that the key doesn't work on his door. I'm not surprised, but I have other tricks up my sleeve.

I pull the key card from my pocket and leverage it into the small space between the door and the frame. It's an interior door so the lock should be fairly easy to pop. When the doorknob turns, and I push it open, I'm shocked how a few online videos I watched this afternoon can teach anybody anything. I still feel guilty for asking Rivers not to join me in the bath, but I knew it was the only time he'd be okay with me being alone. *Safe.*

I rush to his desk and pull the drawers open, rummaging through the files and eliminating them by name first before going through each one. Not that he'll have a file labeled donations for illegal activity, but it's worth a search for something that stands out.

I turn to the file cabinet in the corner and pull the handle, but it doesn't open. *Damn it.* It's locked.

The light comes on, and I spin around. Busted. "Brian?"

"What are you doing here, Stella?"

"I, um," the lie I told the last two guys comes to mind, but he knows better. "How did you know I was here?"

Holding his phone up, he says, "Alarm company. They have to call me as part of the procedure we have in place."

Shit.

"Stella," he starts as he comes closer. Sitting on the other side of the desk where the students sent to see him usually sit, he continues, "I think we got off track with our friendship. Ever since your friend came into the picture, we seem to have lost what we once had."

Still standing where he found me, I eye the desk for anything that will help fend him off to give me a chance to run if needed. I know it will be needed, but my head is playing mind games, toying with the idea that I have a chance to actually get out of this situation alive. "What did we have, Brian?"

"I liked you."

Past tense. "And now?"

He seems to relax under my scrutiny, and a grin appears. "I still like you. I think the sparks we had still exist. Even though Baird's sullied you, I'd still take you."

Oh God. I'm going to be sick. He's not just delusional.

He's dangerous.

Very, very dangerous.

"I don't know what you want me to say." With my thumb, I try to call for help.

Darkness spreads over the lightness of his irises, and he stands. "You push another button on that phone, and I'll kill you right here, and then I'll kill your sister and your father and your boyfriend. Although, Josh has behaved himself, so I think I'll give him your sister to play with first. No doubt your father will love watching that."

The pulled together principal is gone. The upstanding detective is nowhere to be found as hate fills his expression. "Phone on the desk. Now."

There's no room to fight this, and I'll never make it to the door behind him, so I set my phone on the desk between us. With nothing left to lose, I ask, "Did you know I was the daughter of one of your debtors? Did you target him or me first?"

His eyes never leave mine when he angles his head down. The knuckles of his hands whiten as he grips the arms of the chair. "Brown found a bunch of low-level gamblers who felt like bigshots tossing five-dollar chips around like they were a grand. They were easy prey. So easy. I used to run a successful bookie business when I first came out of the police academy. With the connections I made through arrests, I was making money hand over fist."

"How did you end up working for that monster if you were so successful?"

"I discovered when you swim with sharks, you attract whales. Like you, I had no choice. Conrad Baird has bought and paid for half the police force. How do you think I got assigned to his case? Why do you think no charges have been filed after years?"

"And Suthers?"

"No," he says, laughing. "Somehow, that sap still thinks he can change things." He chuckles, and it sounds positively evil. *How did I think this man was good at heart?* "And for the record, I thought I was doing your family a favor by offering you a job. As soon as you graduated, you had a paycheck." Shaking his head, he says, "When your dad drinks, he brags. He used to brag about you, so fucking proud of his daughters. I was the good guy. I was trying to help you and your family out from under the fucking mess your father created." *He believes he's still the good guy? Oh shit. He's more than delusional.*

He sits forward, resting his elbows on his legs while rubbing his hands together. "Your dad wasn't safe until Baird laid eyes on you. You should have never gone with him to sign over the house. Once he heard about you, he didn't care about your father. He didn't care about the debt. He saw something he could make more money off than a three bedroom on the wrong side of the tracks."

"Me." My chest hurts, breathing getting harder in the stifling room. "Is that what you're saying? That you didn't know when I was taken to him?"

"No. Not until after. I found out through Brown. You still showed up at school the next day, acting like nothing happened." A grin begins at one corner and then slides onto the other side of his mouth. "Your bravery is to be admired."

I wasn't brave. I was broken. But I'll never give him the satisfaction of seeing that side of me. Trying to find the man I once thought I knew, I ask, "Was the money worth it?"

"Worth what?"

"My life?" I try to be brave, but I'm terrified, and it was heard in my shaking voice. Standing up, he keeps his eyes on me but doesn't answer. I guess that man is long gone. "Now what?" I ask, dreading the answer because I know how this story ends. He's confessed his sins. There's nowhere to go but down from here.

"Unfortunately, we go for a car ride."

40

Stella

I ONCE HEARD that if attacked, never let the attacker move you to a second location. Your odds for survival go down.

But what if you're living on borrowed time already?

Does the location of your death matter?

Yes.

I'd rather die in my lover's arms than in the trunk of this car.

The hammering in my head causes me to wake up, my eyes bleary as early daylight slips in through the blinds lifted a few inches above the sill. Beige textured paper coats the walls in a high-end design with a polished brass bench anchoring the window.

I squint, trying to remember if this is the hotel or where I am. Moving my arm from my side to behind me on the bed, I feel around for Rivers. When I don't find him, I sit up abruptly, my head pounding from the rush of blood.

"Get up."

I know the voice before I find Yellow sitting in a chair on the other side of the room near the door. On the trust scale, it's sad to say, but I trust Brown more than being alone with Yellow. "Where's Brown?"

"Busy."

Scanning the room once more, I know where I am. My throat hurts as it constricts.

He stands, angered. "The boss is waiting for you."

My body refuses to move, to leave this bed. My head hurts, and my fingers ache from holding the blanket so tight. He charges, taking me down with a blow to the left ear. "Get the fuck up!" he screams loud enough for me to hear in the other ear that's pressed to the mattress.

He's done damage, but it's not my ear that hurts; it's my heart. My body's already gone numb, but I can hear the phantom hum of Rivers's heart next to mine and the feel of his arms around me.

I'm grabbed by the ankles and yanked to the floor before I have time to recover. My side hurts in addition to my ear throbbing. Against my wishes, I'm feeling too much, the pain the least of my concerns.

I move to my feet, and I'm pulled by the arm to the door. Pushed forward against the wall, I feel his dick against my backside. I will not go down without a fight. With a swift swing, I elbow him in the neck, sending him back in pain. I open the door and run right into Brian's hard chest.

Catching me, he wraps his arms around me. "Where are you off to so fast?" he asks with a playful grin as if I'm not a hostage in this house of horrors. How this man was permitted to be around children day in and day out is beyond me. He's just as much monster as Baird. I doubt it will work, but the only thing I can think to do is appeal to his ego. I'm going to hate every single word coming out of my mouth, and I feel as though I'm going to be sick. But I take a deep breath. *This is for my life.*

"I'm sorry, Brian. Your behavior has confused me lately. You've hurt me, but then tell me we could have been something. Do you still believe that? Despite what happened with Baird?"

"Crow is an asshole. You shouldn't have let him touch you. He shouldn't have been able to fuck you in my house." *Oh God. He watched us?* Bile rises to my throat, but I have to push that back.

Yellow goes to grab me, but Brian says, "I'll handle her. Go."

Brian's hold on me tightens, and it reminds me of how he held me in the hallway. That seems so long ago . . . when Yellow is out of earshot, he says, "What are you saying?"

"I'm saying I'm sorry. Sorry that . . . that I confused you. Don't hand me over to Baird. Please help me."

"What's in it for me?"

"What do you want?"

"You know what I want, Stella. I was on your side. I was protecting you. I wanted you, knowing how you chose Conrad over your own dignity."

"Protecting me?"

"Yes," he says, picking pieces of my hair off my face that are sticking for some reason. "I told him I would handle you, take care of you. He agreed. But then . . . well, it's too late now. I can't protect you anymore." He pulls me by the arm down a few doors and stops.

My voice is weak, so weak that I don't even recognize it. I do recognize the door to the bathroom though. "Please don't make me do this. I'll do anything you want, but please—"

"Date?"

Rivers. Rivers. My heart will only ever belong to that man.

Brian starts laughing in my face. "Kidding. It's too late to negotiate." He opens the door and pushes me inside. "You know what to do."

The door is closed behind me, and I stand in the purgatory of cleanliness to prepare for the devil incarnate. I turn toward the mirror and now know why my hair was stuck to my face. Blood from my ear streaks across my cheek, and I lean in to get a closer look. What have I done?

No one knows where I went.

No one knows where I am.

No one will ever know what happened to me until it's too late.

I start the shower and strip off my clothes. There's no point in putting off the inevitable. I clip my hair up after testing how sturdy the plastic tips are. They're too weak and bendable to do any damage. I wash my face. Using the perfumed gel, I cleanse my body, freeing it from the blood, the dirt from where their grimy hands touched me, and free from this world.

No one is going to touch me like they did once before. I'll fight. I'll fight for my life. I pull the clip out and get some of my hair wet because fuck him.

The shower is turned off, and I dry my body. I don't put my yoga pants back on in protest. I've learned that trick won't work anyway. I fix my hair and slip on the heels that have been set next to my clothes on the floor before putting on the robe. I open the door to find Brian still standing there. "Demoted to lackey?"

"No. Making sure none of the perverts here walked in on you."

"And somehow they're a different caliber of criminal than you?"

"Yes."

His answer is direct, so simple but chilling in delivery. I look down the hall, but we're still alone . . . or so it seems. Since he's suddenly feeling so honest, I ask in a whisper, "I want to ask you something, and I need you to tell me the truth. You know as well as I do that I may not walk out of that room once I walk in." His eyes are cast down, his lack of eye contact speaking volumes. "Was I supposed to die last time?"

When he looks back at me, he says, "Yes."

"Then why did I live?"

"Because I promised to keep an eye on you."

"You saved me?"

There's no reply to that question, but he says, "You did everything he never expected. You didn't tell a soul—not your father. Not your sister. Not the police. And as long as you didn't tell anyone, you were safe. He expected you to cry to your father, which would be torture, I assume, for a dad. But you didn't hold it over him." He checks the hall before he whispers, "It was a test that you passed. He wanted to keep you, to sell you to the highest bidder for your loyalty." *To sell me? He's involved in sex slavery? Here . . . the man is evil.*

"I wasn't being loyal. I was living in shame."

"I asked for a favor. The only one I've ever asked for and it was granted."

"Me?"

"You."

"You saved me once, Brian. Will you save me again?"

Dark clouds storm his eyes. "I can't ask for a second favor, or I won't walk out of that room."

"Then there's no sense waiting around for death to show up. Let's go greet the bastard."

When I turn to leave, he takes my wrist, causing me to glance back. For a moment, I think I see the clouds clear, but I have no idea how to read him anymore. "Remember not to ask questions. He hates being asked questioned. You know how this works."

The door is opened, and we walk in. I expect Brown and Yellow to be there, but it's unsettling to only find Yellow. "I know," I say, holding my hand up. I don't want to hear him. "He wants me on the X."

I move around the desk with lead feet unsure of anything that is about to happen. I place my feet on the X and stand there in the robe.

When "the boss" comes in, he's drying his hands on a hand towel that he promptly tosses into a basket near the bathroom. "Ms. Fellowes." He comes to me as if we're old friends, pleased to see me. "How have you been? I've been thinking about you since you had to leave the dinner party early. I hated that you felt ill."

I watch him carefully. He has a good façade, but he slips every once in a while. Those are his moments of weakness when by word or by physically doing something are your only chances to turn the tables. Today, he shows no weakness. "Take the robe off."

With Yellow gawking at me and Brian watching, I stare at the desk in front of me. My hands start shaking and my knees get weak, my guillotine taunting me as I disrobe.

Brian says, "The bird tattoo makes a lot more sense now."

The comment's off the cuff by his light tone, but Baird is swift, angling toward Brian. "Explain."

With his eyes volleying between my tattoo and my eyes, Brian shoves his hands in his pleated khakis. "There's a band called The Crow Brothers." Baird looks back at me as Brian continues, "Her boyfriend is a member of the band."

Baird's eyes seem to light up with some fucked-up delight. "My son likes that band. You can arrange a meeting and tickets."

I didn't know he could be more twisted. I was wrong. The only thing that keeps me from screaming in hopes of waking up from this nightmare is the slip that he's going to let me live.

Baird comes around the desk and runs his finger along my spine. He pushes me forward, a firm hand between my shoulder blades guiding my descent. *Fight.*

"Ow," I whimper when my ear touches the wood.

"Is something wrong with you, Ms. Fellowes?"

Of course, there's something wrong. Like me bent over this desk and you being a money laundering, gambling ring, sex-slave psycho. The fact that I was almost trafficked and somehow saved by the man I thought was the worst I would encounter. That I will never see the reason I breathe again. Or feel his arms around me. So yes, there's fucking something wrong with me. "Yes."

"What?"

"Yellow hit me on the ear. It's still bleeding and hurts against the desk."

His voice aims across the room. "What happened, Yellow?"

"She elbowed me."

He sounds surprised and then laughs. "Elbowed you?"

"Yes, sir."

"But then you laid a hand on my property?"

Me. *Baird's property.* My stomach roils.

Anger's heard in Baird's tone, so this time, Yellow pauses before speaking. "Yes, sir."

The drawer next to my hip is opened, the sharp corner digging into my skin. I don't see what's happening as I lie across the desk waiting to make my move, ready to fight, but I'm assured in my decision.

Gunfire rings out without warning, and I scream, closing my eyes. Just when my eyes reopen, I see Yellow fall to the ground, and Brian yells, "Duck, Stella."

Working on instinct, I slide down to the other side of the desk and bury myself in the opening for the chair. Another gunshot sounds, echoing in the small room. And then one more before Baird slumps against the credenza and slides to the floor, his eyes level with mine. He raises his arm with the gun in his hand, staring straight at me until the life leaves his eyes and his arms falls to the floor.

"Stella?"

I scramble to my knees, slipping off the shoes, and jumping to my feet with the robe in my hands covering me. "Brian?"

Swinging the robe over me as I run, I then drop to my knees beside him. Blood seeps into the cotton of his shirt and spreads wide across his chest. He saved me? "Brian?"

He coughs up blood and gargles, so I help him the best I can, trying to support his head. Then he smiles, and all the smugness from before is gone as he finds the light. "I'm sorry." When he tries to laugh, he spits blood. His eyes find mine, and he says, "He . . . wasn't meant to touch you."

I nod, but I have no words. I'm surrounded by death. I'm surrounded by evil.

Can't get air into my lungs.

"Pray for my soul ... fires ... hell ..."

Prayers won't save his soul.

What do I do? I can't breathe ...

The door flies open, and Suthers rushes in, gun in hand leading the way. "Put your hands up." He scopes out the room, and asks, "Anyone besides you alive?"

I don't know the answer. My vision is shrinking, and my legs feel too weak to stand ...

41

Rivers

Leaning against the cop car, I have my legs crossed at the ankle and my arms over my chest. It's been two hours since I arrived, and I refuse to leave until they release Stella from the scene.

I relaxed once I heard from her. The scene investigators found her phone, and though they're keeping it for evidence, they let her call me on a different one. Once I heard her voice and that she was *okay*, which was bullshit given she passed out for a minute, I breathed a sigh of relief and have been impatiently waiting outside on the street since they won't let me inside to see her.

God, what she said . . . What she did . . . running off . . . I can't believe she risked herself. It makes me furious and desperate to see her, to hold her again.

My brothers were waiting with me until the gathering crowd saw them and started making a scene. A few screams of glee had officers pulling their weapons thinking they were in the middle of another developing scene. They were but not the dangerous kind. Jet and Tulsa signed a few autographs and then left to wait at the hotel with the other guys.

Meadow is at the hotel for safety reasons, and once she heard from Stella, she agreed to stay put for the time being.

Like a vision, I don't trust my eyes when I see an angel coming my way. I push off the car and wipe my eyes. I nearly lost her tonight. I start walking toward her, but there's no way I won't run. I speed up, running toward her as she starts running to me. Right into my arms. I could have lost her again. She could have died or been hurt. Not one second of holding this woman in my arms will ever be taken for granted.

My hands roam her body, making sure she's all in one piece even after setting her down. I look at those big green eyes filled with what I hope are happy tears. I think she's okay. For now. And even though I want to yell at her for leaving me, I think she needs me to carry that burden for a while. So I suck back my anger and go for light. "How are you, Rambo?"

That elicits the laugh I hoped to get. If she can laugh after what she's been through, I know she'll be okay. A crocodile tear breaks free from her lower lid and rolls down her cheek. "I was supposed to die today."

"No. You were meant to live today, or you wouldn't be standing here with me."

She nods while looking behind her, the ambulance's siren blare before pulling around the barricades. Turning back to me when Suthers approaches, she tightens her hands on my sides. I bring her against me and angle toward him, becoming a united front.

He stops a few feet in front of us, his hands jangling keys or change in his pockets from the sound. "I'm not much of a detective it seems."

Stella says, "I think Brian was good at hiding the other side he didn't want people to see."

"I'm sorry I didn't see. It was my job. I just wanted to tell you that I'm sorry you had to go through everything you did."

"You're not to blame." Her arm slides around my back. "Rivers and I have felt the pain that carrying unwarranted blame can do to your soul. I'm alive. No one that died in there today was good." I see through her. My woman with the love bigger than the sun gives him a reprieve so another doesn't suffer like me. I still carry the guilt of my mother's death, but she's right.

I'm not to blame.

That won't take away the pain, but it eases the sting.

She steps forward to shake his hand. When he takes her hand, she covers it with her other, and is determined when she says, "His son has been groomed by his monster of a father."

With the names of the deceased unreleased, a sting was set up to catch Josh Baird before he flew the coup as Suthers called it. When that much money is at play, he could disappear and never be seen again. But as a witness, as an accomplice in his knowledge of his father's operations, he was vital to them to gain more information.

Stella was nervous but was convinced it was the right thing to do. Who says she doesn't wear a cape. I refused to let her do this alone. I can't be in the classroom without blowing her cover, but I can be in the school.

My band, my brothers, my family who extends to Johnny and Tommy all insisted to be here as support despite Stella saying we can't blend in. We're blending into the teacher's lounge just fine, proving her wrong.

I made Stella promise two things: If she felt she was in danger at any point, she would leave immediately, and that when she was ready for the police to come into the classroom, she would FaceTime us so I knew she was safe. With these promises in place, she sent the substitute who had filled in for her today to the lounge to cover the class for her, if necessary.

The sub couldn't be more than a few years older than me. The mug shakes in her hand as she brings it to her mouth, her eyes glued to us. She takes a messy sip and then swirls her finger at us. "Do you always travel in a pack . . . like this? All together?"

"By pack, you mean band?" I look around at Johnny, Jet, Tulsa, Ridge, Tommy, and shrug. "It seems to happen more often than you'd think."

"Can I get a picture?"

Smiling, I wink. "I was just about to ask you for one."

Her cheeks turn bright red. Standing up, the guys and I gather behind her, and Tulsa stretches his arm to get us all in the photo and takes it.

Everyone settles back around the room, drinking coffee while we wait for the action to begin. The sub asks, "So you know Ms. Fellowes?"

"Yes." I try to play it cool, but there's no fucking way I can keep from smiling. "She's my girlfriend, soon-to-be wife." I wiggle my eyebrows.

"Wow. Lucky girl."

Resting forward on my elbows, I say, "Nope. I'm the lucky one."

The screen of my phone lights up, and it's Stella Face-Timing me. I turn to the guys. "Showtime."

When I answer, the phone shows a panoramic view of the classroom. Stella moves back to the chalkboard and continues her lesson. I lean in to try to find the fucker. He's easy to spot—slumped back with his pen, like a dick, poking the side of his cheek as he looks at my Stella like she's there for his personal entertainment. His father just died, but I've lost any sympathy for these psychopaths.

The door swings open and two men—Suthers and a cop in uniform—enter the classroom. Asshole sits straight up when he sees them. Through the commotion, it's hard to hear everything as it goes down, but Suthers holds his badge out as he walks to the prick's desk and stands right in front of him.

When he's told to stand, I rush out of the lounge and up a flight of stairs, taking the steps three at a time. There are a few people in the hall outside the classroom as well as other officers. Working together to put this plan in place, I walk right past them but move to the side when the door is pushed open.

He's walked out by the officer holding him by the handcuffs behind his back. He's struggling and turns to look back over his shoulder. "You'll pay for this, you fucking bitch," the son of a monster yells at my woman.

He has some fucking balls to talk to *my Stella* like that.

My whole reason to live.

Fuck this little fucker.

He never saw me coming. Pinning him to the lockers behind him, I tighten my fingers around his neck. "You'll pay for what you've done, for the thoughts you had the nerve to voice. You'll never fucking talk to her again. Don't even think about her, or you'll never have the ability to use that small dick of yours again."

Just as his face starts turning a deeper shade of red, I

release him. He hacks a lung, but when his eyes come back to mine, they go wide. "What the fuck? Hey! Wait . . . aren't you in The—"

Suthers sweeps him to the side. "Take him away and don't forget to tell him that his father's dead."

The prick's feet stumble, and his head falls forward. "What did you say about my father?"

Another officer takes his other arm, and they move him down the hall. We hear him yelling obscenities at the cops, but I just don't give a shit. Rot in hell, asshole.

Stella comes out of the classroom and nudges my side. Wrapping my arms over her shoulders, I say, "You did the right thing."

"I'm not feeling the satisfaction I thought I would."

"Because you have a heart, unlike that sicko. You've saved a lifetime of women who would have had the unfortunate luck of meeting him. He was like his father, and Meadow was his next target."

She nods, and even though I see how heavy her heart is by the sadness in her eyes, she manages a small smile. "You'll be happy to hear that I'm hanging up my cape. I don't want to be the hero anymore."

Squeezing her tight, I kiss her head and sneak a little ass grab. "I prefer you naked anyway."

I get whacked in the chest and rewarded with the best damn sound in the world—her laughter.

42

Stella

I USED to think that love was easy. My love bloomed for Rivers Crow the day he talked to me in tenth grade. He was easy to like with his charisma and good looks. He was easy to love with his soft heart and kind words. My first taste of true love was loving him. There's definitely something to be said about first love. Sometimes it turns into your forever love and always stays with you.

So despite the terrible role models my parents were on the matter, love came easy for me and stayed for the long haul. We had our bump in the road, though it felt like a cliff at the time, but we're back together and better than ever.

I could say so much about how my life changed this past year, but I don't want to rehash the bad or relive the nightmare. Three months ago, the love of my life decided to take a chance and come back for me.

I'm so glad he did because the one thing I've learned when it comes to love is it may not have always been easy, but he's easy to love.

Rivers's hand tightens around mine. I know he's anxious. I am too. After putting the bad we've both been through behind us we still have a few demons to duel. The problem is that they're all inside his head. I'm not sure how to help battle them other than being here for him.

The car comes to a stop, but he doesn't get out. He doesn't even make a move, not to open the door or look out the window. His gaze stays directed on the bottom of the seat in front of him. "Rivers?" He turns, almost surprised to hear his name, but remains silent. "You're not to blame."

"She died because she felt guilty about not having a cake for me."

"No. That's not true. She wanted you to have the cake. She wanted to give you everything every kid deserves on their birthday. She loved you. You're the boy she used to wake up early just to spend quiet time alone with."

His eyes stay on me, captive to the story. "What?"

"She once told me that on your seventh birthday you woke up early, too early. She knew you would because you always tried to get a peek of your presents, so this time, she woke up early and was waiting for you." I smile as if the memory is one of my own happier times. "She said you were so cute because you thought you were a ninja. When she spotted you, though, you came outside. She held you in her arms as the sun rose. Rivers, she told me she loved that memory so much because for a few moments in time, she had you all to herself and you had her."

This man carries so much guilt that it fills his eyes, hiding the truth from him. "Why did she have to die?"

"I don't have the answer."

"It was a fucking cake. I could have gone without."

"You went without so much already." Running fingers through his hair, I stop and hold the back of his head. "It wasn't about the cake, Rivers. It was about her wanting you to feel special, to celebrate your day."

"If I hadn't let my mother leave, convinced her that a cake wasn't necessary. . . but she insisted. It didn't matter that I was seventeen and practically a grown man. She babied me, insisting that we needed balloons and a cake. It didn't matter that she had just worked a ten-hour shift at one of her shitty jobs. She saw me when she walked in, and I remember the sadness on her face. I remember every moment of that last goodbye and how I begged her to stay."

Will sharing these memories set him free from the pain of them? I'll do anything to help him. "What did she say?"

"She told me to order the pizzas and that she'd be back before they arrived." He tips his head down. "She said to humor her and let her get the cake. I let her walk out that door, and she never returned." His shoulders sag even more as he folds over losing himself in the memory. "She promised she'd return, Stella."

I slide over until I'm practically on top of him, wrapping my arms around his body. "She kept her promise." I rub the spot over his heart. "She is always with you, and she'd be so proud of the man you've become."

The door opens, and Jet stands, angling his head down. "Rivers?"

I kiss the side of his neck and then by his ear, along his cheek until he turns to me and lets me kiss his lips. I cradle his face in the palms of my hands, and say, "She's always been there for you. It's your turn to be there for her."

Rivers nods and steps out of the car, waiting with his hand held back for me. His brother claps his back before walking ahead to catch up with Hannah, Alfie, and his baby, Violet.

We've come this sunshine filled January day to celebrate

her birth, the legacy of her life here to recognize the way she touched all our lives. I've been here before. Actually, many times. I bring flowers every couple of months and lay them on the grass in front of the headstone. I wasn't officially her daughter, but she was a mother in all senses to me.

As we gather around her grave, I read the stone silently to myself:

Louisa Rain Crow

She lived for sunrises.
She lived for her kids.
She had endless love to give.
But most of all, Louisa loved.
She lived and She loved.

"She lived." The words slip out, and that sense of adventure to live life to the fullest fills my soul again. Looking up into the warmth of his eyes, and say, "It's time to grieve and let go of this pain you carry with you every day. It's time to live, Rivers. Just like she did. She lived for every day she got to be with you."

Rivers takes my hand again and says, "And loved. She loved so big like you."

We didn't visit back in November on the day she died. Instead, we celebrated Rivers's birth with a party, family, friends, balloons, and cake because he deserves the sweet life his mother always wanted for him.

And Meadow and I finally got to meet Holli, Johnny's wife, because she hosted the party at their LA home. She's quite extraordinary and made me feel right at home. Sipping on margaritas, Rivers nudged me and asked, "What do you think about moving to LA?"

While spending time in the California sunshine, I realized it wasn't teaching I hated. It was knowing I wasn't helping anyone that changed my view. It was being attacked and believing I made that choice. It was catering to spoiled brats and being taken advantage of that ruined everything. I've walked away, taking a break to figure out what I really want to do. If that's teaching, I can teach anywhere.

Finding happiness again gave me a new perspective. Finding love with Rivers again gave me the life I always dreamed about. I wasn't me without him, and he's not him without me. He was right when he talked about my blood flowing through his veins and his through mine. We're just no good apart. The fairy-tale version would say we're meant to be.

I see it a little differently.

We *are* meant to be. There's no denying that, but what we created together is our own destiny. I turned to him, and said, "I wouldn't have it any other way. If you're in LA, I want to be there too."

"Too," he repeated with a chuckle.

"Too much?" I teased, setting down my cocktail.

Taking me by the hips, he faces me. "Never too much."

There are kisses, and then there are kisses that Rivers gives. "God, I missed these lips on me."

"I can fix that."

"I thought you had?" I ask, my arms going around his neck.

"Nope. I'm just getting started."

EPILOGUE

Rivers

THERE'S SO much to be nervous about, but Stella isn't one of them. In front of millions of people watching the music awards live and in an audience of a thousand or more, we listen as our third category—Record of the Year— is announced.

Anywhere you look in the venue, the biggest bands in the world, including The Resistance, our rival nominees, fill the seats around us.

Around *us*. I still struggle to comprehend how we're actually sitting here as though we belong with these great musicians. I look over my shoulder, half expecting to find security coming down the aisle to remove us as if we're impostors. They aren't coming, and I settle in my seat since I know we won't win against these other amazing bands.

That nomination cliché about being honored just to be here holds true. This feels like a dream come true. Until another dreams happens. "'In Time You'll Be Mine' by The Crow Brothers, off their debut album, *Austin Nights*."

Stella's shoulder bumps my arm. "Rivers."

"What?"

"You won, babe."

"What?"

She starts laughing and shoves me. "Go. Your brothers are already out of their seats."

Huh? Checking for Tulsa, I find his seat empty. Over the clapping, Nikki starts laughing. "Get up there, Rivers. You guys won."

I stand without thinking but turn back to look at Stella. "Love you."

"Love you more. Now go get your award."

Ridge chuckles, still waiting on me to move. With his hand patting my shoulder, we move along the aisle past Nikki and Hannah. All the members of The Resistance are there with their wives, and then Tommy at the end. They give us a standing ovation as we walk by, patting us on the back to congrats.

Since Outlaw Records produced our album, this win is equally as much theirs as it is ours. We all make it on stage, and Jet thanks our family and friends, our band families— The Resistance—Nikki, even the other members of Faris Wheel—who aren't there. This year. But I have no doubt will be here next year.

Tulsa takes his moment in the limelight. In true Tulsa fashion, he tells everyone to be ready for the next record, and that it's going to blow everybody away, which earns him a goodhearted laugh. Ridge steps up to thank the fans and everyone who supported the album and last summer's tour.

I don't need the microphone for the person I want to thank. Her seat is right next to mine this time. She's not shoved in the back but celebrating our victory with tears in her eyes and her hands clasped in front of her mouth.

Before her tears have a chance to fall, I jump down and run back to the second row where our seats reside. There's fifteen seats between me and the woman I live to love and not enough space to get to her fast enough.

Tommy looks up at me from the aisle seat and asks, "What are you doing, Crow?"

"What I should have done years ago." I step up on the armrest of his seat and start my trek back to Stella. "Watch out. Coming through."

I race the tears, but they fall too fast for me to catch as she watches me come back to her. Landing on my feet in the space in front of my empty seat, I hold my hand out. "Rivers?"

When she stands, I kneel before her on one knee, causing her tears to really start flowing. As much as I want to wipe them away and kiss every streak down her face, I stay.

The cheer of the crowd disappears when I kiss her hand. Looking up into the calm green of her eyes, I say, "I've loved you since before I knew you. You became my friend and then the best of those. You became my girl, and then I had the honor of watching you turn into a woman. I've experienced the worst of life, but in your arms, you made me see I had everything I'd ever need. You loved me when I was a scrawny kid. You loved me through the bad times and provided the solace I craved. You own my heart, captivate my soul, and I will never love another like the love I have for you. As a man willing to bow at your feet, to honor you every day for the rest of my life, I will forever be yours faithfully. Star of my night. *Star of my life.* Will you be my wife? Marry me, Stella Lilith."

She wipes a tear from her cheek, and with the prettiest damn smile I've ever seen residing on her sweet lips, she touches my cheek. "I've waited my whole life for you, Rivers. There's not a day I want to spend without you in it. You're my best friend. My lover. And now you'll be my husband. Being your wife will be an honor I'll never take for granted." Hearing the answer I want, I stand and pick her up in my arms. Hovering above me, she says, "Yes. Yes. I love you so much."

The audience erupts in more cheers as I kiss the woman I loved since I was fifteen. I kiss her for the years we had together. I kiss her to make up for the years we spent apart. I kiss her. I kiss her. I kiss her, grateful for the years we have ahead.

And then I pull the ring from my pocket and slip it on her finger. Nikki and Hannah helped me pick it out. Hannah said two carats. Nikki said four. I went with three. The compromise made them happy, and by the look on Stella's face, I did well.

Stella sits in the middle of the living room of the house we're renting down the street from Jet sorting through a box. Meadow and Ridge arrived this morning after driving Stella's stuff from Austin to LA.

They're not currently speaking to each other. I'm not sure what the spat is about, but Stella and I both decide to let it be. They have issues, whether they're serious or not, and one day, they'll have to deal with them.

She pulls a book from the box and holds it up. "Look, Rivers."

Glancing up from the strings, my fingers still on the guitar I've been playing. "*Pride & Prejudice*."

"This is the book I was reading when you talked to me

the first time under the oak tree." She turns it over in her hand a few times and then runs her hand lovingly over the worn fabric cover.

It's how she treats the things and the people she loves— lovingly. "I can buy you a first edition if you want."

"I don't," she says, smiling as she admires her copy. Holding it to her chest, she meets my gaze. "This one has more value than any other ever could."

I start to play a song I wrote for her that made it onto the new album, and she watches me sing from my soul just for her. Something I've noticed that's changed since she moved out here is that she doesn't read sad books anymore. Having experienced more than enough sadness for two lifetimes, every day she chooses happy.

An envelope left behind on the table catches my eyes. "What's this?"

"Money I owe Meadow."

"For what?"

"A silly bet we made once."

Now I'm intrigued. "What was the bet?"

She clams up for a second and then tries to deflect. "Here's the other book, *Until I Met You*."

"Oh no, you don't." I'm on to her. "What was the bet?"

She huffs, exasperated and clearly not wanting to fess up. When her eyes peek up under her dark lashes, she says, "Meadow bet me five dollars that we would end up back together."

For dramatics and a little guilt mixed in, my mouth falls open. "You bet against us?"

"It was a big mistake on my part, but in my defense, I never expected you to show back up looking as sexy as you did." Waving her hand up and down, she giggles. "How did you expect me to react? You're hot."

"You knew what I looked like before I ever showed back up. You said you had stalked me online."

"Stalked is a strong word. *Accurate*, but strong."

I set the guitar down on the couch and go to her. "C'mon, I want to show you strong."

"Are you going to let me watch you work out?" She jumps up excitedly, making me laugh.

"Yes, I want you to keep your eyes on me the whole time we get a good workout in." Grabbing her, I flip her over my shoulder and slap her ass as I carry her to the bedroom.

I toss her onto the mattress, and she immediately starfishes. "Take me, I'm yours."

"Not quite. But as soon as you say I do, you're mine forever."

"I'm already yours forever. The rest is just legalities."

"So sexy when you talk teacher-ese to me. Will you wear the glasses?"

"Only if you'll use the ruler."

Sliding my hands into the front of my jeans, I try to ease the pain as the denim gets too tight. "Fuck yeah, we're using the ruler."

While she scrambles to the nightstand, I take my clothes off and grab the box out from under the bed. I watch as she gets naked and lies there waiting for me. Climbing onto the bed, I hide the box behind me until I can set it out of sight above her head. I hover over her positioned exactly where I want to be, and then push in just enough to tease before I stop again. When she opens her eyes, she says, "I'm ready."

I set the box on her stomach. "Open this first."

"What is it?" she asks, looking at the box as she holds it above her head. The velvet lid is lifted, and her eyes go wide. "Rivers. Oh my God. They're beautiful."

"They're real pearls. You never have to wear fake ones again."

Taking the string of pearls in her hands, her eyes return to mine, as she laughs lightly. "Is this part of the fantasy?"

"Yes, but not the teacher one."

Her smile is so genuine that my heart begins to pound. "Will you put them on me?"

We're in a compromising position, but I'll never deny one of her requests. We angle up enough for me to balance on my knees and elbows. I undo the clasp and wrap the pearls around her neck, fastening it again. She runs her hands along the necklace and lies back. "How do they look?"

"I've never seen a more beautiful sight in my life. The pearls aren't bad either." I wink and then sink deeper. Her body is open like her heart for me.

Mine.

My world embracing me.

Leaning down, I kiss my fiancée, and then whisper, "You're everything to me." My lips touch hers again, but this time, I taste, running my tongue along her lower lip. "My whole life wrapped in a hot as sin present just for me."

Sliding her hands under mine, I fold our fingers together and raise them above her head. "Take me. Take all of me."

I do because when it comes to her, I'm a selfish bastard.

"Rivers?"

Stella calls from the living room, another box open in front of her as she continues to go through her stuff from the move despite my protesting. I could have lain in bed with her all night . . . or done more if she was up for another round. After washing up our dinner dishes, I lean on the counter in the kitchen. "What's up?"

"What's this?" she asks, holding up a brown answering machine.

"A relic." I laugh. "Need more wine?"

"Need? No. Want? Yes. Please," she says, giving me a smile. I walk over with the bottle and top her glass up. "Thanks. But for real, this isn't mine. I never owned an answering machine."

I take another look at the machine she sets on the coffee table and stiffen. "Where'd you get that?"

She shrugs. "I don't know. It was in this box. There are some of your things in here, too. A trophy . . . photos from elementary school . . ." The blood rushes in my ears as I stare at the machine. "You were so cute. Here's your crown . . ."

"That's a box from my mom's house."

"Oh." She stops and looks at the contents. "That would make sense." When she looks up at me, she laments. "I remember now. When I threw out your stuff after 'the incident' I couldn't throw away this box that was left behind. I didn't find it until I moved from that apartment." Her fingers are still in air quotes when she asks, "What's wrong?"

"After her death, we got rid of almost everything. We were stupid kids who didn't know how to appreciate things. But that's my mom's answering machine."

Her voice.

I bend down and pick it up. Lifting the cover, the tape is still intact. I walk to the counter in the kitchen and plug it into the socket. The lights come on and a loud beep sounds before the tape starts spinning and then stops abruptly. The number one flashes on the screen and keeps flashing.

Stella's hand warms me as she stands beside me, rubbing my back. I take a deep breath and then exhale before reaching forward and pushing play. "I know you don't want a cake or this hoopla to celebrate your big day." *My mom.*

I push stop and drop my head to the cool marble, closing my eyes and remembering how beautiful my mom looked that day. After a long shift, she gave me nothing but big smiles and happiness, willing to do anything to make me smile in return. *Did I?*

"Are you okay, babe?"

I'm not sure if she can see me, but I nod. "I smiled. When she was walking out the door. I remember. I smiled for her."

She asks, "When was this left?"

"When she was driving home from work. I never heard it. I walked in from being with you that day, and she got home shortly after I did. Tulsa was in his room, and Jet was coming over for dinner. She always left messages for me because I was the only one who would check the machine, but I didn't that day."

Stella stands quietly still rubbing my back. Raising my head, I push play again, bracing my palms to the hard surface, and listening to my mom from her last day. "But you deserve the hoopla, my handsome man, because I won't get to spoil you when you're away at college. I'm so proud of you. So proud to be your mom. Anyway, I'm on my way home from work now, so I'll see you in about twenty minutes. Sorry I've been working a lot more lately and not gotten as much time with you. Sunrise coffee date with your mom tomorrow? See you soon. Love you forever." A tear hits the top of my hand when I close my eyes again.

The message ends, and Stella turns me, wrapping her

arms around me. I hold her against me, finally free of the burden I've carried with me. I got more than a sign. I got the words I prayed for, begged to hear, the words I needed to be freed from the pain that tried to bury me.

She loved me.

She was proud.

She was also right about Stella. I say, "She told me that one day I should marry you."

"She was a smart woman." The light, happy tone of her voice makes me grin.

I chuckle while inhaling her sweet orange scent and remembering that day Stella shared her lunch with me under the oak tree. Miracles happen in mysterious ways, but it's no mystery that the star of my life is the one who helped me see that I have everything I'll ever need right here in my arms.

Her hand slips into mine, and she rests her other on my shoulder as mine finds her hip. Although no music is playing, we start dancing in the kitchen together, and ask, "What do you think about having a couple of kids?"

"I think we should plan the wedding first."

I cock an eyebrow. "I thought the wedding was just legalities?"

"Being married to you will always be more than a piece of paper."

"So that's a yes to starting a family?"

"Wait, what?"

I spin her and then take her hand, pulling her back into the hallway that leads to the bedroom. "Come on, it will be fun."

"You are so much like your brothers."

"Let's not talk about my brothers when I want to talk about being inside you." Her head goes back when she laughs, her silky brown hair dipping almost to her fine ass. "Or better yet, let's not talk at all. I have plans that include my mouth on your body." I reach around and hold her by the head and the ass, bringing her to me. "How'd I get so lucky?"

"There was no luck involved. You owned my heart the moment you said, 'Hi, I play guitar.'"

I kiss her before I pull back to look in her green seas that bring me peace. "And together we created our own destiny."

THE CROW BROTHERS

If you loved spending time with Rivers Crow, make sure to meet his brothers and bandmate in their own novels.

Jet Crow in Spark.

Tulsa Crow in Tulsa.

Dave "Ridge" Carson in Ridge: Coming September.

———————

Turn the page for a sneak peek of Jet Crow in Spark.

JET CROW - SPARK

Prologue

Subtle scents of cinnamon mix with the taste of whiskey on her skin. I lick her from collarbone to the back of her ear, her moans enticing me to take more than a gentle share of what I want.

I'm well past hooking up with groupies, but something drew me to the beautiful brunette. Under the bright spotlight of that stage, my eyes found hers as I sang about finding the missing piece of me. Maybe it was the way she pretended not to care—catching my eyes and then turning away as if she was too shy to come speak to me, but too good to be bothered. It didn't matter. I was already caught up in her as much as she was caught up in me.

The set ended, and I made my way over to the mystery woman, the one who hid in the dark of the bar just as two shots were served. I took the shot of Fireball and then took her home shortly after.

Fuck. She feels good.

Hard little body, but soft in all the right places. Tits that fill my large hands and legs that spread enough for me to squeeze between her thighs. I bet she wouldn't reach my shoulders in heels. Speaking of, "Keep them on."

I like the feel of the leather against my lower back, the hard heel scraping across my skin when she tries to power play me by tightening around my waist and pulling me closer. I didn't ask her to my bedroom. I didn't have a chance. What started out as laughing while we shared a two a.m. snack of Cheetos, hummus, and whiskey turned into me eating her as a snack on top of my kitchen counter. I don't ever do that with a one-nighter, but damn if she didn't make me want to break more rules with her.

She kisses me like a woman in need of water, taking as much as she wants while pressing her heels into my ass. The heat between us emanates until I'm dragging my shirt off to try to cool down.

I knew she was different the moment she opened her mouth back at the bar. "You sing rock with so much soul. Who hurt you?"

"No one gets close enough to do me any harm."

"That's a pity."

"It's a pity I've never been hurt?"

"No, it's a pity you've never loved anyone enough to get hurt."

My heart started beating for what felt like the first time as I looked into her sultry eyes. I could blame the booze, but I can't lie to myself. She had me thinking twice about things I never considered once before.

Who was this woman?

Even with our stomachs full, we weren't satisfied. She dragged me by the belt down the hall to my bedroom. Her clothes were off and mine quickly followed before we tumbled into bed.

Fast. I want to fuck her fast and hard, but every time our eyes connect, there's such sadness found in her grays that I slow down. Wanting her to hold the contact, I cup her cheek. "Hannah?"

Her eyes slowly open, the long lashes framing the lust I find between them. "What?" she asks between heavy breaths.

"Are you okay?"

"I'm good."

"Just making sure."

She runs her hands up my neck and into the hair on the back of my head. "I'm sure." Pulling me down to her, our mouths are just a few inches apart when she whispers, "I want you. I want to do this."

Shy isn't something I'd call her, considering we were in my bed two hours after meeting. I like a woman who knows what she wants, and Hannah knows. And fuck if it isn't a turn-on that she wants me.

I nod before kissing her, getting lost in the soft caresses of her tongue mingling with mine and the feel of her nails lightly scraping my scalp as she holds me close.

We don't know each other, but I already know when I slip my fingers under the lace and into her wetness, she purrs for me. When I kiss behind her left ear, her back arches. When I press my erection against her to seek relief, her kisses become more frenzied.

When I slide my bare chest down hers, leaving a wet trail of kisses and taking the lace that divides us down as I go lower, her breath audibly catches. My body reacts—hardening for her, craving her.

Reaching over, she takes the glass of whiskey on the nightstand and sips, her eyes staying on mine as I slip the thong from her ankles and spread her legs wider. And somehow, desire replaces her sadness. In the dim light, her gray eyes appear bluer. I close my eyes and breathe her in —cinnamon.

She hands me the glass, and I take it. Finishing the amber liquid, I let it coat my mouth and burn on the way down. The ice clatters in the glass, so I fish it out and let it roll around my tongue while she watches. Placing it between my lips, I run it between hers. Her fingers tighten in my hair, tugging, urging me for more. "You like that, baby?"

"So much."

I crush the ice and swallow, ready to swallow her instead. I take her sweet pussy with my mouth, kissing and sucking until she's squirming under me. I flick my gaze up and visually trace her breasts and then go higher to see the underside of her jaw as she presses her head into the pillow beneath her.

Playing her body with my tongue like my fingers play my guitar, I set her on fire, feeling the burn deep inside. "I want to be buried inside you."

"I want that, Jet. I want you," she says, her body sinking into the mattress as she comes back to me from the high.

I grab a condom from where I tossed a few on the night-stand when we came crashing in here on a high of alcohol to continue what was started in the kitchen. Sticking the packet between my teeth, I rip it open and sit up.

Hannah lifts on her elbows, eyeing my body unashamedly. "Three crows," she says, eyeing my tattoos. "For three brothers."

"We all have them."

"They're sexy on your bicep." A wry grin appears. "How are you so fit if you drink every night?"

Chuckling, I continue to cover my cock and reply, "I do a lot of damn sit-ups."

"Every last damn one you do is worth it."

"What's your trick for staying in shape?" I ask, bending over and biting her hip just enough to tease her into thinking I'll break the skin. I won't, but I like the indentation from my teeth on her body.

"I like to fuck."

Shit. "You've got a dirty mouth."

"Maybe Jet Crow's just the one to help me clean it up."

Positioning myself above her, I angle my hips until I'm pressing against her entrance. "I have no intention of keeping this clean when it's so much more fun to play dirty."

Lying back, her chest rises and falls heavy with each breath. Her words starting to stick to her throat when she speaks. "With that handsome face, I have no doubt you use your looks to get what you want."

"I know how to use more than my looks," I start, pushing in just enough to feel her heat wash through me, "to get what I want." I push the rest of the way when her thighs butterfly for me. Seated deep inside her body, I close my eyes, the warm sensations taking over. On instinct, I move, and she moans.

I pick up my pace, but when I rise up on my elbows, I pause. *Fuck.* I shake my head.

"What is it, Jet? What's wrong?"

"Nothing," I'm quick to reply, hoping she doesn't see how much she's affecting me. What the fuck? I just met her, but when I close my eyes, it's not just the high of good sex taking over my mind. Normally, I don't pay a lot of attention to the body beneath me. Why should I? They only want me for one thing. But with Hannah? The girl with the haunted eyes? I want to erase the sadness. I want to replace her melancholy with other emotions.

What. The. Fuck?

Just fucking move.

We have chemistry, but I want more than just a physical connection with this woman. I want to know why she was alone tonight. Why she was drinking shots at the bar? Why she ordered me one before she knew me? I just want to know her.

Fucking move, Crow.

I do. Finally. But it's tainted with thoughts of tomorrow and hoping she stays tonight. Fuck.

This is just sex. Sex. Just a good time. *Focus.*

God, she feels amazing. *Too good.* "So good."

A warm hand caresses my cheek, and I open my eyes to find hers on me already. She smiles. "So good." Lifting up, she kisses me, dragging me out of my head and into her world. Her mystery is an aphrodisiac, and I want to learn all her secrets. Will she let me into her mind? It's a place I could lose myself forever in if I'm not careful.

Hannah isn't just another pretty face. She won me over the first time I saw her with that come-hither stare and devilish tilt of her lips.

We exhaust ourselves, pouring my soul into hers while hers fills me. As I hold her in the aftermath of ecstasy, I whisper into her hair, "Stay."

Turning her head, there's just enough light to see a flicker of happiness flaming in her eyes. "Ask me tomorrow," she replies with a small teasing smile as she closes her eyes and snuggles her back to my chest.

"I will."

I did. When her eyes open the next morning, I toss my cigarette out the window, lean forward, and ask her to stay.

While she gets dressed, I tell her I want to know her mind as well as I know her body. I confess too much too soon, more than I have to anyone in years.

She listened with a sly smile peeking through, her eyes brighter in the daylight, her worries seem to have lifted. When she kneels before me, she says, "You were the best time I ever had."

I'm tempted to tell her she's my worst. I hate feeling this way—reliant. Somehow, I've kept my emotions in check, a lock without a key for years.

Then she shows up with the right bow and shoulder, her cuts and tip fitting inside, the anatomy of a key made to unlock the deepest parts of me.

My chance starts slipping away as she does. I offer her coffee, to make her breakfast, and then I offer her a ride back to her car downtown where she parked behind the small bar where we met. I offer her anything to keep her from leaving. I don't offer my heart and I don't beg, but I offer her what I can.

The blue electric car surprises me. I mistakenly took her for a sports car or something less reliable and more rebellious. Her sexually carefree demeanor juxtaposed against her mysterious side fascinates me. Hearing the alarm click off and watching her open the car door, I know she's different. I felt it last night; not just in the way we connected, but in the way she makes me feel. "Maybe I'll see you around?"

"Maybe. I just moved here."

"I can show you around."

"I don't have a lot of free time right now, so I don't get out much."

Her jeans hug the curves of her hips, and I like the way she'd knotted my band's shirt, causing it to hug her upper body and exposing the skin of her stomach. Those boots that rubbed against my ass last night look just as sexy on her today. "Well, if you do, maybe you can come see the band play again."

Just before she slides into the driver's seat, she stops and looks back at me. Resting my elbow out the open window, I watch the sway of her hips as she comes back to me. *Come back to me.*

She lifts up on her toes and kisses me, our tongues meeting slick against each other's. Leaning back, she says, "I had a good time with you, Jet." Lowering back on her heels, she looks disappointed, that sadness making her eyes gray again. I miss the fire of the blue.

"I had a good time, too."

"My life is complicated. It's really not even my own these days."

I'm pathetic for saying anything to get more time with her, but it's worth a shot to explore our connection from last night. "Maybe I can help uncomplicate things."

"I wish you could. My cousin is sick, and I'm here to help her out. She needs me, but she also has a young son. His mom's illness has taken a toll. I need to be there for him."

"Sorry to hear that."

When she touches me, I savor the feel of her nails trailing through my hair. For a foolish split second, I think she's changed her mind, my chest feeling fuller as hope expands. Then the bubble bursts as she says, "If I get some free time, you'll be the first person I look up."

"We could make it easy and exchange numbers."

"That comes with expectations, and I don't want to hurt or disappoint you. If last night is all we get, it was pretty damn good."

"Yeah," I reply, already disappointed I won't know how to contact her. I sit back, take her hand, and bring it to my lips. I kiss it once and then again, pressing the tip of my tongue to her skin. "Take care of yourself."

Maybe I don't hide my feelings as well as I thought. Lifting up once more, she kisses my temple, then whispers, "The weather is too nice for such a sorrowful goodbye."

"Then let's not say it at all."

Nodding, she pushes away gently and returns to her car, opens the door, and slips in. With one foot still firmly on the ground, she looks back. "Take care of yourself, Jet."

Want to read more of this second chance single dad romance? Spark is available now.

ALSO BY S.L. SCOTT

To keep up to date with her writing and more, her website is
www.slscottauthor.com

To receive the Scott Scoop about all of her publishing adventures,
free books, giveaways, steals and more, sign up here:
http://bit.ly/2TheScoop

Join S.L.'s Facebook group here: S.L. Scott Books

The Crow Brothers

Spark

Tulsa

Rivers

Hard to Resist Series

The Resistance

The Reckoning

The Redemption

The Revolution

The Rebellion

The Kingwood Duet

SAVAGE

SAVIOR

SACRED

SOLACE

Talk to Me Duet

Sweet Talk

Dirty Talk

Welcome to Paradise Series

Good Vibrations

Good Intentions

Good Sensations

Happy Endings

Welcome to Paradise Series

From the Inside Out Series

Scorned

Jealousy

Dylan

Austin

From the Inside Out Compilation

Stand Alone Books

Everest

Missing Grace

Until I Met You

Drunk on Love

Naturally, Charlie

A Prior Engagement

Lost in Translation

Sleeping with Mr. Sexy

Morning Glory

ON A PERSONAL NOTE

Thank you so much for reading my books. Your support and kindness make this a road worth traveling.

To my amazing team of beta readers: Lynsey Johnson and Andrea Johnston - Thank You! You are not only encouraging but inspiring.

My editing team is truly the most incredible wizards. Thank you Marion, Marla, Jenny, and Kristen. You are incredible who help me not only stay sane, but make my words SHINE.

Thank you so my family who loses endless hours of time with me to the stories and characters that live in my head and insist on me recording their stories. You are my rocks, my heart, and always my whole soul <3

XO,

S.

ABOUT THE AUTHOR

To keep up to date with her writing and more, her website is www.slscottauthor.com to receive her newsletter with all of her publishing adventures and giveaways, sign up for her newsletter: http://bit.ly/2TheScoop

Instagram: S.L.Scott

For more information, please visit:
https://www.slscottauthor.com/